Tania Car... ...um for ... husband-and-wife
writing tea... ...f M... ...Waites, who were
shortlisted ... the 2010 Theaksto... ...for their debut
The Surrog...

4

Also by Tania Carver

The Surrogate

The Creeper

CAGE of BONES

TANIA CARVER

sphere

SPHERE

First published in Great Britain in 2011 by Sphere
Reprinted 2011 (four times)

A CIP catalogue record for this book
is available from the British Library.

Typeset in Plantin by M Rules
Printed and bound in Great Britain by
Clays Ltd, St Ives plc

Papers used by Sphere are from well-managed forests
and other responsible sources.

MIX
Paper from
responsible sources
FSC® C104740

Sphere
An imprint of
Little, Brown Book Group
100 Victoria Embankment
London EC4Y 0DY

An Hachette UK Company
www.hachette.co.uk

www.littlebrown.co.uk

CAGE of BONES

PART ONE

SUMMER COLD

1

It was a house of secrets. Dark secrets, old secrets. Bad secrets.

Cam knew it as soon as he saw it. Felt it, sensed it. Not just derelict but desolate, collapsing under the weight of its own despair. A solid shadow, deeper than black.

The old house was on a patch of ground just by the river, opposite the Old Siege House pub and restaurant at the bottom of East Hill in Colchester. Beside where an old mill had been converted into a set of fancy apartments. It was an area of old buildings, some dating back to Elizabethan times, mostly all sympathetically restored. The area had managed to retain some character and the properties were starting to go for inflated prices. There was a demand for more of the same. Or at least a cheap contemporary copy.

But first the area had to be cleared. And that was where Cam came in.

His back to the morning traffic, walking down a single-track road, he had felt good. His first job after three months claiming Jobseeker's Allowance. A labourer with a building and demolition company. Seventeen years old, one of the few from his class to actually get a job. Not what he wanted; he loved reading and wished he could have gone to university, studied English. But he was realistic. Kids like him didn't go to university. Especially not now. Still, he should be grateful to be working, to be busy. Happy to be anywhere except at home watching *Jeremy Kyle* become *Cash in the Attic*.

He had passed an old brick wall on his right, behind which a grand Georgian house had been renovated, turned into offices. All gleaming white sash windows, polished brass plaques, ornamental trees guarding the huge front door before the curling gravel drive. Cars for the office staff were parked on his left, their engines still ticking, cooling.

Cam imagined himself driving a car like that one day, working in an office like that one day too. Having a secretary, even playing golf. Well maybe not the golf. But something like that. Perhaps they would love his work at the demolition company so much he'd be promoted. Move on up the company until he was top man.

Cam smiled. Walked on.

Then the trees overhead closed in, darkening the morning, chilling the air, and Cam's smile faded. The traffic noise diminished, absorbed by the trees. Old and thick-trunked, they deadened the mechanical rushing sounds of vehicles, replaced them with the natural white noise of rustling leaves. Cut off from the road, the noise of the leaves increased, shushing and whispering all around him. The sunlight barely glinted through the dark overhead canopy. Cam's smile disappeared completely. He shivered. Felt suddenly alone.

Beyond the cars was a wasteland. Poured concrete posts, heavy, moulded from old oil drums. Chained together, bordering a weed-infested gravel patch. The first line of defence, keeping people away from the building.

Then the fence.

4

He stopped before it. Sturdy, heavy mesh panels anchored into solid concrete bases. The surrounding bushes and weeds had grown through and around it, pulling it towards them, trying to claim it for themselves. 'Dangerous: Keep Out' and 'Do Not Trespass' notices were attached to it by plastic ties, barely visible amongst the green. Warnings to the curious. Cam didn't look at them. He was just glad he wasn't doing this at night. Place was creepy enough in the daytime.

Behind the fence was rubble and weeds, fighting for space, dominance. And beyond all that was the house itself. Cam took a good look at it.

A solid black shadow, absorbing the daylight, holding it within. Giving away nothing. Then he saw something rise from the side of the building, slap down again with a leathery sound. Like huge crow's wings. A horror-film monster. He jumped, gasped.

Cam turned, thinking of running away. Stopped. Tried to get hold of himself. This was ridiculous. It was morning, and it was just an old house. He looked at it again. Studied it, confronted it. Hoped his scrutiny would take its power away.

It was more like an old barn or storage house. And it was old. Very old. Black wooden slats cladded the exterior, most of them askew or collapsing with age and disrepair, leaving exposed lath-work and bare brick underneath. What he had taken for crow's wings was a huge sheet of black plastic attached to one side of the building. A cheap makeshift repair, now tattered and useless, left hanging beyond its useful life.

There were huge gaps in the roof tiles, exposing the aged, water-damaged skeletons of beams and joists. At the far end was a one-storey extension, blackened plasterwork, rotted wooden window frames. A crumbling brick wall exposed a flat concrete area. Beyond that was the River Colne, dirty brown, plastic debris and greasy scum bobbing slowly along.

So close to the road, the town, and he could have been anywhere. Or nowhere.

Just a house, Cam told himself. Just a house. Nothing more.

'What you waitin' for?' A voice behind him, loud and angry-sounding.

Cam jumped, startled. He turned.

'Come on, get a move on. We're on the clock here.' The newcomer looked at his watch to emphasise the point. 'Shift it.'

'Sorry . . .' Cam found his voice. 'Sorry, Gav . . .'

His boss had been following him down the path. Cam was so wrapped up in the house that he hadn't even noticed. Galvanised into action by Gav's words, pleased to have some reinforcements, he pushed and pulled at the fence, tried to get it to budge. Sharp branches slapped at his face and limbs. Leathery green tendrils seemed to wrap themselves round his arms and legs, tugged at him. Cam felt panic, unreasonable but insistent, rise within him. He gave one final heave and eventually, sweating from the exertion, his knuckles red and sore from the metal and green from the foliage, he managed to make a gap wide enough to squeeze through.

'Yeah, that's right,' said Gav behind him. 'Just make enough room for yourself, you skinny little bastard. Selfish twat.'

Cam thought of answering, explaining his sudden panic, his irrational, instant fear of the building before them, apologising even. Had the breath in his mouth ready, but didn't use it. Gav was just joking. In his own way. Funny and charming, he thought himself, while other people just found him loud and offensive. Plus he wouldn't understand why Cam was so suddenly scared. But then Cam didn't understand it either.

Just a simple job, Gav had said. A two-man crew, do a recce, decide how best to demolish the place, plan it, do it. Clear the land to cram in yet another development of boxy new houses and flats. The last thing Colchester needed, Cam thought, more boxy new houses and flats. But he tried to have no opinion on it. Because he needed the job. And because some of those boxy little houses weren't bad. He quite fancied living in one of them.

Cam heard the fence rattle and clang behind him, felt it vibrate and shake. He also heard curses and expletives, as Gav forced his steroid-pumped body through as loudly as possible. Cam, reluctant to enter the house alone, waited for him. The other man joined him, stood beside him looking at it.

'What d'you think?' Gav said, sweating from the exertion.

'Like the House of Secrets,' said Cam, instantly regretting it.

Gav turned to him, a sneering smile on his lips. 'The what?'

Cam began to stammer. 'Th-th-the House of Secrets. It's from a comic.'

'Bit too old for comics, aren't you?'

Cam blushed. 'Read it when I was a kid. It was a … a horror comic. These two brothers. Cain and Abel. Abel lived in the House of Secrets. Cain lived in the House of Mystery. With this graveyard between them.' He paused. Gav hadn't said anything, so he continued. 'Cain was always killin' Abel. But he was always back to life for the next issue.'

He expected Gav to say something, insult him in some way. Take the piss. But he didn't.

'Cain and Abel,' said Gav. 'That's the Bible, that. First murderer, first victim.'

Cam just looked at him, eyes wide in surprise.

'What? Just 'cos I work in demolition doesn't mean I'm thick.' Gav looked away from Cam, beyond the fence, across the path.

'Hey look,' he said, pointing. He laughed. 'There's another. That must be your House of Mystery.'

7

Cam looked. Gav was right. There was another building further down the road in even worse repair than the one they were standing in front of. It looked like a row of old terraced houses, boarded up and falling apart, the foliage reclaiming it. Eerie and isolated. Even the graffiti that covered it looked half-hearted.

And in between, thought Cam, *the graveyard*.

They stood in silence. Cam eventually found his voice.

'Creepy place,' he said, 'innit? Like . . . like somethin's happened here.'

'What, like an old Indian burial ground or somethin'?' Gav laughed. 'You're too sensitive, you. An' weird.' He sniffed. 'Now come on,' he said. 'We better get crackin'. 'Cos it'll be bloody murder if you don't get a move on. We ain't got all day. Let's get inside.'

Gav stepped in front of Cam, crossed towards the boarded-up doorway. Cam followed reluctantly. As he did so, he saw something on Gav's face that he hadn't seen before. Something that the mouthing off and bravado didn't cover.

Fear.

2

Up close, the house looked – and felt – even worse.

The back wall was covered with tarpaulin panels. Over the years, the edges had peeled away from the wood and brickwork, and now they resembled a line of hooded cloaks hanging on a row of pegs, just waiting to be worn to some sacrificial black mass.

Cam shivered again.

In amongst the cloaks were the remains of a doorway. Frame rotted, eaten away from the ground up, paint flaked off and blown away. The door it held looked flimsy enough too, missing paint showing wood that looked like shredded wheat.

'Go on, get it open.'

Gav's voice behind Cam.

Cam reached out, turned the handle, pushed. Nothing. Pushed again, slightly harder this time. Still wouldn't budge. And again, more force this time. Nothing. He stopped, turned to Gav. Hoping that would be the end of it. That they could leave now. Return to the sun, the warmth.

Gav had other ideas. 'Useless twat, give it here.'

He twisted the handle, pushed. Hard. Nothing. Anger,

never far from the surface of Gav's steroid-addled psyche, was rising within him, reddening his face, making him tense his arms. He stepped back, shoulder-charged the door. A splintering sound, but it held firm. The sound was encouragement enough. Gav did it again. And again.

The door resisted, but eventually, with a loud crack and a shriek of breaking timber, gave.

Gav stood there, bent double, hands on knees, panting.

'Go on then, kid . . . in you go . . . '

Cam looked between Gav and the darkness. Reluctantly, he entered.

It took a few seconds for his eyes to adjust to the gloom after the bright morning sunshine outside. And once they had, it was pretty much as he would have expected. Razor blades of dusty light cut through the gaps in the wood and brickwork of the walls, illuminating a desolate, dank space.

The boards beneath Cam's feet creaked as he put pressure on them. He was wary about entering further in case the floor gave way beneath him. A shadow loomed behind him.

'Come on, get movin'.'

Cam stepped further into the house.

'Jesus Christ . . . ' Gav again. 'That smell . . . '

Cam hadn't noticed he had been holding his breath. He let the air out of his lungs, breathed in. And immediately gagged. The stench was awful, almost physical in its putrid power.

'God . . . ' said Gav. 'Smells like someone died in here . . . '

'Don't say that.'

Gav looked at him, about to make a joke. But Cam could tell he was becoming just as scared. Gav said nothing.

'Let's look around.' Cam was surprised at the strength in his voice, the bravery of the statement. But it had nothing to do with bravery. He just wanted to get this over with as quickly as possible. The sooner this house was demolished, the better.

Cam, still wary of the floorboards, moved further into the room. The smell was overpowering. Cam hated to admit it, but Gav had been right. It smelled like someone had died in there.

There was a set of stairs off to the left of the room, leading upwards. They looked, if anything, even riskier than the floorboards. Directly ahead was a doorway through to another room. It had no door, and Cam was aware of quick, darting movements in the shadows at his feet as he moved slowly towards it. Rats. He hoped.

The remains of a kitchen were decaying in the next room, cabinets empty, doors missing or hanging by half-hinges, lino underfoot broken and missing.

'Anything there?' said Gav from the main room.

'Kitchen,' said Cam. 'Or it was once.' At the far end of the room was another doorway. Cam moved towards it. There was a door in this one. Closed. And it looked newer, sturdier than the rest of the inside. He reached down. The handle looked newer too.

Heart skipping a beat, he turned it.

A sudden light came from behind him. He jumped, screamed, shut his eyes.

'It's a torch, you soft bastard,' said Gav.

Cam forced his heart rate to slow down. Gav swung the torch round the main room. The small black shadows scuttled away. They *were* rats. But something else had been there. Among the debris of the falling-apart building, the bricks, old concrete and cement, pieces of wood and broken furniture, were more recent leavings. Pizza cartons. Fastfood wrappings. Newspapers. Gav shone his torch down on them.

'Look at that,' he said. 'The date. Couple of weeks ago. Recent . . . '

The bad feeling Cam had been harbouring increased. 'Let's get out of here, Gav. Come on. This . . . this isn't right.'

Gav frowned angrily, fighting the fear inside himself, not wanting to show it. 'Bollocks. Just some old tramp or somethin' been dossin' down here. Come on.' He pointed to the door. 'What's in there?'

'Toilet?'

'Open it.'

Cam, sweating now, turned the handle.

It wasn't a toilet. It was another flight of stairs, this time leading down. The darkness sucked away what light there was like a black hole.

'Gav . . .'

Cam stood back to let Gav see. Gav drew level. The two of them in the cramped kitchen filled it, made the place seem claustrophobic. Gav shone the torch into the dark stairwell. The two of them looked at other.

'Go on then,' said Gav, licking his lips.

Dry from the steroids, thought Cam. Or fear.

Cam opened his mouth, wanted to complain, but knew it would be no use. Putting his hand out to steady himself against the wall, he began to make his way downwards.

The wall was clammy, cold. He felt damp flaking plaster and paint beneath his palm. The steps creaked as he placed his feet on them, felt soft at times.

He reached the bottom. Felt hard-packed earth beneath his boots, a low ceiling above his head. The smell was worse down here; corruption allied to a pervasive dampness that made his skin itch and tingle unpleasantly.

He crouched and looked round. Saw shadow on shadow. Behind him, Gav started to move down the stairs, swinging the beam of his torch as he did so. Cam caught flashes of illumination, made out something at the far end of the cellar.

'What . . . what's that?' He pointed. Gav stopped descending, stayed where he was on the stairs.

'What's what?'

'Over there, it's . . . '

Something glimpsed in the beam's swinging light. Quickly, then gone. A construction of some sort, criss-cross.

And behind it, within it, some kind of movement.

'Come on,' said Gav, 'let's get out of here.'

'Just a minute.' Cam surprised himself with the strength in his voice. His heart was hammering, blood pounding round his body, but fear or no fear, he wanted to know what he had seen.

'What d'you mean, just a minute? Come on, we're goin'.'

'Wait.' Cam's voice, stronger now. 'Point the torch over there, in the corner.'

'Why?' Panic creeping into Gav's voice now.

'Because there's something over there.'

Gav, grumbling, reluctantly did so. The beam illuminated a cage, built into one whole wall of the cellar. The bars were the colour of stained teeth, tied together with what looked like strips of old leather.

'Jesus . . . ' Gav tried to back away, found he couldn't move. 'A cage . . . What's . . . what's a cage doin' down here?'

Cam didn't answer. He didn't know the answer. Fascinated, he started to move towards it.

'Where you goin'?'

'Just . . . I saw something . . . ' Cam kept walking. Slowly. 'Keep the torch pointed at the cage. Let me see . . . '

Something moved in the corner. Shifted. A shadow with substance and bulk.

'There's somethin' in there . . . ' Gav, no longer hiding the fear in his voice.

Cam stopped walking. Stood rooted to the spot, staring. He glanced round, back to Gav.

13

'Keep the torch there.'

Cam reached the cage. Extended a hand, touched it. The smell was worse in this corner. Animal waste, plus corruption. The bars themselves stank. Cam leaned in close, smelled them. Like old bones in a butcher's shop.

He froze.

Old bones. That was exactly what they were.

'Come on! I'm goin'.'

The beam wavered as Gav turned, indicated the way back upstairs.

'Give me a minute,' Cam shouted back. 'I just want to—'

He didn't get to say what he wanted to do. With a clanking rattling of chains, the thing in the cage sprang at the bars, roaring. It grabbed Cam by the arm, the neck.

Cam screamed, tried to pull away. Couldn't. The grip was too strong.

He tried to shout for Gav to help him, but the words came out as one solid block of noise.

The pain increased. He looked down, saw that the thing in the cage had sunk its teeth into his arm.

Cam screamed even louder.

Suddenly he was in the dark. Gav had left him, run back up the stairs, taking the torch with him.

Cam felt the teeth bite further into his arm, accompanied by a snarl, like a hungry dog feasting. He grabbed his own neck, felt fingers digging in, tried to prise them away.

The snarling increased.

Cam pulled harder on the fingers. Felt something snap.

An animal howl of pain. The grip on his arm loosened slightly.

He pulled another finger back. Heard another snap.

The grip on his arm slackened, the pain eased.

Realising that he wouldn't get another chance, Cam pulled

14

as hard as he could. His neck was freed, then his arm. Not bothering to look behind him, he ran for the stairs.

All the way up, not caring if they gave way underneath him, just desperate to be out of the house.

Then, once upstairs, straight through the kitchen, the main room and out of the door.

And running.

As far away from the house as possible.

Because, before Gav had taken the torch and run, Cam had seen what was there.

A child. A feral child.

In a cage of bones.

3

Faith ran.

Through the trees, into the forest. Squinting at the sudden daylight, pushing herself as hard as she could, running as fast as she was able. The ground hard and uneven beneath her bare feet, her chest hammering. Arms windmilling wildly, breath barked out in ragged, harsh bursts. Anything to gain momentum, move faster.

Get away from *him*.

Escape from *him*.

She ran on. Not knowing where she was going, not stopping to think. This way and that. Wherever there was a clearing between the trees, a space large enough to force herself through, she went. Just trying to put as much distance as possible between herself and . . .

Him.

Her feet were cut by branches and stones, the soles searing anew with pain each time she landed them hard on the forest floor. Branches and vines slapped at her. Stung. Brambles and thorns tore at her skin, tried to slow her down, pull her back. Claim her for the forest. She ignored them, fought them off.

Told herself she felt nothing. No pain, no agony. She would have time for that later. Once she had put distance between herself and ...

Faith reached a clearing, slowed down. Hands on thighs, bent double, head down, she gulped in air as hard as she could. No good. She tried, but her body couldn't do it. Her lungs were burning, seared, but not big enough to take in the amount of air she needed. She cursed herself for being so unfit. For smoking and drinking and not taking any exercise. A pleading mantra ran through her head:

Pleasegodletmegetoutofthis ... pleaseplease ... please ... Ipromise ... please ... IpromiseIpromise ... I'llbeI'llbe ... anythingjust ...Iwon'tIwon't ... please ...

Eyes screwed tight shut, she concentrated.

Pleasepleaseplease ...

She saw Ben in her mind's eye. Her son. Smiling at her. Like an image from a different world. She'd left Donna to look after him. Gone to work.

And how had she got from there to here? How had she got into this? How? She knew. She had thought she had been clever. Standing in New Town, her usual spot. Making it look like a pick-up, like work. Knowing it was anything but. Feeling a bit protected thinking he'd be on CCTV somewhere.

And then the drive. Faith was used to getting into men's cars. She knew the risks. But with the insurance she'd put in place, she'd doubted there was much risk in this one. Not for her, anyway. Because Donna would know what to do. Faith could count on Donna.

But he had hit the town limits and kept going. She had asked him where, and he had told her. Somewhere private. Somewhere they could talk. Where he could get what he wanted and she could get what she wanted.

Yeah, she had thought. Heard that one before.

17

But it hadn't worked out like that. Not at all.

He had taken her somewhere private, all right. Then ... nothing. Until she woke up. In that place. That horrible place. Like something from a horror film. Cold. And dark. And ...

Oh God.

The bones. She remembered the bones.

And in that moment she knew where he had taken her.

Back there. Back home.

And she had let him. She was so cross with herself for allowing herself to make such a stupid, simple mistake that her anger gave her the energy to attempt to escape. And she had. She wasn't stupid. She knew what he had done. One look at that place told her that. If she stayed, she would have no future.

So she had run. Not stopping to look back, or pause to check where she was. Not even noticing she was naked. Just ran. Out into the forest, the open. It was daylight by that time. She had been there all night.

Faith straightened up. Listened. Tried to hear something beyond her own ragged breath. Some sound of her pursuer.

Nothing.

Her body relaxed. Air came more freely into her. Her heart rose slightly. She began to feel the pain in her body. Feel normal again.

Then she heard it. The crack of dry twigs. Footfalls. Heavy. Not caring whether she heard or not. Knowing he was going to find her. She couldn't stay where she was. She had to keep moving.

Looking round, she quickly decided where the sound was coming from, turned and headed in the opposite direction.

Her feet hammering down hard on the earth, pain starting anew, body racked and burning, feeling worse for stopping, not better.

And on. Running, running, running. Arms pumping, legs pounding. Not stopping. Not looking back. Moving forward, ever forward. Her son in her mind's eye. Running towards him.

And then . . . other sounds. In front of her, not behind her.

She slowed, nearly stopping. Listened again, tried to make them out over the top of her laboured, painful breathing.

She knew what the sounds were. She smiled.

Traffic.

She was near to a road.

Smiling, she ran all the harder.

Then: another sound. Behind her this time.

She risked a glance over her shoulder. And there he was.

Faith hadn't expected him to move so fast, given the size of him. But he was barrelling towards her, knocking branches out of way as though they weren't there. Like that Vinnie Jones character in the X-Men film she had watched once with her son.

'Oh no, oh God . . . '

She ran all the harder. Away from him. Towards the traffic.

The forest floor began to slope downwards. There was an incline leading towards the road. Faith ran down it. Brambles and thorns were thick here. They tore at her, attempted to hold her back. She ignored them, refused to feel her arms, legs, as they were ripped open. Some snagged her, refusing to give way. She kept on running, letting them gouge out large lumps of bleeding flesh.

No time for that. Only for escape. Escape . . .

The road was in sight. The cars speeding past. She could see them. And, in a few seconds, touch them. Her feet ran all the faster.

And then, just as she was about to break free from the thorns, he was on her.

She screamed, tried to pull away. Felt his hot breath on her neck. His strong, meaty, sweaty grip on her shoulders. Fingers like heavy metal bolts digging into her skin.

She screamed again. Knowing she couldn't match him in strength, she became an eel, twisting and writhing away from his grip. Something she had picked up years ago, used when a customer tried to get a bit too handy. There was another move she knew too.

Squirming and turning in his grasp, she managed to bring her heel up, right into his groin. He might be big and strong, she thought, but there was no way he wouldn't feel that.

And he did. Grunting, he loosened his grip slightly.

It was all Faith needed. She pushed her body sharply back against him, knocking him off balance, releasing his grip further, then ran.

Towards the road.

She reached the kerb, glanced back. He was following. She allowed herself a small smile of triumph.

She had escaped. Got away. Yes, she—

Didn't see the VW Passat coming round a blind corner, straight towards her.

Too fast to stop or change direction.

It hit her, sending her body into the windscreen, shattering it, then over the roof of the car, landing in the road behind, her pelvis shattering, twisting the lower part of her body away from the top. The next car, a BMW 4x4, tried to swerve and missed her torso, but wasn't as lucky with her legs. The thick tyres crushed them as the driver slammed on the brakes.

Faith had no idea what had happened. No time to think. All she saw was daylight, the sky far away, yet near at hand. Then her son's face once more, smiling at her. Like an image from another world.

And a few seconds later, it was.

4

Whenever Detective Inspector Phil Brennan thought he had seen every kind of horror that humans could inflict on humans, something would hit him with the force of a right hook to the gut to remind him that he hadn't. And that he would never fail to be surprised and sickened, no matter how long he lived.

When he looked into that cellar and saw the cage, he felt that blow to the gut once more.

'Oh my God . . .'

As DI with Essex Police's Major Incident Squad – MIS – he had witnessed on a regular basis the damaged and the deranged destroy themselves and others with tragic inevitability. Seen loving family homes mutate into abattoirs. Comforted victims whose lives had ended even though they still lived. Attended crime scenes so horrific they gave a glimpse of hell.

And this ranked as one of the worst.

Not because of the usual stuff. Gore and dismemberment. Emotion and anger made corporeal. A savage and senseless loss of life. Here, the passion and rage of murder was absent. Although he imagined it would have been there in time. No.

This was a different kind of horror. A calculated, deliberate horror. Thoughtful and precise and vicious.

The worst kind.

Phil stood on the hard-packed dark earth and stared at it, shivering from more than just the cellar's cold.

Arc lights had been hastily erected at either wall, dispelling the Hammer Films gloom, replacing it with deadeningly bright illumination that revealed everything, conversely making it all the more horrific in the process.

The blue-suited CSI team worked in the glare of the lights. They were all around him, attempting to spin samples and specimens into the slenderest of narrative threads, building the biggest story from the smallest particles.

Phil himself was similarly dressed, standing still and staring. Taking in what was before him. Trying to process it. Knowing he would have to hunt down the person responsible for it.

The cellar floor was strewn with flower petals. The arc lights showed up the varying colours: blue, red, white, yellow. All turning brown, curling, dying. All from different kinds of flowers. Around the walls were bunches of wilting blooms, bound together, placed in clusters at regular intervals, like little roadside memorials. The smell, in that small space, was overpowering.

Above them, daubed on the walls, were symbols. Swirling and Cabalistic. Phil had initially thought they were some kind of pentagram, an indication of devil worship. But he had examined them more closely and found that wasn't the case. They weren't like any Satanic designs he had come across. He couldn't say what they were, but they made him feel uncomfortable looking at them. As though he had seen them before and knew what they were. And didn't like them. He shuddered, kept looking round.

In the centre of the space was what looked like a workbench. Wooden surface, with adjustable metal legs. Old. Well used, but well looked after. Phil leaned forward, examined it. It had been kept clean, but the wood was stained darker in places, the surface scarred and chipped with blade marks and heavy, angry gashes. He suppressed a shudder.

And there, behind the bench, at the far end of the cellar, was the cage. He moved closer, stood before it like an astronaut confronted by an alien artefact, unsure whether to worship it or destroy it. It took up nearly a third of the cellar. Floor to wall to ceiling. The bones embedded, cemented. Bound tightly together with what looked like some kind of hide. Varying in size, but all quite long and substantial. Precisely worked and integrated. A solid construction, criss-crossing to form neat, even-sized squares. It had been there a long time. Some of the bones were worn and smooth, time-leached from white to grey. Some were much newer, almost white. And it had been well maintained over the years. Sections had been repaired, the newer, paler bones standing out, at odds with the rest. Old, splintered ones strengthened and bound. A smaller frame set into the larger one served as a door, hinged on one side by bindings, a chain and padlock securing it on the other side.

The bones . . . Their selection based on size and shape . . . The method of joining them together . . . He tried to imagine the work involved, the time taken, the kind of mind that had created such a thing . . . Failed. Shook his head, concentrated, examined it all the harder.

'Built to last, that.' A voice at Phil's side. 'British craftsmanship.'

He turned. DS Mickey Philips was standing next to him. The flippancy of his tone was only perfunctory. It didn't reach Mickey's eyes. He was equally awed and repelled by the structure.

'Why bone?'

'What?'

'Must be a reason, Mickey. Whoever did this must be telling us something.'

'Yeah. But what?'

'I don't know. But they could have used wood, metal, whatever. They chose bone. Why?'

'Dunno. Why?'

'I don't know either.' Phil's eyes roved over the cage. 'Yet.' He looked round the cellar once more. Took in the flowers, the workbench. 'This cage, this whole place . . . like a murder scene without the murder.'

'Yeah,' said Mickey. 'Good job we got the call. Just in time.'

Phil looked at the stains on the workbench. 'This time.'

They turned back to the cage. Eyes fixed on that, not on each other. Phil broke his gaze, turned to Mickey.

'Where's the child now?'

'At the hospital, with Anni,' Mickey said.

Anni Hepburn, Phil's DC.

Mickey sighed, frowned. 'Jesus, what a state that kid must be in . . .'

Mickey Philips was still regarded as the new boy in the MIS, the team that Phil headed up. But he had been there long enough to earn his place. The more Phil worked with him, the more he found him a mass of contradictions. He looked the complete opposite of Phil. Always immaculately suited and tied, in contrast to Phil's more carefree approach of jacket, waistcoat, jeans and casual shirt; his hair neatly razored short, unlike Phil's spikes and quiff, and his shoes always polished, as opposed to Phil's Converses or, if the weather was really bad, scuffed old Red Wings. A bull-necked nightclub bouncer to Phil's hip university lecturer.

But there was something that set Mickey Philips apart from

24

other coppers, and that was why Phil had wanted him on his team. He was one of the new breed of coppers, a graduate rather than a grafter, but he didn't conform to type. Most of them Phil dismissed as promotion-hungry politicians, but Mickey wasn't like that. He was tough when he had to be, aggressive even, but not brutal. He was also articulate and erudite, qualities that didn't always go down well in the force, and he had done his best to hide them when necessary. It was only since working for Phil that he had felt relaxed enough to allow that side of him to show. And even then he tended to ration its appearances.

'I'll, er . . . go and see if I'm needed upstairs.' The cage made Mickey visibly uncomfortable.

'It's a ritual,' said Phil.

Mickey didn't move. Waited for what Phil would say next.

'Isn't it?' He gestured round. 'All this. Deliberately set up for a ritual.'

'The murder of that kid?'

'I'd put money on it. And we've stopped it. Taken the would-be victim away, averted a death.'

'Good for us.'

'Yeah,' said Phil. He didn't sound convinced. 'Good for us. Question is, what does this guy do next?'

Mickey said nothing.

'I think we're going to need some help on this one . . .'

5

'Come in. Sit down.' Marina Esposito smiled. It wasn't returned.

The woman across from her sat. The desk in Marina's office was pushed back against the far wall. She had tried to make the room in the Southway police station as warm and characterful as possible: prints on the walls, easy chairs, rug on the floor. Not a luxury, thought Marina, but a necessity. No one ever came to see her because they were happy.

'So ...' She looked down at the file before her. She knew the woman's name. Probably knew more about her than she realised. 'How are you, Rose?'

Detective Sergeant Rose Martin gave a brisk smile. 'Fine.'

'You feel ready to return to work?'

'Absolutely.' She closed her eyes, rolled her neck round on her shoulders. Marina heard a faint clicking noise. 'Been off too long. Starting to go mad watching daytime TV.'

'*Diagnosis Murder*'ll do that to anyone.'

Marina knew just how long Rose had been off. She herself had been involved in the same case, five months previously. The Creeper, so christened by the media, was a murderous

26

predator. He had kidnapped Rose, tied her up and subjected her to sexual torture. She had tried to escape, but it was only after the intervention of Phil Brennan that she was actually freed.

Rose had been under Phil's command. But Marina knew he hadn't wanted her, chosen her or even liked her. He had found her manipulative, devious and problematically aggressive. In the course of the Creeper investigation, Rose Martin had instigated an affair with his boss, the previous DCI, in order to further her career. He had been completely besotted with her. The decisions he had made at her request had resulted in his near-fatal stabbing, and he was subsequently invalided out of the force. Even worse, from Phil's perspective, recklessly endangering the lives of the team in the process.

But everything had been neatly brushed over. Spun out simplistically to give the media its heroes and villains. Phil the hero. Rose Martin the brave but tragic heroine. The Creeper the villain. DCI Ben Fenwick the unfortunate casualty.

Marina was professional enough not to take her partner's word for things, to judge for herself. But she had been there. She knew the whole messy truth. And she had agreed with him about Rose Martin.

But she put all that to one side, remained impartial. Did her job.

Rose looked good, Marina had to admit. Tall, her dark hair curled and styled, she wore a blue two-piece suit, jacket and pencil skirt, spike heels and a cream silk blouse. Power-dressed, thought Marina. A strong physical presence in the room. Ready for a fight. But also rested, recuperated and rehabilitated. Ready to return to work.

On Marina's recommendation.

Marina looked down at the file before her once more. Moved a heavy strand of hair that had fallen across her face back over her ear. She was slightly smaller than Rose Martin and dressed completely differently, but she didn't allow the other woman's strong presence to intimidate her. Marina, with her long, dark, wavy hair and Italian features, favoured lace and velvet, full peasant skirts and diaphanous blouses, cowboy boots and scarves. She knew she was often portrayed as a caricature, exactly what some on the force expected a psychologist to be like, but she didn't care. Even played up to it sometimes, enjoyed it. Just because she worked for the police didn't mean she had to think and dress like them. And besides, her record spoke for itself.

'Right,' she said, nodding, 'been off too long. And what have you been doing with your time? Besides watching Dick Van Dyke?'

'Worked out.' Rose Martin kept eye contact. 'Kept fit. Active. Anything to stave off the boredom. I'm itching to get back.'

'Itching.' Marina nodded once more.

'Look,' said Rose, irritation creeping into her voice, the shield of her features slipping. 'I got over . . . what happened fairly quickly. Dealt with it. Months ago. I've been ready to return to work for ages.'

'You realise that when – or if – you do return, it may not be back on the front line?'

Rose bristled at the suggestion. 'There's no reason why not.'

'I'm just advising you. Be aware of the possibilities.'

'But I'm ready to go back. I can feel it. Look, before all this, I'd taken the inspector's exam and passed. I was waiting for promotion. If they knew what was good for them, I'd be back straight away as a DI. I should be. I've spoken to DCI Glass and he agrees with me.'

Interesting, thought Marina. DCI Glass was Ben Fenwick's replacement. She wondered in how many ways.

28

She nodded once more, said nothing. Rose Martin's attitude was typical of a lot of officers she saw. They felt they could handle themselves. Reached a point where they found their convalescence too constricting, where they knew they were ready for the challenge of the job, raring to go once more. And if any problems came up, if they had flashbacks, they could always rely on their old inner strength to pull them through.

Even in the comparatively short time that Marina had been doing the job, she had seen too many of them try that, only to crash and burn. Their inner strength had deserted them at the first opportunity. They had crumpled, folded. Been back at square one.

She leaned forward in her armchair. 'Look, Rose. I don't want to seem negative, but it's easy to think you can just walk back into work like nothing's happened and pick up where you left off.'

Rose leaned forward too. 'I know myself. I know how I feel. I know when I'm damaged and when I'm good. And I'm good now.'

'It's not that simple.'

'Never is, is it?' Rose gave a harsh laugh. Nodded. 'This is about Phil Brennan, isn't it? I know what he thinks of me. And if anyone's blocking me coming back, it'll be him.'

Marina sighed. Didn't bother to hide it. 'I'm a psychologist, Rose. Bound by the oaths of the medical profession. Do you really want me to add "paranoid delusions" to your file?'

Rose Martin sat back, stared at Marina.

Marina leaned forward once more. 'Look, Rose. Over the last five months, you've refused to talk to me. Ignored all attempts to let me help you.'

'Because I didn't need help. I've coped on my own.'

'So you say. You wouldn't even attend the anger-management course I recommended.'

Rose Martin's eyes flashed at the words. 'I didn't need your help,' she repeated.

Marina sighed. 'I just wanted to say, I know how you feel.'

Rose snorted once more. 'Is this the bit where you try to be my friend? Tell me you're the only person who understands me?'

Marina looked at the notes in her lap, deciding. She looked up again. 'No, it's not, Rose.' Steel in her voice hiding a battened-down anger at the other woman's manner. 'This is the bit where I put professionalism aside for a while and deviate from the script. Forget that I'm a psychologist and you're a police officer. Where we talk as one human being to another.'

Rose said nothing.

'I do know what you're going through, Rose. Because the same thing happened to me. It was before your time here, but the circumstances were very similar. If you don't believe me, check it out.'

Marina paused, tried not to let the memories overwhelm her. She continued.

'And I did what you did. I thought I could cope. Just get on with things again, live my life like nothing had happened. I tried. And I couldn't.' She bit back the emotion in her voice.

The shield slipped. Rose frowned, interested. 'What happened?'

Marina shrugged. 'I coped. Eventually. Took a while. Longer than I thought it would. Longer than I felt it should have done. It wasn't easy. But I got there. In time.'

The two women sat in silence together. Then Rose's phone rang.

She answered it, even though Marina had started to speak, to tell her it should have been switched off. Marina watched the other woman's face. It changed from initial hostility to polite interest. A smile then split her features as she listened.

She took a notebook and pen from her bag, wrote something down. Hung up. Turned to Marina.

'That was DCI Glass. He has a case he needs me to work on.'

Marina nodded, noting her words. *Needs.* 'Right. When would this be?'

'Straight away. Shortage of staff. He thinks I'm ready.'

'Does he?'

Another smile from Rose Martin. Triumphant. Adrenalised.

Marina shrugged. 'You'd better go, then.'

'Don't you have to write a report on me?'

'Doesn't seem a lot of point now, does there?'

Rose left the room.

Marina shook her head, clearing Rose Martin out of it. She checked when her next appointment was, looked at her watch. Thought about what she'd be having for lunch. Wondered what her daughter Josephina was getting up to with her grandparents. Then her phone rang.

She answered. DC Anni Hepburn.

'You busy?' Then, before she could answer, 'You want a distraction?'

Marina leaned forward. 'What's up?'

Anni's voice became hesitant. 'I'm at the hospital. The General. And I could do with a bit of help . . .'

6

Paul had left him in the cave. Stuck in as far as he could push him. Tried to push everything in after him. Stopper him up. He hoped he would never come out.

Right at the far end, the black, dank far end. With the crying and the sobbing and the wailing of the lost souls. With the hideous dirt-encrusted earth creatures. The back of the cave. Away from the light. As far away from the light as he could get.

It was Paul's turn to be out. To put his face to the light. Close his eyes. Breathe in the air. Remind himself of what was important. That he could still live like this. That he could still live with his face to the sun if he wanted to. Close his eyes. Breathe. Relax. He still could. He just had to believe in it enough.

Not be dragged back. Into the cave again.

Into the dark.

He closed his eyes. Sat on the floor. Back in place. His sacred space. His special place. He tried to relax. Couldn't.

Because of the noise out there. The people. What were they doing? Rushing round, talking in loud voices, their cars screeching, their voices coming through the air. Talk. Talking, talking. Always talking. Not saying anything. Like radio static. Just noise. Horrible noise. Giving him a headache.

And then he had seen the boy.

Dragged out of the sacrifice house. Kicking, screaming. Pulling, pushing. Crying.

And Paul had hid his face in his hands. Put his arms round his head, over his ears. Blocking out the sound. The noise of the boy. The crying boy.

'No . . . no . . .'

Because that wasn't what it was about. Never had been. Never. No . . . Not that. He had tried to stop that. Tried to . . .

And look where it had got him.

The boy had kept screaming.

Paul sang to himself, chanted words, rocking back and forward, warding off the noise, keeping the bad spirits away. Songs from the old days. The happy days. Good-times songs. Community songs. Together songs.

But it didn't work. He still heard the boy's cries. Imagined his tears. Felt his fear.

Eventually the noise stopped. The boy stopped screaming. Or stopped screaming outside. Just the blue suits and their noise left.

He dared to watch. Gave a small peek. Saw them going into the sacrifice house.

Knew what they were going to find.

Ducked back down again, heart pounding.

Knew what they were going to find. Knew . . .

And knew something else too. They would keep looking. Come to his house next. Find him. And then . . . And then . . .

He couldn't have that. Not that. No.

So he curled up, small as he could. Back to a child, back in the womb.

Back when he was happy.
Curled up. And hoped they wouldn't find him.
At least he wasn't in the cave.
That was something.

7

'Right,' said Phil. 'Plan of action.'

He wanted to go above ground, feel sunlight on his skin, breathe in clean air. But he couldn't. Not yet.

He turned to Mickey. 'What did we get from the guy who called it in?'

Mickey checked his notes. 'Two of them. Demolition team. House was going to be turned into a housing estate. They've both been taken to hospital. Kid who got bitten needed some attention. Kept going on about old comics. Shock, probably.'

Phil frowned. 'Comics?'

'House of Secrets and House of Mystery,' said Mickey, not needing to look at his notes. 'Two brothers who keep killing each other. With a graveyard between them.'

'Right. We need . . . '

Phil trailed off, his eyes drawn back to the cage. The deliberate horror transfixing him. The cage, the flowers, the symbols on the wall, the altar-like bench . . . Arc-lit, the cellar held a palpable sense of anticipation, a stage set waiting for actors, unaware that the performance is cancelled. His gut churned in repulsion. But there was something else, some other feeling it invoked within him. Fascination. The workmanship, the craft, the dedication . . . the cage was a beautiful piece of work.

He moved closer, wanting to feel the worn bone beneath his fingers. To touch it, explore it, caress it even. But to simultaneously run as far and as fast as he could from it. He kept staring, riveted, head spinning in wonder, stomach churning in revulsion. Acting on something he couldn't explain or identify within him, he reached out a latex-gloved hand.

'Boss?'

Phil blinked. Mickey's voice called him back.

'Look. You'll want to see this.'

A uniform was pointing to a corner, shining his flashlight on it. Phil and Mickey stepped closer. Hidden behind a bunch of flowers were gardening tools. A trowel, a small hand fork and a scythe.

'Oh God,' said Phil.

Mickey peered in closer. 'Have they been sharpened?'

The tools were old, well-worn. Phil checked the edges. They were silver bright. Razored sharp. They reflected the beam of the flashlight, glinting round the cellar.

'Get Forensics to examine them,' Phil said. 'That brown staining? I reckon it's blood.'

'You think he's done this before?' said Mickey.

'Looks that way,' Phil said. He turned. Away from the tools, the flowers, the cage. 'Right. A plan. We need a plan.' He could still feel the cage's presence behind him. Like a pair of unblinking eyes boring into him, giving him the mental equivalent of an itch between his shoulder blades, something he couldn't identify and reach, couldn't satisfy . . .

'Are the Birdies here yet?' Phil asked.

'Should be up top,' said Mickey.

'Let's go then.'

He gave one last look at the cage. Tried to see it as what it was. A hideous, horrific prison. He looked at its floor. In the corner was a bucket, the stench coming off it in waves indicating that it had been the boy's toilet. Beside that were two old plastic bowls. Both filthy and scarred, one with the traces of something inside it, smeared round the rim. Bones sticking out of it, smaller ones than those of the cage. Food. The other contained some dark, brackish water.

Phil wished his partner were there. Marina Esposito, police psychologist. They had worked on several cases together, where their professional relationship had developed into something more intimate. But that wasn't why he wanted her now. She would be able to help with the investigation, track down the perpetrator. Help him work out why someone had done this. And that, he hoped, would make it much easier to turn that 'why' into a 'who'.

He kept staring at the cage. It stirred something within him, something he couldn't name or identify. Like a memory remaining annoyingly out of reach. But not good. He knew that much.

He thought harder. It was coming to him, reaching through the fog of his memory like a ghost from a horror film . . .

Then he felt it. That familiar tightening round his chest. Like his heart was being squeezed by an iron fist. And he knew he had to get upstairs as quickly as possible.

He ran ahead of Mickey, exited the house. Out into the open air. The daylight, the sunshine he had craved. He didn't even feel it.

Phil stood against the side of the building, waiting for the feeling to subside. Why? he thought. Why now? Nothing had happened; he hadn't done anything to exert himself. Why here? Why now?

He took a deep breath. Waited a few seconds. His panic

attacks had become much less frequent recently. He put that down to his newly settled home life with Marina and their daughter Josephina. His job hadn't got any easier, less distressing or less involving. But now he had people he loved and who loved him. And a happy home to go to at the end of the working day. That was as much as he had ever asked for and more than he ever thought he would get.

Because Phil had never believed in long-term happiness. His own upbringing – children's homes and foster homes, fear and violence – had put paid to that. He wasn't taking anything for granted and didn't know how long this would last, but he was enjoying it. Every nerve-racking second. If this was happiness, then it was the happiness of the tightrope walker managing to keep his balance.

He opened his eyes. Mickey was standing before him, concern on his features.

'Boss? You OK?'

Phil took a deep breath, another. Waited until he trusted himself to speak.

'I'm fine, Mickey, fine.' He put the panic attack to the back of his mind, along with the cage and the niggling, unreachable thoughts it had triggered. 'Come on. We've got work to do.'

8

Donna felt an insistent prodding in her shoulder. She ignored it, turned over, hoping it would stop.

It didn't.

'Donna . . .'

The prodding again. More insistent this time, harder. The voice saying her name louder. 'Donna . . .'

Donna opened her eyes. Closed them again. 'Just a few more minutes, Ben. Let Auntie Donna sleep.' Christ, listen to her. Auntie Donna. Must be desperate.

She closed her eyes, hoped he would do as he was told. Knew he wouldn't.

''M hungry . . .'

Anger coursed through Donna Warren's body. Her first response was to lash out with a fist, smack this kid square in the face, remind him that life wasn't fucking fair and that just because he was hungry didn't mean he was going to get fed. Who did he think she was? His mother, for Christ's sake?

She closed her eyes tight, knowing at the same time that he wasn't going to be fooled by that.

Her arm snaked slowly out from under her, patted the other side of the bed. 'Where's your mother?' Donna's voice sounded slurred, like an old-school VHS tape at the wrong speed.

But Ben understood. 'Don' know ... Get up. 'M hungry ...'

Donna sighed. No good. She would have to get up. The anger subsided. Poor little bastard. Wasn't his fault his mother hadn't come home last night. No, but when she did turn up, Donna would be so fucking angry with her ... Leaving her alone with her kid like that. Saying she wouldn't be long.

She swung out of bed, planted her feet on the floor. The cold penetrated her numbness. She gave a small shiver. Her head spun. Too much booze the night before. Cider and vodka cocktails. Home-made. With blackcurrant. Had seemed like a good idea at the time, especially with Bench and Tommer turning up, supplying the weed and the charlie. Faith should have been there. Didn't know what she had missed. And she could have helped sort them both out, instead of getting all secretive on her and going out. As it was, Donna did the two of them herself. The drugs and booze needed paying for. Fair's fair. She didn't mind. Much.

She looked at Ben, standing there in his washed-out Spider-Man pyjamas, knowing he wasn't the first kid to have worn them. 'All right ...' She pulled her dressing gown around her. 'I'm comin' ...'

By the time she made her way downstairs, bones creaking like a woman at least ten, if not twenty, years older than the thirty-two she was, Ben was already down there. He'd probably been through the kitchen cupboards, seen what was there, helped himself, even. And he still wanted her to cook for him. Little bastard.

She stopped in the living room, looked at the mess from the

previous night. Just like them. Turn up, trash the house, piss off. But she couldn't complain. She had helped them do it. And the place wasn't exactly tidy to begin with.

She reached the kitchen, looked in the fridge, found some bacon.

'You wanna bacon sandwich?'

Sitting at the table expectantly, Ben's eyes lit up. 'Yeah . . . '

'Well make me one an' all.'

Ben frowned as Donna laughed at her own joke. 'Put the kettle on. D'you know how to do that?'

He nodded, took the kettle to the sink, filled it with water, crossed back to the counter, flicked the switch.

'Good lad.'

He smiled, enjoying the praise.

Donna put the pan on the gas, started to cook the bacon.

'Some Coke in the fridge. Get yourself some.'

Ben did. Donna went back to cooking. He wasn't a bad kid. She had known worse. She had *been* worse. But he still wasn't her responsibility. And she would let Faith know in no uncertain fucking terms as soon as she bothered to turn up.

She served up the bacon sandwiches, slathering margarine and ketchup on Ben's white bread first. He wolfed his down. Donna lit a fag to accompany hers. Rubbed her eyes.

'You got to go to school today?' she said to the boy.

He shrugged, nodded. 'S'posed to.'

Christ, what an upheaval. Donna's head was ringing. The sandwich and the fag hadn't helped. 'Well you've got a day off today.'

Ben smiled.

Sooner Faith came back, sooner she could go back to bed. Once she'd given her a bollocking, of course. Made sure she knew she owed Donna for this.

She sipped her tea, dragged smoke deep within her lungs. Started to feel human again.

Unaware that Faith wouldn't be coming back.

Unaware of the large black car sitting outside her house.

Waiting.

9

'So . . . let me get this straight. He was found in a cage?'

DC Anni Hepburn stared straight at the bed, nodded.

'Of bones?'

Anni nodded again.

Marina Esposito looked at the woman speaking, gauging her response to the words. Hoping it tallied with her own.

'My God . . .'

It did.

The child was lying on the bed before them. An under-nourished, skeletal frame, his closed eyes black-rimmed, haunted-looking. He carried an ingrained residue of filth in his skin and hair. His already pale skin was bone-white where a patch on his arm had been swabbed clean and a feeding drip inserted. His broken fingers had been temporarily splinted and set. He was sleeping, heavily sedated, in the private hospital room. The lights had been taken right down so as not to sear his eyes when he woke up. The machines and monitors provided the only illumination.

Beyond formal questions of process and procedure, Marina didn't know what to think. Didn't want to allow herself to conjecture. So she stuck with formality.

'Dr Ubha.'

The doctor drew herself away from the child in front of her. Marina could tell this was already out of the woman's frame of reference.

'What's been done for the boy so far?'

Dr Ubha seemed relieved to receive questions she could answer. 'The first thing we did was to stabilise the patient. Checked his height and weight. Treated his cuts and abrasions. Set his broken fingers. Then we took samples.'

'Samples?'

'Blood, hair, fingernail scrapings.' She swallowed, eyes flicking back to the boy in the bed. 'Anal. We should have the results later today or tomorrow.'

'What's your first opinion?' said Anni.

Dr Ubha shrugged. 'Impossible to say at the moment. I need to get a full blood count, check for markers of infection, nutritional deficiencies . . . he needs a bone density scan, his hips, his joints . . .' She sighed. 'His teeth are in terrible shape. He must be in a lot of pain.'

'Apparently he bit one of the demolition team,' said Anni.

Dr Ubha raised her eyebrows. 'It's a wonder his teeth didn't fall out.'

'Anything for us to go on?' asked Anni.

Dr Ubha shook her head once more. 'Nothing much beyond what you see before you. He's been in that cage, or something like it, for quite a while. It's a long time since he's seen daylight, had decent food, anything like that. We'll have to wait until he comes round to see how socialised he is. My guess is, not too much. There is something, though. Something odd.'

'You mean odder?' said Anni.

'Yes. Right. I see what you mean.' Dr Ubha pointed to where his feet were under the covers. 'There was something

44

on the sole of his right foot. We thought it was a scar at first, but when I looked at it more closely, it seemed to have been deliberately made.'

'Deliberately scarred?' said Marina.

Dr Ubha nodded. 'Looks that way. Like a . . . brand.'

'A brand?' said Anni. 'Like you'd do with cattle?'

Dr Ubha said nothing. Shook her head. 'Never seen anything like this before.'

Marina looked at the child in the bed. Her hand went to her stomach as she thought of her own. She had vowed never to get pregnant. The tough upbringing she had endured plus the horrors she saw on a regular basis as part of her job all reminded her that bringing a child into the world – the world she worked in – was one of the stupidest, most selfish things a person could do. And then she found herself pregnant. It was unplanned, unwanted. And to make matters worse, the father wasn't her partner; it was Phil Brennan. Everything about it had been wrong. But now, nearly two years on, things were different. Her life had changed for the better. Phil was now her partner. Their daughter was nearly one. And it took something like the sight of the boy in the bed to remind her that while bringing a child into the world might not be the most stupid, selfish thing imaginable, it was one of the most terrifying.

The gloom of the room was getting to her. 'Shall we step outside?'

10

The antiseptic air in the corridor and the harsh overhead strip lighting felt warm and welcoming in contrast to the dismal darkness of the boy's room. Judging from the way the other two women were unconsciously gulping in deep breaths, Marina reckoned they must have felt it too.

Marina had come straight away, as soon as Anni had hung up. No further appointments for a while, and the tone of Anni's voice told her that this was not only urgent but important. More important than yet another assessment of whether some stroppy, self-deluded officer was fit to return to active duty.

Marina enjoyed working with Anni. She knew how hard it was to be a woman and have any success in the force, but to be a black woman in an area where there were hardly any took real determination. And Anni had plenty of that. But she was also bright enough not to let it show.

It was clear she was on Phil's team. The denim jacket, cargo trousers and dyed blonde hair said that she had embraced the unorthodoxy and creativity he encouraged. From that had come confidence. But not arrogance. And that, Marina had discovered, was a rare trait in a police detective.

Phil's team. When she thought about it, Marina reckoned she must be a part of that now. Especially as the police force was now her official employer.

Josephina, the daughter she and Phil Brennan shared, was approaching her first birthday. And, both of them being working professionals in fulfilling careers, they had agreed to share parenting duties equally. Feeding, cleaning, upbringing. They wouldn't fall into outmoded patriarchal systems. They were a partnership; they would do things together.

It hadn't lasted. Not because of any stubbornness or ideological need, but just because of circumstances. They had fallen into the pattern of most first-time parents. One working, one staying at home. Phil had kept working. He did his share but he still walked out the door in the morning, had something else in his life, could compartmentalise. Marina had tried, and found that she couldn't. Work had been too demanding. So she had stayed at home with the baby. And she had begun to resent him for that.

So when the vacancy for an in-house criminal psychologist with the police force based in Colchester came up, she had jumped at the chance. She knew she could do this job. She had expected resistance or antagonism from Phil, put off telling him. She needn't have worried. He was totally supportive, even gave her a reference. And when she was offered the job, he was the one who sorted out daily childcare for Josephina with his adoptive parents, Don and Eileen Brennan. They had been thrilled to have the baby with them.

So it was a winner all round. Marina and Phil kept both their careers and their relationship going, Don and Eileen felt involved and needed and Josephina got more than her share of attention. And evenings together felt, to Marina and to Phil too, she knew, even more special with just the three of them.

'I'm a working mother with a career and a family,' Marina

47

had said to him, smiling. 'I'm having it all, the *Daily Mail*'s worst nightmare. Worth doing just for that.'

Phil had laughed, agreed. Marina smiled at the memory.

Things were going well. Too well. This had never happened to her before. Something had to come along and spoil it. Something always did.

'You OK?' Anni's voice.

Marina turned, blinked, pulled out of her reverie. Back to the corridor. 'Yeah, fine. Just thinking.'

Anni turned to the doctor. 'I brought Marina in because she's a psychologist.'

'And I think we'll need you,' said Dr Ubha.

'I'm not a child psychologist, though,' said Marina. 'I'm with the police.'

Dr Ubha glanced at the closed door. 'With what's happened to that poor boy, I think we'll need you anyway.'

'I agree,' said Anni. 'You should be on the team for this one. Even if you can't help with the boy himself, you can help find who put him there. You know what makes this kind of person tick.'

Marina nodded. Josephina's smiling face came into her mind. She blinked it away. Swallowed hard. Concentrated. 'What can I do?'

'I need to start checking on missing children,' said Anni. 'Go at it that way. And check that, that . . . ' she could barely bring herself to say the word, 'that thing on his foot. See if there's been anything similar anywhere else. If you can stay here and—'

A noise emanated from the boy's room. A scream. The three women stared at each other.

'He's waking up,' said Anni. 'Come on.'

They ran back inside the room.

11

The white tent had already been erected at the side of the house. Keeping their findings safe and onlookers away. Phil began stripping off his blue suit. Mickey did likewise.

'Like a personal sauna, these things,' Mickey said. 'Must lose half a stone every crime scene I come to.'

Phil gave a distracted smile in acknowledgement, checked his breathing. Fine. He looked up. The ambulances and Police Incident Units were parked at the top of the path, the area taped off, so the gawpers had gathered on the bridge. Peering over, necks craning. Trying for a glimpse of something dangerous or thrilling or exciting. A vicarious kick out of being close to violence but far enough away to be untouched by it. As though his work was some kind of sporting spectacle.

'Like they're watching TV,' said Mickey, reading his mind.

'Our audience,' said Phil. 'As though this is all a kind of showbiz.' Then he thought of the cellar. Laid out like a stage set. The analogy didn't feel appropriate any more.

'Boss?'

Phil turned. The Birdies had arrived. DC Adrian Wren and

DS Jane Gosling. Inevitably paired together because of their surnames. And their physical appearance didn't help: Adrian stick thin, Jane much larger. They looked like a music-hall double act. But they were two of Phil's best officers.

Phil called them over. 'Adrian, Jane, good to see you both.'

They nodded their greetings.

'Right,' he said, addressing the group. 'The CSIs are going to take over this area. Having been down there, I think we've got our work cut out for us.'

'In what way?' DS Jane Gosling frowned.

He explained what he had seen in the cellar. 'We don't know what kind of bones the cage is made from. Hopefully we will soon.'

'Could they be human?' asked DC Adrian Wren.

'Don't rule anything out,' said Phil. 'Not until we know for definite. But some of them have been there for years. And the way it was laid out, there's a sense of ritual interrupted. Whoever's responsible, it looks like he knew what he was doing. Chances are he'll have done it before. So we need to know who owns the house, what sort of history it's got, what hands it's passed through, everything.'

'Might be able to help there,' said Mickey. He flipped through his notebook. 'One of the two guys who called it in. Gave me the name of the demolition firm. George Byers. Based in New Town. They'll know who owns the place. Might have had some dealings with them.'

'Good place to start.' Phil looked behind him at the big Georgian building. Faces were at windows, necks craning to see what was happening. 'Before you do, find out what that place is. Who works there, what they do, if they saw anything or anyone going to and from this house. Someone must have seen something.'

Mickey, making notes, nodded again. So did Adrian.

Phil was still aware of being watched. He looked the other way. A concrete path, chipped, cracked and sprouting weeds, sided by a chain-link fence struggling to withstand an assault from the bushes, trees and weeds threatening to spill out over it. The path led past another dilapidated house. 'What's down there?'

'Council allotments,' said Mickey, following his gaze.

Phil looked again at the house on the opposite side of the path. Saw that it was in fact a small row of terraced houses, two-storey, in a terminal state of disrepair. The roofs were down to skeletal frames, the meat of tiles and fat of insulation starved off them. The windows and doors boarded up, the wood warped, aged down to grey. Gutters and drains rust-stained. The outside walls graffitied and tagged, filthy. And all around the terrace, weeds and vegetation making a bid for reclamation.

'Jane, stay here. Co-ordinate with Forensics. Sorry, CSIs. Wouldn't want to upset them.'

Thin smiles. Forensics had recently been rebranded as CSIs in line with the TV series. Made them feel more glamorous. On the outside at least.

'Anni's at the hospital with the kid. He's still sleeping. No response. She'll be looking into missing children, children's homes, runaways.'

Another look round. The gawpers were still on the bridge. Nearby, but a world away. And Phil reckoned that deep down, they knew that. When they had seen enough they could walk away, taking the frisson of adventure back with them to their normal world. Plus a sense of thankfulness that what was happening down there wasn't happening to them. But Phil couldn't walk away.

And neither could the boy in the cellar.

'I'll check that house over there.' He looked round his team. 'We ready?'

They were.

'Right. 'Let's go.'

Then Phil's phone rang.

12

Rose Martin swallowed hard. Then again. Felt that rush, that tingle of adrenalin, that she hadn't experienced in months. This was where she belonged. Back. Working.

Since the call, everything had felt good. Right. She had pulled up to the Road Closed sign on Colchester Road just outside the village of Wakes Colne, holding her warrant card up to the windscreen, being allowed access where all other vehicles were being turned away. She felt that indescribable power that being above civilians gave her. She had missed it.

She pulled her car up to the crime-scene tape, flashing her warrant card again, silencing the nearest uniform's entreaty to turn away. Just ducking under the tape, walking along the closed-off country road, her heels echoing, had been thrilling. The trees either side of the road seemed to bend in, beckoning her towards the crime scene.

She looked ahead. A 4x4 had ploughed into the banked up roadside, its left front side crumpled. Behind it, blue-suited CSIs stood and knelt in the road alongside uniforms. All attention directed downwards. She speeded up. Eager to rejoin her clan, immerse herself in that life once more. Lead them.

Then she stopped dead. Looked at them once more. Crouching. Kneeling. The body. There would be the body.

Her chest was gripped by a sudden fear; her arms began to shake. Her feet wouldn't move forward. She wanted to turn, run back to her car, put herself on the other side of the tape once more. Forget about it. Hide herself away.

Marina was right. She had said this would happen.

Marina. Rose closed her eyes, controlled her breathing. Nothing that woman or her bastard boyfriend had to say was of any relevance to her. She would prove them wrong. Show them that she was strong enough to return, cool-headed and unafraid of anything the job could throw at her. She would show them.

The shaking subsided. Her breathing returned to normal. She flexed her fingers, regaining control of her body, willing it. Yes. She would show them.

She started walking again, the viaduct behind her, the leaves on the trees slowly moving, rubbing together, like jazz brushes over drum skins. She moved slowly at first, then with purpose. She reached the gathering of uniforms and blue suits. Held up her warrant card.

'DS Martin,' she said, slightly too loudly, ensuring they all saw her ID. She cleared her throat. 'What have we got here?'

A plain-suited man she hadn't spotted stood upright. He crossed towards her. 'Hello, Rose,' he said. 'Good to see you.' He stretched out his hand for her to shake. She took it.

Her superior officer. Acting DCI Brian Glass.

Glass offered her a smile. A small one, as if rationed. A quick flicker across his lips, then gone. Back to business.

She knew him by reputation. A no-nonsense, by-the-book copper. Always well turned out, but not flashily so. Respectably suited, as if he dressed for court or cameras. Hair short and tidy but not severe, greying at the temples. Methodical, diligent, got results by hard work. Straight-backed, well-built; his aftershave could have been Eau D'Alpha Male. Tanned, healthy-looking. Very tanned, in fact, thought Rose. Not just a copper's copper, but a copper copper.

She smiled inwardly at that thought. Noticed his eyes make a quick detour to her breasts. Smiling inwardly once more, she pushed them further out in as unconscious a way as possible. She knew what her weapons were. Wasn't above deploying them strategically.

Another smile flashed across his lips. Appreciative, this time. And in that instant Rose knew that this was her case. She could ask of him anything that she wanted. And get it. Because underneath that straight exterior, he was just another bloke.

She had him. Right where she wanted him. Maybe not immediately, but she could work on him. And that work wouldn't go unrewarded.

Yes. This was going to be a good case.

13

Phil walked away from the group, put his phone to his ear.

'Phil? Just a quick call. About Josephina. Wondering what time you'll be picking her up.'

He knew the voice straight away. Don Brennan, his adoptive father.

'Hi, Don.'

Don Brennan picked up on the tone of Phil's voice. 'Sorry, you busy? This a bad time?'

Phil looked around. Orders given, his team were all moving away from him. He put his head down, covered the mouthpiece. 'Kind of.'

Don's voice changed immediately. 'What's happened?'

Don was an ex-copper. Responsible for Phil's upbringing and for Phil's career choice. He had also found it difficult to let go. Phil could understand that and tried to keep him informed as much as possible. When he could. He often joked with him, said that telling him about his day at work made him feel like the head of the CIA giving security briefings to a former US president.

Phil had suggested Don apply to work in the cold-case unit, but Don hadn't been interested, said it wasn't real police work, just an approximation of it. Something to appease the old-timers with. Give them a pat on the head and a sticker. Phil felt sure he would change his mind at some point.

Phil hesitated before speaking. He didn't want to say too much about an ongoing investigation, but he also didn't want to patronise the man he regarded as his father.

'Someone been murdered?'

'Wish it was that simple. I'm down on East Hill. We've found a child. It's . . . not good.'

'Abused?'

'Probably. But alive. In the cellar of a house. In a cage.'

Phil expected Don to ask further questions but he was greeted with silence.

'You there?'

'Yes, yes . . . I'm still here. In a cage, you say?' There was now no vestige whatsoever of the doting grandfather in Don's voice. He was back in the day, back on the force. 'What kind of cage?'

Again Phil hesitated before speaking. 'It's . . . bone. A cage made of bones.'

Phil heard nothing but the taut, static hum of silence.

'Listen, Don, I'll have to call you back later. Are you OK with Josephina for a while? I don't know how long we'll be with this.'

'Yes, yes, fine . . . ' Don sounded distracted. 'You just . . . just call whenever.'

'Will do.' Phil looked at his watch, at the house by the allotments. 'Look, I've got to go. I'll give you a ring later, OK?'

Don said that was OK and Phil broke the connection.

His father had sounded strange, but Phil didn't have time to dwell on that now. He looked at the house once more. Made his way towards it.

14

Don Brennan was in the kitchen. Sitting at the table. He replaced the phone, sat staring at it. His hand absently rubbing the stubble on his chin.

A cage . . . made of bones . . .

He heard sounds from the living room. A cheerful children's song being sung on the TV. His wife Eileen talking to Josephina. And Josephina herself answering, her phrasing still unformed, just enjoying the sounds she could make, the novelty of communication. Laughing like all life had to offer was good.

A cage . . . made of bones . . .

He didn't know how long he sat there, lost in his own thoughts, memories, but gradually became aware of a shadow standing before him, blotting out the light coming in from the garden.

'What's the matter? You all right?'

He looked up. Eileen. She read his eyes. Knew something wasn't right. Sat down next to him. Behind them, the TV continued to play cheerfully.

'What's happened?'

He sighed. 'Just spoke to Phil. He's at a house down on East Hill.' He fell silent, unsure how to say the next words.

'And?' Eileen, eager for news, even if it was bad.

'There was a cage in there. With a child in. A cage of bones ...'

Eileen's hand went to her mouth. 'Oh my God ... oh no ...'

They sat there, not speaking, not moving, while garden sunlight cast shadows round them and a contented child played in the next room, unaware that the world could ever be a bad place.

15

'Where's the body?' Rose Martin said, trying not to look at the ground.

Glass looked round, back to Rose. 'Taken away. I didn't think you needed to see it. Very nasty.'

A flame of anger flared inside her. *He* didn't think she needed to see it? *He* didn't? She took a moment, composed herself. It was probably the right thing, she thought. She didn't need to see a body, not her first day back. And she could hardly have refused if it had been there. Instant loss of respect. She waited until the anger subsided before speaking. 'Four-by-fours tend to do that,' she said.

'They will,' Glass said, 'especially when they're the second car to hit.' He turned to her. 'I didn't think you should see the results of that. Not on your first day back.'

She nodded. 'Right. Thank you.' Gave a small laugh. 'Just what I was thinking.'

He smiled again. 'No problem. Body's in the mortuary if you need to see it. Give Nick Lines a call.'

His hand touched her shoulder. Just briefly, then away. Her anger flared again. Should she make something of it? Ask him whether he would have done that to a male colleague? No, she decided. She didn't want any trouble. Not yet.

But it meant he knew. Of course he knew; everyone at the station knew. And he'd made up his mind based on that. The affair with Ben had ended up common knowledge. No doubt, she had thought, rumours would do the rounds about the speed of her return being because she was now Glass's lover. Let them. She could take it.

And if this new boss thought he had a chance with her as well . . . She could play her part, play along. Let him think he had a chance, even. See what she could get out of it. A tactical deployment of weapons.

'So what have we got here?' Rose said, snapping on her latex gloves.

'Road accident,' said Glass, looking down at where deep black tyre tracks had come to a sudden, unexpected halt, the back of the 4x4. 'Woman ran out in front of that car over there,' he said, pointing to a VW Passat stuck in the banked side of the road, 'then this one came along, finished the job. Dead virtually on impact. Woman who was driving's in a right state.'

'I can imagine,' said Rose, not doing so. 'She over there?' She pointed to the ambulance parked at the side of the road.

'They both are.'

A blonde woman who looked like a dishevelled footballer's wife was sitting in the back of the ambulance. Blanket draped over her shoulders, she was staring off into the middle distance, but her eyes appeared more inward-looking than they had probably ever been in her life.

Next to her was a middle-aged man, dressed in a business suit and looking equally dishevelled. Neither of them was looking at each other.

'They been any help?' asked Rose.

'Both said the same thing. This woman came running down the bank out of the trees. Didn't stop. Probably going too fast. First car, the man, couldn't swerve out of the way, tried to stop but there wasn't time so just ploughed into her. Up and over the bonnet. Four-by-four hit her when she landed. Finished the job.'

Rose looked down at the ground once more. It was dark from more than just tyre tracks. She swallowed hard, pleased there was no body to see. Tried not to let the sight of the blood that was there disturb her. Questions, she thought. Keep it at bay with questions.

'Happened this morning, you said?'

Glass nodded.

'What time?'

'Early. Very early. About sunrise, not much after. Six-ish.'

'And what were our drivers doing out at that time?'

A smile crossed Glass's features. 'Lovers. They'd spent the night together. At a motel. He was off to work, she was off to get the kids up for school. Told poor old hubby she'd been with a sick friend all night.'

Rose smiled too. 'So, the victim. Do we know who she is yet?'

'One of the uniforms found a Visa Electron card in the woods. Name of . . .' he checked his notebook, 'Faith Luscombe.'

'Faith Luscombe . . .' Rose took out her phone, turned to Glass. 'You checked her out?'

'First thing I did. She's known to us. Got a record. Soliciting.'

'Where?'

'Colchester. New Town.'

'Bit out of the way, up here.'

'Not necessarily,' he said. 'She was naked when she met her death. Might have been working.'

62

'Could be,' said Rose. 'Out here with a client, parked up in there somewhere, got a bit rough, she ran away ...' She looked at the steep bank. 'Down that slope, into this car. Then that one.' She suppressed a shudder. 'Makes sense. So we should be looking for a clearing up there, a car. A place where she was running from. Any other witnesses.'

Another touch of her shoulder. 'That's what you're here for.'

'Right,' she said.

'We know how she died,' he said, taking his hand away. 'What we need to find out is how she got here. Throw some light on the matter.'

'We'll need to get in the woods, have a comb through.'

'Uniforms have done that already. That's how the card turned up.'

'I'll need to get them in there again. See what else we can find.'

Glass pulled a slightly pained expression. 'Well ... that might be difficult. We're down on numbers at the moment. Budget cuts for one thing. And we're a bit stretched. What with all that activity down on East Hill.'

Rose nodded, kept her face straight. Felt anger welling up inside again. Phil bloody Brennan. Once more, he had taken priority. She tamped the anger down, forced a smile. She knew how to get her own way.

She moved close to Glass. Arched her back once more. 'Oh come on, Brian, I'm sure you could get some extra bodies in to help here ...'

Glass looked at her, face flat, expressionless. 'DS Martin, I would if I could. But it's just not possible. If you want to look in the woods again, you'll have to do it yourself. Personally, I would accept what the uniforms found for now and move on.'

Rose backed off. Angry with him, angry with herself. 'Right,' she said. 'Fine. You got an address for her?'

He gave it to her. 'And the name of the person she lives with. Donna Warren.'

'Do we know her?'

'Oh yes. Faith's partner in crime.'

'OK.' She made a note.

Glass looked at his watch. 'Better get a move on. I don't think anyone's going to be losing sleep over some prostitute who got herself killed, so let's get this one wrapped up soon as, eh? Shouldn't take you too long.'

'Fine,' she said. 'I'll just have a word with our couple over there, then get over to New Town.'

Glass stayed where he was. Rose thought something else was expected of her.

'Thanks for this opportunity ...' she almost called him Brian, 'DCI Glass. I—'

He cut her off. 'There's something else.' His face impassive.

Her heart skipped a beat. She waited.

'I'm promoting you.'

She wasn't sure she had heard him properly. 'What?'

'I'm promoting you. Provisionally, anyway.'

'I ...'

'You had applied for promotion before your ... absence. I'd like to put it through.'

'I don't know what to say ...'

'Thank you would be nice.'

She laughed, grinned. 'Thank you.'

He didn't. 'You're welcome. Right, DI Martin, this arrangement will become permanent once you've completed this assignment.'

'Right.'

He looked straight at her, eyes boring into hers. 'To my sat-isfaction. Understand?'

And suddenly she understood. Do what he wanted. That

was what he meant. And she would. She wanted that promotion. 'Don't worry,' she said. 'I won't let you down.'

'I know you won't,' he said, and turned away.

First day back on the job and she had been promoted. And because of that she didn't care that Phil bloody bastard Brennan was taking precedence. She would show him. She would show all of them.

She walked over to the couple in the ambulance. Notepad at the ready.

She would show him. Show all of them.

16

The day fell away as Phil stepped carefully through the doorway of the run-down house.

The depressing ruin draped itself around him, sucking out the light. The floorboards creaked under his feet. He put his weight down slowly on each one, testing to see whether the wood had rotted, unsure if there was a cellar beneath and if so what it might contain.

The boards held. He moved slowly into the hallway. The smell struck him first. Neglect. Damp. Terminal decay. The close, fetid air clung to his face like a cold death mask. He pulled on latex gloves. Work-required, but in any case the thought of touching anything in this place felt like a contamination.

Phil couldn't shake an irrational sense of unease. He analysed it: it didn't make sense. He had attended much more dangerous crime scenes before. Some where his life had been in danger. A few that had been so bad his body had been crippled by panic attacks. So why was this – an empty old house – so bad? He couldn't explain. But he knew he felt it.

Into what would once have been, he guessed, the living

room. Nothing lived in it now. At least nothing human. Small shadows scurried away at the sides of his feet, disappeared down cracks, holes. He took out a pocket flashlight, swept it over the floor. Some of the boards were missing, rotted and caved in. But no cellar.

The room was empty of everything but detritus. Old pizza boxes and mouldering kebab wrappers were slowly breaking themselves down into compost. Rusting high-strength lager cans, empty bottles sticky with dust. Cigarette ends, both legal and illegal, were dotted around. Human consumption. And in the corner, the inevitable conclusion. Human waste. As old and atrophied as everything else in the room.

Damp cardboard and a festering, mouldering blanket had been a bed. Stained and crumpled pages from old, well-used porn mags at the side. Bedtime reading. From the patina of dust coating every surface, no one had been there for a while.

Two broken, unboarded windows on the far side of the room explained how the previous inhabitants had made their entrance and exit. Phil thought he heard something. A scuffling movement from somewhere. He straightened up, listened.

'Hello?'

No reply. Just the dying echo of his voice through the ruin.

Heart beating faster, he turned right, into another room, that had once been a kitchen. Most of the cabinets were still in place, as was the remains of a cooker in the corner and an old fridge, the door open, hanging off. The walls, he noticed, had once been a cheerful yellow. But the vibrancy was gone, the fight given up. They were now streaked black with mould. A back door led out into a garden. He tried the handle. It didn't budge. A thick wooden board had been nailed over the glass panels.

He swept the room with his flashlight, peered into the corners, the cabinets, even inside the oven. Nothing. He turned back into the main living room. Tried to imagine what the house had once been like. Couldn't. The decay was too pervasive.

Turning left, he went into another hallway. Stairs led upwards. He took them.

Three doors presented themselves on a small landing. He chose the right-hand one. Found the wreck of a small bathroom. The sink smashed off the wall, the toilet pan cracked in two. The bath now a breeding ground for mould and mildew.

He opened the door on his left. The main bedroom. The room was completely bare. Peeling, damp walls, rotted wood, boarded windows. No furniture, just dirt and dust. The walls had been painted, not papered. Originally emerald green, it looked like. And the floor, too. Phil swung his flashlight again. There was something on the wall. He stepped in to examine it.

The same design they had found on the wall of the cellar beside the cage. Not a pentagram, but something . . . not right. And seeing it again, something clicked inside Phil. Something deep and hard, either lodging or dislodging. A tumbler in a vault combination falling into place.

He recognised it. He didn't know what it was, but there was part of him that recognised it. Then the familiar constrictions started in his chest. Not a full-blown panic attack, just something low and rumbling. A sense of unease. He didn't know what the symbol was, but it meant nothing good to him.

Trying to head the attack off, he backed out of the room. Tried the third door.

And immediately found himself thrown back out on to the landing.

His back and head hurt from contact with the bare wood, his chest from the force of the blow. It had knocked the wind out of his lungs. He tried to get his breath, gagged as he breathed in. The stink was awful. He opened his eyes. A vision of humanity – as wrecked as the house was – was on top of him. Screaming, hitting him about the head.

Phil didn't have time to think, to do anything but react instinctively, use his urge for self-preservation. His arms were pinned at his sides, as much by his own body as by his assailant. He brought his knee up between his attacker's legs, hard. The man gave a yelp of pain, like a wounded animal, drew back. Stopped hitting him as his hands went to his groin.

Phil knew this was only temporary, that his attacker would recommence soon, so he pressed the advantage. He brought his right fist up, straight into the man's face. Felt it connect with nose cartilage. Saw blood spurt.

Glad he had remembered the latex gloves, he punched again. His assailant had no fight left in him. With another scream of pain, he dragged himself hurriedly off Phil, ran down the stairs. Phil got slowly to his feet, breathing in through his mouth. The smell was still in his nostrils.

He turned and, knowing that what he had seen on the wall would keep for later, gave chase.

The man was already out of the front door, running down the gravel drive, Phil after him, shouting for help. He reached the first house, headed towards the road. He saw the uniforms, the incident vehicles, the crowds ahead and turned. Made for the allotments.

Four uniforms gave chase. Phil joined them. Together they pursued what looked like a running bundle of rags

It was no contest. The officers brought him to the ground before he reached the allotment gates. Phil arrived in time to stand over them.

'Right. Let's get him on his feet.'

They helped the man to stand. Phil got a good look at him. He was older than expected. Although that might have been the long grey hair and beard. His clothing was in ruins and tatters, his features filthy and scabbed. His bleeding nose made him look even worse. And the smell. Like he was decomposing before them. Phil hadn't thought it possible to decay that much and still live.

The fight had gone out of him now. He was whimpering.

'Come on,' said Phil, turning. 'Let's take him somewhere, have a chat.'

Phil hoped he had found the perpetrator, the child's abductor. But looking at the wreck of humanity before him, he doubted it.

17

'Please, Detective . . . Philips, is it?'

Mickey nodded. 'Detective Sergeant Philips. Major Incident Squad.'

'Right, Detective Sergeant.' Her eyes widened slightly. 'Sounds important. Please, take a seat.'

Mickey extended his hand, then, realising how awkward the gesture was, he quickly retracted it and sat, hoping she hadn't noticed. The tiny smile on her lips told him she had. Not a good start.

He looked at the woman opposite him. Mid-thirties, he reckoned, well-built but curvy. Wearing a figure-hugging and enhancing black dress; long brown hair highlighted blonde. As he got settled, she flashed him a larger smile that had, he presumed, seen plenty of service on the local great-and-good cocktail circuit. And was used to seeing its magic work.

She held out her hand. 'I'm Lynn Windsor,' she said, her voice as confident as her smile. 'Senior Partner, Fenton Associates.'

He stood slightly, shook hands. She was good, he thought.

Had managed a seemingly effortless domination of the situation. He had ground to gain.

They were in an office on the first floor of the Georgian house. Adrian Wren had been tasked with talking to the occupants, but word came through that someone of senior rank was required. Since Phil was indisposed, that was Mickey.

Walking through, Mickey had noticed that the inside of the building was as tastefully decorated as the exterior. The floors were wooden, the walls neutral. They held paintings that were clearly original, but not original enough to command huge sums, gallery space or column inches. The office furniture managed to look both expensive and minimal.

The ground floor was taken up by a firm of accountants. On the next two floors were Fenton Associates, solicitors, and above them on the smallest, cramped floor, a marketing company. There was an air of excitement in the law offices as suited and tied people, normally more at home with spreadsheets and files, craned their collective necks to see what was going on opposite. When Mickey entered, they transferred their attention to him.

'So, Detective Philips, your uniformed officers have been questioning my staff. I presume it's in connection with whatever's going on down there.' She pointed to the window.

'That's right.'

'And what is that, exactly?' Taking charge again.

'I'm afraid I can't say at the moment.'

'Oh please, Detective Philips. We're all legal professionals here.'

Mickey thought for a moment. 'Fenton Associates. I've not heard of you before.'

'No reason why you should,' said Lynn Windsor. 'We're corporate, not criminal. We cover most of East Anglia. Specialise in blue-chip companies.' She smiled again. 'We don't bail out New Town drug dealers.'

Mickey smiled. 'Must be why we've never met before.'

'Must be.' She straightened up. He tried hard not to look at her breasts. Failed. 'And what do you do, Detective Sergeant? Catch criminals? Solve murders?' Her smiled widened, became more teasing. 'Deal with major incidents?'

Mickey felt uncomfortable. She had him again. He was sure he was blushing. 'That sort of thing, yeah.'

She raised an eyebrow. 'Keep up the good work.'

'Er, thanks ...' Mickey looked down at his notepad, tried to hide his discomfort. 'You, er, wanted to see me, Ms Windsor?'

She sat back, smiling. Thinking. Those breasts of hers were large, Mickey noticed once more. 'Call me Lynn, please. Sounds like you're talking to my mother. And I can call you ...?'

'Mickey.' He looked quickly away, hoping he hadn't been caught staring. If he had, she didn't let on.

'So,' she said, 'you want my help and the co-operation of my staff, but you won't tell me what's happened.'

'I'm afraid ...'

The smile dropped. She became businesslike. 'I appreciate what you're saying, but perhaps you should see things from my side.'

Mickey waited.

'What if one of my staff has seen something? Something that places them in danger?'

'Might they have done?'

Lynn Windsor shrugged. Mickey tried not to watch her breasts move as she did so. 'I don't know. Perhaps they could identify someone who might later come back to harm them. Or say something that could inadvertently incriminate them even though they're innocent?'

Mickey gave a small smile. 'You've been watching too much TV.'

'Really? You're saying that never happens in real life?'

'Not as often as you think. Not really.'

She leaned back, eyes on him all the time. Mickey felt like he was being appraised. Like there was more to this conversation than the words on the surface. But he didn't know what.

'I'm a solicitor and you're a police officer,' she said. 'We both know it does happen. Before any of my staff speak, I would need guarantees of protection.'

'You can have them,' he said. 'If it comes to that. But I doubt it. It's just routine questioning.'

'And we can't ask what's going on? We heard a lot of screaming down there earlier today. What was that?'

He opened his mouth to reply.

'You can't say,' she said. 'Right.' She sat forward, steepled her fingers. Eyes never leaving him. Mind seemingly made up. 'All right, then. Ask me what you want to know.'

He asked her. Had she seen anyone entering or leaving the crumbling building? Only occasional workmen. They had erected the fence, put up the signs. Had there been anyone there recently? Not that she had seen. What about the other houses? The ones down below? Her expression changed.

'Ah.' She sat back. 'There was . . . someone down there.'

'Who?'

'A tramp, I think. A homeless person. Someone was living in that derelict house, the one at the end of the garden. We would find evidence that someone had tried to break into this building at night. We assumed it was him. We initiated legal proceedings, got him to leave. Then we contacted the council, asked them to board it up. That seemed to take care of the problem.'

Mickey glanced at his notebook, ready to ask another question. Lynn Windsor silenced him. 'I'm afraid that's all the time I can spare today. I have a client coming in.' She stood up, came round the desk. Smiled once more, held her eyes on his. 'But if there's anything I can do to help ... ' She handed him her card. 'Anything further you want to ask me ... '

He stood, went to take her card. Noticed she wasn't wearing a wedding ring. Was about to speak when his eye was drawn to someone walking past the office window. A tall man, middle-aged, well-dressed. He didn't look happy. Another middle-aged man was ushering him quickly into the next office along.

'Who's that?' said Mickey. He was sure he recognised him.

Lynn Windsor's gaze followed his. 'One of our clients.' Her smile had disappeared. 'I'm afraid I have work to do. You'll have to leave.'

'What's his name?'

Lynn Windsor's smile returned. But it was hard, professional. No warmth to it. 'I'm afraid I can't give that out. Some of our clients prefer to remain anonymous. We have to respect their wishes.'

'Right ... '

She placed her hand on the small of his back, ushering him out of the office. At the doorway she stopped. Body blocking his view of the next office along. 'Do you have a card? Some way for me to get in touch with you?'

'Uh, yes ... ' He dug into his jacket, handed one over.

'Thank you. If I think of anything else, can I call you?' Eyes full on him. 'Or you can call me ... '

Mickey was flustered once more. 'Yeah ... sure.'

Another dazzling smile. 'I'd like that.' She turned, motioned to a pretty girl seated at a desk. 'Stephanie will see you out.'

Mickey said goodbye and left.

Head spinning from the encounter. Hoping he would see her again. Wondering just who the man was. He couldn't think of where he had seen him.

But he knew it wasn't good news.

18

At least he had stopped screaming, thought Anni. That was something.

The boy from the cage lay in front of them. Completely still, eyes wide open, staring straight ahead. Like an animal hiding in plain view, frozen. Thinking that if he couldn't see them, they couldn't see him.

Anni tried another smile. 'What's your name?'

Nothing. Just those eyes, unblinking.

Dr Ubha was standing behind them both, monitoring the situation. She had been first in the room when they heard the screaming. Had ducked to avoid a plastic tumbler aimed at her head. When they had stepped into the darkened room, they had seen a water jug lying on its side where he had thrown it, the floor wet. He was kicking, thrashing, trying to pull the feeding drip from the back of his hand, escape from the tightly made bed covers.

Dr Ubha went straight up to the boy. On seeing her approach, he forgot the drip and, eyes brimming with panic and fear, grabbed her arms to fight her off. Anni had been at her side in an instant, ready to assist, but the doctor, sensing that the boy's reaction was born of terror rather than aggression, had pulled away from him and stepped back. Once she did that, his hands had dropped.

Seeing he had no means of escape through the door with the three women there, he had backed himself up against the headboard of the bed, tried to push himself through it. Gasping and sobbing as he did so. But, Anni had noticed, there was no violence. And he hadn't spoken. Just the staring. And silence.

Realising he wasn't going to attack again, Anni exchanged a glance with Marina and moved forward, making to sit in the chair beside the bed. The child pushed himself even further back, whimpering once more, trembling now in fear. Eyes moving from staring at nothing to being directly on Anni. She stopped, chilled when they met hers. She had come across people in distress through her work, on an almost daily basis. But she had never encountered such depths of terror in anyone. She flinched inwardly, not wanting to think about what the boy had seen, experienced.

'OK ... ' Eyes averted from his, she backed off. Took a chair from behind her and slowly brought it up to the bottom of the bed. The boy didn't take his eyes off her all the time she was moving. She sat. Looked at him. Managed to smile.

'Hello,' she said. 'I'm Anni. What's your name?'

Nothing.

'You do have a name, don't you?'

Nothing. Just those eyes, that stare ...

Anni could cope with traumatised women, rape victims, abused wives, but children were a blind spot. She had been trained to deal with them and always followed her training, but it wasn't something that came naturally to her. Usually she found something she could relate to, some shared commonality on which to start a dialogue, build a relationship. It could be anything from difficulties with siblings or school to football or even *Doctor Who*. Anything. But it was all book-learned, not natural. And he kept staring at her. Those eyes ... Maybe if she had children of her own. That might be different. But she didn't, and although her sister had a couple, she lived in Wales and they weren't close.

She felt another chair being pulled up next to her. Marina sat down. Anni immediately felt more relaxed.

Marina smiled at the boy. 'Hello.'

Anni didn't know how she had managed it, but something in Marina's smile connected with the boy. He didn't reply, but neither did he look as scared as he had done.

'I'm Marina.' She gave another smile. If she had seen the depths of fear in his eyes, thought Anni, she wasn't letting it show. 'Don't worry. You won't have to remember all these names. How are you feeling? Do you hurt anywhere?'

The boy forgot his need to escape and shifted slightly as if testing his body in response to the question. He held up his bandaged hand.

'Yes, you've broken your fingers. But they'll mend.'

He still didn't speak, but he didn't express any great discomfort either. He looked at the tube going into the back of his hand. Frowned. Moved his other hand towards it.

'I think it's better if you leave that where it is,' Marina said, her voice calm and warm yet authoritative. 'It's feeding you. Making you big and strong.'

The boy's hand fell back.

'It's a little bit uncomfortable. But it'll make you feel a lot better, I promise you.' Another smile. Reassuring. 'That's better.' Marina leaned forward towards the boy, not threatening his space, just showing she was interested in him. 'Now, I've told you my name, Marina, why don't you tell me yours?'

The boy's eyes darted between the three women.

'We're not going to hurt you. But it would be nice if I knew what to call you, don't you think?'

Again the boy's eyes darted. But this time the fear seemed to be lessening. Like he was deciding whether he could trust them or not. He began moving his mouth. At first Anni took it for another unconscious fear response, but she quickly realised that he was trying to form sounds, words.

She waited, hardly daring to move, while the boy's mouth twisted.

'Fff . . . ' His front teeth looked rotten, painful as he placed them on his lower lip, tried to make a sound. 'Fff . . . Ffinnn . . . '

They waited. He offered nothing more.

'Finn?' said Marina. 'You're called Finn?'

Another glance between the three of them. Then a small nod of the head.

Anni let out a breath she was unaware of holding. She stole a glance at Marina, saw a glint of joy, triumph in her eye.

'Well hello, Finn,' said Marina, still smiling. 'It's a pleasure to meet you.'

The boy seemed to relax slightly. His mouth kept twisting, trying to form more words, or just repeat the same one.

'Ffinn . . . Finn . . . '

'Very good,' said Marina, an encouraging teacher. 'So where are you from, Finn?'

More tortuous mouth-twisting. 'Thhh . . . Gahh . . . denn . . . '

Anni and Marina stole a glance at each other. 'The . . . Garden?' said Marina. 'Is that where you're from?'

Another nervous look between the pair of them, then a nod.

The Garden, thought Anni. Her mind was immediately working. Checking through a mental Rolodex for a match. Children's homes, care homes, residential, secure units, YOIs, anything that would match ... The Garden ... She came up with nothing.

Marina was about to ask another question, but Finn's mouth was twisting again. She kept silent, waited.

'Mmm ... mmoth ... eh ... moth ... er ... '

'Mother?' said Marina. 'Your mother?'

Another nod.

'What about her? Is she ... is she looking for you?'

Finn frowned. A dark shadow covered his face. His mouth twisted once more. 'Thh ... thhuh ... god ... thuh god ... nerrr ... '

'The gardener?' said Marina. 'Your mother is the gardener?'

Finn shook his head viciously. 'Nnnuh ... nnnuh ... ' The darkness was seeping back into his eyes. The terror.

'Your mother,' Marina persisted, trying to head off those dark thoughts. 'Tell me about your mother, Finn. Is she ... is she in the Garden? Would we find her in the Garden?'

Finn's eyes snapped open wide once more. The terror dissipating. He nodded.

'Right. Where is the Garden, Finn?'

He twisted his mouth, searched for words.

They waited.

And Marina's phone went.

Finn jumped, screamed, pushed himself back into the headboard.

'It's all right,' said Marina. 'All right ... ' Although inwardly she was cursing. She stood up, walked into the corridor to take the call.

Anni remained with Finn. She tried the smile Marina had used. Hoped it would work. 'Hey, it's OK, Finn. It's just a phone. Just a phone call.'

The boy was calming down. Anni was stunned – had he

81

never seen a mobile phone before? Or any phone? 'It's OK,' she said once more, hoping her words would soothe.

Marina pocketed her phone, motioned to Anni from the doorway. 'That was Phil. He wants me at the crime scene.'

'Didn't you tell him what was happening here?'

'I did, but . . . ' She shrugged.

'You're doing great. He was just about to tell us where he was from.'

'Perhaps. If he knows, which I doubt. Anni, he can barely speak. I mean, I'm doing the best I can, but I'm limited. This isn't my area. They really need a professional child psychologist to come in and work with him. It'll take time.'

Anni looked once more at the boy lying there. A lost boy. Her heart went out to him.

'I'd better go,' said Marina. 'Keep talking to him. Ask about his mother. But don't let him talk about this gardener, that seems to upset him.' Then she too looked at Finn. 'I'll just say goodbye to him first.'

19

Phil was getting nowhere.

He stared at the wreck of a man in front of him, exasperated, lost for words. Tried again. 'OK . . . look.' He sighed. 'I'm not going to hurt you. You're not in any trouble. We just need some help.'

The man stared off over Phil's shoulder. Seeing something Phil couldn't, something that wasn't even in the room. Phil tried not to let his exasperation show.

They were sitting opposite each other on folding chairs in the back of the incident support van. Phil hadn't noticed how cramped those vans were. Or how badly ventilated. But he did now. With a vengeance.

The tramp smelled like parts of him were dying. Like he was decomposing before Phil's eyes. When he stood up, Phil wouldn't have been surprised if he left some body part behind. His clothes were just the tattered ghosts of the garments they had once been. Shirts, T-shirts and vests had been wrapped around him, the layers solidifying into one filthy mass. His trousers were ill-fitting and torn, scabbed and ulcerated legs peeking out from beneath. His boots were holed, his feet sockless.

And his face. Phil was usually good at spotting people's ages and backgrounds. Physical tics and tells always gave them away. But he had no idea with this man. The lines on his face were deepened and ingrained by dirt, like permanent comic-strip etchings. His skin was reddened by various abuses. His hair long, greying and filthy, like his beard. Ravaged, scarred and weather-beaten, he could have been anything from forties to seventies.

Phil tried again, his voice as calm and unthreatening as possible. He didn't think it a good idea to tell the tramp he was the prime suspect in a kidnapping and possible murder inquiry. 'So what's your name?'

The tramp swivelled his head towards Phil, eyes coming slowly into focus. He stared blankly ahead.

'Do you have a name? What would you like me to call you?'

'Paul.'

Result. 'Paul. Good. I'm Phil.' He leaned forward. 'Right, Paul, what were you doing in that house? Is that where you live?'

'I live . . . By God's grace, I live . . . '

'Right. And by God's grace, do you live in that house? The one where I found you?'

A sigh, as if mention of the house brought with it a great burden on his soul. 'My . . . house.'

'Your house. Right.'

His voice rose. 'In my house there are many mansions . . . '

Here we go, thought Phil. This was what he had dreaded. 'There are. Yes. So you live there, where I found you?'

Another blank look, then Paul put his head back as if remembering. Then a nod.

'Good. That's fine. That's great. Maybe you could help me, Paul. You know the house opposite yours? The one we've been going in and out of all day?'

Paul's face darkened, eyes came together. Fear crept over his features.

'What's the matter, Paul? Is there something wrong with that house?'

He shrank back from Phil, as if trying to physically get away from his words. 'No . . . no . . . There was . . . there was . . . evil in there . . .'

Phil leaned forward. This was it, he thought. Getting somewhere. Even if the tramp was addled. 'Evil? What kind of evil?'

'There was . . . No. I can't . . . can't say . . .'

'Why can't you say? Paul, why can't you say?'

'Because he'll . . . come back and I . . . No . . . he's evil, evil . . .'

'Evil? The man in the other house is evil? The house we were in?'

Paul's brow creased. He seemed confused by the question but continued anyway. 'A man. With a dream. Of love. The love of creation . . . Of creation . . .'

Phil leaned back, suppressed a sigh. He had thought he was going to be given a lead. Instead it was just a story from the tramp's damaged mind.

'Was this man evil? Is he the one you meant?'

Paul stared off somewhere, kept talking as if he hadn't heard Phil.

'This man . . . he . . . he shared that love with others . . . And it was good . . . But then . . . the bad, the evil . . . men . . . came . . .'

Paul stopped talking. Phil leaned forward once more. 'Where did the bad men come, Paul? To the house? The house you live in? Or the one opposite? Which one d'you mean?'

Another frown. 'The bad men . . . Serpents in paradise . . .' Paul frowned once more, face screwed up as if he was about

85

to cry. 'I just ... just want to see the sun ... ' He trailed off into a troubled silence, chewing his lower lip with rotted teeth, head moving slowly from side to side, body beginning to rock back and forth.

'But ... what about the evil?' Phil knew his words weren't reaching him.

Paul's voice, although as broken and ravaged as the rest of him, held traces of education and perhaps erudition. The echoes of someone else, the person he had once been. Phil reflected on that, knew that was why he didn't allow his first response, to dismiss the story as just a deranged ramble, to take hold. Paul's words nagged at him. He thought of the designs on the wall of the house and in the cellar. They looked to have been drawn by two different hands, but they were the same kind of design. Something mystical, but not quite a pentagram. And now Paul's words. Serpents in paradise ...

Again something gnawed at Phil. Something he couldn't quite reach.

He tried a different line of questioning. 'That design on the wall of your house,' he said. 'Did you draw that?'

Paul stopped rocking, looked at him quizzically.

'On the wall. That design. What does it mean, Paul?'

'It's ... life. It's ... everything ... '

He fell back into silence. Rocking backwards and forwards, mouth moving with words he wouldn't speak.

Phil tried to talk to him again but got no response. He sensed he would get no more from him for a while now. He stood up.

'Just stay here a minute, please, Paul. I'll be back soon.'

He turned, left the van, glad of the fresh air. He popped a mint into his mouth to take away the smell. One of the Birdies could chat to Paul next. See how they got on with him.

Phil didn't think the tramp was the man they were looking

for. Instinct told him that, and he had learned to rely on instinct. He thought Paul might know something, but whatever that was wasn't going to be unearthed quickly. If at all.

He checked his watch. Time for Marina. Good. He was looking forward to seeing her.

And also not. Because something was wrong. Inside of him. That house ... it had touched something deep within him, something dark, twisted. Unpleasant.

Something soul-deep that he couldn't understand.

But something he didn't want Marina to see.

Not until he understood it better himself.

So he waited for her. In trepidation.

20

As soon as the door opened, Rose knew she had been sized up, made.

Copper. Filth.

But that was OK. Because Rose had made equally strong, instant assumptions about the woman before her too.

Druggie. Whore.

She held up her warrant card. 'Detective Sergeant Rose Martin. Donna Warren?'

The woman gave a grudging nod of acknowledgement.

'Could I come in, please?'

The woman's attitude was aggressive, confrontational. Strong as a physical barrier. Her body language tensed and rigid, preparing to fight.

That'll all change when she hears what I have to say, thought Rose.

'I ain't done nothin'. I ain't been out.'

Rose looked round. A small, shabby house in a nondescript street just off Barrack Street in New Town. Terraced houses squashed together, old cars and vans bumper to bumper either side of the road. The street was gated on one side by a convenience store, its windows barred, a chalkboard advertising the latest cheap deals on full-strength lager and cider. And opposite that a fried chicken and pizza fast-food restaurant, closed, the smell of cheap stale oil perfuming the air. Gang tags adorned the walls. A big, dark sedan, expensive-looking, sat incongruously amongst the MOT failures and dodgers that filled the street. The local drug dealer's, Rose assumed.

She felt anger rise at this woman's attitude.

'Could I come in, please? It's best if we talk inside.'

Without removing her gaze and without seeming to move, Donna Warren let Rose in. Closed the door behind her.

The inside didn't look any better. Rose had felt nothing but disdain for this woman since knocking on her door, but now she felt that disdain was justified. The place was a mess. The front door led straight into the living room. A sofa sat against one wall, old with ingrained dirt; the armrests were shiny and threadbare and had been used as ashtrays. Pizza cartons sat open and festering on the sofa. Stained mugs and empty bottles lay on the floor. Dirty ashtrays with dead fag and spliff ends were dotted about. And in amongst all this were a scattering of children's toys, old, used, broken. Underneath, the carpet was filthy. A big old silver box of an off-brand TV dominated one corner. DVDs spilled out underneath it.

Rose wasn't asked to sit down. She didn't want to. She stood, facing Donna Warren. The woman had her arms folded across her chest. Rose looked at her.

She had been on plenty of police training courses. Diversity. Ethnicity. Equality. Treating everyone she came into contact with as a police officer with respect no matter what the circumstances or how the individual behaved. She had nodded along with the rest of them, paid lip service to the idea, as was expected of her. But she hadn't believed it. Not one word of it. Because, as the sort of people she came into contact with realised, that respect had to be earned. And they did very little to earn it.

Like Donna Warren. The hardness of her features, the tension in her posture. Her Primark clothes and her home-dyed hair. Her indiscriminate racial origins, her mongrel skin colour. She reeked of substance abuse and her body looked well-used and sold. Rose wondered just how desperate a man would have to be to pay to have sex with Donna Warren.

'Had a party in here?' she asked.

'What d'you want?' Donna Warren's voice was still strident, but now there was a slight shake to it. Like she's worked out why I'm here, thought Rose.

'You might want to sit down.'

Donna Warren remained standing.

Rose made a play of checking her notebook. 'Does ... Faith Luscombe live here?'

'Yes.' Another waver to her voice. 'Have you ... where is she?'

Rose looked at her notebook. Donna Warren spoke before she could say anything further.

'Have you run her in again? That it?' Her voice getting stronger, feeding on the anger of her words. 'Come to take her kid away, that it?'

'She's got a child?' said Rose.

'Little boy. I'm looking after him.'

'Well you might have to look after him a while longer.' Rose hated the next bit. Even with people like Donna Warren. She slipped into the voice she had been taught to use on another course. 'I'm afraid Faith's dead.'

21

'What? What you talkin' about, dead?' Donna spat the words out rapidly, another shield. 'She's not dead.'

'I'm afraid she is, Donna. Would you like to sit down now?'

Donna was about to sit down, then stopped herself. 'What for? Ain't gonna bring her back, is it?'

'No. But we could talk about it.'

Donna, not wanting to give ground or show weakness before a police officer, reluctantly lowered herself into an armchair. Rose perched on the edge of the sofa, hoping she wouldn't stain her clothes or catch something.

'What . . . what happened?'

'She was hit by a car. Out in Wakes Colne. On the way to Halstead.'

Donna frowned. 'Wakes Colne? Halstead? What was she doin' out there?'

'I don't know, Donna. Perhaps you could tell me.'

Donna looked at her, about to speak. Then changed her mind.

Rose tried to prompt. 'It'll help if you can tell me where she was last night.'

'Help how? Won't bring her back, will it?'

Stupid bitch, thought Rose. She was getting angry all over again. She felt like getting up and leaving, but stopped herself. This was a chance, a case. She could prove she was fit to return to work, that she was worthy of the rank of DI. She stayed where she was, bit back her natural reaction, kept her voice calm and consoling.

'I know this is difficult for you, Donna, but if you could co-operate with me, it would be a great help.'

Donna said nothing.

'Where was Faith last night, Donna?'

Rose watched the battle being fought on Donna's face. Talk or not talk. Go against years of conditioning, of not helping the police, in order to help her friend. She didn't let it show, but she quite enjoyed seeing it.

'Please, Donna. I know you haven't had good experiences with the police in the past—'

'You know that, do you?'

'Yes. I know that. I've read your record. And I've read Faith's too. But this isn't about that. This is about finding out what she was doing in Wakes Colne last night.'

Silence from Donna. Rose waited.

'Tell me,' Donna said eventually, her voice weary. 'Tell me what happened.'

'She was killed early this morning. She ran out of a clump of trees on to the road. By the viaduct. She was hit by a car. She died almost instantly.' She thought it best not to mention the second car.

Donna's eyes glazed over. She blinked. Hard. Her lower lip trembled. Her breathing changed.

Here it comes, thought Rose.

But it didn't. Donna took control of herself, looked up. Shields down, composure regained. Still blinking, but clearly willing the tears not to fall.

A tiny part of Rose admired her for it.

'What was she running from?' Donna's next words.

Rose's grudging admiration for the woman increased slightly. Whatever else she was – and a glance round the living room showed that – she was bright.

'Well that's what I hoped you might be able to help me with.'

Donna said nothing, retreated into silence.

Rose leaned forward, nearly toppled off the edge of the sofa. Hid her irritation. 'Come on, Donna. Just tell me. Was she out working? Seeing punters? Scoring? What?'

At the mention of scoring, Donna gave Rose a fierce death-ray stare. 'She wasn't an addict.' Her voice rising, a growl at the edges.

Course she wasn't, darling, thought Rose. 'I'm not saying she was, Donna. I'm just asking you where she went last night.'

'She was getting help, that's what she was doin'. She wasn't a junkie.'

'Getting help? Last night?'

Donna paused. 'No. Not last night. She was goin' to get help. St Quinlan's Trust. Down there. Had a place booked.'

Rose felt a tiny victory inside. She had caught Donna in a lie. She tried not to rub it in. 'So she did have a problem with drugs?'

'No.' Another pause from Donna. 'She has a kid. She was usin'. Just a bit, on an' off. Wanted to get clean, properly clean, for him.'

Rose nodded. 'Right. And where is this child now?'

Donna nodded towards the stairs.

Silence fell once more.

'So,' said Rose. 'Last night. Where was Faith? Not at St Quinlan's, I take it?'

Donna shook her head. 'She went out. One last time, she said. I told her not to bother. But no. One last time. Just to make a bit. Tide her over. Till she got clean an' could get a job.' Donna's head dropped, her shoulders slumped. 'One last time . . .'

Rose waited while Donna composed herself. She felt nothing positive for the woman before her. She didn't see her as someone who had lost a friend. She felt no sympathy. Rose had a strict definition of right and wrong. If a woman sold her body – for whatever reason – that was disgusting. If she willingly offered herself up to the kind of man who did what he did with her, then she had no one to blame but herself for what happened. And Rose felt nothing for that woman but anger.

Then she thought of her ex-lover, DCI Ben Fenwick. She hadn't found him particularly attractive, but she'd still slept with him. Willingly offered herself up to him. But that was different, she told herself. She had something to gain from that.

She shook the thought from her head. It only made her feel more angry.

Donna was getting a grip on herself. It took longer this time, was more of an effort. But she managed it. Thinking she might not make such a good recovery next time, Rose hurried her questioning along.

'So do you have any idea who she could have seen last night?'

Donna shook her head.

'Did she have regulars? Did she say anything about seeing one of them?'

'No. Nothin' like that. Just said she was goin' out. Makin' a bit of money.'

'And what did you do last night?'

Donna sat immediately upright. 'None of your fuckin' business.'

I'll bet, thought Rose. 'What about boyfriends? Pimps? Anyone like that?'

Something passed across Donna's eyes. Too quick for Rose to read it. 'Yeah,' she said. 'There was an ex. Used to turn her out sometimes. Make her go out to work. He was the one got her on the pipe, know what I mean?'

Rose felt that familiar burn inside. She was on to something. 'Got a name?'

'Daryl. Daryl Kent.'

'And where can I find him?'

'What, now? The Shakespeare. He's always there. Playin' pool.'

'Right.' She stood up. Glad to have a focus for her anger. 'I'm sorry, Donna. Did Faith have any family?'

Donna shook her head, kept her eyes averted. 'She had me. I'm all she's got. An' Ben.' Voice small, cracked.

'Family Liaison'll be in touch soon.'

Donna shrugged: whatever.

'I'm . . . sorry.' The word dredged reluctantly from her.

Donna said nothing. Crossed to the door, opened it.

Rose left.

Out on the street, she gulped in what passed for clean air off Barrack Street then set off walking to meet Daryl Kent. The big car was still parked opposite. She ignored it.

Just glad to get away from the place.

22

The man behind the desk was nervous, Mickey thought. But he doubted it was because the police were there to see him. More to do with his firm losing money.

'Look,' Colin Byers said, sitting back, 'it's awful and all that, but I don't see what I can do for you. I mean, we were just contracted for the demolition.'

'But you can tell us who contracted you.'

Mickey Philips sat opposite the desk. George Byers Demolition was the first place on his list. It was a one-storey brick building on Magdalen Street in New Town. Low and open-plan, it sat between a car dealership and a fireplace and door reclaimer. It had a cracked concrete forecourt with lorries and vans on it, and the building itself was just like Mickey had expected. Office-surplus furniture, tabloids lying round, a calendar with a semi-naked girl on it. No finesse. Stripped to the bones.

Colin Byers looked like the product of his environment. The son of the owner of the company, as he had explained, and now running it since his father's retirement, he was a heavy-set middle-aged man, thinning on top, wearing metal-framed glasses and a maroon polo shirt with the company logo on it.

He sighed, scratched his ear. 'Look, Detective Sergeant, all I can give you is the name of the buildin' firm. We're sub-contractors. You'd be better off contactin' the Land Registry.'

'I have,' said Mickey, strictly speaking telling a lie. He hadn't contacted them; Milhouse had done it for him. 'All they could tell me was that the property is registered to a holding company in London. We're looking into that now. In the meantime, Mr Byers, I'd just like a little help. I appreciate you've got your job to do, but so do I. The sooner you talk to me, the sooner I'll be off.'

'Yeah. And I'm out of pocket now because of this.' Byers sighed. Put his hands behind his head, smoothed down what remained of his hair. Came to a decision. 'I know this one, as it happens. Took it myself. Lyalls. The builders. Wanted a couple of semi-derelict properties dismantled down East Hill. Area cleared for a new housin' development. Easy job, really. Might be a bit of asbestos removal, uprooting some trees, landscapin', nothing worse than that. And now this.'

Mickey made a note of the building company's name.

'So now we can't work there, can we?'

'It looks that way.'

'How long you gonna be, then?'

'I've no idea,' said Mickey. 'The area's going to be thoroughly searched. Could be days. Could be weeks.'

The expression on Byers' face told Mickey what he thought of that.

'Thanks for your time,' Mickey said, and let himself out.

Outside he checked his pad, looking for directions. The day had turned colder, chilly autumn notes carried on the wind.

He turned right, going back to where he had parked the car. Magdalen Street was the main stretch of road linking

New Town to the town centre. He walked past tattooists, Afro-Caribbean hair stylists and corner shops. Most of the people on the street paid him no mind, although a few gave him sharp, furtive looks then dodged out of his way. He recognised a few faces. Knew he had dealt with them on a professional basis.

He walked to where Magdalen Street turned into Barrack Street. The area became more run-down, the buildings less well-kept, the shops dirtier. He was standing at the lights, about to cross and head down Brook Street to find his car, when he spotted someone he knew.

Rose Martin, walking along the street opposite.

His first instinct was to turn round, walk as far away from her as possible. He hadn't known her long, but the impression she had made on him wasn't a good one. However, he couldn't. Because she was looking straight at him. He would have to talk to her.

She crossed the road, approached him. Smiled.

'Hello, Mickey. Long time no see.'

'Didn't know you lived round here, Rose.'

She gave a small, stifled laugh. 'Me? Live round here? You're joking, aren't you? No. I'm working.'

'Oh good,' he said, relieved that she was no longer with the police. 'What as?'

She frowned, gave him a quizzical look. 'As a police officer. What else would I be doing?'

Mickey was lost for words. He knew what she had gone through, how she had been put on long-term sick. Everyone knew it. And most people never expected her to return.

'That surprised you, didn't it?'

'Well, yeah ... What happened?'

'Glass brought me back.'

'You're not working on ... '

A dark cloud passed over her features. 'No. Oh God, no. No, it's a road accident. Well, we think it's an accident. Dead woman.' She gestured back the way she had come. 'Lived down there. Prossie.'

'Right.'

They stood there looking at each other. Nothing more to say.

'Well,' she said, 'I'd better get on. Nice to see you, Mickey. I'm sure we'll be seeing more of each other soon.'

God, he hoped not. 'Yeah. Sure, Rose.'

She was turning to go, stopped. 'Oh, and it's Detective Inspector now. I've been promoted. Bye.'

She smiled, turned and walked away.

Mickey was left standing there, absorbing that last piece of information. The pedestrian crossing sounded. He just stared at it, unmoving.

'Detective Inspector . . . Jesus Christ . . . '

23

'So how is he?'

Marina walked up to the tape at the bottom of East Hill, phone clamped to her ear. She heard Anni's voice.

'Asleep again. Didn't stay awake much after you went. He's exhausted.'

'Did he say anything more?'

'Nothing. I'm still here, but if he's not moving, I might leave a uniform to look after him, or get someone from, I don't know, Family Liaison? I'm at a bit of a loss.'

'He needs a psychologist.'

'Yeah, well he had one. Very briefly. But she had to go.'

Marina smiled. 'We'll talk later.'

She pocketed the phone, held up her ID, ducked under the tape.

She felt the eyes of the crowd on the bridge watching her as she did so. Knew that media crews would be in there too. They would all be wondering who she was, what she was doing there. She felt like a celeb on a red carpet. It gave her quite a thrill. Probably more than she would have liked in light of what she was there for.

Of course the media crews might know who she was, she thought. A couple of high-profile cases would do that.

She looked round, scanning the area for Phil. Didn't see him. There was an air of quiet urgency about the place. The white tent was up and blue-suited CSIs were going about their work with a calm, concentrated commitment. Uniforms were there too. She spotted Adrian Wren, waved at him, moved over to ask where Phil was. Before she could do so, another figure detached himself from a conversation with two uniforms and turned to her.

'Marina. Good to see you.' Brian Glass was smiling, holding out his arms as if welcoming her to his party. He looked round, then back to her. 'I'm afraid Phil's busy at the moment. Was it him you were looking for?'

When Glass had first arrived at Southway, Marina had done her best to like him. But he hadn't made it easy. He was the kind of copper she hated working with. The kind that was all business. There was a strand of officer, she had reasoned, and unfortunately it was a dominant one in the force, that had a little more of their personality surgically removed with each higher rank they made. And Glass was no exception. There was no spark, no inner life to the man that she could detect. She had told Phil that Glass reminded her of a supporting CTU character in an episode of *24*; there to wear a suit and give orders but have no discernible characteristics beyond that.

Still, he had made encouraging noises about her work and the job of the psychologist in the police force in general. At least to her face. In times of budget cuts, plenty of higher-ups thought a psychologist was not a necessity but a luxury. That anything she offered could be outsourced, bought in when needed at a fraction of the cost. Irrespective of the results she achieved, the standard of the work she did. So she was polite to him, but wary. It seemed like a healthy way to proceed.

'Yes,' she said, 'I was looking for Phil.'

'Can I pass on a message?'

He was making her feel like she was being troublesome, the interfering wife bringing her husband's forgotten packed lunch to work for him. Not, she thought, because he was belittling her on purpose, but just because he was innately sexist that way.

'I'll wait,' she said. 'He wants me to look at the crime scene with him. See if I can help him with leads.'

'Good, good. Fine. All offers of help gratefully received.' He brought his brows together in a thoughtful manner. 'What's happening with the boy? The one from the cellar?'

'Anni's with him now. He came round. I talked to him but didn't get much. He kept asking for his mother.'

'His mother?'

She nodded. 'As far as I could tell. But wherever he's been, he's been there a while. He can barely speak. Hardly communicate. There's a lot of damage there. A hell of a lot. It's going to be a while before we can get anything coherent from him.'

He nodded. 'Right. Good. Good work, Marina.'

She said nothing.

'Keep at it.' A smile. Marina imagined he thought it was the kind Churchill must have given to rally the troops.

'I will,' she said. He made to walk away. She stopped him. 'Oh, by the way, I'm glad I caught you. There's something I wanted to talk to you about.'

He looked at her quizzically. Waited.

'Rose Martin.'

His attitude changed, his voice guarded. 'What about her?'

'You've returned her to work. I don't think she's ready.'

He straightened up. Expression closed. 'In your opinion.'

'In my professional opinion as her psychologist, yes. She's

still exhibiting signs of stress, of trauma. She's not emotionally ready to handle the demands of her job. At least not back on the front line.'

'Well, thank you for your comments, Marina,' he said, nodding. 'You know I value your input greatly. I'm sure you'll put them all in your report. I'll read them then.'

Marina felt her face redden, her hands shake. She controlled her anger, kept talking. 'With all due respect, Brian, you've put her back on front-line duty and I hear you've promoted her too.'

He held his hands up as if in surrender. 'That wasn't my doing, I'm afraid. The ball was in motion before I got here.' He looked at her, and she detected sincerity in his gaze. Or a good facsimile of it. His voice dropped. 'Look, Marina. Sometimes I have to make decisions that are unpopular, or that people who don't have full access to the facts may find ... contentious. Rose Martin is a fine officer. In my opinion' – he highlighted the words, as if he had spoken in italics – 'she is fit to return to work. The case she is working is fairly routine. I'm sure she'll be fine. And with budget cuts, we need all the bodies we can get.'

He smiled, as if that was the final word.

'Fine. Well I just wanted you to know that I have officially voiced concerns, that's all.'

'Noted.' He smiled. 'That's what we pay you for.'

Any further conversation was abruptly halted. Phil Brennan was walking towards them.

'Ah,' said Glass. 'Here he is. I'll leave you to it. Good luck.' He walked away.

'Tit,' Marina said. Then felt guilty. He wasn't that bad. There had been worse DCIs.

Forgetting Glass, she turned, smiling, to face Phil. Her heart still rose when she saw him. Even here, even like this. Or perhaps even more so. After all, they had met during a case, so it seemed like a natural habitat to them. Working together. Just like old times. It felt right.

And sometimes she just couldn't believe her luck that she had him.

But as soon as he approached and she saw him clearly, her smile faded.

24

'Phil?' Her hand straight on his arm, concern in her eyes. 'You OK?'

He shook his head as if coming out a trance, seeing her for the first time. 'Marina. Hi.' He stopped before her.

Her voice dropped. 'What's the matter? You look like you've, I don't know. Seen a ghost.'

His eyes went out of focus for a few seconds before zoning back in on her. 'No. I'm ... I'm fine. Just ... fine.'

She was about to ask him again, but he spoke before she could.

'We'd better get a move on,' he said, not bringing his eyes into contact with hers. 'I've asked the forensic teams to give us a few minutes alone in there. I'll come with you, show you round. Tell you whether they've moved anything, what was in the original places. That sort of thing.'

'Fine ... ' She was still looking at him, curious. Phil was a man of raging emotional torrents – because of his upbringing, both good and bad. It was one of the things that had first attracted her to him. The damage she felt an immediate connection with. The passion he had she wanted to share with him. But she knew that because of his job, for the most part he kept his emotions tightly bound. Didn't let anyone glimpse inside.

But he had never done that to her before. Never kept her out. And that was what she felt he was doing now.

One last attempt. 'Phil?'

'I'm fine.' He pulled his arm away. 'I'm fine. I'm just . . . tired.'

She looked at him, said nothing. Felt the tightrope she was on begin to waver.

'Right,' he said, clapping his hands together as if to break a spell, 'you up for this?'

'Why wouldn't I be? It's my job.' Frosty. Clearly unhappy.

If Phil picked up on that, he didn't acknowledge it. 'OK. Good. Come on then, let's go.'

He turned, walked towards the house. She followed. Putting her relationship aside, ready to enter the house as a professional.

Compartmentalising.

She would deal with the rest later.

25

'Watch your step down here. It's pretty rickety.'

Phil led the way, Marina behind him. The arc lights had been left on, the trailing cables leading up the wooden stairs to outside generators. There was space for only one person at a time, so he moved carefully, aware of her behind him.

He was angry with himself. What he had seen in the other house had spooked him, unsettled him, though he didn't know why. But he knew the answer was within him somewhere. And until he found it, he couldn't share it with anyone else. Not even Marina.

He hated keeping anything from her. It broke his heart to see the concern on her face, knowing he couldn't say anything. He just hoped she would understand. Later.

He reached the cellar floor, Marina a few seconds after him.

'This is it,' he said. Waiting while she took it all in, trying to see it through her eyes.

She looked round, her eyes widening as she saw the cage. 'Oh my God . . .'

'Exactly. My reaction too.' That sense of unease returned as he looked at it once more. His mind was trying to subconsciously connect it with the diagram on the wall . . .

No. He couldn't see it.

Marina gave another scan. 'And the flowers? Was this how you found them?'

Phil looked at the floor. Some of the petals had been gathered up, removed. A few had been trampled on by Forensics.

'No, they were all over the floor. Strewn.'

She smiled. 'Strewn. I think you've won the award for most unexpected word of the day.'

He reddened slightly. 'What can I say? I'm honoured.'

Her smile faded as she went back to work. Concentrating.

'There were a few bunches, though.' He pointed round the walls. The bunches were still there, where he had found them. Wilting, dying.

'In those exact locations?'

'Just about, yes.'

She nodded, staying in the one place, looking round three hundred and sixty degrees. She took it all in. The flowers, the cage. The workbench. The gardening tools. The markings on the wall. Her lips began to move as she spoke to herself.

Phil had seen her do this before. Mentally processing information, working out what she saw, interpreting the scene before her. He had never ceased to be amazed at how she did it, or the accuracy of her results.

She walked round the cellar. Plastic gloves on her hands, paper booties over her shoes. She knelt down, examined one of the bunches of flowers. 'Roses . . . red, blue, yellow . . . ' Then another. 'Carnations, red, blue, yellow, same colours . . . and here, petunias, chrysanthemums, same colours . . . ' Looked round once more. 'And left on the floor to decay. Go brown . . . '

'What does that mean?'

'Whoever did this either grew them himself or bought them somewhere. I'm leaning towards growing them himself. There's a ... horticultural sense to the place. Those gardening tools over there ...'

Marina crossed to the workbench. Looked down at it, the tools on the surface. 'Has any of this been disturbed?'

Phil crossed over, stood beside her. He could smell her perfume. Made him want to hold her. 'I think one of the tools has been taken away for forensic examination. I asked them to leave the others for a bit.'

She nodded, lips moving all the time. She picked up the scythe, examined it slowly. 'They've been ... adapted. They're not for gardening. Not been used for gardening in a very long time.'

'My thoughts exactly.'

'And this workbench ...' She knelt down beside it, put her face to it. Sniffed the scarred, pitted surface, eyes closed. Remained in place afterwards. 'Hmm ...' Did it once more. 'Earthy ... but more ...'

She stood up, dusting down her skirt. Turned, looked at the wall behind her. Crossed to it. Examined the painted design. Touched it.

'We thought it was a pentagram at first,' said Phil. 'But it's clearly not.'

'No,' Marina said, absorbed, her fingers, eyes following the lines of the design, 'it's not. More like a star. But I can see how you could make that mistake. Would be an easy conclusion to jump to ... if you weren't open-minded and imaginative ...'

Phil said nothing. Had she just paid him a compliment?

She pressed her face to the wall. Sniffed.

'Not paint. Not ...' She turned to Phil. 'Has this been analysed?'

'Not yet. They'll have taken a sample. Don't know when we can get results. Any ideas on what it is?'

'I'm guessing ... something of the earth ... a plant concoction? Bodily fluids, even? All mixed together? I don't know ... something along those lines, though, I'd guess ... '

Marina straightened up, looked round once more. Crossed to the cage. Examined it closely. Turned, looked behind her at the bench, then over at the flowers bunched round the walls. Then the design on the wall. She began to walk towards the bunches of flowers, taking slow, deliberate steps to get to each one. Her mouth moving all the time, brow furrowed as if performing advanced mathematical calculations.

She stood in the centre of the cellar, stretched out her arms as far as she could, rotated them, straining her fingertips. Half pagan priest, half yoga teacher. Holding her breath as she did so.

Phil watched her all the time. Fascinated. He loved this woman so much it scared him sometimes.

Right,' she said. 'Here goes.'

26

The shadows were lengthening in Don and Eileen Brennan's kitchen. Outside, darkness descended like a grey blanket thrown over the sun.

They sat at the table. Silence between them like a huge block of ice.

A different silence from the next room. Peaceful. Tranquil. Josephina having a nap. The TV off.

Eileen sighed, reached for her tea. It had gone cold. She still drank it.

Don sat unmoving. The sun's dying rays playing over his face, hollowing out his features, haunting him.

Eileen placed her mug gently down on the coaster. Flowers of the British Isles. A present from a friend's holiday. She didn't see the colours. 'We have to ... we've got to do something ... '

Her voice thrown out, dying away in the silence.

'We can't just let him ... go on. Find out what it's ... '

'And what d'you suggest we do?' Don turning, looking at her. Like an Easter Island head come to life. 'What can we do?'

'I don't know. Just . . . something.'

'You mean tell him?'

'Yes, maybe.' Eileen's eyes widened. The dying daylight glinting, fearful.

Don shook his head. Pulling back from the dark. 'I don't think we could . . . We couldn't . . . Not after what . . . '

Eileen sighed. 'Then what do we do instead?' she said. 'Because he's going to find out, Don. Sooner or later.'

Don said nothing. His face halfway into the darkness.

Eileen leaned towards him. Breaking the ice between them. Her voice as low as the light in the room. 'He'll find out anyway. And he'll know we haven't told him. Then how will we feel? How will *he* feel?'

Don said nothing. Eileen watched him. Gave another sigh.

She looked down at her mug once more. Made to drink from it. Remembered it was cold. Replaced it where it had been.

Silence. Darkness descended.

Then a cry from the other room. Josephina waking up.

Eileen looked at the doorway, back to Don. 'And what about her?'

'Don't, Eileen.'

'What about that poor little girl in there? Doesn't she have a right to know too?'

'Eileen . . . '

'What, Don, what?'

Josephina's cries became louder.

'I can't. It's too . . . I can't. And you know it.'

'Don. He has to know. That's all there is to it.'

And louder.

Don put his head down, shook it slowly.

More cries. Eileen put her head to one side, eyes never leaving Don. 'I'm coming, love. Grandma's coming.'

The cries eased slightly. Eileen stood up.

'It's time, Don. And you know it.'

She left the room.

Don didn't move.

The sun disappeared completely.

27

'This is just preliminary,' Marina said. 'Just so we have something to go on for now. First impressions.'

'Fine,' said Phil. 'Whatever you've got.'

'Right. The boy hasn't been here long,' Marina said, turning, staring at the cage.

'No?'

'No.' She pointed. 'That's a holding cell. He would have been transferred here. That cage has been like that for a long time. Very long time.'

'How long?'

'I'll come to that. The boy was brought here for . . . something. Nothing good. This is a killer's lair. However he dresses it up. It's a slaughterhouse.'

She closed her eyes, turned on the spot, breathing in deeply.

'The anticipation . . . he brings them here to . . . ' Another deep breath. 'He's building the anticipation for himself. Letting it, letting it . . . the ritual. Yes. That's it. It's all about the ritual. Not just aspects he's developed in his own mind, though . . . no . . . his own fetish, no . . . ' Another breath. She dropped to her knees, looking round. 'Something more than that . . . '

Phil didn't dare to speak. It was almost like Marina was in a trance, receiving communications from the spirit world. He knew how ridiculous that sounded, but still the image persisted.

'Getting himself in the right place, the right . . . frame of mind, getting ready to enjoy it, but no. More than that. More. The flowers . . . Yes . . . The right . . . time . . . '

She opened her eyes. 'It's about time. Ritual.' She looked round at the bunches of flowers by the walls. 'The flowers, they're . . . it's . . . a growth cycle. Living, blooming, dying. Perennials.' She pointed to the wall. 'And that design. You were right, it's not a pentagram, not Satanic. It's . . . I don't know. Some kind of calendar? Could that be it?'

'With the star shape . . . '

'Overlaying that. But it's not a pentagram. More a . . . logo, I think.' Surprise in her voice.

She closed her eyes once more. 'But the child . . . What does that mean? Readiness? Fruition? Is the child part of that growth cycle?'

She crossed to the bench.

'The tools, gardening tools . . . symbolic, yes, symbolic . . . but what? Planting, getting ready to grow? Cutting down? Adapted to, to surgical instruments . . . Yes . . . flowers, nature, everything natural . . . pruning? Growth cycle, yes . . . '

She turned to Phil, addressed him directly. 'The cage. The bones. You think they're human?'

Startled, it took him a few seconds to respond. 'Well, we think there's a good chance . . . '

'Right.' She turned away again. 'Old, some of them. Old. Been there years, decades, probably . . . yes . . . ' She moved up close to the cage. Stared at it. 'What does this mean?

115

Planning. That's what it means. Planning. Preparation.' She closed her eyes. 'A controlled – and controlling – intellect is at work here. He's clever. He's patient. A strategist. He's been planning this for a long time.'

'You think . . . he's been doing this for a while?'

'I do.'

'How long?'

She straightened up. Opened her eyes wide. Stared once more at the bars of the cage. Like she was waiting for them to speak to her.

'Years.' She reached out, touched the bones. 'Decades . . .' Incredulity, fear in her voice. 'Never been caught . . .'

She shook her head.

'A record, would he keep a record . . . probably not. At least, not in the way we understand it. No, I don't . . . unless . . .' She turned round once more. Looked at the back of the room. 'The flowers . . . different blooms, different times of year . . . the flowers . . . Maybe they're . . . I don't know . . .'

Then turning, back to the cage.

'There's a confidence about what's been happening here. What he's been doing.' She reached out once more, touching the bones. 'This . . . this is a progression. And that's fine, that's what an established pattern . . . what usually happens. But often in cases of a serial nature, the perpetrator begins to unravel the more he goes on. Like he wants to make mistakes, wants to be caught, stopped . . .' She stroked the bone bars. 'But not here . . .' Stroking and stroking. Gently, slowly. 'Here . . . is control. Ritual. Honed. Perfection. The quest for perfection . . .' Still stroking. Caressing. 'Perpetrators often stop when they get older,' she said, her voice almost at a whisper, 'but not here. Not him. He's been doing this a long time. For a reason.'

'What reason?'

116

'I don't know. But he thinks it's an important one. More than just for his own gratification.'

'But I thought all serial killing had sex at the heart of it.'

'Yeah, pretty much.'

'So?'

I'm not saying he doesn't get his kicks from this. Just that he's gone so much further than that. And there's something else.'

'What?'

'I don't think he's going to stop.'

28

'Unless we stop him,' said Phil. 'Catch him and stop him.'

'Yes,' said Marina, turning to him as if released from a trance. 'There is that.' She gave a small, tight smile. 'But that's your job.'

'No pressure there, then,' said Phil, looking to Marina like he was composed entirely of pressure. He looked to have aged years since she had seen him in the morning.

She had to say something, talk to him. 'Look, Phil, what's—'

'Please,' said Phil, his voice small, barely a whisper. 'Not here. Not now.'

'But when?' She gently placed her hand on his arm. 'What's the matter?'

He sighed. Like Atlas shrugging. 'I can't . . .'

'Phil. This is me you're talking to. Me.' Eyes locked on his. 'You can tell me.'

His eyes tried to stay on hers, kept jumping round like they were being electrocuted. 'I . . . I can't. Not now.' Then another sigh. 'I don't even . . .' He snapped his head up. 'No. Come on. Let's . . . we've got work to do. Come on.'

'OK . . . but—'

'How did he get here?' Phil's voice sudden, abrupt.

'What?'

'The boy. How did he get in here? If this was a holding cell, he can't have been here for long.'

She looked at him. He had never closed her out like this before. 'Right,' she said. 'OK. The boy. Well . . . OK. What I think. He couldn't just walk in with him, in broad daylight, could he?'

'I doubt it. And there's a fence all the way round. No entrance.'

'So the road is out. Unless it was at night, and that might have looked suspicious. There's the other path down to the allotments; where does that lead?'

'To a housing estate on the Hythe. But it's badly lit, over-grown, lots of bushes. Mugger's paradise. And it's alongside the river.'

'There you are, then.'

'What, he came down the path?'

'No. The river. This house backs on to the river. He could have moored a boat beside the house, got the boy out of there.'

Phil rubbed his chin, paced the cellar floor. 'It would fit . . .' He turned to Marina. 'What you said before. Nature. Cycles. Could the river have anything to do with that?'

'Very possibly.'

'Right . . .' More pacing. 'Then there's just one more thing.'

'What?'

'Where did he get the boy from?'

Marina gave a thin smile. 'That's for you to find out. You're the policeman. I'm just the profiler.'

'But you've spoken to him.'

'I know. And he's a long way from telling us anything useful.'

They stood in silence.

'I'll get an official report made up,' she said eventually. Looked at her watch. 'I'd better pick up Josephina.'

Phil told her he had spoken to Don. He and Eileen were holding on to her a bit longer.

'Good. That helps.'

Another silence. Marina looked at Phil. His eyes were roving round the cellar. Not because he was looking for anything in particular, she thought, but because he was avoiding looking at her. Why? He wouldn't talk to her, tell her what was wrong. Had coming down here, seeing the cage and the boy, upset him that much? Did he just not want to say that in front of his team? She hoped so. Hoped it was something like that.

Anything more than that, she didn't want to contemplate.

She reached out her hand once more. Perhaps anticipating it, he turned.

'Come on,' he said, 'let's go.' Walked up the cellar steps. She stood for a minute, watching him go.

This wasn't like him. Not at all. It must be something big for him to keep it from her, whatever it was.

After all, she was bound to him. She knew that, had never felt it for any other person. A real, true love. A soulmate's bond. But with that came fear. Of something going wrong. Of one of them dying.

Or of some darkness enveloping them. They were two damaged souls who had recognised each other, clung together. What if that darkness returned? Resurfaced, destroyed everything they had in the present?

The tightrope fraying and fraying . . .

29

It was an ordinary meeting room. Air-conditioned. Blinds drawn. Rectangular table. Chairs set around it. Even a tall jug of water on the table, short glasses nestling next to it. An ordinary meeting room.

But no ordinary meeting.

The Elders had been meeting for years. Decades. Firstly, in the open air. Decisions made round a campfire. Then shifting inside, the smell of newly sawn wood permeating their meetings. The floors and walls bare and hard, the furniture functional. Then moving on to warm wood-panelled rooms. Old, oiled and polished wooden tables. Carved chairs. And ceremonial robes.

Those had been the best years.

And then the years in between.

And now this. Conference rooms. Board rooms. Ordinary rooms.

The faces had changed. But the names remained the same. And four. Always four.

The fifth . . . absent. As always.

There had been no welcomes beyond common courtesy.

No catch-ups, no jokes. Just silence. Tension zinging in the air like taut steel cable in a high wind. The room cold from more than just air-conditioning.

One of them had to start.

'I think I speak for everyone here,' the Lawmaker said, 'when I say, what the fuck did you think you were doing?'

The ice was broken but the room was still cold. The words expressed what the others had been thinking. They wanted answers.

'Please,' said the Portreeve, customarily positioned at the head of table, 'try and keep emotion out of this. It clouds the issue.' He turned to the subject of the inquiry. 'But the Lawmaker is right and the point needs answering. What did you think you were doing, Missionary?'

'Do we still need these stupid names? Can't we all talk properly for once?' A shake of the head from the Missionary.

'We need them,' said the Portreeve. 'You know we do.'

'They're practical as well,' said the Teacher. 'Stops anyone listening in from gathering evidence against us. Should that arise.'

'So I say again, Missionary,' said the Lawmaker, 'what did you think you were doing?'

'You know we need money,' said the Missionary. 'For this deal to go ahead. And we need this deal. Otherwise we're all . . . well, you know. So I just thought I'd dispose of one of the old properties. We don't use it any more; valuable real estate, that.'

The Lawmaker leaned forward. 'And you didn't think to tell any of us about this?'

'I didn't think it was important.'

The other three stared at the Missionary.

Not used to begging, the Missionary gave a good approximation of it. 'Look, I was miles away. I didn't want the deal to go south; what was I supposed to do? I did what I thought was best for all of us. Thought I'd get a thank-you. Didn't think I'd get this.'

They kept staring at him.

'I mean,' the Missionary said, 'I didn't think he'd still be at it, did I? Not now, not after all this time.'

'Really?' The Teacher spoke. 'Are you that naïve? Or just stupid?'

'How was I supposed to know?'

'Did you think he'd just stop? That he'd ever change? You of all people should know better.'

The Missionary sighed. 'I'm sorry. I just ... didn't think.'

The Teacher leaned forward. 'The cage is still there.'

The Missionary shuddered. 'Yeah. Well ... I thought he'd have ... others.'

'He does,' said the Lawmaker. 'Reserve ones.'

'Then why couldn't he have—'

'Because everyone has their favourite.' The Portreeve spoke in a voice to end all argument. 'He's no different in that respect. All part of the ritual.'

'I didn't think there still was a ritual. I thought, you know, the deal going through and all that, looking to the future ...'

'This is getting us nowhere,' said the Lawmaker. 'We need to know what's happening now. We need damage limitation. We need a plan.'

'You're right,' said the Portreeve. 'Progress report. Suggestions.'

'I see it like this,' said the Lawmaker. 'There are three distinct areas we need to look at. One. What's going on with the police investigation into the cage and the boy. Two. Making sure none of this impacts on the shipment arriving safely. Three. Making sure the ritual goes ahead.'

The Missionary looked confused. 'The ritual's still going ahead? After all this?'

'Has to,' said the Lawmaker. 'Too important not to. For him. He's very angry at what happened. Very angry.'

'The Missionary shuddered. 'Right. Yes. Couldn't we just . . . ' Knowing what the answer would be, he let the words trail away.

The Teacher didn't speak, just stared at him.

The Missionary sighed once more. 'God, what a mess.' Then looked up, eyes dancing. 'Wait. Does it have to be that one? Couldn't he use another one?'

'You know better than to ask that.' The Portreeve shook his head. 'It has to be the chosen child. The ritual demands it.' Leaning forward. Ghost of a smile. 'Or would you like to suggest your idea to him yourself?'

'So we have no option,' said the Teacher. 'We need to get the child back.'

'And,' said the Portreeve, 'the police investigation has to be controlled.'

All eyes turned to the Lawmaker. Who gave a slow, weary smile. 'All down to me, then. Again.'

'Is the woman still a threat to us?' asked the Teacher.

'No,' said the Lawmaker. 'She met with a nasty accident this morning.'

'Good,' said the Teacher. 'One less problem to worry about. It is, isn't it?'

'It's being taken care of. I don't think there'll be repercussions.'

'Christ, what a mess,' said the Missionary.

'Of your making,' said the Teacher.

'This is getting us nowhere,' said the Lawmaker. 'We need to think, to plan. Come on, focus, concentrate. This is the most important thing you'll do all year.'

They all sat back, thinking.

The only noise in the room the low murmur of air-conditioning.

Then, focused and concentrated, they began to talk.

Eventually, they had their plan.

30

Donna put the mug to her lips. Too hot. She set it back on the table at the side of the sofa. Took the cigarette from the ashtray, placed it between her lips, dragged down. Heard the paper curl and burn, felt the smoke fill her body. Took it way down. Blew out a stream of smoke, clouding her view of the living room. She held it in her fingers, looked at the glowing tip. The alcohol and drug tremble in her hands was subsiding, the tea and nicotine helping. She took another drag, curled her legs beneath her, looked at Ben playing on the floor.

Escape. That was what she was thinking about. Escape.

And Faith.

And the lies she had told the police bitch.

Escape. Donna knew all about it. Wrote the fucking book on it. If there was anything she was an expert in, that was it.

Escape.

That was how she had ended up where she was. How all the girls had ended up there, if they were honest. Which they weren't, most of the time. Not to people who didn't matter. And they were the ones they dealt with most of the time. Punters. Police. Council. Sometimes all three.

But escape. Running away. They were all running away from something. Herself included. Abusive husbands. Rapist fathers. Or fathers, uncles and friends. Families that weren't. Running. Always running.

That was why they were all such fucking messes. Herself included. Running away, needing to escape.

Escaping into anything. A different life. Being a different person. Different name. And the ways of escape. Pills. Booze. The rock and the pipe. The herb. Lovely, all of it. Comedowns could be a bastard, but so what? Just score some more. Get high again.

Escape.

Another mouthful of tea. Cool enough to drink. Another deep draw.

Faith always said she was running. Escaping from something. Always had her stories. Donna never paid much attention. She had her own stories. Sometimes she told them. And when she did, she always changed them. Never the same one twice. But they were always the truth. At least they were at the time.

But Faith's stories. The same every time. Running from something big. Had to escape. Couldn't say anything, but had to escape.

Donna had never really listened. *If it's that big,* she had said, *why don't you go to the papers? The TV? Get yourself on there?*

Faith had just laughed. *You think they're not in on it? It's huge, I'm telling you. Massive. They're all in it together.*

Donna had laughed then.

Keep me head down. Best way. Keep meself safe. And Ben. Especially Ben. 'Cos that's who they want really. If somethin' happened to me, it would be him they'd want.

And that had been that. Donna had let her go on. Silly girl. Silly little stupid messed-up girl.

Lots of the girls talked like that. Booze fantasies. Crack dreams. Spliff psychosis. And they were all true, the stories, all real. Donna never paid it much mind. Her stories were true too. When she was telling them.

But Faith . . . she hadn't let up. Ever.

If somethin' happens to me, she had said one night, eyes pin-wheeling on skunk and vodka shots, *anythin', an accident, anythin'. Somethin' happens . . . it'll be them. After me. They'll have got me. An' if they do that, an' if that happens . . . You've got to promise me . . . promise me . . .*

Donna had taken a hit off the skunk and promised her.

Haven't told you what yet. Promise me . . . you'll look after Ben. Don't let them take Ben. Whatever you do, don't let them take Ben.

Donna had thought she was talking shit, but looking in her eyes, her bloodshot, broken eyes, she had seen that her best friend was completely serious.

So she had promised her. Whatever.

Faith had seemed relieved. *They will come, you know. In a big car. Two of them. Both men. Wearin' suits. Like Jehovah's Witnesses. But they're not. They're not . . .*

And then the drunken tears had started.

Promise me . . . promise me . . .

And Donna had promised once more.

She sucked the fag down to the filter, crushed it in the ash-tray.

That copper. Martin. Hard-faced bitch. Fancied herself too. But she wasn't as hard as she thought. Donna was good at reading people. She had to be in her line of work. Too many girls had got into the wrong car only to be found up in the woods at the Stour estuary with their brains smashed in by a claw hammer. So she had taught herself to read people. And Martin had been easy.

128

Easy to read.

Even easier to lie to and get away with it.

There was something behind her eyes. Some kind of damage. Hurt. And anger. Lots of anger. Donna would put money on there being a man behind it. Which was why she had sent her after Daryl.

She smiled.

Wished she could be there when Martin stomped in, accused him of being a pimp, of having something to do with Faith's death. Oh, that would be priceless. Because Daryl *was* their pimp. Or used to be. Pimp and ex. She hoped he would get into something with Martin. Knew he would. Hoped that the bitch copper was angry enough and psycho enough to make something of it.

She wouldn't like to put money on the outcome of that one.

She smiled, took a mouthful of tea. Grimaced. It was cold. She uncurled from the sofa and crossed to the window. Looked out.

And there it was. A big car. On the opposite side of the road.

A shiver ran through Donna. Her stomach flipped over.

Coincidence, she thought. The council out looking for benefit fiddlers again.

She looked closer. Two men sitting in it. Both wearing suits. Neither Jehovah's Witnesses.

They were looking at her house. They were waiting.

Shit. Shit shit shit.

Her hands began to shake from more than last night's booze and drugs. She had to do something. Anything.

Ben was still playing on the floor. Absorbed in his own world of make-believe. She looked again at the window, then down to the boy.

Thought of her friend. That silly girl. That silly little stupid messed-up girl.

Tears sprang to the corners of her eyes. She hadn't grieved for Faith. Her best friend. Her lover. And she wouldn't now. Things like that didn't touch Donna. She told herself so all the time. She was too hard for that. She had to be.

She wiped her face with the back of her hand, ran her hand down her jeans.

'Come on, Ben, get your stuff together. We're goin' out.'

'We goin' to see Mum?'

Donna felt the tears threaten again, pushed them back down. 'No. We're not. We're . . . goin' out.' She forced a smile. 'It'll be an adventure. We're runnin' away. Come on.'

The little boy stood up, went upstairs. Donna looked round, tried to think what to do next. They had to get away. Far away. They needed a car . . .

She smiled. Went into the kitchen. Took out the biggest, sharpest kitchen knife she had. She never used it for cooking. But it came in handy to scare off psycho punters.

A car. She knew just how to get one . . .

31

The pub had large rectangular windows. Huge, bare. Inviting passers-by to look in, saying to the world: we have nothing to hide. Nothing untoward goes on in here. We're a friendly, happy place. Come on in.

Rose Martin knew that was nowhere near the truth.

The Shakespeare liked to think of itself as one of the roughest pubs in Colchester. Villains and criminals were drawn to it like the terminally self-deluded and desperate were to *X Factor* auditions. And like those *X Factor* auditionees, the pub's clientele were a similarly hopeless and pathetic bunch. Petty and low-level, bungling and inept. The pub nurtured these no-hopers, fuelled their delusions, lubricated their lack of success until failures talked themselves into winners. Kings of a cut-price castle. Until the real world hit them like an icy blast from the North Sea.

Until closing time came.

Rose Martin had dealt with this place many times in a professional capacity, both in uniform and out. Mopping-up operations on a weekend, banging heads together, proving she was a tougher uniformed officer than her male colleagues. Or then with CID, chasing after one of the failures who believed – wrongly, of course – he was ready to move up a league.

She knew this place.

As she walked in, she felt the adrenalin rise within her. An old response kicking in, her hands automatically clenching into fists, body going into fight-or-flight.

Fight, definitely.

She had also attracted attention. Made immediately as filth. May as well have a big neon sign round her neck. The solitary drinkers dotted round the place had either looked up at her as she entered or put their heads down, eyes averted. On tables of two or more, hands had swept the surface, gone underneath, where they would stay until she had left. A gang of lads clustered round the pool table stopped playing, stared. Gripped their pool cues like tribal warriors holding spears.

She moved further into the pub. The air was rank. Cigarette smoke no longer disguising wood ingrained and rotted by stale beer, or a toilet that hadn't been recently cleaned, or a deep-fat fryer that hadn't changed its oil since Tony Blair was prime minister.

The walls were drab, bare. Chairs that had survived being used as Saturday-night brawling weapons clustered round old, scarred tables. Vinyl banquettes lined the walls, a patchwork of gaffer-covered slashes.

Rose walked up to the bar. The barman was large and neckless. His stubble-shaved head went straight into his faded Hawaiian shirt. His face was as open and welcoming as an evangelical church to a married gay couple.

She showed him her warrant card. She needn't have done. 'I'm looking for Daryl Kent. He in? I was told he'd be here.'

The barman appeared to be thinking. Weighing up being a grass against not co-operating with someone who could get his pub investigated. He settled for nodding in the direction of the youths playing pool.

'Which one?' she said.

'Dark lad. White hoodie.' His lips didn't move as he spoke.

She nodded by way of thanks and crossed the floor to the pool table. Spotted Daryl Kent straight away. He was mixed race and angry about it. Or at least angry about something. His eyes narrowed, features set into a scowl. Body tensed, ready to leap, begging for trouble.

'Daryl Kent?'

He checked his gang first, a quick look either side. They moved in closer behind him, pool cues gripped tight. He looked back at Rose. 'Who's askin'?'

She showed him her warrant card. 'Detective Inspector Rose Martin.'

'Five-O.' Pleased with himself, like he'd just unravelled Fermat's Last Theorem.

She waited. 'Daryl Kent.' A statement not a question.

A small nod. 'Yeah.'

'Can we talk?'

Another look round. 'Talk here. My bredrin's safe.'

Rose inwardly rolled her eyes. Talking like a New York gangster or a Jamaican yardie when he had probably been no further than Marks Tey.

'You were Faith Luscombe's boyfriend. Right?'

He shrugged.

'That a yes?'

'Yeah. Some. Not no more. Bitch was skanky.'

'Certainly isn't no more, Daryl, because she's dead.'

It was like she had slapped him. Suddenly a different persona appeared. Shock passed over his features, followed by fear. Suddenly she sensed he was uncomfortable with his bredrin around him.

'Seriously?' His voice small, incredulous. A child's response.

'Seriously. Where were you last night, Daryl? Or this morning?'

He backed away from her, into the pool table. Fear spreading over his features. 'Naw, naw . . . not me. You ain't stitchin' me up for it.'

'Where were you, Daryl?'

Another look at his bredrin. They had dropped back away from him. Suddenly not that close. Rose was enjoying herself now. Putting this arrogant twat in his place.

'With my . . . my new woman.'

'What, your mum?' She couldn't resist it.

His bredrin sniggered. Daryl became angry.

'Not my mum. Cheeky bitch. My new woman. Denise. Was round at her place.'

'Right. And do you pimp her out as well?'

'What?' Shock and incredulity.

'Get her to have paid sex with other men and then take her money off her? I thought you of all people would know what a pimp does.'

'I ain't no pimp.'

'No?' Rose's anger was increasing. 'I hate liars, Daryl. I really do. Such a lack of respect, being lied to. But you know what? I hate pimps most of all. Scum. Lowest of the low. Cowards, living off women. Too lazy to get themselves work.'

'I ain't no pimp!'

'Liar.'

'No I ain't . . . ' Another look round to his bredrin, who weren't helping him. They had drifted away from him now. He was on his own. His anger increased. Rose saw his lips move, eyes dart. Trying desperately to think of a comeback. 'But if I was a pimp,' he said, 'I'd turn you out. Show you some respect for talking to me like that.'

And that did it. All the excuse she needed.

She was on him. One arm locked round his neck, the other pulling his own arm up behind his back, stretching it as far as it would go. He cried out in pain. She felt his muscles tearing, heard something pop.

'Take it outside,' the barman said from the safety of the bar.

'Fuck off,' said Rose, then turned her attention back to Daryl. 'Now, where were we? Oh yes. Liars and pimps. I hate both of them. And that's you, Daryl. Now talk. You were Faith's boyfriend. Did you pimp her out?'

'No . . . '

She pulled harder. He screamed. 'Did you?'

'No . . . ' he gasped out.

It sounded like the truth, she thought reluctantly. He was too weak to keep lying while she was doing this. She kept going. 'Where were you last night?'

'With Denise, I told you . . . '

She pulled again.

'All right, all right . . . at home. At my mum's . . . '

'That's better.'

'Wait . . . wait . . . '

Rose waited.

'Did . . . Donna send you? Did . . . she tell you that? Bitch . . . '

A sudden realisation hit Rose. She had been played. Read, wound up and sent after Daryl. Donna had played her.

'Why's she a bitch, Daryl?' Wanting to let go of him, not knowing how to. Not knowing how to let herself go.

'Because . . . she hates me. Always hated me . . . hated me bein' with Faith, mad lezzer wanted her for herself. An' she got her an' all . . . '

Played.

It was a hateful feeling.

135

She gave him one last twist. He cried out and she let him go. He slumped to the floor beneath the pool table, gasping and crying. 'You're a psycho, a fuckin' psycho . . .'

'And you're still scum,' she said, and walked out.

Away down the street, not knowing where she was going, just moving, letting the adrenalin subside.

Played. She couldn't believe it.

Dissatisfied and unfulfilled. That was how she felt. She had been made a fool of. Hadn't learned what she wanted to know. And she had assaulted an innocent man. Well, she doubted he was innocent. But he was in this instance.

That didn't bother her. That wasn't upsetting her. She was only angry about being lied to. She could have kept on hurting him. Making him scream.

In fact, she had wanted to.

And she didn't know how she felt about that.

So she just kept on walking.

32

Mickey hadn't had much luck or help at the demolition firm and it seemed to be continuing at the building firm. He was becoming irritated.

He leaned across the desk. 'Look, I realise your boss isn't here; you've said that enough times. I just want to know when he'll be back and when I can talk to him.'

The girl behind the desk just stared once more.

He was in the offices of Lyalls, the building contractors. He had checked them out. Once one of the East of England's biggest firms, when the credit crunch hit they had found it hard going and the original owners had sold the company. But judging by the billboards and the blown-up photos adorning the walls of the reception area in the offices on Middleborough, they were still fronting, still looking prosperous. Still claiming to be responsible for the majority of new build going on in the town. Despite the fact that most of the projects had been completed a few years ago.

However, thought Mickey, whatever success the company had had didn't stretch to them hiring a receptionist capable of independent thought.

She was pretty enough, beautiful even. He gave her that. In fact his first instinct had been to try and use whatever charm he had on her, but after her first, smiley response, all rictus grin and dead eyes, he had tried a more formal approach. That hadn't worked either.

It was clear that whatever gifts she did possess were restricted to applying perfect make-up and choosing and wearing the right clothes, which, while looking suitably corporate, accentuated her gym-trim figure and showed just enough cleavage to distract from the fact that she was there primarily to stonewall.

'I don't know,' she said. 'Can't say. Sometimes Mr Balchunas is out all day.'

'And sometimes he isn't. Right. Is there anyone else I can talk to? Anyone else who can help me?'

'Umm . . . ' She shook her head.

'OK.' Mickey took out a card, handed it to her. He spoke slowly. 'Can you make sure he gets this, please? Tell him to call this number when he gets back.' He underlined it with his finger to make sure she understood him. 'Tell him it's important.'

He waited until she had nodded, then turned, left the building.

Outside, he checked his watch. Back at the station, Milhouse was ploughing his way through computerised lists trying to find names behind the holding company that owned the property. Mickey seemed to be having no luck using up shoe leather. Time to call it a day, he thought.

As he did so, a car pulled up. Jag, chauffeur-driven. The suited driver got out, opened the back door. A small, dark man got out. Small but, Mickey noticed, compact. Solid. And well-dressed. Like a street fighter who had learned how to use his skills in business. He still looked like he could handle himself.

But not at the moment. His eyes darted round nervously. They alighted on Mickey.

'Mr Balchunas? Karolis Balchunas?'

The man jumped. 'What? Yes, who are you?' Spoken with an accent. Mickey couldn't place it.

He showed his warrant card, gave his name. 'Could I have a quick word, please?'

The man's distress increased. Mickey sensed Balchunas was about to fob him off, brush him aside, but he stood his ground, took strength from stillness, didn't move.

It worked. Balchunas sighed. 'Come in, please. But I'm very busy, I can't give you long.'

'This'll only take a few minutes, sir.'

Balchunas turned, entered the building, Mickey following.

He turned as the car pull away. And stopped.

There was another passenger. He ducked his head away as if not wanting to be seen, but too late. Mickey had glimpsed him. And recognised him.

The man from the solicitors' offices. The one he knew but couldn't give a name to.

Mickey's stomach gave a small lurch. Something was happening here. He didn't yet know what, but there was a pattern emerging.

Hurrying, he followed Balchunas inside.

33

Anni couldn't concentrate. She was sitting outside the boy's room, waiting. It wasn't a skill she was proficient at at the best of times. And this wasn't the best of times.

She felt out of her depth on this one. That was why she had called Marina in. But now Marina had left, and in her place was a child psychologist Dr Ubha had brought in. Jenny Swan seemed a pleasant enough woman, middle-aged, dyed blonde hair, curvy and handsome-looking. Probably a stunner in her youth, now more like a trendy grandma.

Anni had briefed her as much as she could, told her it was still early in the investigation and he was going to take a lot of working with. Jenny Swan had nodded as Anni talked, took it all in, asked questions.

'I think it's better if I work with him alone.'

Anni had nodded. 'Fine.' She felt happier about that.

Jenny Swan had then walked through the door to the room, smiling at the boy as she went in, putting him at ease as much as she could.

The door had closed behind her and Anni had been left outside.

When Anni had been in the room while Marina was talking to the boy, she had felt distinctly uncomfortable. She had been trained to work with abused children – her remit as a reactive DC in the Major Incident Squad encompassed that. But this boy was especially difficult. She felt it strongly from him, like a kind of chemical repellent.

All her usual tricks had failed. She could find no commonality with this boy. Nothing she could get a handle on. Nothing she could find to engage him with. Like he was from a completely different tribe. Or race, even. Species.

He gave her the creeps. She felt guilty admitting it, but it was true.

Anni knew what traumatised kids were like. She'd worked with enough of them. They weren't the airbrushed, doe-eyed victims the tabloids liked to portray. They were fractured, damaged individuals, sometimes irredeemably so. Occasionally they could be helped, put back on track with the right care and support, but she had seen too many of them go straight from hellish childhoods to secure units to young offenders institutions to adult prisons. Their crimes escalating each time, externalising the abuse they had suffered, taking it out on someone else.

But this boy . . . he was beyond even that. From what she had seen of him, he was a breed apart and she couldn't begin to get a handle on him.

The door opened. Jenny Swan emerged, closed it quietly behind her.

Anni stood up. 'How is he?'

The strain was showing on her face already. 'Not . . . happy. He's calmed down since he first came here and is communicating, after a fashion. I think your colleague helped to open him up.'

'Did he tell you anything? Anything we could use?'

She looked momentarily unhappy about Anni's question, the conflicting interest showing in her eyes. 'I . . . it's too early to say. Nothing yet, I don't think.'

'He talked about his mother before.'

'And now. He's very concerned that she should be safe.'

'Did he manage a description, anything like that? Talk about a place where she might be?'

'The garden, that's all he said. She's in the garden.'

Anni nodded. Nothing more than Marina had got out of him. 'Thank you, Jenny.'

Anni turned away, checked her watch. There should be a uniform coming to relieve her soon for the night shift.

'Oh, there is one other thing.'

She turned, waited.

'Wherever this boy has been, wherever he's been kept, it's far away from the rest of society. And I don't need an examination to know he's been forced to do things against his will.'

'Such as?'

Jenny sighed. 'I . . . wouldn't like to speculate. But my guess is something horrific. Sustained and repeated, too. And something else.'

'What?'

'Wherever he's been kept, he and his mother, they weren't the only ones.'

Anni frowned. 'Oh my God.'

'Exactly.'

34

Balchunas sat behind his desk. The room, like the reception foyer, was covered with photos of developments. Amongst these were framed certificates, citations and awards. Statuettes sat on a shelf over the filing cabinets, in front of photos of Balchunas shaking hands with politicians and celebrities. He looked the same in every photo – beamingly thrilled to be there; they looked the same in every photo – bemused and startled.

Balchunas fidgeted. He couldn't get comfortable, shuffling round on the seat, making the leather squeak. He picked things up off the desk, played with them, put them down again. He fiddled with cuffs, the edges of his shirt. In response, Mickey sat as still as possible. Waited.

'I can't give you long, I'm afraid, Detective ... I'm sorry, what was your name again?'

'Detective Sergeant Philips. That's all right, Mr Balchunas, I won't need long. Just a couple of questions.'

'Fire away.' His smile was shaky, his voice resigned.

'You know about the discovery at the property at the bottom of East Hill? On the land you were going to build a new housing estate on?'

Balchunas sighed, fidgeted some more. 'Yes, yes, terrible business. Shocking.' His eyes strayed away from Mickey, on to a photo of Karolis Balchunas shaking hands with Boris Johnson. In the flashlight, only one of them seemed pleased about it.

'I'd just like to know who owns the property, the land that you're building on. Is that you?'

'No, no. Not us. We're just the contractors. We just build. Sometimes we own the land, but not in this instance.'

'So who does?'

'I . . . don't know.'

'You don't know.'

'No.' Shaking his head, building the point emphatically. 'No. I don't.'

Mickey frowned. 'Do you often build properties and not know who owns the land?'

More shuffling, more fidgeting. 'No . . . '

'Then why in this case?'

'I . . . look. Have you tried the Land Registry? They would know.'

'And you wouldn't?'

'I could find out. It would take time . . . '

Mickey leaned forward. 'Mr Balchunas, is there something you're not telling me? Because if there is, I may see it as obstructing an investigation.'

Anger flared in Balchunas' face. His cheeks flushed. Fists clenched. 'Who's your superior officer, Sergeant?' His voice suddenly strong, clear.

Mickey didn't answer straight away. Just nodded to himself. This was following a pattern. Whenever he questioned anyone who had money, who perceived themselves as having status or influence, that line always came up. But only when they were asked something they didn't want made public knowledge. A fact they were ashamed of.

Or of losing control over.

'Can I take it you're not going to answer the question, sir?'

'Are you going to answer mine? I have friends in the police force, Sergeant. High-ranking ones. Important ones.' He gestured towards his framed photos. Unfortunately he alighted on Philip Glenister posing as DCI Gene Hunt.

Mickey thought of giving Phil's name, the person he regarded as the boss, but didn't think that was senior enough to impress Balchunas. So gave him another.

'DCI Brian Glass.'

Balchunas sat back, face impassive. 'I'd like you to leave, Detective Sergeant. I'm a busy man. I have work to do. Especially in light of what's happened today. I could stand to lose an awful lot of money.'

'I appreciate that, Mr Balchunas, but—'

'I am not legally obliged to tell you anything. Any further questions can be put to me through my solicitors.'

'Who are?'

'Fenton Associates.'

Fenton Associates. Lynn Windsor's firm. Based at the Georgian house at the bottom of East Hill.

'Right, sir.' Mickey stood up, turned to the door. Turned back. 'Just one more thing.'

Balchunas waited, seemingly holding his breath.

'The person in the back of your car.'

Fear flashed across his eyes once more.

'Person?'

'Yes. The man in the car with you. You got out, it drove away. With him in it. Who is he?'

Balchunas' mouth moved but no sound came out.

'Mr Balchunas?'

'There . . . there was no other person. There was just me.'

'You're lying to me. Sir. There was a man in the back of that car. And I'd like to know who he is.'

Balchunas stood up. Anger in his eyes. 'Get out. Now. Or I will have you reported to your superior. I'll have my solicitor on you for harassing me. Go on. Get out.'

Mickey felt anger of his own rising. Tamped it down. 'I'm going, Mr Balchunas. But I doubt this is the last you'll hear from me.'

Mickey left.

Outside, walking down Middleborough, he tried to piece things together. Couldn't. There was something just out of reach, something he couldn't quite get.

But he knew that if he could remember who that man in the car was, it would all become a lot clearer.

35

Paul was shaken. He had to sit down.

They had let him go. They'd had to. Couldn't even keep him as a witness, because he'd seen nothing. Or at least nothing he wanted to tell them. Because if he did, he would have to think about things too much and it would all start to fall in. No more sun on his face, no more breathing in the open air. No more relaxing. No. It would be back in the cave for him and he didn't want that. Didn't want that ever again.

But they had kept on. And on and on. And on. They had told him things, waited for him to respond. To make their minds up about whether he was telling the truth from what he said and the way he said it. And he didn't want that. He couldn't have that.

Because if they didn't like what he said or the way he said it, they would put him in a cell and never let him out again.

And that would be as bad as the cave.

Or nearly as bad. At least he might be on his own there. Just Paul. No Gardener. That would be something.

But he had said nothing. Given them nothing. Because they were the dogs. The earth. He was the wind. The butterfly.

'I'm the butterfly . . .'

He hadn't realised he had spoken aloud. People tried to pretend he hadn't said anything, that they hadn't seen him. Just glimpsed him out of the corners of their eyes and hurried on by. Made him invisible.

He didn't care.

He walked up the street. Shops and people with bags. Going into shops to get more bags. And more. Hurrying before the shops closed, said they couldn't have any more stuff till tomorrow. They would wait and then start again. That was their lives.

But not his. Never his. Because he had a joy within him they would never have. Could never know.

He said all this to himself as he walked up the street. Words coming out between his ruined teeth. Words only he knew the meaning of. Words they would never understand.

Up the street and away.

He could hear the cave calling. Knew who was there. What he would do. But Paul was soft. That was his trouble. He would go in, see if he was all right. See if he had changed, if he was ready to come out and be nice. Go from Cain to Abel. And sometimes he would say he was. But he was tricking Paul. Being nice just to get out. Then he would be the same as he always was. Bad. Bad man. Evil. The serpent in paradise. And he would throw Paul in the cave. And Paul would sit there in the dark. Crying, wailing. Feeling guilty for what he had done. Trying to find his way out. To see the sin and breathe the air. But there would be no way out. Not until the Gardener decided to let him out.

And Paul fell for it every time.

Every time.

Like this time. He knew he would fall for it. He always did. Because he was weak. He used to think it wasn't weakness, it was meekness. For they shall inherit the Earth. But he had tried that. And look what had happened. That was where the Gardener had come from. And the rest of them.

So he hurried away from the people.

Because as hard as he tried to resist it, the cave was calling. And he knew he would have to open it.

36

Donna closed the door behind her, hard. It felt loud. Final.

She looked down at Ben standing beside her. The little boy was wearing all his best clothes, his new – or new to him – coat on and fastened up to the neck. He looked up at her, eyes uncomprehending but trusting. A shiver of maternal feeling ran through Donna. It was one thing to look after herself. But now she had him to think about.

'You all right, then?' she said to him.

He nodded.

'You remember what to do?'

Nodded again. 'What you do,' he said. 'What you tell me to do.'

She managed a grim smile, hoped it didn't scare him. 'Good. Come on.'

She had packed a holdall with as much stuff as she could manage. She slung it over her shoulder, kept it in place with one hand, held Ben's hand in the other. She looked over at the car. It was still there, the two men sitting in the front, pretending not to look at her.

Donna set off down the road, away from the main entrance on to Barrack Street. It was starting to get dark. The grey in the sky deepening, the sodium lights casting the street in pools of orange.

They passed the car, Donna looking through the windscreen at the two men. Both big, both wearing suits.

Just like Faith had said.

She swallowed hard, gave Ben the signal and started to run.

Initially, nothing happened. Then she heard car doors opening, slamming closed. Feet running behind her. They were coming.

Still gripping Ben's hand hard, Donna ran down the road and round a corner. There were no houses down here. It was a walkway, a cut-through to another street. Bushes pushing against a chain-link fence on one side, the high wall of a graffitied garage on the other.

She raced down the cut, still holding the bag on her shoulder. Glad she was wearing trainers. Ben was running as fast as he could, trying to keep up with her. They reached a corner, ran round it. Stopped.

It was a longer alley, bushes on both sides, fast-food debris, plastic bottles lying around, broken glass sparkling like uncut diamonds in the weak reflected light of the occasional street lamp. It was deserted.

'Get behind me. Quick.'

Ben obeyed, holding on to Donna's leg, gripping it tight.

'Don't cling on to me, just stand there.'

He dropped his hands, did as he was told.

Donna waited, flattened against the fence, chest heaving from the exercise. If she got out of this, she told herself, she would never smoke again. Or cut down at least.

All she could hear was her own breathing.

She felt inside her jacket pocket, did an inventory with her fingers. All there. Good. She took out a small cylinder, held it tight in her hand.

Then she heard them, above her own ragged breathing, the pounding of feet on tarmac. She braced herself. Knew she would get only one chance at this, had to do it properly.

The first one arrived. She didn't even stop to look at him, see if she recognised him. She just pointed her pepper spray, let him have it full in the eyes.

It took him a couple of seconds to realise what had happened, but once the shock subsided and the pain kicked in, he flung his head back, clawing at his eyes. He dropped to his knees, head forward. Gasping, screaming.

The other one arrived then. She turned to him, ready to give him the same treatment. But he was too quick for her. He had quickly sized up the situation, decided the same thing wasn't going to happen to him. He looked straight at her, anger in his eyes. Punched out his fist. Knocked the can flying from her hand.

Advanced on her.

He smiled. He had her.

Or so he thought.

Heart beating so fast she thought her chest would explode, she reached into her pocket for Plan B. Brought it out.

The kitchen knife.

Gripped it tight. Felt the heft of it in her hand, saw the light glint off the long, sharp, heavy blade.

Didn't hesitate. Just thrust it outwards, sliced at him. As hard and as fast as she could.

He stood there, shocked, unmoving. Looked down at his chest. Blood began to seep through his white shirt from his left shoulder down to the top of his belt. He looked at her, surprise on his face.

Donna was shocked at the sight too. Couldn't quite

comprehend that she had actually done that, that she was responsible for it. But she recovered quickly. Saw that it had only slowed him down, not stopped him. Slashed him again.

The blood began to pump now, more quickly, soaking the white fabric to a deep red.

Donna looked at the knife, at the man in front of her. He was starting to topple forward, falling to one knee, his hand trying to hold himself together. He looked up at her. The smile was a distant memory. Incomprehension had given way to shock, which had now given up its place for terror. Fear in his eyes.

And Donna felt a surge of strength. She knew now what it must be like to be a man. To have that sense of control, that power. It was a new feeling to her. And she loved it.

She looked at the knife again. She wanted to slash him once more, keep slashing, until there was nothing left of him but ribbons of blood and flesh. Make him answer. Make him pay for the years of pain and abuse she had suffered at the hands of men.

The knife went towards him once more. He cowered away.

She stopped herself. Reminded herself she was doing this for a reason, a purpose.

'Give me your car keys. Now.' Shouting, adrenalin raising her voice.

He did so, taking the keys out, throwing them on the ground.

'Pick them up, Ben.'

She looked behind her at the little boy. He was standing there, hands covering his face, shaking.

'They're bad men, Ben,' she urged him. 'They're going to hurt us. We have to do this. Quick.'

He didn't move. Couldn't move.

'Oh for God's sake,' she said, and bent down herself to pick the keys up. 'Now your wallets. Just the cash.'

Neither of them moved; they just lay there, groaning.

'Now!' She brandished the knife once more. It worked.

They both dug into their pockets, flung their wallets on the ground. She bent down, took the cash out. Didn't look at it as she pocketed it, but it felt like a couple of hundred there.

'Now phones.'

They did so. She picked them up, threw them over the hedge.

'Right,' she said to Ben. 'Come on.'

She grabbed his hand, pulled him along with her. It was like dragging a small slab of granite.

They ran back the way they had come. The car was still parked there. Donna ran towards it, threw the holdall on to the back seat. Told Ben to get in the passenger side. He did so, moving numbly.

Donna got behind the wheel.

Drove away as fast as she could.

37

The phone rang. And the rest of the world fell away as the Teacher heard the voice.

'You're not supposed to call. Not here.'

'I know,' said the Lawmaker. 'And I wouldn't be. Unless it was important.'

The Teacher sighed. 'What? I thought we had it all arranged. A plan.'

'We did. But things have changed since then. Very quickly.'

The younger one's heart skipped a beat. 'How?'

'The investigation seems to be picking up things we don't want it to. Talking to people we'd rather they didn't.'

'Can't you fix it?'

'Of course. But it takes time. And there's been an added complication. The woman who died.'

'The accident.'

'Right. Her ... partner, shall we say ... has disappeared. Taken that boy with her.'

'But she doesn't—'

'We don't know what she knows. We can't take the chance.'

The Teacher sighed. 'We should stick to the original plan. Let the others do their part.'

'I agree. But there's more we could be doing.'

The Teacher felt the chill in the words. Knew that further argument was futile. 'What do you want to do?'

'We stick to what we've already arranged. As far as that goes.' The Lawmaker's voice dropped, became conspiratorial. 'But I think our Missionary friend may have made his final mission.'

'How d'you mean?'

'I think he's been recognised. Even after all this time. And if that's the case, it won't take them long to put a name to the face. And then . . . well. Do I need to tell you?'

Silence.

'It won't be a question of damage limitation any more. It'll be the end. Of everything. We don't need the Missionary any more. He's done his part, the deal's been struck. We've already got our new partner, could even be the next Missionary. So the current one would just be . . . in the way.'

'What are you suggesting?'

A chuckle. 'That's what I like about you. So pragmatic. The Missionary is removed. Permanently.'

'How? Not one of us, surely.'

'Of course not. But I imagine the Gardener isn't too happy at the moment. Waiting for his ritual to go ahead, not knowing whether he's going to get his victim returned to him or not, he's going to have a lot of pent-up energy. He's going to need a release.'

'But on the Missionary . . . '

'Poetic, don't you think?'

'Would he do it?'

The Lawmaker laughed. What do you think? The Missionary will be on . . . gardening leave. Permanently.'

The Teacher thought about it. 'Does the Portreeve know?'

'Not yet.'

'*Will* he know?'

'Eventually. They'll all find out.'

'So why tell me?'

'Because the Portreeve is the past. And you're the future. And it's always wise to invest in the future.'

The Teacher could find no words.

'We'll talk tomorrow. Remember, you still have a part to play.'

'I hadn't forgotten.'

'Looking forward to it?'

'I'll tell you later.'

'We'll speak soon.'

The phone went dead.

The Teacher put the phone away. The real world, held in abeyance for the duration of the call, started up again.

But it didn't feel real. It didn't feel right.

It felt like an illusion.

It felt like . . . nothing at all.

38

Phil ducked under the tape, dodged the waiting news crews, walked away from the crime scene. His Audi was parked on the opposite side of the road.

Marina was going back to the station in her own car. Just as well, he thought. He had felt uncomfortable around her. And he had felt bad keeping what he was feeling from her. The trouble was, he still didn't know what exactly he *was* feeling. Just that it wasn't good.

As he reached his car, he heard his name being called. He turned. Saw Don Brennan walking over the bridge towards him.

'There you are,' said Don.

'Don.' Phil walked away from the car to join him on the bridge. With the lack of action, bodies or blood down below, the gawpers had thinned out. 'What brings you here?'

Don shrugged, smiled, tried for casual. 'Oh, you know. Just out for a walk. Bit of exercise.'

'And you ended up here.'

Another smile. 'Can't keep away, can I?'

Phil looked at the man he regarded as his father. He was in

his sixties but kept himself fit. He hadn't succumbed to the expanding waistline and strawberry nose that cursed so many ageing coppers, those who couldn't deal with the lack of focus and direction once the pension cheques started and the excitement of the job abruptly ceased. He played tennis, badminton. Still had a full head of hair, now white. Still dressed well. Not for him the beige windcheater and elasticated trousers. Instead, a plaid shirt, tweed jacket and jeans.

Don looked down at the house, the white tent. 'Brings it all back,' he said, smiling with the corners of his mouth.

Phil waited. He doubted this was just an accidental meeting.

Don looked away from the crime scene, back at Phil. 'How's it going?'

'Early days,' said Phil. 'You know how it is.' He was going to add *or was*, but decided to leave it. Sure that Don didn't need any more reminding.

Don nodded. 'Kid in a cage, wasn't it? That what you said?'

'That's right,' said Phil.

'What, down there? In that house?' Don looked once more at the crime scene.

'That's the one,' said Phil, his eyes following.

'Any leads? Anything?'

'Nothing yet. Early days, like I said.' Phil turned back to Don. 'Are you really just here by chance, Don?'

Don looked down at the bridge's stone balustrade, his own hands. Then back up to Phil. 'I just thought ... you know, you're always saying I should come back, get in with the cold-case squad, that kind of thing ... '

'Yeah. We've talked about this before.'

'I know that. And I've always said no. But ... ' His eyes flicked down to the crime scene. Phil could tell he was tempted to keep looking, but he brought his gaze back up.

'Well, I was thinking. You were saying about how short-staffed you were. Cuts and that.'

'Yes.' Phil could see where this was going.

'Well I just thought . . . ' He shrugged. 'You could use all the help you can get.'

'You want to work this case? With me? Be on the team? That what you're saying?'

Another shrug. 'If you'll have me.'

'And what would you do, exactly?'

'You know. Filing. Office stuff. Bit of legwork.' He looked away again. Phil couldn't see his eyes. 'Check out the files, the archives, see if this kind of thing's happened before. Any connections . . . '

He didn't look back at Phil. Phil couldn't read his expression.

'D'you think it has?' said Phil. 'Does it remind you of anything?'

'Don't know. I could have a look.' He tapped his head, looking at Phil at last. 'Get the old brain cells going again.'

Phil didn't know what to say. He was sure from his body language that Don had some ulterior motive. But he also knew that if he asked him, he would just deny it. Still, something about this case was stopping Phil from thinking straight. It might be good to have someone he could trust and rely on alongside him.

'You sure you can stand working with me?'

Don gave a small laugh. 'Why wouldn't I? Taught you everything you know.'

Phil smiled. 'OK. I'll have a word with Glass, see what he says.'

Don frowned. 'Glass? Brian Glass?'

'That's him. D'you know him?'

'Years ago. He was uniform when I was CID.' He nodded,

memories screening behind his eyes like old movies. Again the sides of his mouth curled into a smile. Not a happy one, Phil thought. 'Yeah, I remember him. Doubt he'd remember me, though.'

'We'll see. I'll give him a call.'

Phil detached himself from the side of the bridge. Looked at Don. 'I've got to go. Marina'll pop round for Josephina in a while, yeah?'

He went back to his car.

Head like a badly tuned radio.

39

Darkness had fallen. And cold with it: the air catching the breath unexpectedly after a warm day. And with the cold, fog. Drifting, swirling, rendering the world in dark, Impressionistic hues.

But the Gardener didn't notice any of that. He didn't care. He was out of the cave. That was all that mattered.

He stood by the gates, staring upwards. Breath a cloud of steam, his personal fog machine.

Out again. That stupid weak fool Paul. The Gardener laughed. He loved the man really. Paul had saved his life. Stepped in at a time when it was all falling apart. Showed him there was a different way. A better way. A purer way. And he would always be grateful to him for that. Always.

But he was a fool. And a soft-headed, soft-hearted one too. He had hope. Even now. Even after everything that had happened. And that was why he would never win. He would put the Gardener in the cave. Yes. But he would let him out again. Always.

Yes. Always.

The Gardener nodded to himself. Eyes never leaving the house before him.

Big. Old. Lights on in lots of rooms. Making it look inviting. Warm. Big gravel drive curving round before it. Grounds at the side. Grass. Trees. Deer in the trees. He had seen them. They had seen him too. Run from him. Scared.

Good. They should be.

He had received the call. Been told what to do.

He hated being told what to do. Hated it. Especially with what had happened today. The sacrifice house gone. The boy taken. How had that been allowed to happen? Didn't they know how important it was? To him? To them? All of them?

They had said they did. And that they would make everything all right. Get the boy back. Use the other sacrifice house. They had better, he had told them. They had to.

Or it would be their turn next.

They knew that. But first they wanted him to do something for them. And for himself too.

They had told him what it was.

And he had smiled.

He would have done it anyway if they had asked. Enjoyed it. But he didn't tell them that. Made them bargain. Give him what he wanted. Needed. It was only right.

And they would keep their promises.

As he would keep his.

He looked up at the building once more. Saw what it once had been. Heard the voices of ghosts, glimpsed them all around. Then saw it for what it had become. And the voices stilled. Now there was . . . nothing.

He moved towards it. Knew the secret way in. Knew everything about the place.

Pulled his hood on. Felt his breath against the inside. A truer skin than his own flesh.

Felt inside his pocket for the blade.

Smiled inside the hood.

Like God had kept his promise to Abraham, he would make sure they kept their promise to him.

And he would enjoy it while he did it.

40

He took a sip of his drink. Rolled it round his mouth. Good. Fine. Smiled. Took another one. Settled back in his chair. Relaxed.

They'd never find him here. Here of all places. Never think to look.

Not that they were looking for him.

Nah. Everything was fine.

Or it would be.

Bit of a misunderstanding, that was all. Just like he'd told them. Needed the money for the deal to go through. No problem. It would all be sorted out soon. Because no matter what the filth had found – or thought they'd found, because they didn't have a clue yet – it could all go away with money. Just like the old days. Bung a bit here and there, a few favours, pay for some blind eyes, that was it. Bish, bosh, and free to go about your business. Didn't know what all the fuss was about. Especially now. Not with—

'Robin?' A voice from the bathroom. He'd almost forgotten she was there.

'Yeah?'

'I am nearly ready.'

'Can't wait to see you, sweetheart. Bet you look spectacular.'

She should. Money he'd paid for her. And she'd better *be* spectacular an' all. Because East Europeans were always the best. Had a reputation to keep up.

Another mouthful of whisky. God, that was smooth. Just slipped down like silk on fire. No after-burn at all.

He smiled, gave a small laugh to himself. Robin. A little joke he played with himself. His nom de plume. His alias. Robin Banks. Still made him laugh to think of it. Irony and all that.

He put the whisky on a side table, stretched out in the seat, hands behind his head. Ankles crossed. He looked down his body. Bespoke Savile Row suit. Hand-made Italian leather shoes. Silk socks. Shirts from Jermyn Street. If you're going to do it, do it properly.

He sighed. He'd fronted it round the table, stuck it out when their questions had got a bit too close. Tried to play it down, look relaxed. But he needed that deal to go through. Desperately. Things had reached the end the way they were, no question. But it would take a bit of vision to move on to the next step. And vision, unlike cash, was one thing he had plenty of.

But there was still that niggling doubt, that feeling that it was all a house of cards that could come crashing down any second.

He brushed all that away. Didn't need doubts. Never had them, never had need of them; too old to start entertaining them now.

But still . . .

He sighed. 'You ready in there yet?'

'Nearly . . . '

'Well hurry up. Any longer an' I'll have had too much to drink. An' if that happens, that's your fuckin' tip gone, darlin'.'

He heard an angry slamming of cosmetics from behind the closed door. He smiled. Good. Get 'em angry. Fire 'em up. He liked it when they had a bit of spirit to them. Made it more memorable.

And made his job easier, if he was honest. At his age, that was a relief.

'Now come on. I'm takin' my little blue pill. Don't wanna waste it.'

He slipped the pill into his mouth, swallowed it down with a shot of whisky. Hoped he'd timed it right. One time, he'd got it all wrong. Barely able to get hard when the bird was there, walking around like a fucking flagpole all the next day.

He put the glass back on the table. Noticed it was empty. Picked up the phone, called room service. Asked for another bottle.

Sat back. Waited.

There was a knock at the door.

'Blimey, that was quick.'

He levered himself out of the chair, legs stiff, crossed the room. Opened the door.

'Must be some kind of record,' he started to say. 'I only just—'

And stopped.

'Oh no. Oh no . . . '

He had seen who it was.

And what he held in his hand.

'Oh no . . . not you, no . . . '

The figure advanced into the room. Slammed the door behind him.

'Look, I'm sorry, right . . . ' He backed away from the intruder. 'I didn't know you were still . . . in there . . . '

The figure kept advancing towards him. He could hear that broken, ragged breathing, smell that rotted, loamy smell. Hadn't encountered either for years. The memory made him shiver.

'Come on, not me ... I mean, not me ...'

The figure kept advancing. He was pushed against the far wall.

This is it, he thought. *This is the end. Unless I do something. Unless I find some way of fighting back.*

He reached across to the table, found the empty whisky bottle. Picked it up by the neck, swung it at his assailant.

Who ducked. The bottle missed his head, glanced off his shoulder. A grunt, a huff, but nothing else. Still advancing.

And then he felt his erection starting. Thanks a fuckin' bunch, he thought. What perfect timing. He pulled at his crotch, trying futilely to rearrange himself.

If his assailant noticed, he didn't show it. Just swung the blade up above his head.

'No ... no ...'

Brought it down.

Hack.

And again.

Hack.

And again.

Hack.

Until soon all that was left of him was his erection.

The figure turned, left.

Not noticing the muffled screams and sobs coming from the bathroom.

Dissolving away into the night.

41

Marina heard the door, opened her eyes. Checked the clock. Blinking green numerals told her it was nearly half one.

Phil coming home.

She hadn't slept.

The call had come earlier. Marina had picked Josephina up from Eileen, brought her home. She had felt something strange about Eileen's mood, a diffidence, a reserve. A fear, even. But hadn't felt it was quite her place to ask if there was anything wrong.

So home after that, feeding the baby, playing with her, putting her to bed. Then starting on her report of the cellar. And that was when the phone had rung. Phil.

'Listen,' he had said, voice sounding remarkably like Eileen's, 'I'm going to be late.'

Marina didn't know why, but she had expected this kind of call. Something to keep him out. Something to keep him away from her.

'OK.'

She heard the hum of atmospherics coming down the phone line. A swirling silence between them.

'There's . . . there's been a murder. Out at the Halstead Manor Hotel. Nasty one too.'

'What happened?'

'One of the guests. Carved up. Really badly. It's . . . I'm there now.'

'Right. So . . . what time will you be home?'

'Late. I can't see . . . ' A sigh. 'Late. This is a bad one.'

More atmospherics.

'Well I'll . . . will you have eaten?'

'I'll grab something on the way. Don't worry. About me.'

Silence then, as she bit back what she wanted to say. The atmospherics, the swirling, came from her inside her own head this time.

I do worry, she wanted to say. *Especially now. Since you've pulled so far away from me so suddenly. I should worry. I do worry.*

'OK.' All she could manage.

More silence. The phone line. His and hers.

'I'll not wait up for you, then.'

'Best not to.'

Silence. Rising to deafening.

'OK. See you later,' said Marina. 'Or not.'

They said their goodbyes. Hung up on each other. Marina put the phone down, looked round the living room.

They were really starting to make it theirs. It had been painted, furniture moved in. Old stuff discarded, new stuff chosen together. No longer living out of boxes, they'd arranged and shelved their books and CDs, integrating them all together. Marina had joked that Phil would want every-thing placed alphabetically. He had laughed and replied no. Let's arrange them as if they're at a dinner party.

'Put books together by writers we think would get on. Same with CDs. A kind of thematic consistency.' He had smiled at her as he said the words, gently teasing, the kind of thing she would say to him.

And that was how they had arranged things. Spent the best part of a day doing it.

And at the end she had loved him even more.

But that was then. This was a new Phil. A closed, cold Phil. A keeper of secrets. A non-communicator. She wasn't used to this. She was throwing herself out there, at him, and he was ignoring her. Pretending she wasn't there. It unnerved her, unsettled her.

Scared her.

And now here he was, coming in.

She heard him climbing the stairs, quietly. Heard the door to Josephina's room open, knew he was checking in on her. Then the door of their bedroom opened.

What to do? Pretend to be asleep, or talk to him?

She lay on her side, away from him, as she always did.

She heard him undressing, using the bathroom. Felt him get into bed next to her. Expected to feel his body up against her, arm round her waist, the way they always slept.

Felt nothing.

She wanted to move, turn to him, ask what was wrong, where he was.

But didn't. Just stayed where she was. And she knew why. Not because she was scared of asking the question.

Just of hearing the answer.

So she lay there, awake. Pretending to be asleep. And knew that Phil was doing exactly the same.

And the night dragged on.

PART TWO

AUTUMN FALLS

42

Phil tried to move. Couldn't.

Something round his neck restraining him, holding him back. His fingers went to it. Found cold, rusted metal. Sharp edges digging in. Tightly clamped, just enough space to breathe.

He tugged. Felt his throat constrict.

Put his hands behind his head, his neck, looking for something – anything – that could give him purchase. Found only rusted chain. Heard the clanking in his ears, the weight of it in his hands as he pulled. Pulled again.

Nothing. It wouldn't budge.

His heart was hammering, chest beginning to ache. Like the other, more familiar metal band was wrapping itself round him, tightening, tightening . . .

He gasped, tried to hold down the pain, keep breathing . . .

Keep breathing . . .

Hands behind his head, he pulled the chain once more. Hard as he could. Felt nothing but the coldness of metal in his hands. Dead. Heavy. Unyielding. Felt his chest burning.

His eyes closed. Hot tears forming behind his eyelids.

Heard himself shout out:

No . . . no . . . let me . . . let me go, let me go . . .

No sound emerged. Shouting only in his head.

Please . . .

Nothing. Just his inner screams, inner pain.

He dropped the chain, opened his eyes. And saw what was before him.

And when he knew where he was, his heart thumped harder, chest ached fiercer.

He was in the cage. The cage of bones.

No . . .

Screamed, at the top of his lungs.

Silent.

Hands outstretched now, clamped tight round the bone bars. Pulling hard, harder . . .

He could feel the age in them, the smoothness. And the strength. Nothing gave. The cage held firm. He pulled again, pushed, rattled back and forth.

Nothing.

Another scream.

Another silence.

And then, at the far end of the cellar, a shadow amongst shadows, he saw someone. A figure moving closer. Slowly, slowly closer. Weak light glinting off metal. A sickle held in an outstretched fist. Moving slowly, rotating. Backwards . . . forwards . . .

Backwards . . . forwards . . .

Swinging slowly.

No . . . no . . . please no . . .

Silence. Impenetrable. Deafening.

Something else about the figure. A reason for its slow motion. It was dragging one leg. Throwing it out, limping painfully on it. But coming steadily forward.

Slowly . . . inexorably.

Phil's hands went into overdrive. Pulling at the chain. Pulling at the bars.

Nothing. And nothing.

He stopped. Exhausted. And saw the face of the advancing figure.

Screamed again.

There was no face. Just sacking. Tatters. A rough scarecrow's head, sewn crudely together to resemble a man's. Slash for a mouth, but nothing for eyes. Just darkness. Two black holes.

Phil screamed once more.

He saw the rest of the figure now. Tattered from head to foot. Sacking. Hessian. Crudely stitched and sewn together. Patched. Filthy. A leather apron tied at the front. Old and dark-stained.

The sickle was raised. The moon blade shivering in the pale, weak light.

The tattered face loomed close, right up to the bars. Phil saw the eyes. Nothing there. Just deep, dark, empty black holes.

The blade glittered.

Was brought back.

Phil screamed.

The blade was brought down.

Phil screamed again, sobbing now.

Again. Again. Again.

Screaming, sobbing.

Silence.

'Phil . . . Phil . . . '

His heart was pounding, his chest burning. He couldn't

177

suck in enough air. His lungs didn't feel big enough. Sweat covered his body, hot and prickly.

'Phil . . .'

He opened his eyes. Saw Marina's anxious face, her eyes staring into his.

'What . . . what . . . happened?' His voice. He had found his voice.

'You had a nightmare.' Marina's hand on his arm, rubbing slowly, her skin cool and soothing against his own, uncomfortably hot.

'Nightmare . . . nightmare . . .' Gasping out words, gulping in air, struggling to sit up.

'Just a nightmare. That's all.' Her hand stroking him. The feel of it reassuring. 'Come on. Don't talk. It's fine. Everything's fine.'

Phil turned his head, looked to where Marina was. The room was dark. But he could see her. The shape of her head. Her eyes. Her beautiful eyes shining out of the darkness.

'Nightmare,' he gasped.

'That's right.' The stroke of her hand soothing, comforting. The closeness of her, their intimacy, reaching him. Calming him. 'A nightmare. Come on.'

She pulled his body down to the bed once more. He felt her arms encircle his chest, her head on his shoulder. Legs pressed against his. A living, breathing cage of bones. Enfolding him. Protecting him.

'Just a nightmare, that's all.'

He nodded. She settled down with him. From the rhythm of her breathing and the weight of her arm, he could tell that she was soon asleep. He lay there awake. Staring ahead. Looking into the darkness. Wary for any shadows within shadows.

A nightmare. Just a nightmare.

Except it wasn't. Phil knew that. He could feel it. He didn't know how, but he could feel it.

No. Not just a nightmare.

It was so much worse than that.

43

Mickey sat in his chair, leaning back, toying with his pen, watching the rest of the team enter for the morning briefing. Bought-in large cappuccino resting beside him – four shots of espresso zinging him up to the hilt.

The bright late-September morning sun streamed through the blinds. Still clinging on to the idea of summer, not wanting to relinquish its grip, hand over to autumn in earnest.

Despite not finishing until late the night before, and being completely exhausted when he had finally hit the bed in his flat, Mickey hadn't slept much. He hardly ever did when he was working a big case, and this one seemed to be developing into just that.

And then there was what he'd seen at the hotel. Those images would take some dislodging in his mind. The body of what had once been a man lay in a heap beside the far wall of the room. Butchered. The only word to describe it. The body sliced into, hacked to pieces, blood everywhere, the room redecorated in arterial sprays and splatters.

'Someone must have really hated him, whoever he was,' Mickey had said to Phil, looking from the doorway at the body. The SOCOs hadn't allowed them anywhere nearer than that. They were going to be a long time with this one. This was, Mickey knew, a forensic worker's dream.

Phil had kept staring. 'Yeah. Whoever he was.'

'Any ID?'

Phil had answered, never taking his eyes off the body. 'Adam Weaver is the name in the wallet. But he signed in under the name Robin Banks.'

'What?' said Mickey. 'He a Clash fan or something?'

'Could be, who knows? He'd been booked in for a few days, had bought himself a bit of company last night.' Phil pointed to the bathroom. 'That's who raised the alarm.'

'Ah,' Mickey had said, understanding.

'Apparently,' said Phil, 'she was in the bathroom getting changed when there was a knock at the room door. After that she heard him screaming.'

'And she didn't look out?'

Phil shook his head. 'Locked the bathroom door. Hid behind the shower curtain. Didn't see a thing. Then phoned 999.'

Mickey frowned. 'She had her phone in there with her?'

A ghost of a smile troubled Phil's lips. 'Taking photos for her boyfriend, apparently. Said it was an arrangement they had.'

Mickey's turn to smile. 'Classy. So he was here on business, then? Adam Weaver?'

'What he said. We'll get it looked into.'

Mickey looked again at the man lying on the floor. There wasn't much of him left to recognise or make an identification from. But from the sweep of his grey hair, the first thing Mickey thought was, *that's the guy I saw yesterday*. Then he shook his head. Seeing him everywhere now.

'What?' Phil looked at him. 'What did you say?'

'Er . . . nothing.' Mickey hadn't realised he had spoken his thoughts out loud.

Phil kept looking at him. Waiting.

'Nothing.'

'You had a thought there, Mickey. Your first response. Your copper's intuition. What was it?'

Mickey tried to smile, laugh it off. 'Well, I saw this guy. In the solicitors' offices first. And I recognised him. Or thought I did. Couldn't place him. Anyway, I didn't waste too much time on it, kept going.'

He paused. Phil waited.

'And then . . . ' Mickey sighed. It felt ridiculous saying this aloud. 'I saw him again. At the building firm. In a car with Balchunas. I asked Balchunas who he was. He got angry. Asked me to leave.'

'And now he's here. Dead.'

'If it's him.'

Phil looked again at the dead body. 'D'you believe in coincidence, Mickey? When murder's involved?'

Mickey didn't reply. He knew a rhetorical question when he heard one.

Now he dropped the pen. Blinked. He had been slipping away. He took a mouthful of coffee. Two. Looked around the room once more.

The incident room of the Major Incident Squad was filling up. When a big investigation was under way, they moved into the bar. He could imagine, given the press of bodies in the room and the escalation in importance of what they were working on, that they would be in there soon.

They were all here. The Birdies, sitting together as usual. Milhouse, dragged blinking and squinting away from his computer, forced to interact with real people against his will. Anni. Sitting opposite Mickey. She looked up. Smiled.

He returned it. Held it for a second too long. Just as she did.

Every time he saw her – which was just about every day – the word that came into his head was 'nearly'. They had nearly gone out together. Nearly gone for a drink. Or dinner. Or the cinema. They had nearly kissed. They had nearly gone to bed together. Nearly. Always nearly. There was definitely an attraction there. No question. And it was reciprocated, too. But neither one of them would make the final move towards the other. As if something – fear of rejection, fear of losing friendship, fear of losing mutual respect if it went wrong, he couldn't say what exactly – was holding them back.

Maybe it was all of those things. Maybe none, something he didn't even realise. Whatever, it had kept their relationship as just good friends. Who smiled at each other and held it for too long.

Then Glass entered. Took his place before the group, plonking a heavy-looking file down on the desk, digging into his briefcase for something to supplement it. No banter, no chat, just business. All business, as usual.

And then Phil arrived. With Marina. Mickey frowned. The pair of them entered together but couldn't have looked further apart. They sat down next to each other but still managed to maintain a distance.

Lovers' tiff, thought Mickey, risking a glance at Anni. From the expression on her face, she had picked up on it too. That was the trouble with having relationships with people at work, he thought sadly: if they went wrong, the fallout was awful.

Another glance at Anni. From the way she looked at him briefly, then away, it seemed like she was having similar thoughts.

'Right, good morning, everyone,' said Glass. Getting attention just with his voice.

Everyone looked at him, waited.

Mickey took a mouthful of coffee. Another. Blinked. Felt the caffeine jolt through his body.

'We ready? Let's start.'

Another quick glance at Anni, who was staring straight ahead, eyes on Glass. Mickey did the same.

He was ready.

44

'OK,' said Glass, 'I think the first thing I should say is that we are now dealing with two ongoing major crimes, and we will be investigating them simultaneously.'

Phil said nothing. Just waited his turn to speak. Before Glass arrived, Phil had always led the briefings. He wasn't the most senior officer in the team, but as a reactive DI, his role was the most hands-on. Glass had changed that. He had stated, brooking no argument, that he should be the one to host the briefings. Even when he didn't know directly what they were about.

'Phil here,' said Glass, pointing.

Phil looked up as his name was mentioned.

'Detective Inspector Phil Brennan will be running both investigations.' He looked at Phil, made a rising gesture with his hand, as if he was a stage illusionist performing an act of levitation. Phil rose, walked to the front.

He tried to push last night's nightmare out of his mind. Keep his recent fears securely locked up. Concentrate on his team, on the job he had to do. Work through it, don't give in to it.

He looked at the assembled faces, his gaze falling on Marina. The concern in her eyes for him, the worry. The love. He felt a thudding of shame from within his chest, pangs of guilt at the way he was treating her. Something was going wrong within him. Very wrong. He didn't know what. And the one person who could help him ... he couldn't tell her. Because he didn't know *how* to tell her. Because he didn't understand it himself.

He knew what she must suspect. What she must think of him. And he had to do something about it. Before those feelings crystallised. Before she pulled away from him the way he had from her.

Before they fell apart.

Concentrate on the team, he thought once more. On the job. On the work before him. The rest will have to wait.

'OK,' Phil said, eyes scanning those before him, 'as you're well aware, last night there was a murder at the Halstead Manor Hotel. The photos are here if you'd like to see them and you haven't had any breakfast. But I wouldn't advise it unless you need to. Because someone did a very thorough and brutal job on the victim.'

Adrian Wren frowned, spoke.

'Halstead Manor ... Isn't that the place that used to have that commune in it?'

'Years ago,' said Glass. 'I was on the team investigating that. One of my first jobs as a uniform. I remember it well. But I doubt that's relevant.'

Adrian nodded, as if a bet had been confirmed. Phil waited, made sure there was nothing else from Glass. Continued.

'The victim's name was Adam Weaver. However, he was signed in to the hotel as Robin Banks.'

A ripple of laughter.

'Yes, I know,' said Phil. 'Adam Weaver was a businessman,

living in Lithuania. We don't know what he was over here for, but we're in the process of investigating. We do know that he was on the board of the company who own the hotel.'

Phil was aware of Glass leaning forward, listening more intently to his words.

'And there's something else,' Phil continued. He looked to his DS. 'Mickey?'

Mickey cleared his throat. 'Yeah,' he said, not standing up but turning to address the rest of the group. 'Adam Weaver. I think I saw this man yesterday. At the offices of Fenton Associates, the solicitors' practice just beside the house where we found the kid in the cage. And then again later, at the building contractors. He was in a car with Karolis Balchunas, guy who runs the company.'

Anni looked up. 'So the two things are related?'

Phil became aware of Glass scrutinising him. He ignored him.

'We don't know,' said Phil. 'But we've had a look into Mr Balchunas and he's Lithuanian too. So are most of the staff he employs.'

Glass cleared his throat. 'So a businessman living in Lithuania is murdered while visiting another Lithuanian businessman living here. How is that related to the boy in the cellar?'

'I don't know,' said Phil. 'But we'll find out if it is.'

'Looking at it logically,' said Glass, 'it sounds like a business rival waiting until Weaver's out of the country to do the dirty deed, somewhere he can't be investigated. I'm sure he had rivals in Lithuania. Like the Wild West over there.'

'You might be right, sir,' said Phil, clearly irritated at the interruption, 'and we'll be looking into it. That's one avenue. The other is that it's connected with what we discovered yesterday.'

Glass shrugged.

'We're keeping an open mind.' Phil looked again at his DS. 'Thanks, Mickey.'

Mickey nodded, making eye contact as he did so.

Phil knew what that look meant. Mickey was grateful to him for not mentioning the fact that he had recognised Weaver from somewhere else. That was an angle that the two of them had agreed Mickey should work on his own. If it panned out, great. Another lead. If it didn't, well these things happened in police work.

'Could it have been a professional hit?' asked Anni.

'Well,' said Phil, 'I have to say, there didn't seem to be anything professional about it. It was one of the most horrific murders I've ever seen. Ferocious. You usually see something like that only if it's personal. So we don't know yet. Not until we have more information.'

'What about leads? Clues?' Adrian this time.

'Nothing much,' said Jane Gosling. 'But someone answering the description of the tramp we pulled in yesterday was seen in the area.'

'What?' Phil looked at the assembled faces. 'I thought he was still being questioned. On whose say-so was he released?'

Glass leaned forward. 'On mine.'

Phil looked puzzled and a little angry. 'Why?'

Glass held up his hands. 'Did you think he was our murderer?'

'No, but—'

'Exactly. So I let him go.'

'But he could have seen something. Could have known something.'

'There was nothing more he could tell us,' said Glass. 'He was questioned thoroughly. I'm sure everyone who spoke to him agrees that whoever got that boy into the cellar was

188

younger and fitter than the tramp. And more capable of planning. Our chap wasn't even capable of being a fully functioning human being. And certainly not strong enough.'

'Couldn't he have been on drugs?' said Mickey.

'Almost certainly,' said Glass.

'Well you never know,' continued Mickey, backing up his boss, 'once they get something inside them . . . '

Glass was clearly irritated at being questioned. 'I let him go. It was my decision and I stand by it. We move on.'

'And now,' said Phil, 'he turns up at a hotel where one of the guests is murdered.'

Glass's voice was rising. 'If it was the same man, Detective Inspector.'

'Let's follow it up. See if it was.'

Glass said nothing. But the silence made it clear what he thought of Phil's words. Phil waited for another interruption, but none came.

'Please continue, Detective Inspector.'

Phil continued.

'So that's where we are with it. We're looking at Weaver's life. Looking for enemies, both here and abroad. Friends also. We're now following up on sightings of the tramp, too. We're not letting anything go.'

'Thank you,' said Glass. He stood up, ready to take over.

'I'm not quite finished,' said Phil.

Glass sat down again, reluctantly.

'I realise that we're operating two cases simultaneously. I also know that usually they would both be upgraded, given a proper operating budget. Of course, in these straitened times, that might not be possible.' He looked at Glass, who made no response. 'Well, bearing that in mind, I've asked an old friend of mine to join us. A retired detective who's put in a fair few years' service. We've been trying to get him back to go over cold cases for ages, and he's agreed to give us a hand working on these two.'

Phil looked at the double doors.

'Don Brennan.'

On cue, Don entered.

And Glass's agitation increased massively.

45

Phil noticed Glass's response straight away. Don didn't. He just walked into the room, smiled and nodded, found an empty chair, sat down.

'Thanks, Don,' said Phil, smiling. 'Good to see you.'

'Thanks for asking me.'

Phil was surprised. As soon as Don had entered the room, the years seemed to have fallen away from him. He was no longer Phil's adoptive father and Josephina's grandad, but a police officer again. Even his walk was different. Stronger. More purposeful.

And then there was the effect he had had on Glass. Out of character. Maybe Glass didn't like Phil exercising his authority. Well, tough. Phil had already cleared it with him, mentioned Don by name. Glass had given the go-ahead. Perhaps he hadn't been expecting such a public announcement.

Phil put it to the back of his mind, continued.

'Right,' he said. 'Anni. The boy?'

'Yeah. Right.' Anni stood up. Addressed the room. 'Well I think we're in this for the long haul.' She looked down at her notes, looked up again. 'There's a child psychologist been brought in.' She hesitated, looked at Marina. 'Perhaps Marina could tell you the technicalities better than me.'

'We'll hear your impressions first, Detective Constable Hepburn,' said Glass. 'We can come to the technicalities later.'

Anni paused, looked apologetically at Marina, who shrugged, gave her a small smile. Anni, bolstered by this, continued. 'As I said, there's been a child psychologist brought in by Dr Ubha. Marina talked to the boy first, though.'

She raised her eyebrows, giving Marina a signal to speak. Phil knew what his DC was doing. A subtle dig at the DCI. With Anni's gesture and Mickey backing him earlier, he felt a small swell of pride in his team.

'Yes,' said Marina, not standing, 'I tried to talk to him. Very traumatised. In a very, very bad way. He's been down there, or somewhere similar, for a long time. And from the way he was talking, I don't think he was alone.'

Silence in the room. Marina continued.

'He kept talking about his mother. Worried about her. Wanted to see her.'

'Natural in a boy who's been taken away,' said Glass, interrupting.

Marina didn't look at him, kept going. 'True, but I got the impression they had been imprisoned together.'

'We've checked missing persons lists,' said Jane from the back. 'Nothing. No one matching the boy's description. Started on children's homes, social services, nothing so far.'

'He's going to be in hospital for a while,' said Anni. 'He's very weak. They're working with him. Hopefully he'll be able to tell us something, give us something to go on. And we've got some of his medical results back too.' She sighed. 'He's malnourished to virtually Third World levels, and is a potential breeding ground for so many infections. The hospital have pumped him full of antibiotics. Wherever he's come from, it's left him in a hell of a state.'

Phil could tell, from the softness in her voice, that the boy had got to her. He wasn't surprised. Seeing a child in that state would do the same thing to anyone with a spark of humanity.

'We've also got back preliminary DNA results on him,' Anni said. 'No match. On anything. Not even a close match. It's like he just . . . doesn't exist. But since we don't know who he is or why he was there, we have to assume that he matters to someone. We're keeping a twenty-four-hour watch on his room.'

'Thanks, Anni.'

'There is one more thing.' She took out a photo, placed it before her. 'This was on his foot. Some kind of scar. Looks like a brand.'

'What?' said Mickey. 'Like you do with cattle?'

'Seems that way,' said Anni. 'I've started checking, seeing if any other bodies have turned up with similar markings. Nothing so far.'

She sat down.

'Forensics from the cellar haven't come back to us yet,' said Phil. 'They're still doing tests to decide whether the bones are human or not, and same for the dried blood we found. So. Marina?' He looked over at her. When his eyes hit, she jumped as if he had made physical contact. His heart broke a little more. 'Would you like to give us your report on the crime scene?'

Marina stood up, eyes on her report. Phil was grateful for that. He was sure that everyone in the room knew something was up with them. Sure that everyone was watching and listening to them, and not for the right reasons.

'Yes,' she said. 'Well, most of you know what was there

193

apart from the boy. The cage. The implements. The flowers. I've been focusing on the Cabalistic markings on the wall. Checking them out. I think if we can understand what they mean, we can go some way towards understanding why the boy was there and who put him there.'

Glass nodded, listening.

'All the evidence would indicate that it's some kind of calendar. A growth cycle. The flowers point to that too. There seemed to be equinoxes, solstices marked. In fact, one's happening about now. If that's the case, then it looks like the boy is important. Very important. Whoever put him there has plans for him that include the equinox.'

'D'you mean a sacrifice? Something like that?' said Mickey.

Marina shrugged. 'I couldn't speculate, but it might well be. The boy was imprisoned, as if waiting for something. The cage was a holding cell. I think he was kept somewhere else beforehand. Only moved there for the ritual. The flowers point to that too. They're very specific colours. Red, blue, yellow. My guess is they represent bodily secretions. Blue and red for blood, yellow for urine, and they're all decaying, turning brown. I'll let you work that one out.'

No one laughed.

'But why there?' Mickey again. 'Why that place?'

'I don't know. It must have some significance to the person carrying out the ritual. I do think, though, that in finding the boy, we stopped a murder.'

Silence in the room.

'Might he try again?' asked Anni.

'Very likely. As I said, there's only a small window of opportunity in this equinox, if that's what he's working towards, and I strongly suspect he is.'

'Will he try to get the boy back?' asked Mickey.

'He might. Or perhaps try to find another boy. We've got

the rest of today and tomorrow. It's my opinion that he'll strike within that time.'

'Where?' Mickey again.

'I don't know. He operates from somewhere safe, somewhere that's secure for him. Somewhere that means something to him. The cellar was laid out the way it was because of the ritual. And that's important to him. He must have taken a long time preparing it, getting it just the way he wanted it. He's going to be spending all his time between now and tomorrow night finding another place, getting it ready.'

'And going after the boy?' asked Mickey.

'Or a boy.'

Silence round the room.

'Something else,' said Marina. Everyone listened. 'He's done this before. Solstices, equinoxes . . . four a year. And not just this year.'

Silence once more. Phil was thinking about comics. House of Mystery. House of Secrets. With a graveyard in between.

'Right,' he said. 'We've got our work cut out for us. We're up against the clock with this one. If Marina's right, and from the look of the evidence we must assume she is, there's going to be an abduction and murder before tomorrow night. We keep doing what we're doing. Working on the boy, keeping him safe in hospital. Following the paper trail for the house's ownership. And don't forget about Adam Weaver. We've still got him to look into.'

He scanned them all once more. Had a sudden, intense flashback to his nightmare. That face, moving towards him, those dark, deep eyes, the blade coming down . . .

He jumped, shook himself out of it. Looked round. They were waiting for him to speak.

'I want radar,' he said. 'On the space in between the two houses. Check for soundings. For bodies. That's it. We can do

195

this. Let's go.' Hoping he sounded more confident than he felt.

Dismissed, they all rose, made for the door.

Phil saw Marina stand later than the rest. Pack her things slowly. She's waiting for me, he thought. She wants to talk. Now. About what's wrong.

She began to move towards him.

Phil waited. Steeling himself.

A tap on his shoulder. He turned. Glass. 'Phil? Word in my office, please.'

The DCI didn't look pleased. He turned, walked out.

Phil, giving Marina only the smallest of smiles, followed him.

46

Donna opened her eyes. Tried to move her head. As she did so, a rod of pain pushed up through her spine. She gasped, cried out.

That was what she got, she thought, for sleeping inside a stolen car.

She turned over, groaning, rotating her shoulders as she did so, stretching her legs in the cramped space. Trying to coax her limbs into action, get the blood pumping again. Her body was now angled away from the window, into the car, looking towards the passenger seat. A pair of round blue eyes stared back at her.

Ben.

Scared, cold. Uncomprehending, but still trusting.

Donna didn't know how that made her feel. She wasn't the boy's mother, so she shouldn't have to feel responsible for him. But then she had dragged him away with her, so perhaps she should.

She sighed. All too fucking much.

He was still staring at her, shivering.

'What'sa matter? You cold?'

He nodded, eyes unblinking, never leaving her face.

'Told you to keep warm, didn't I? Put more clothes on.' She looked at him again. He seemed to be wearing all the clothes he had brought with him.

'Auntie Donna . . . ' His voice tremulous, wavering.

She cut him off. 'I've told you before, Ben, I'm not your auntie.' Another sigh. Irritation building with it. 'I'm just Donna. Right?'

He nodded. 'Donna . . . '

'What?' The kid was becoming tedious.

'When are we goin' to see my mum?'

'I'm . . . ' She opened the car door. 'I'm just goin' for a smoke.'

She got out of the car, slowly unfolding herself out of her curled, cramped state. She shivered. Looked round. The September sun was rising high in the sky. Shining. She shivered again, pulled her jacket round her. Giving off light, but not heat.

She had no idea where she was. She had driven the car as fast and as far as she could from her house. But hadn't known where to go. At first she had decided on a hotel; use the money she had taken from her attackers to pay for it. But that idea hadn't lasted long. A hotel would be the first place they would look for her. Especially after she'd cut one of them. Her description would be out there, her face on all the news programmes, in the papers. The internet, even. So no. That was out.

But she had needed to go somewhere. Out of the town centre, through Stanway. She saw the sign for the turn-off to the zoo. Told Ben about it. He had asked if they could go there, and for a second she had thought seriously about it. Drive to the zoo. Catch the last hour before chucking-out time. Find somewhere to hide, spend the night there.

Brilliant. Last place they would expect her to go. But that idea hadn't lasted long either. Her mind had bombarded itself with all the things that could go wrong almost before she had thought of them.

So she had turned off at the new retail park roundabout, taken the road away from Colchester, down to the A12. To London and beyond. Resigned to putting as much distance between herself and the town as possible.

And on the way, going through Stanway, she had seen a turn-off. Between two tree-rich gardens in a row of nondescript houses. Wooded either side. On impulse, she had turned down it.

At first it was just a single-track country road. A few houses on one side, detached, exclusive-looking, she thought. The kind of thing she'd seen on *Grand Designs*. Big cars parked in front, 4x4s. Paula couldn't understand that. All that money and they bought something hidden away, somewhere people couldn't see. She wouldn't do that, if she had the money. She'd buy the biggest, gaudiest house. Put lights on it. Round it. Make sure no one could miss the fucker. Make sure everyone knew she was minted. Wasn't just some failure.

But anyway.

She had kept on down that road. Not looking back. Just seeing where it took her. The car swayed from side to side as the road became more uneven, as pockmarks turned to craters, tarmac ran out and became hard-packed dirt and stones. The trees thinned out too. Soon there were none. And the countryside opened up around them.

The road bisected two fields with a view of miles around. It was so pastoral and peaceful, so unlike Donna's day-to-day life in Colchester, that she could have just parked up, stayed there. Looked out over the calm, serene landscape. Forever.

But she didn't. She kept going.

Trees began to multiply, and she was soon in a forest. The road stopped completely. And that was where she decided to spend the night.

Ben had complained he was hungry, so she had turned the car round, driven back to the retail park, ordered two McDonald's. She knew she was taking a risk, but he was starting to complain and she knew he wouldn't stop until he was fed, so it was a risk she had had to take.

Then back to the forest. And the night, with much pain and discomfort and hardly any sleep, became morning. Now she stood, smoking a fag, wondering just what the hell she had done.

Ben stared at her from inside the car, kneeling on the seat, face pressed against the window. She turned away from him. He opened the door, got out to join her.

'Where's my mum?'

Donna didn't answer.

'I want my mum. Where is she? You said we'd be meetin' her.'

Had she? Had she said that? She wished she had brought something to drink. Or a bit of puff. Just to tide her over. Keep her going.

'Where is she?'

God, that kid . . .

Donna had put up with him for the sake of Faith. She hadn't thought of herself as gay. A lezzer. A dyke. A rug-muncher. She had done stuff, lezzie stuff before. Yeah, course she had. But that was for punters, for their enjoyment, their money. Not for fun. Faith had been her partner in all of that. Neither minded; they liked each other. Were good friends. Donna felt relaxed with Faith, open. Probably more so than with anyone else in her life. So when Daryl had been kicked to the kerb and Faith and Ben had nowhere to go, it had been the natural thing for them to move in with Donna. It was a small house. And Ben needed his own room. So it had been even more natural for Faith to move in with Donna. Share a room. Share a bed.

And do the kind of things they'd done for money, for the enjoyment of punters, for their own enjoyment. And if that made Donna a lezzer, a dyke, then so what? Whatever. Faith would never beat her up. Never take her money. Never force her out on the street to work while she sat at home or in the pub or spent the money she'd made trying to impress some slag.

And now Faith was gone. And Donna was all alone.

'Where? Where is she?'

Donna turned, stared hard at the little boy. And something in her snapped. Some anger, long-dammed, needed sudden, sharp release. 'She's gone, right? Fuckin' gone. She's not comin' back, 'cos she's—'

She stopped. Looked at him. He was standing there like he had been hit. His mouth began to tremble, eyes began to tear over.

'Look, I'm sorry, I . . . '

The tears came. Huge, racking sobs came screaming out, totally unconscious and inconsolable, like only a child could do when faced with the biggest loss of his life. Donna realised that she felt exactly the same. And she could do nothing but join him.

'I'm sorry,' she said, gasping between sobs, 'I'm sorry, I didn't . . . I didn't mean to . . . '

She hugged him. He let her. Reluctantly at first, then, realising he had nowhere else to go, collapsing into her.

'I'm scared,' he said eventually, once the tears had subsided.

'So am I,' Donna whispered. 'So am I.'

He looked at her. 'What are we goin' to do now?'

It was almost too painful to return the look. But she had to. 'I don't know,' she said. 'I just don't know . . .'

47

Paul had done it. Gone and done it. And now he was sorry. Like he knew he would be.

He had gone back up to the cave. Let the Gardener out.

He had told himself he wouldn't give in. Not this time. Wouldn't listen to the crying and the promises. Oh no. No matter how much the Gardener screamed and sobbed. About how he was going to be good from now on, how he wouldn't hurt anyone any more. If Paul would just let him out. He was sorry, so sorry . . .

Same old thing, same old words, same old pleas, time after time after time.

And it always worked.

Because the Gardener knew that Paul was weak. And he played on that weakness, wore him down with guilt until he opened the cave up, let him out again.

And of course the Gardener never kept any of his promises. As soon as he was out, he threw Paul inside and picked up where he had left off. And Paul would have to track him down, find him and haul him away again before he did more damage.

But now he had got him back inside the cave.

Now he could relax.

Paul knew what the Gardener had done this time. The Gardener had told him. Told him it was his duty. His divine duty. And that Paul should understand. And Paul would try to explain again.

'No . . . you . . . What you do, it's . . . it's wrong. It's . . . evil. Not what I meant. No, no, no . . . not what I meant . . . '

And the Gardener, back in the cave, would pretend to listen. Then pretend to cry. And Paul would have to come away so he couldn't hear it. Because God was love. And *he* was love. And he would let him out again.

So he sat outside the cave. And tried to relax.

Breathe in the air. Feel the sun on his face. Hear the river go past, lapping at the bank. Watch the water. See the leaves fall on it.

Relax.

Don't think about the Gardener. Don't think about letting him out.

Ignore his cries. Listen to the water.

Relax.

Just relax.

And don't think about what the Gardener had done.

And what he was going to do.

As soon as Paul let him out again.

48

Rose was angry. Really angry.

Anger was nothing new to her, but this kind was. Sudden and quick. And very, very deep. With a scattergun aim.

Glass had phoned her earlier in the morning. She had been up. It felt like she was always up. Since she had been put on long-term sick, she had had trouble sleeping. More than she had told Marina or any of the police doctors. Much more. Insomnia. Bad, verging on the chronic. She had tried over-the-counter remedies. Prescription pills from her GP. Drinking excessively before bed. Exercising until she was too physically exhausted to move. A long, hot, relaxing bath, even. And nothing had worked.

So she had learned to live with the lack of sleep. Learned to lie in bed at night staring at the ceiling, the walls. Closing her eyes, letting the film play on the backs of her eyelids. The same one. Always the same one.

That day in the boat, unable to move, those hands on her body . . . Fighting, losing . . .

Her eyes would open. And there would be the walls, the

ceiling. Her bedroom. Just the silence, the shadows. And Rose. Alone. Always alone.

She had even tried to lose herself in sex. Not love – she didn't want that level of intimacy, didn't want anyone seeing behind the shield, couldn't cope with it – but sex. Just to feel exhilarated, wanted. Alive. To have another body next to her to keep the shadows, the darkness at bay. To let her sleep. That hadn't worked either. She had soon found that she couldn't bear anyone to touch her. And she hated to have anyone next to her for the night. She would lie awake watching them sleep, wondering how long it would be before their hands were on her body, forcing her, fighting with her . . .

No.

So she had coped with the silence, the shadows, on her own. Alone. She had no choice. And if she was being honest with herself, she wouldn't say she was cured. She would just say she was stronger. Better armoured.

And that was enough. It had to be.

But she was also angry. Especially after Glass's call.

'Just a catch-up. Checking in. Seeing how your case is progressing.' As businesslike as ever, but did she catch a hint that he was thinking about her at home? Wondering what she was wearing, perhaps? She put it out of her mind. Just imagination.

She thought of the previous day. The fight in the pub. Obviously nothing had been said. She hadn't been reported. 'Fine,' she said. 'Just running down a few leads today. Ex-boyfriends, that kind of thing. Nothing concrete yet.'

She was sitting on the edge of the unmade bed. It seemed like this room, not even the rest of the flat, was her world. The TV in the corner, clothes, both clean and soiled, piled and thrown on the floor. Old mugs, ringed with coffee stains, sat on half-read paperback books. Plates with hard, curling crusts poked out from under the bed. She sighed.

'Time scale? Any ideas?'

'Early days,' she said, kicking an empty white wine bottle under the bed, hearing it roll to a stop, clink against another one already under there. 'But it won't take long, I don't think. Something'll break soon.'

'Good. Good.'

'I thought we were meeting this morning? Having a proper catch-up?'

'Yes . . . ' Glass's voice became cautious, guarded. 'Bit difficult. All kicked off here.'

She stood up. 'But I thought I was coming in to the station.'

'No.' Said quickly. Sharply. 'Like I said, it's all got busy here. A couple of cases taking up all the space, the manpower. I think it's best we talk this way. For the time being.'

And that was when the anger started to rise. Because she realised as he spoke what he was doing. Sidelining her. And she knew who had all the office space, whose cases were getting the upgraded treatment. Oh yes. She didn't even have to ask.

'Right,' she said. 'Fine. I'll call when there's news.'

And broke the connection. Threw the phone on the bed. Sat down beside it.

Phil Brennan. Fucking Phil Brennan again. Always him. Always. She had a special streak of hatred reserved just for him. Because he was everything she saw herself as not being. Successful. Popular. Promotable. Yes, she knew she had been promoted, but even so. It happened more easily for him. It always had.

She looked round the room again. Her world. Everything she had, all that she had to show for her life.

She had never wanted to be a police officer. Not really. It

was something she had done to impress her dad. He had been a DCI in the Met. Well-regarded. Well-decorated. One of the finest thief-takers of his time. That was what everyone said about him. That was what he said himself. But with a few more profanities thrown in.

And she had looked up to him. Admired him. But from a distance. It had always been that way, even before the divorce. He had always been out. Working, or networking, he called it. His mother had come to resent it. Partying, she said. Getting freebies off slags. He had laughed it off at first, told her she didn't know what she was talking about. It was the way the job worked, the culture. He had to go, had to be seen at those places, those parties. Her mother had said nothing then. Just glared at him in silent resentment. Let things continue that way.

She turned a blind eye to the whoring, the drinking. But she reluctantly accepted the unexpected presents, the bonuses. Holidays, home improvements, new cars. All on the sudden windfalls. She wasn't stupid. She knew her silence was being bought. And she entered into that complicity, albeit grudgingly. As long as the two worlds were separate, then she didn't need to know the other one existed.

The house of glass and cards held. For years and years. Until one world invaded the other. Until her mother found she had been given a dose of the clap.

She had confronted Rose's father about it. How could he? How the hell could he? The money, yes, a blind eye. The drinking, she had said nothing. Even fucking those slags … that was one thing, but bringing it home, into the family, *infecting her*, that was … that was something else. That was intolerable.

Her father had tried shrug it off. Just one of those things.

Her mother wouldn't let him. Kept on at him. On and on, all those years of silent resentment, bottled hatred, slewing out. Shouting that she could see at last. That the scales had fallen from her eyes, that she was blind no more.

That was when he had walked out. But not before he had hit her. Hard. Smashed her to the ground, left her lying in teeth, blood and agony on the kitchen floor. Years of silent, pent-up hatred coming out of him, too.

And Rose had been left. Brought up along with her brother by her shattered mother. Now silent, withdrawn, almost catatonic for the rest of her life.

Rose should have grown up to hate her father. And she did. But she hated her mother more. The spineless way she had given up on life, the way she drifted through the years like a ghost that wasn't yet dead. When she was finally diagnosed with cancer, she seemed to find it a relief. An excuse for her to stop living. And Rose never forgave her for that. Never stopped resenting her.

And never stopped trying to impress her father, either.

That was why she had enrolled in the police force. Just to impress him. But it hadn't worked. Living with his third wife, in declining health somewhere on the south coast, he hadn't contacted her in years. She had thought he would reappear when she was in the papers following the Creeper incident, but no. Nothing. Maybe he had died too. She hoped so.

She stood up once more, made her way to the shower. Thought of going for a run, channelling some of that anger, that energy. Decided against it. She would channel it another way.

Real police work. Visit the mortuary, take a look at Faith Luscombe's body. Check the CCTV cameras for New Town and roads leading out to Wakes Colne.

Then pay a return visit to Donna Warren.
Show her she wasn't a fucking idiot.
The water hit her, nice and hot.
But it could never be hot enough for Rose.

49

'Hold your nerve. That's all. Just hold your nerve.' The voice on the other end of the phone sighed. Tried to keep its temper, not let its exasperation show.

'But . . . ' The Portreeve wasn't happy.

Another sigh.

'You've got the easy bit,' said the Lawmaker. 'You're doing nothing. Even the Teacher is doing more than you.'

Silence from the Portreeve.

'Bet you wished you hadn't phoned me now.'

No reply. The Lawmaker took that as a yes.

'You didn't tell me,' said the Portreeve. 'You sanctioned . . . what happened, and you didn't tell me about it. Did you tell anyone else?'

'The Teacher knew.'

'And why didn't the Teacher tell me?'

'Because I said not to. I said I would talk to you. I knew what your reaction would be. And this is it.'

'But this is a step too far. This is . . . implicating us too much.'

'It isn't. Weaver was becoming a liability. Unpredictable.

We didn't know what he was going to do next. He needed to be taken care of. What better way than this? Misdirection. No one will care about our shipment arriving now. Pressure's off.'

'And what about ... There should be four of us. Who's going to be the new Missionary?'

'I would have thought that was an easy one. Our foreign friend is perfectly situated.'

'But what if he ... refuses?'

'Refuses? Why would he do that?'

Silence again from the Portreeve.

'Look,' said the Lawmaker, 'you just keep doing what you're supposed to be doing. Keep organising. I'm taking care of things here and the Teacher's part comes in soon. Everything will go ahead as planned.'

'And the boy? What's happening with the boy?'

The Lawmaker gave a laugh. It wasn't pleasant. 'All taken care of. It's a beautiful plan. And we won't be implicated in the slightest.'

'Should I know about it?'

'Do you want to?'

The Portreeve didn't reply.

'Thought not.'

Silence.

'Look. Hold your nerve. You know what you have to do. Weaver will take the blame for everything. We'll ensure that. And once that's done, we'll get the Gardener taken care of too.'

'Should I not ask about that either?'

'Up to you. But let's be honest here. We don't need him any more. Not with what's happening. Or with what's happened. He's just ... an irritant. He'll be dealt with too.'

'Be careful,' said the Portreeve. 'He's dangerous.'

The Lawmaker laughed. 'So am I. Keep the faith. We'll talk soon.'

The phone went dead.

The Portreeve sat staring at it. Wondering how such a mundane piece of plastic, metal and glass could have such a powerful effect on him.

He stood up. Took a deep breath. Another. Hands flexing, expanding. And again. Another breath.

Decided what to do.

Another breath. Held, let out slowly.

Decided there was no choice.

There was no turning back.

The Portreeve was ready.

50

The hotel stood in its own grounds. Sixteenth-century or thereabouts, Phil reckoned. A one-time country house for the landed gentry turned country retreat for the moneyed classes. It looked warm, seductive, nestled in amongst the trees, curving gravel drive before it. The kind of place that flattered a customer's good taste for choosing it. The kind of place he would take Marina for a weekend.

So why did it give him the same feeling he got when he had first looked at the house with the bone cage?

He pulled the Audi up to the front, feeling and hearing the gravel beneath the wheels. He switched off the engine, silencing Band of Horses singing about monsters, and stared. It was like he had driven on to a film set. The hotel itself looked like some costume-drama backdrop, the police presence shifting the genre. *Downton Abbey* to *Inspector Morse*.

The hotel unsettled him the more he looked at it. He replayed the meeting he had just had with Glass. That had been unsettling in its own way too.

At first, Phil had just been relieved to get into Glass's office, avoid Marina's questions. But once inside, the look on the DCI's face showed he had been called in for a specific reason. And he didn't get the feeling it was an altogether good one.

'Sit down, please, Phil,' Glass had said, looking up from his computer screen.

Phil had done so.

'Right . . . ' Glass stared at a file on the desk in front of him. Avoiding eye contact, Phil thought. Not a good start. He looked up. 'I'm seeing the Super today. In Chelmsford.'

Glass paused. Phil felt he was expected to say something. 'Yeah?'

'Yes.' Glass continued. 'I think he's going to tell me officially that this job is mine. Full time.' He leaned back in the chair. Phil could still see his predecessor sitting there.

'Congratulations,' said Phil.

Glass gave a tiny smile, a slight nod of the head, as if accepting his due. 'Thank you.' The smile disappeared. 'That being the case, I thought we should have a little chat.'

Phil thought he was expected to say something else, but decided against it. Waited in silence instead.

Taking Phil's silence for deference, Glass continued. 'It seems like we're going to have to work together, Phil. And I feel it only fair to warn you that I'll be running things very differently from my predecessor.'

Here we go, thought Phil. He tried for lightness in his response. 'Anything I should be concerned about?' he said.

The smile again. Twice in one meeting from someone who normally rationed them, thought Phil. Not a good sign. 'That depends. Clearly we're going to have to work together. But as the senior officer, I have to tell you there are going to be some changes round here.'

Phil felt a prickle of anger at Glass's words. 'Are you unhappy with my performance in some way?'

'No. Not at all. You've got virtually a hundred per cent arrest rate.'

Phil said nothing. It was true.

Glass leaned forward. 'But then this is MIS.'

Phil's anger was definitely rising now. 'What's that supposed to mean?'

Glass sat back. 'Clue's in the name. Major incidents. They're always the easy ones to clear up, aren't they?' He continued before Phil could reply. 'For instance, murder. You find a body, you ask who killed them. The person with most to gain. You question them. They confess. Case closed. Not so difficult, is it?'

'So what are you getting at?' Phil said.

'Just that. Cases like that don't seem very major to me. Your team have a lot of resources. Others may get jealous.'

'What are you talking about? We have the resources we need to get the job done. Have you seen the cases we've dealt with over the past few years? Have you seen the ones we're dealing with now?'

Glass put his hands up in what was supposed to represent mock-surrender, but it wasn't in his physical repertoire. 'All I'm saying is that you're very well-funded. In such straitened times as these, that funding could be eyed jealously by others as a luxury.'

'So ... you're reallocating the MIS budget, is that it? Where?'

'Phil,' Glass said, leaning forward, hands together in a gesture that looked to be learned from management classes, 'let's not be hasty.' He gestured to the file in front of him. 'I've made a study of you and your team. Your results speak for themselves, of course, but ... let's be straight. You run your team as though it's your own private fiefdom.'

Phil couldn't believe what he was hearing. 'What?'

'In the briefing just now. You questioned me. In front of the whole team.'

'So? You'd let someone go – a witness, or even a suspect – and not informed me.'

'Some would say that's what the briefing was for. For everyone to catch up on developments.'

'Something like that I should have known about. I should have been consulted. It wasn't proper procedure.'

Glass stared at him. 'As I said. There will be some changes in procedure from now on.'

'Including not keeping me informed of what's going on? Taking decisions above my head about my investigations and not informing me?'

Glass's voice dropped. 'Detective Inspector, you may have had a certain amount of latitude and leeway from your former DCI, but you won't be getting that with me. We do things by the book. My book. There'll be no room for mavericks in my department. You or your team.'

Phil's voice was rising. 'There are no mavericks on my team.'

'That's open to debate.'

'No it isn't.' Phil leaned forward too. 'What problems have you got with my team?'

Glass looked at the file. 'Their attitude borders on insubordination. I—'

Phil jumped in over the top of him. 'No it doesn't. I encourage creativity and free thinking. And the results bear that out. More crimes are solved by taking a lateral approach.'

Glass's eyes hardened. 'I can see where they get it from. You have a pernicious hold on them. Miss Jean Brodie syndrome.' A quick glance down, then back up again. 'They're in thrall to you.'

'Thrall?' Phil nearly laughed out loud. 'Are we in a nine-teenth-century novel suddenly?'

Glass's voice became cold. 'You're dressed in a manner more like a student than a police officer. You're insubordinate. You're rude to your superiors. And from what I've seen, your procedures sail dangerously close to the wind.'

'I get results. Virtually one hundred per cent. You said it yourself.'

Glass sat back, his voice dangerously low. 'Once I've spoken to the Super, I'll be putting my stamp on this place. You can still get results. But we'll get them my way.'

'And if I don't want to get them your way?'

'No one's irreplaceable.'

Phil stared at him. Wanted to hit him. Instead, he spoke. 'By the way,' he said, suppressing any anger that could make his voice waver, 'Mickey spoke to me earlier. Said you've brought Rose Martin back on board.'

Glass looked momentarily wrong-footed, lost for words. He quickly recovered his composure. 'What of it?'

'Why?'

'She's not on your team. That's no business of yours.'

'Yes it is. She was a DS on my team at one point and she's been on long-term sick. There's no way she's ready to come back. No way she's competent.'

'I made the decision in consultation with her psychologist.'

Knowing Marina, Phil doubted that. 'Stevie bloody Wonder could see she's not ready to return yet.'

Glass looked like he wanted to hit him. 'Thank you for your opinion. Noted.'

Phil bit back his initial reply. 'And you've promoted her to DI as well?'

Glass's face turned red. 'How did you know that?'

'Is it supposed to be a secret?'

'What happens with other officers is none of your business.'

'You're making a big mistake.'

The ghost of a smile. 'Again, thank you for your opinion.'

There was so much more Phil wanted to say, felt he needed to say. But he knew there would be no point. He would be going round in circles. He looked at his watch.

'Am I keeping you from something important?'

'Yeah,' said Phil, rising. 'I've got one of those murders to solve. But don't worry. They're really simple. I'll be done by lunchtime.'

He turned, left the office before Glass could say anything else.

And now he was staring at the hotel.

Swallowing down the fluttering in his chest, he got out of the car. Tried to put his conversation with Glass out of his mind. Concentrate on his job. Took a couple of deep breaths, ducked under the tape, walked towards the main entrance, ID held aloft.

Here we go, he thought.

No one barred his way.

51

Completely different, thought Phil. Different shape, size, age, everything. Completely different to the house at the bottom of East Hill. The cage. Completely.

But he still couldn't shake the feeling.

Giving himself a mental talking-to for being so stupid, he walked towards the hotel.

It was a beautiful building, he admitted that much. He stepped through the front door, found himself in a wood-panelled reception area, stone-flagged floor. The wood was aged but well-preserved, the stone floor worn by centuries of feet. Clearly authentic, he decided. He flashed his card.

'DI Brennan,' he said to the girl behind the desk. 'Is Jane Gosling here?'

The girl was very attractive, dressed in a smart dark uniform suit, white blouse beneath, cut to emphasise her cleavage. Dark hair pulled back, large earrings. Well made up. She creased her brow. Even her frown was pretty.

'Is she . . . a guest . . . here?' Voice heavily inflected.

East European, thought Phil, but he couldn't place her more specifically than that.

'No,' he said, 'she's the police officer in charge of this murder investigation.'

'Oh. Yes.' She looked round for another member of staff, beckoned over a young man with spiked hair and an eager face, told him to take her place behind the desk.

'Come with me, please.' She walked round to Phil's side of the desk, went through another doorway that led to the main section of the hotel.

Phil knew from the night before where the room was, but didn't want to appear as the kind of arrogant policeman he hated, so he followed her. Tried hard to take his eyes from her pencil-skirted legs and spike heels. She walked like he imagined Marilyn Monroe must have walked. If she had been on sand, the dots of her heels would have been in a straight line.

He picked his eyes up, looked round. The wood panelling and worn flags persisted. They reached a central area with a huge old fireplace, the fire unlit. Then up a wide, high stair-case. The panelling gave way to plastered walls, stained-glass windows. Even a suit of armour.

Phil looked through a set of double doors to an old wooden doorway that seemed even more aged than the rest of the hotel.

'What's in there?'

'The chapel,' said the girl.

'Chapel?'

'Yes. It was Knights Templar chapel. Very old.' She looked round. 'You would like to look in?'

'Yeah. Please.'

They crossed the floor. She opened the door. They stepped inside.

The first thing Phil noticed was the cold. The walls were heavy old stone. The windows stained glass, the floor flagged.

It was like stepping even further back in time. He could feel the history in the place.

'Nice,' he said to the girl. 'How old is it?'

'Oh, it is . . . very old,' she said, turning her head quickly, favouring him with a quick smile. 'I do not know . . . '

'Right,' he said. He looked over at the far wall. A huge wooden door stood there, so old and heavy it looked like the chapel had been built round it. 'Where does that lead?'

'Nowhere. Is . . . blocked off.'

'Right.'

'Would you . . .?' She pointed back the way they had entered.

Phil followed her out and up the stairs.

They kept walking. 'Can I ask, where are you from? That accent isn't from round here.'

Another smile. 'Lithuania,' she said. 'I come here to work.'

'Right. Enjoying it?'

She didn't turn round this time. 'Is OK.' Then perhaps thinking she should have said more, 'Is fun.'

'Good.'

They walked in silence until they reached the room. 'In here . . . ' Her expression darkened as she showed him the doorway. He would have worked out which one it was. The only one with crime-scene tape across it.

Phil thanked her, and she turned, walked away down the hall. Her heels perfect dots in the carpet once more. Phil turned to the doorway.

'OK to come in?' he called.

'Get yourself suited first,' came the reply.

A plastic-wrapped bundle was thrown into the hallway. Phil undid it, put it on, zipped up. Entered.

DS Jane Gosling was already in there, looking round. 'See anything you like?' she said.

Phil noticed how different it looked from the previous night. The body was gone, for one thing. Down to the mortuary to be rendered down to its component parts, weighed and examined, quantified and analysed. Adam Weaver no longer a person, just a dead organism. A human watch, broken beyond repair, lacking a set of instructions as to why it had stopped ticking.

Phil hated the aftermath of a murder scene. He often found it worse than when the body was still there. The absence of life more disturbing than the loss of it. A murder presented an end, but also a beginning. Because that was where his job started. But the aftermath showed that life went on. And in a way that was worse. Because one day that would be him.

He shook his head. He had been having increasingly morbid thoughts since the birth of Josephina. Because her existence reminded him that one day there would be a world without him in it. But she would go on. He knew that was right, the way things were meant to be. But that didn't make it any easier.

'Catch me up, then,' he said, focusing on the job in hand. 'Any progress?'

'Not a lot,' said Jane. 'We've canvassed the other rooms, asked the guests if they saw or heard anything suspicious. Nothing. Not until the girl started screaming.'

'Staff?'

She shook her head. 'Same thing. No one saw or heard anything. Until the screaming.'

Phil nodded, looked round once more. Saw the emptiness. Felt the absence. Tried to think in absolutes, not abstracts. Weaver's suit jacket was still on the bed, his other clothes in the wardrobe. The woman's underwear was discarded on the bed next to a selection of sex toys. The wrapping and packaging beside them showing they had just been bought for her.

Phil frowned. Something . . .

'Jane,' he said. 'Where was the girl from? The one in the room here?'

Jane Gosling shrugged. 'Dunno.'

'What was her name?'

She checked her notebook. 'Maria. And then . . . Oh God, I can't read it. Here, have a look.'

Phil looked.

'Luko . . . sevic . . . ius . . . ichius?' Jane read. 'Something like that. Eastern European, it looks like.'

'D'you know where, exactly? What country?'

Another check of her notes. 'Lithuania, she said.' Jane looked at him, frowned. 'Hey, why does that ring a bell?'

'Because Weaver lived in Lithuania. And the staff here, the woman who let me up was Lithuanian. And the builder Mickey spoke to . . .'

'A pattern,' said Jane. 'Or a coincidence?'

'Don't know,' said Phil. 'Don't know what it is yet.' His eyes travelled round the room once more. He had to get out. 'I'm just going to have a look round the grounds. See if anything comes to me.'

He left the room.

Outside, the air felt colder than the previous day. Summer losing the fight against autumn. The leaves starting to brown and redden. He walked round the corner of the hotel, by the kitchens. Past the bins and skips. Some outbuildings were dotted around. Old, but lacking the preserved charm of the rest of the place. Where the staff live, he thought. Behind them was the river.

He walked down to it, stood on the bank, staring at it.

Something else was hitting him. Hard. Not just a feeling, an emotion, but something more solid. More tangible. A memory.

His heart skipped a beat at the realisation of what it was. He looked up and down the river again, back to the hotel. Looked at the roof, the chimneys against the trees, the skyline.

And he knew what the memory was telling him.

He had been here before.

52

Samuel Lister walked down the hospital corridor. Enjoyed the looks he received. Smiles. All smiles. And the best thing was, even if they didn't like him, they smiled.

He enjoyed everything about his job. Well, most things. Dealing with the staff under him, endless meetings, that kind of thing bored him. But the rest more than compensated for it. The lavish dinners and parties. The golf. The car he drove at the hospital's expense. The money. Oh yes, the money.

And the perks. Those lovely little perks.

There was a lot to be said for being the hospital's staff director and workforce manager.

Walking down the corridor, enjoying the sound of his heels echoing behind him, he planned his day. Meeting for the rest of the morning. Could he get out of it? What was it again? Budget strategy planning. Best not. Although anything that needed implementing could be done at a lower level. Middle management. That was what they were there for.

Then what? Lunch in town, discussing expansion plans with a friend on the council. All on expenses. Then perhaps a quick round of golf over at Colne Valley Golf Club. Yes. That sounded like not a bad day after all.

Lister nodded to a nurse. Smiled. She returned it, that kind of up from under thing with her eyes. He liked that. Made them look demure but knowing. Clean on the outside, dirty on the inside. Lovely.

He checked her out as she went past. Young, pretty. Not too curvy. Just his type. Budding. That was the word he used to describe them, budding.

He slowed down, watched her walk away, the slow, languorous swing of her narrow hips, her pert bottom. Budding. Lovely.

He waited until she had turned a corner, was out of view, then continued on.

Thinking of the nurse who had just passed, his mind hopped on, made connections. He wished it could be like the old days, he thought. When nurses' uniforms were more like something out of Ann Summers, something that a young man could get quite worked up about, fetishise, even. Not like they were now. All functional and plain. Nothing to get worked up about. He should try and bring that up at a meeting. Claim it was for the good of the patients, the morale in the hospital.

He remembered a dentist friend he knew. Only employed fit, slim young dental nurses. Made them wear uniforms that were this side of a tribunal away from see-through. Made sure they co-ordinated their underwear too. White. Lacy. He had marvelled at his friend, asked how he got away with it. Got away with it? He had a list longer than the war dead on the Cenotaph in Whitehall of people wanting to be his patients. He had pointed to the Merc parked outside the restaurant they were in. That was paid for, he had said, entirely by middle-aged men's fantasies.

Lister smiled at the memory. He should definitely try something similar here.

His phone sounded, jolting him out of his reverie.

Probably Jerry, he thought, confirming this afternoon's golf session.

He took the iPhone from his jacket pocket, opened it.

'Hello.'

Nothing. Just crackling.

'Hello?' He sighed. Probably one of those automated things. Telling him not to hang up, press this button to be put through to a premium-rate line in Sri Lanka or something. He was about to switch off when a voice spoke.

'Hello, Samuel.'

At first he couldn't place it. Then he did. And it was like reality crumbled around him.

'What . . . what d'you want?' He stopped walking, cupped the phone in his hand so anyone passing couldn't see him, hear him speak. 'Why are you calling me?'

'I need a favour, Samuel.'

'You can't have one.' His throat was suddenly dry. His voice sounded uneven and cracked. An arid desert floor.

'I can and I will.'

Lister sighed, looked round. Expected the rest of the world to have stopped just because his had. But it went on around him as usual.

'No. You can't. I'm . . . I'm going to hang up now.'

'No you're not, Samuel. People who say they're going to hang up never do. They just . . . stay there. Waiting. Is that what you're doing, Samuel?'

'I'm . . . I'm hanging up. Now.' Weakly, as he made no effort to end the call.

'Oh. You're still there, Samuel. Why would that be?'

Another look round. Surely everyone was staring. Pointing

228

and laughing, wondering why the staff director and workforce manager was sweating and stammering in the corridor. But no one was pointing or laughing. In fact everyone was ignoring him, just getting on with their own lives.

'I'm ... I'm ...'

'You're going to do what I tell you, Samuel. You know you are. What you did came with a price. You know that. You were told that at the time. You agreed to it. Happily, if I remember. Well now it's time to pay.'

'I ... I ... What if I won't?'

A chuckle. 'Does that really need answering?'

Lister sighed. 'I'm ... I'm going to my office now. Call me back there.'

Without waiting for a reply, he broke the connection, pocketed the phone. Looked around once more.

His first thought was to run. Hard. Fast. As far away as quickly as possible. But he knew that couldn't happen. He knew they would catch up with him wherever he went. Not even bother to catch up with him. Just say a few words to the right people, let things take their course.

Another sigh. Heart fluttering, he walked quickly to his office. People nodded, smiled at him on the way. He managed to return their greetings. How? he thought. How could he do that? Pretend everything was fine on the surface while inside he was consumed by turmoil? He knew how. The thought was sudden. It arrived with the heavy, final clunk of a key in a cell-door lock.

Because he had done already. Quite a few times. Kept his normal, everyday world going smoothly while under the surface he did ... other things. And now they had caught up with him. When worlds collide.

He reached his office, went straight in, told his secretary to hold his calls. Closed the door behind him. Sat at his desk. Waited.

The call wasn't long in coming.

'What . . . what d'you want?' He knew who it was without checking.

'Just what I said, Samuel. You owe. Time to pay.'

'I . . . I can't . . .' Close to tears now. Ready to just give up.

'You can. And you will.'

He opened his mouth to speak, but couldn't think of an answer to give. There was no answer to give.

Silence.

Eventually, a sigh. 'All right. What . . . what d'you want me to do?'

The voice on the phone told him.

And Samuel Lister knew that whatever happened next didn't matter.

This was the end for him.

53

'Well I'm sorry, but that's the way it is, I'm afraid.' Lynn Windsor turned her back on Mickey, began to walk away from him as if he'd been dismissed.

I don't think so, thought Mickey, following.

He was back in the solicitors' offices, following up his previous call. Finding out what he could about Adam Weaver. He wasn't getting very far. Lynn Windsor was stonewalling.

'Lynn, don't walk away from me, please.'

She stopped, turned. Sighed, exasperated. Her face looked different from the previous day. Harder, set. No flirtation in her manner, just business to get on with. Once she had dealt with Mickey the irritant.

'I need to talk to you. I need to talk to your boss. Adam Weaver. I saw him here yesterday, going into a meeting. I saw him again last night. And he was very dead.'

Her eyes widened. 'Dead?'

'Haven't you seen today's news? Read a paper?'

'No . . . '

'He was found dead in his hotel last night. Murdered.'

She turned away from him. 'Oh my God . . . '

'Yeah. So I'm following up every lead I can.'

Lynn Windsor's head was down, eyes on the floor. Her shoulders heaved as she sighed. She looked up.

'You'd ... you'd better ... better step inside my office.'

She entered her office. Mickey followed, closing the door behind him. They sat down at either side of the desk.

'Right,' she said. She leafed through a pile of papers in a distracted manner, not making eye contact with him. 'Tell me again what happened and what you want.'

'I want to know why Adam Weaver was here yesterday. Who he was seeing, what he was discussing, what business he had.'

'He was seeing my boss. As to what they were discussing ... ' She shrugged. 'I'm afraid I couldn't say.'

'Could I talk to your boss, please.' No question, just a statement.

'He's ... not here at the moment. Out all day. Don't know when he'll be back.' She looked up at him, eyes on him, darting quickly away. 'Sorry.'

Mickey knew when he was being lied to. He also knew when stating that fact helped him and when it didn't. He didn't think now was the right time. Wouldn't get results.

'I will have to talk to him. At some point.'

'Well I'll run it by him, see if he's OK with that.'

'Lynn, it's not a question as to whether he's OK with it. This is a murder investigation. I can get a warrant if I have to.'

Yeah, he thought, I could. But it's a hell of a lot of effort just to have a conversation. He was sure Lynn knew that too, but if she did, she wasn't letting on.

'I realise that,' she said, 'but it's not my decision to make. As I said, I'll put it to him.'

'Thank you. Appreciated.' He gave a smile.

She returned it. Briefly.

'Of course, whether he'll be able to tell you anything . . . I couldn't say. Client confidentiality and all that.'

'Of course,' said Mickey. He sensed that was as much as he was going to get, dropped it. Gave her another smile. 'Well, thank you.'

She smiled too, nodded.

Mickey looked at Lynn Windsor, head down, rearranging papers on her desk, toying with a paper clip in her fingers, and knew there was something wrong. Or at least something she was unhappy about. Tense.

'You OK?' he said.

She jumped. Dropped the paper clip. 'Yes. Of course. Why wouldn't I be?'

'I don't know.' He smiled, sat back. Not professional interest, the move said, more personal. 'You just seem a bit . . . distracted.'

'Oh. Yes.' Head down once more. Another sigh. 'I suppose . . . ' She looked up again. 'Just . . . split up with my boyfriend.'

'Oh. I'm sorry.'

She nodded. Looked at the papers on her desk. Looked up again. 'Have you got . . . anyone, Detective?'

Mickey felt his cheeks reddening. Anni's face came into his mind's eye. 'Erm, no. Not really.'

She raised an eyebrow. 'Not really?'

'No.' Anni's face disappeared. He felt the beginnings of an erection. 'No. There's no one.'

Lynn Windsor nodded. Sat back, crossed her legs. Smiled. Mickey's eyes were immediately drawn to her breasts. He tried not to look. Failed. Kept his eyes glued to hers.

She smiled again, well aware of what he had just done. 'I've still got your number . . . Mickey.'

He swallowed. His throat had gone dry. 'Yeah, yes. You have.'

'Shall I call you if there are ... developments?'

'I ...' The room suddenly felt very hot. Uncomfortable. 'Yes. That would be ... I'd ... yes.'

He couldn't believe the way he was behaving. This was textbook, he thought. The kind of scenario every copper dreamed about. How many pub tales and fantasies had revolved around this kind of situation? And here he was, tongue-tied and blushing. Not very Sweeney.

'Good.' She smiled again. 'I might just do that.'

He returned the smile. She looked away.

'Well, I'd better get on with some work.' She stood up. 'Very nice to see you again. Good luck, and ... I'll be in touch.'

'I ... I look forward to it.'

Mickey got up and left the room.

Outside, he shook his head as he walked away.

'I look forward to it,' he said out loud. 'Tit.'

But he was smiling as he said it.

54

Phil walked the grounds of the hotel. He didn't need a guide.

The place felt familiar to him, but it was a kind of dream familiarity. Like he had never visited in real life or during waking hours, but knew his way round none the less.

Phil was firmly a rationalist, didn't believe in any kind of psychic phenomena. Even turned the TV off, swearing at it, when *Most Haunted* came on. But standing in the grounds, the trees around him, the river behind him, the way he was feeling now, what he was experiencing . . . he couldn't say. All bets were off.

He put his palm on the nearest tree. A huge old oak. Felt . . . he didn't know what. Rough bark, lichen, on a physical level. But beyond that, age, the centuries that the tree had stood there for. Something that had been living long before him and would continue to do so long after he had gone. A permanence. A rightness with nature.

Hand still in place, he closed his eyes. Tried to feel beyond that, reach for something else, some reason for the connection he was experiencing to this area, this place. Eyes closed tight, screwed up. He felt . . . he felt . . . nothing.

Opened his eyes again. Took his hand away quickly, hoping no one had seen him do it. The kind of behaviour Glass would use against him. Mark him down as a tree hugger, a liberal, even. A danger to the team. A maverick. Phil would have smiled if he thought Glass wouldn't have meant it.

The hotel was beyond the trees. Beyond that was a golf course. Phil felt no affinity with that, no reason to go there. Strange. He wondered why. Apart from the fact that he hated golf. So following his instinct, he turned and walked down towards the river.

The water, flowing fast, clear, looked cold. The trees on both sides of the bank were losing their leaves, carpeting the forest floor or dropping into the water, the current bearing them away.

It was Phil's favourite time of the year. He would have found the view beautiful, calming, restful. If not for the nagging inside his head.

And the murder inquiry.

He walked down to the river's edge. The bank showed roots, twisted and gnarled, bare where the moving water had eroded the earth. Sticking out ready to catch the ankle of an unobservant walker.

On the opposite side, a tree had been uprooted and fallen backwards. Probably in a storm or during a harsh winter. It was quite remarkable. The roots had fanned out into a large semicircle, making a natural bay for the water to run into. Or an animal amphitheatre, he thought, smiling. Where the woodland creatures could perform *Tales of the Riverbank*.

He looked further into it. Saw the twisting roots, but became aware of something beyond them. He knelt down on his side of the bank, tried to peer closer. Tunnels. He could see tunnels. Probably an animal. Rabbits or badgers, something like that. A nesting habitat.

Tunnels. Phil sat up straight. The word hit him with an almost physical power. Tunnels.

Why? What did that mean?

He didn't know. But he thought he should find out. He stood up, brushing dirt from his jeans, looked around. Tunnels.

Being guided by the word and his own instincts, he started to walk upstream.

The natural footpath beside the river began to narrow and eventually petered out. Thorned brambles and branches barred the way forward. Phil peered through. He could see that the hotel's land continued, the boundary in the distance. Pulling his jacket over his face, he plunged into the trees.

The thorns pulled at his clothing and, where they could, his exposed skin. He felt the barbs dig in, rip flesh as he tried to pull away. Like being shot repeatedly with an air rifle. Branches slapped him, stung where they hit. But he kept going, driven by the thought – the memory – in his head that remained just out of reach.

The forest became denser. Branches and leaves overhead blotting out the sunlight. To his right, the river seemed further away than previously, the bank more built-up, a steeper drop down to the water. He turned, moved towards it.

As he did so, he checked the ground. There were indentations in the earth, the leaves. He knelt down, examined them. Footprints. Someone had taken the same route. And not so long ago, he reckoned.

Phil looked upwards, around him. Examined his surroundings in closer detail. Branches showed signs of having been bent back and broken, some snapped off altogether. He looked at the tracks, the broken foliage. Followed the trail.

It brought him to the river's edge. He looked round.

Listened. No sign of anything, no sound except the movement of the water. The hotel, the murder scene, seemed far away.

He reached the edge of the bank. There was a drop down to the river, probably higher than he was tall. He looked down at the footprints. They went to the edge and stopped. Phil knelt down. There was scuffing on the ground, as though someone had climbed over the edge, taken some of the earth with them. He looked down. Saw only the river.

He thought. A boat? Was that how they had got out of here? So why hadn't the uniforms looked for signs? Had they just given up at the end of the footpath? He closed his eyes. Tried to think, imagine himself in the killer's position.

Come up the river by boat ... moor it ... climb up the bank, through the trees, down to the hotel ... slip inside ... up to the room ... and out again the same way ...

Phil focused. Examined his theory further.

The killer must have known the layout of the hotel. Known a way in, found the room and out again without being seen. Been confident enough of not being tracked into the forest. Sure enough of himself to get a boat away from the scene without being spotted.

Something nagged at him.

Tunnels ...

He knelt down again, looked over the edge of the bank. The noise of the water increased, mingled with the sound of rushing blood in his head as he leaned further over. He edged forward, scoping the bank side.

Grabbing on to a protruding root, he swung himself over the edge, began to climb down. Jumped the last little bit of the way, got his feet wet in the shallow siding of the river. There was a tunnel right before him. Or at least a cave-like entrance. Dark, overgrown with the tendrils of weeds, roots sticking out at the entrance.

He looked inside. Felt his heart miss a beat.
A shadow detached itself from the dark. Became larger.
Someone was coming towards him.
Fast.

55

Phil braced himself, wanting to turn, run, escape. But knowing he couldn't do that. Knowing that his training – his job – should leave him ready to handle whoever it was coming towards him.

Out of the cave mouth flew a bundle of rags. It took Phil a few seconds, but he recognised it as Paul. The tramp he had interviewed the day before.

'Wait,' Phil shouted. 'I just want to talk . . . ' He ran backwards, twisted and fell. The water splashed up around him, cold penetrating to his skin straight away like icy underwear. He looked round for something – anything – that he could use to defend himself. Pulled at a root that was sticking out of the face of the bank, but it wouldn't budge.

Paul didn't stop.

Phil managed to get to his feet again, felt the weight of the cold water in his sodden clothes dragging him down. If the tramp hit him, forced him into the water, he might not be in a position to fight back.

'Please, I just want to talk . . . Please . . . ' He held his hands up, showing he had no weapon. 'Please, Paul, please . . . '

The figure paused.

Phil pressed home the advantage. 'I'm not armed, I'm just here by myself. There's no one else with me. Come on, Paul. I'm not going to hurt you. I just want to talk to you.'

He hoped that would be enough.

He looked at the tramp standing before him. Blinking in the sunlight, confused by Phil's presence.

'Why . . . are you here?'

'I'm . . .' Phil ran his hand through his hair, decided how to approach this. The truth. Try that. 'Well, Paul, I'm here at the hotel.' He gestured. 'Back there. There's been a murder. And I'm investigating it.'

Paul looked at him, frowning. Phil couldn't tell under the filth and hair, but there seemed to be some conflicting emotions moving across his features.

'Murder . . .'

'That's right. A murder.'

Paul began to nod. 'Yes . . .'

'Let's . . .' keeping his eyes on him all the time he was speaking, 'let's sit down, Paul. Get comfortable.'

Not wanting to get his clothes any dirtier or wetter than they already were, Phil found a tree root to sit on. Brushed it before he sat. Paul settled on the ground.

'So, Paul . . . twice in two days. What are you doing here? Long way out for you.'

Paul looked round, brow furrowed as if listening, waiting for the trees to give him answers. 'I . . . Heaven.'

Phil nodded. Here we go again. 'Heaven. How d'you mean?'

Paul spread his arms out. 'Here. Heaven. Can relax.'

'Right. And how did you get here?'

Paul looked at the river. 'I was brought here. On the water.'

'You mean you travelled on the river, yes? In a boat?'

241

Paul looked at Phil then. Right in the eye, unblinking. 'You think I'm mad, don't you?' His voice calm, controlled.

The directness of the question threw Phil off balance. 'Well, I ...'

Paul shook his head. 'You don't have to answer. I know you do. They all do. *You* all do. And that's fine.' He nodded. 'Yeah. Fine. 'Cos maybe I am.' A laugh. Or at least an approximation of one. 'Should be. Everything that's ... all that's ... you know ...'

Phil ignored the gathering cold in his clothes, leaned forward. 'What d'you mean?'

Paul looked round once more. 'Heaven. This place. Heaven. Or it was. Until ...'

'Until what, Paul?'

Paul snapped his attention back to Phil. 'I told you. Yesterday.' He turned away once more.

Phil thought. What had Paul said? It had all sounded so rambling at the time. Allegorical, even. 'You said that,' said Phil. 'But that's all you said. Heaven until the bad men came.'

Paul nodded. 'I did. Yes. I did. Yes. I did. Evil. Evil. Yes.'

'Was it here, Paul? Was it here that the bad men came?'

Paul looked round once more, taking counsel from the trees, nodded slowly. 'Yes. Here. Heaven up here. In the Garden.'

'The garden? The garden of the hotel?'

'It's not a hotel.'

'What is it, then?'

'The Garden.' Said like Phil was stupid for even asking. 'Always has been. Always will be.'

'Right.' The Garden ... Something in that name too, though Phil couldn't quite place it. He took a risk. Abandoned his chosen line of questioning, his training, everything. Asked Paul a direct question.

'Paul, when I came here last night, and again today, I felt something.'

Paul gave him a sidelong look. Eyes narrowed. He said nothing.

Phil continued. 'I don't know what, I can't really explain it.'

'I think you can.' Paul's voice had changed. He spoke with sudden sanity, clarity. Noticing this, emboldened by it, Phil went on.

'I felt like . . . like I'd been here before. Like I knew my way round.'

'Go on.'

'But I couldn't. I've never been here in my life. How could that happen?'

'Perhaps you have been here before. But perhaps you don't remember it.'

'How can I not remember it?'

Paul leaned forward. A light danced in his eyes. A charismatic light. Not mad; deeply sane. Phil found it comforting. He was surprised, to say the least. 'Perhaps you choose not to remember it. Or part of you has chosen not to remember it, and the other part is trying to break through.' He sat back.

Phil thought about the words. They made sense. Sitting here, he thought, wet through, by a river in a forest with a tramp, the words made sense.

'You have to listen to yourself,' Paul went on. 'Trust yourself. The answer is there.'

'Where?'

Paul leaned forward. Placed his index finger on Phil's chest. Pushed slightly. Phil felt the equivalent of a mild electric shock pass through his body. 'There.'

Paul sat back once more. Said nothing further.

Phil felt like he was on the verge of something. Answers.

243

'I've been having these dreams ... The cage in the cellar ... in the dream, I'm in it ... '

Paul's features clouded. 'No. No ... ' His voice small, head shaking with it.

Phil pressed on. 'Are those ... those dreams ... are they part of it?'

'No ... Don't ... No ... I don't want to talk about that.'

'But ... '

'Navaho. They say dreams are a way of keeping in touch. You dream of someone, you're keeping in touch.'

'But I'm ... '

'You're dreaming of someone. Don't. You don't want to meet them. Not now. Not ever. Not since the Garden got replanted.' Paul stood up. 'I have to go now.'

Phil stood also. 'Please. Don't go. I need to ... I have to talk to you. About the murder at the hotel. About yesterday.'

'I didn't do it. But I'm not sorry he's dead.' More nods. 'Bad thing. But I'm not.' He walked along the side of the river, heading upstream. 'I'm going now. Please don't follow me.'

Phil tried going after him, but Paul was soon lost in the foliage, and Phil became stuck, entangled in the thorny branches of a low-hanging tree. By the time he had extricated himself, Paul had gone.

Phil looked at the mouth of the cave where Paul had been sitting. Saw the remains of a campfire in the entrance. A few trails of dead smoke rising up from it, scuff marks in the earth at the sides where he had kicked dirt over it to damp it down. The ground here looked flattened, like Paul came here a lot.

Phil looked inside the cave, but saw nothing. Only darkness.

Finding nothing more, and remembering that Glass didn't think Paul was a suspect, Phil turned. Made his way back to the hotel.

As he walked, he heard Paul's words zinging round his head.

They should have made things clearer.

But Phil just felt more confused than ever.

56

Don Brennan walked down the corridor at Southway, the years falling away with every stride. It felt good to be back. Very good.

He had dressed for the occasion. Pulled his good suit out of the wardrobe, a deep blue worsted, unbagged it and was surprised to find it still fitted him. The trousers a little tight in the waist, perhaps, pulling the legs up a tiny bit short, the cuffs resting on the tops of his shoes, and skinnier than he would have liked, and the jacket straining to be fastened, but it was nothing too noticeable. He would just have to keep his jacket open, that was all. And, he thought with a smile, from what he'd seen, the drainpipe look was back in again.

When he had left the house that morning, Eileen had given him the kind of smile he hadn't seen in years. Proud that he was going to work. To be useful. Then the expression on her face had clouded over, as she was reminded of the reality of the situation. Of why he was going back.

'Are you sure there isn't another way?' she had said.

He had told her there wasn't. And that she knew there wasn't.

She had nodded. 'Just be careful. That's all. I want you to come home safe.' She had reached out to him, stroked his lapel. 'I want all of my family safely home.'

'That's why I'm doing this,' he had replied.

She had kissed him then, holding his arm as if not wanting to let him go, but eventually relenting, knowing she had no choice.

And he had walked out of the door. And back on to the job.

It had changed. He couldn't deny it. But the principle seemed to be the same: catch the villains. Or at least he hoped it was. The team seemed so hidebound by compliance rules and procedures that he was surprised any policing got done. Even on what was fast becoming a high-profile case. It had been going that way when he retired; now a copper could drown under the amount of forms he had to fill in.

The overuse of computers didn't faze him, though. He had one at home, used it a lot. Eileen was always on at him. Spending more time with the machine than he did with her. Colchester's premier silver surfer. And he was. Paying bills online, ordering the weekly shop, forwarding email jokes. Even making his own Christmas and birthday cards.

The one thing that really bothered him above all else was the jargon. He knew that all workplaces developed their own ways of speaking, so that to outsiders it could sound like a convention of evangelical Christians. But this was something else. The terminology from his era was still pretty much intact, but it had been allied to a kind of management speak. When Glass had started to talk in the morning briefing about goal orientation and – that most hateful of words – solutions, Don had wanted to stick his fingers down his throat. But he hadn't. At least not yet.

He gave a grim smile. Glass. I've got your number, sunshine, he thought.

He turned another corner, looked round. Should be just about here, he thought, if they hadn't moved it.

He saw the door ahead of him. Felt a quickening in his heart rate, mirrored it in his step. He reached the door. Tried the handle. Locked.

He had expected as much.

He reached into his pocket, took out his key ring. A quick glance round to see if anyone was coming – no, thankfully not many people ventured into this area of the building – and he slipped the key in.

Please still fit, please . . .

It did. The key turned. The door opened.

He had had the key cut when he was still on the force. The records room was always difficult to get anything out of. Chits had to be completed, requests made, and, like the slowest library in the world, eventually someone would turn up with the correct box. Or more often than not, the incorrect one. So he and a few of his colleagues had got their own keys cut. Not strictly legal, or even following procedure, but when they were working a case, it could often mean the difference between catching a criminal and letting them go. And it could all be covered up afterwards. So no harm done. Not really.

Criminal records were now on the Police National Computer and just a click away. As were police personnel records. But previous case files, especially ones that went back over thirty years, were kept here. And that was what he wanted.

Don slipped inside the room, closed the door behind him. Found the light switch. And once the overhead strips had come to life, looked around.

Rows and rows of metal shelves piled with boxes and boxes of files. Supposedly in order, but Don could tell from the way some boxes were sticking out at angles or had their lids missing or had just been left in haphazard piles in the aisles, their paper cascading all around them, that it wasn't necessarily so.

Still, he had to believe that what he was looking for was accessible. Otherwise he was in for a long day. And probably night.

He could have told them in the office that he was coming here. That he wanted to cross-reference something with the cases they were working on. But he hadn't. He didn't know who on Phil's team he could trust. He knew who he couldn't. That was a given. But until things became clearer, he was on his own.

He put on his reading glasses, walked up to the nearest shelf. Scrutinised the date that had been written there. Began walking.

He resisted the temptation to look in any of the other boxes apart from the one he was searching for. There was a sizeable part of his life in this room. Memories of a career held in paper and cardboard. Maybe he would take a look. But that was for another day. For now he had something specific to do.

It took some searching, but eventually he found it. A small shiver of triumph ran through his body as he did so. He took the box down, placed it on the floor. Squatted down beside it. Opened it. Took out the file on top, started to read.

Felt that surge of adrenalin course through him again.

Yes. This was it. This was the right box. Oh yes.

He read on. Closed the folder, took out another one.

And felt the adrenalin surge even faster.

Smiled.

'Gotcha,' he said out loud.

He was about to take out another folder, go through that, when the door swung open.

57

Marina walked into the main MIS office. It didn't feel right somehow.

Usually when the team were working on big cases, they based themselves in the bar, extra bodies were drafted and briefed, overtime allocated. The whole thing upgraded. But not this time. It seemed to Marina that Glass was actively working against that. Trying to keep two investigations going in as small a way as possible. It went beyond budget balancing and penny-pinching, she thought. It was as if Phil's team were being punished for something.

The team were still working hard – possibly even harder, if the activity in the office was anything to go by – but there seemed to be something missing. And Marina reckoned she knew what that was.

Phil. Or his leadership, at least.

He was absent from the office in more ways than one. She still didn't know what was wrong with him. She had thought at first it must be their relationship. Some problem with that. With her, even. But seeing him at work showed it went deeper than that. He was distracted, mumbling when he should be giving clear orders. Absent when he should be present.

And she couldn't work like this any longer.

She took out her phone. Hit speed-dial. Waited.

He picked up.

'Hey,' she said, 'where are you?'

'Home,' he replied.

'What? What are you doing there?'

'I, uh . . . ' His voice trailed away.

'You what?'

'I got wet. Needed to change my clothes.'

She asked the obvious question next.

'Chasing a suspect. Up at the hotel. Well, I thought he was a suspect. But he . . . yeah . . . '

Marina sighed. 'Phil. We need to talk.'

Silence.

'We do.' She turned away from the rest of the office, cupped her hand over the mouthpiece so no one could overhear. 'Whatever's going on, you need to talk to me about it.'

More silence.

Her voice dropped further. 'I thought it was about us. Just about us. But I've seen how you are at work. And Phil, it's not right. You need to talk to me. Whatever's going on, you need to talk to me.' Her voice even lower. 'We're in this together. Remember?'

A sigh. She waited.

'Yeah,' he said, eventually. 'You're right, I . . . ' Another sigh. 'I don't know . . . I just . . . don't know . . . '

'Well at least we're communicating,' she said.

She heard him laugh. 'Yeah.' Then another sigh. 'Oh God . . . '

'Look. We don't have to talk about it now. Let's do it later. OK?'

'Marina, you don't understand. It's . . . I don't know.'

'OK. We'll talk it through. Get it sorted.'

There was another silence on the line.

'Glass was on at me earlier,' he said.

'Joy,' she said. 'What did he want?'

'Well, amongst other things, I'm not smart enough. I need to dress more like a copper.'

'How horrible.'

'That's what I thought. So I'm having a look through the wardrobe now. Trying to find something . . . ' He tailed off again.

'Phil? You there? Phil?'

'Oh yes,' he said. 'Oh, that's just perfect.'

'What is?'

He gave a little laugh. 'Glass should be careful what he wishes for. He might just get it. Or my version of it, anyway.'

Marina smiled. This was more like the old Phil back again.

'Can't wait to see it.'

Another silence. Then, at last: 'I think I'm . . . ' his voice shrinking with each word, 'I'm . . . cracking up . . . '

Marina felt her heart break. 'Oh, Phil . . . '

'I just . . . I'm . . . I'm losing it . . . '

She started to talk again, but he cut her off.

'I've got to get ready. Get back to work. I'm going to the hospital to check on the kid. See Anni. Anything to avoid Glass. I'll . . . I'll see you later.'

And he hung up.

Marina was left with a dead handset. She slipped it into her pocket, didn't move. The office was still in full swing, activity all around her, but she couldn't move. Stood still as a statue.

Then she snapped herself out of it. No. She had to do something.

She had to find Don, talk to him. Maybe he could help her, shed some light on what was wrong with Phil.

She left the incident room.

Set off down the corridor looking for him.

58

Rose Martin had driven up and down the street three times. Not because she was practising any kind of surveillance. Just because she couldn't find a parking space. And now that she had finally found one – at the opposite end of the street, nearly round the corner, useless if she did want to do surveillance – she was angry.

Very angry.

She had done some checking before coming back here. Found out a few things about Faith Luscombe. She had gone into the town centre, to the main CCTV control room. Asked to see footage from two nights previous of New Town. Specifically the corner Faith Luscombe had been working from.

Nothing. No cameras on that stretch. Probably why Faith had chosen it. From what Donna Warren had told her, Rose had worked out what time Faith had been there, and from her ultimate destination had worked out the route the car would have taken out of town. That kind of requisitioning would take time, she was told. She gave her best smile, flashed a bit of cleavage and said she would be very grateful if it was done as quickly as possible. They would see what they could do.

Her next stop had been to see Nick Lines at the mortuary. He hadn't been pleased to see her, although with his bald head and cadaverous appearance, he never looked pleased to see anyone. She asked to look at Faith Luscombe's body.

'If you're sure,' he had said. 'It's not pretty.'

'I can take it,' she had said, not sure if she could.

He was right. It wasn't pretty. Rose struggled to keep her eyes on it.

'Is there . . . anything you've picked up about it?'

'We haven't done a post-mortem, if that's what you mean,' he said. 'It wasn't requested. Cause of death was being mangled by two cars. No surprises there.'

'So nothing unusual?' She felt her heart sinking. She had been sure there would be something. Hoped there would be something.

'Just this,' he said, pointing to the sole of her right foot. 'This mark. Looks like a brand.'

'A brand? Like a cow?'

'Could be,' he said. 'Some of the extreme body modification crowd go in for it too. One step up from the ubiquity of tattoos. And much more painful, of course.'

'Would she have been into that, d'you think?'

He frowned. 'Not sure. If it had been on her arm or body, I'd have said yes. Show it off, flaunt it. But on the sole of her foot? I don't know.'

'Have you seen anything like it before?'

'Never. Not like this, anyway.'

She thanked him for his time and asked for a photo of the brand. Then went to see Donna Warren once more.

She turned the ignition off, sat there in silence for a few seconds. Counting her breaths. Slowly in, two, three, four, slowly out, two, three, four. Controlling herself. Like Marina had encouraged her to do. She didn't want to give the woman credit for anything, but this had helped. Simple really; she should have thought of it herself. Take a few seconds, breathe, calm herself down. Then, if there was still some residual anger hanging round in her system, channel it into whatever she was about to do. Simple.

Especially when it involved Donna Warren. Channelling rage in her direction would be a pleasure.

Rose hated being made a fool of. Always had done. Refused to put up with it. All the way through training at Hendon, she had worked hard to make sure she was never the butt of jokes. Never bullied or picked on. She always stood up for herself, always gave as good as she got. Sometimes too much so. When her attitude began to be commented on, to threaten her future plans, she knew she had to rein it in, find new coping mechanisms. And she had done. It was obvious, really. Subsume the rage, channel it. Into career advancement. Into making sure she was better than the rest of her year at everything she did. Into being the youngest DI in the Met. The highest flyer.

But it hadn't quite worked out that way.

And none of it was her fault.

She checked her wing mirror, looked down the street at Donna's house. Studied it. Sat like that for several minutes. There was nothing to see. No one came or went; she didn't see anyone at the windows or the door. Nothing.

Rose ran a few options through her mind. Quickly rejected all but one.

She nodded to herself. Got out of the car, locked it, began walking down the street. Hyper-vigilant all the time.

She needn't have been. No one watched her, approached her, moved away from her. The only other people she saw were a young couple, both wearing tracksuits but, from the unfit, lumpen shape of their bodies, going nowhere near a gym. They were coming down the road pushing a buggy with a child inside it, bulging Aldi bags hanging from the handlebars.

Rose smiled to herself. *I might have a few issues*, she thought, *but at least I'm not as bad as them.*

She approached Donna's front door. Stood before it. Before she could raise her hand to knock, she felt that old familiar rage bubbling up inside her. Looked at her hand. It was shaking. She put it in her jeans pocket, breathed in slowly once more. Out once more.

When she was composed, she knocked.

As soon as her hand was away from the door, her stance changed. She was ready. When the cheap whore arrived, opened the door, Rose would be on her. Inside, door closed behind her, and then her lesson could start. See what happened when you played Rose Martin for an idiot. See how far that attitude got her. She wouldn't do that again in a hurry. No. She'd be begging and pleading for another chance, screaming how sorry she was. How she'd never do it again. Yeah. Just wait. Just you see.

Nothing. No answer.

Sighing in irritation, Rose tried the door again. Waited. Nothing.

Another angry sigh. Not in. After all that, not in.

Rose looked round, hoping to see Donna walking towards her. Didn't happen. Even the lumpen couple and their child had disappeared. No one about.

Rose turned back to the door. Smiled.

She could still give Donna a surprise. In fact, this way, the surprise would be that much bigger. A much better way to show Donna just who was in charge. She would be terrified.

Giving a last check over her shoulder, making sure there was no one about, no one watching her, Rose turned back to the door. Took out a set of lockpicks in a leather case.

Got to work on Donna's front door.

So happy with herself, she could have whistled.

59

Marina found the door to the records room. Turned the handle. Open. She went inside.

'Don? You in here?'

No reply.

She looked down the first aisle. It was exactly as she had expected it to be. Long rows of shelving piled with old cardboard boxes. Dark in there, especially for daytime. Bad, infrequent overhead lighting. Several of the tubes were buzzing, flickering. Strobing the room.

Like in a horror film, she thought.

Then mentally pinched herself. *Don't be so stupid.* This was Southway police station in Colchester. Not *The Living Dead at the Manchester Morgue.*

She paused, listening. Called again.

'Don? You there?'

A noise. Down at the end of one of the aisles. Someone was in there with her.

'Don, it's Marina. Are you . . . '

A figure detached itself from the shadowed end of the aisle. Moved towards her.

'Don? Is that you?'

The figure moved into a pool of flickering light.

Marina let loose a breath she didn't realise she had been holding. 'It is you. I thought for a minute it was ...' She stopped, sentence unfinished. 'What have you got there, Don? What are you doing?'

Don was frantically stuffing something inside his jacket. From the look on his face, it appeared that he wasn't pleased to be caught doing it.

'Marina ...' The flickering overhead light picked out his eyes, lit by a strange cast. Not a pleasant one.

Marina was beginning to get scared. This wasn't the kindly old grandfather who looked after her daughter. This was ... someone she had never seen before.

'Don, what are you ...'

Papers successfully hidden inside his jacket, he advanced towards her.

60

Donna turned the car off Barrack Street into her own road. Slowly eased it along, looking for a parking space. One foot hovering over the accelerator, ready to drive off, speed away at the first sign of trouble.

Ben sat next to her, silent but full of unanswered questions. He had started asking them as soon as she had stopped crying and let him go, standing outside the car earlier that day. She hadn't had the strength to argue, shout or contradict him. She had even tried to answer him, although what she could tell him was limited. But something the boy had said had made her think. At first she had dismissed it, but once she had stopped and thought, she realised that what he had said might be important.

'Have you got her storybook?'

'No,' Donna had said straight away, not knowing what he was talking about. 'No storybooks.'

'Mum always had her storybook.' Ben had sat down on the ground on his own. Kicking at the hard-packed dirt of the forest floor with the heel of his shoe, working up a cloud of dust and grit. 'She wrote in it all the time. Said it was her life story. Said it was important to someone.'

'Yeah, well we don't have it, so it can't be.'

More kicking, more dust. 'Said it was important, though. Said someone would want to read it one day and pay her for it.'

'Yeah.' Donna had lit up a fag, ignoring the boy. Just about everyone she knew thought their life story was fascinating. Thought it was so unique someone would pay a lot of money for it. Well Donna had read misery memoirs. Knew there was nothing unique about them. W. H. Smith had a whole section of them. Tragic Lives. Why the hell would anyone want to read about someone else's tragic life? Losers.

But no wonder Faith wanted to write about hers. There must be a lot of money in that kind of shit.

'That's where she went, isn't it?' Ben had stopped kicking the dirt. He looked up at Donna. 'When she went out. She was going to sell her storybook.'

Donna had been about to answer the boy, give him some dismissive reply, not even diverting breath from her fag. But she stopped. Thought about what he had said.

'She told you that? She was going to sell her storybook?'

Ben nodded, head down, fascinated once again by the dust.

Donna didn't move. Stared straight ahead. Thinking. About what the boy had said. About what it meant. About all the vague stories Faith had told her in their time together: her childhood, her escape, her life with Ben. All the drunken stoned hints she'd dropped about her plan, how she was going to get revenge and make money in the process. About how she would sober up and pretend she had never said anything.

But just because she hadn't said anything didn't mean she hadn't been doing anything . . .

Donna dropped the fag at her feet, ground it out.

'Tell me about this book, Ben. Tell me all about it . . . '

And he had. As much as he had known.

And that was why they had come back to the house.

A few days ago, Donna would have said the book didn't exist. Or if it did, it was just some fairy story Faith had made up. But after the things she had been through, the fear she had encountered, the loss . . . she was willing to believe anything now.

She found a space down from her house, pulled in. Checked the street. Both directions. Nothing that looked suspicious. Nothing that screamed law. She had seen enough stakeouts – been caught in enough – to know what to look for. And she prided herself on her street sense. She knew just which punter to go with, which one to drop if she got a bad vibe about him, thought he would hurt her and not pay. And she was always right. Always.

But she saw nothing on the street. Nothing – and no one – that got her senses tingling.

She switched the engine off, turned to Ben. 'Right then, kid. Where did your mum keep this book, d'you know?'

He shook his head. Then thought a little. Eyes screwed up tight, trying to work it out. Bless him, thought Donna. The kid really wanted to help.

'My room,' he said at last. 'Or yours. And Mum's.'

'Right.' Another look up and down the street. 'You stay here, then. Keep your head down, don't talk to anyone. Don't let anyone know you're here, OK? Just be as quiet as you can.'

'But I want to come with you.'

'I know you do, kid. But it's better if you stay here.'

'Might them men be waitin' in the house?' Fear in his voice.

Christ, she thought, *I hope not.* 'No,' she said, hopefully sounding more confident than she felt. 'I'll not be long. Soon as I get the book, I'll be straight back out.'

''Cos I'm strong,' Ben said. 'If they attack you, I'll defend you. I will.'

Donna looked at the boy. Saw fear on his features. Bravery, too. He had lost his mother. And he didn't want to lose her too. Emotions swirled round inside Donna. Loss. Responsibility. Protection. She had never felt like this before. All the things she had tried to avoid, to keep herself immune from. Here, now, all together. She was all over the place.

She opened her jacket. The kitchen knife glinted. 'Still got this. Don't worry. You just keep your head down. Won't be long.'

She thought about kissing him, decided against it. She wasn't ready for that yet. Even though her heart was saying she was.

Donna crossed the street, found the front-door key and, with another quick look round, was in the house, door closed behind her. She stood with her back to it, listened. Nothing. Only the sound of the street outside, her own heavy breathing.

She scoped the living room. Exactly as she had left it. Or it seemed to be. She looked for little things, ornaments, magazines, things only she would know the correct positioning of, indicators of whether someone had been there, moving things and trying not to let it show. She could find nothing out of the ordinary. She went upstairs.

Towards their bedroom.

Her bedroom. She had to get used to saying it.

She stopped, looked round. Something felt wrong. She didn't know what, but it wasn't right. Fingering the knife in her pocket, she entered the room.

Crossed to the chest of drawers, opened the top one. The underwear drawer she shared with Faith.

Had shared with Faith.

The things in it were always neatly rolled. Now, they were all over the place.

She checked the top of the chest of drawers. Saw fingerprints in the dust. Clean smudges, small but unmistakable, telling her that someone had been there. She opened the second drawer. Same as the first. everything thrown around.

Opened the third. Neat. Just like she had left it.

She closed it again. Thought. Two messed-up drawers, one neat one. Someone was looking for something. Probably the same as her: the book. And they had stopped. Which meant one of two things. Either they had found it, in which case they must have left, or ...

They were still looking for it.

And she had disturbed them.

Donna turned, tried to get the knife out of her jacket pocket. Too slow. An arm gripped her round the neck, pulled her down; a hand pushed her arm behind her back up to her shoulder blades. She felt her bones creak.

'Thought you'd fuck me over, eh? Thought you were cleverer than me, you little whore, did you?' Another pull on her arm. 'Well, you feeling clever now?'

Donna knew just who it was. That bitch policewoman.

She pulled her arm further.

Donna screamed.

61

M ickey stared at the photo. Stared, stared, *stared* . . .
Got him.

Adam Weaver's identity had been in his mind constantly,
yet just tantalisingly – and irritatingly – out of reach. But now
he had him. Mickey had known it was only a matter of time.
Known that once he'd started his mental Rolodex spinning, it
would come to him eventually.

And it had.

He got up from his desk, wanting to punch the air. Do a lap
of honour round the incident room. Down a large whisky.

Glass stared over at him. Frowned. 'Everything all right,
DS Philips?'

Mickey gave a small smile. 'Everything's fine, sir, thanks.'
Then felt he needed more. 'Thanks for asking.'

Glass's eyes narrowed. Unsure of whether Mickey was
taking the piss or not. Mickey just nodded at the DCI, then
put his head back down, returned to what was in front of him.

Adam Weaver. Well, well, well. Robin Banks indeed.

He looked round the office once more, news almost bursting from him. He wanted to tell someone, needed to share it.

But none of his usual confidants were around. Anni was off at the hospital; the boss was out. And he certainly didn't want to share it with Glass. He looked at his watch, picked up his phone, went outside.

Through the double doors, into the car park.

Phil answered. 'What you got, Mickey?' Noise in the background. In the car, Mickey guessed. Listening to one of his God-awful CDs. Mickey tried to listen, make it out. He should know it; after all, he'd been subjected to the stuff enough times. Midlake? Band of Horses? Probably. Sounded a bit like them. You could hear the beard in the voice. Might even be Warren Zevon, although Mickey felt sure that was something Phil played just to annoy him. He couldn't really like it.

'I've got him, boss. Weaver. I've got him.'

The music faded away. 'Tell me.'

'Well I'm pretty sure, anyway. His real name's Richard Shaw.'

'Richard Shaw, Richard Shaw . . . I know that name . . . '

'Yeah, you probably will. When I was in the Met, I was on the team working a case against these north London gangsters. Was a big one, loads of us on it. Been trying to get a conviction for years. Eventually we caught one of the inner retinue, got him bang on. Made him a deal. He turned grass.'

'Was it the Shaws who did the electric shock thing with an old field telephone?'

'That was the Richardsons.'

'The maniac with the hammer?'

'That was the Richardsons too.'

'What did the Shaws have? What was their USP?'

'Fear, mainly. They used anything that came to hand. Everyone knew that if they stepped out of line, that was it, they were gone. Vicious bunch of bastards. Anyway, it looked like we had this case against them. Richard Shaw. And his old man, also Richard Shaw. Tricky Dicky, the old guy was called. Used to be a real big noise back in the day.'

'And which one have we got?'

'The son.'

'Why's he turned up here?'

'Well,' said Mickey, 'that's the thing. We were moving in on them, building this case, knowing we were only going to get one shot at it, knowing it had to be a good one, the best – and then . . . nothing. They disappeared.'

'What, the whole family?'

'Whole lot. Just vanished. Like that. Thin air. And it wasn't the first time.'

'What d'you mean?'

'The father, Tricky Dicky, had pulled a disappearing act years earlier. He was vicious. A stone psychopath. At the time, everyone thought he'd been murdered.'

'But?'

'No body. No trace. Nothing. Which isn't unusual, of course. But no one knew where he'd gone. And then his son did the same thing.'

'What about Spain?'

'Our first thought. But Shaw Junior and his crowd never turned up there. No one saw them. There wasn't even any word about them arriving secretly. Nothing.'

'So what, then?'

'Well, rumour had it they'd been taken out of the country. But not Spain, like I just said. Other rumours had it that they were all dead. Young Richard had ordered a hit on whoever squealed, and anyone who got in the way was just collateral damage. But like I say, these were just rumours. No one knew where any of them had gone.'

'Until now.'

'Until now.'

'Brilliant work, Mickey. A real breakthrough. Well done.'

Mickey smiled. 'Thanks, boss.'

'What you going to do now?'

'Get back on it. Hunt down all the files I can about the Shaws. See if anything matches, if I can get a handle on what's happening here.'

'Good stuff.' Phil gave a small laugh. 'You must be keen. That'll involve paperwork, you know.'

'I know.'

It was well known just how much Mickey detested paperwork. Even among naturally report-writing-averse police officers, Mickey's hatred of it was legendary.

'What about you, boss?'

'I'm just off to the hospital. See Anni. Find out what's happening with the kid.'

'Right. We'll catch up later. Give my regards to Anni.'

Mickey didn't know if Phil had heard, but he did hear the volume on the music being pushed back up as the call was broken. Midlake. Definitely. Or Band of Horses.

Mickey turned, making his way back into the building. Nearly jumped out of his skin.

Glass was standing right behind him.

Mickey actually clutched his chest. 'God . . . '

Glass smiled. 'Just me.'

Mickey said nothing. Tried to walk past him. Glass put a restraining hand on his chest.

'Just a moment, Detective Sergeant.'

Mickey stopped, waited. He really disliked the man. The previous one had been bad enough, but Glass . . . He should have been perfect. Mickey should have responded well to him. A straight-down-the line copper. No-nonsense. But he hadn't. Maybe he had worked with Phil too long. Adopted his methods.

'Who was that on the phone? DI Brennan?'

Mickey knew it was a bad idea to lie. Even if he didn't want to tell the truth. 'Yes, sir.'

Glass nodded, as if a suspicion was confirmed. 'And why did you have to call him out here? Isn't the office good enough?'

'Don't know, sir. I had something to tell him. This felt like the best way.'

'And what would that be, Detective Sergeant?'

Mickey knew he was taking a chance with what he was about to say, but he said it anyway. 'I'm afraid I can't tell you, sir. DI Brennan asked me to look into an aspect of the investigation that was potentially ... sensitive. I was following his orders.'

Glass clearly didn't like the answer but had to accept it. He nodded, face unhappy. 'And where is DI Brennan now?'

Mickey had to tell the truth this time. No option. 'On his way to the hospital.'

'Thank you.'

Mickey made to go. Glass stopped him again.

'You're a first-rate detective. Don't let certain ... associations come before achieving your potential. Do you understand what I'm saying, Detective Sergeant?'

'I think so, sir. But I'd better get back to work.'

He walked back into the building, trying to put the encounter, and Glass's disturbing final words, out of his mind.

Focus on finding out everything he could about Richard Shaw.

Doing his job, he thought, would be the best way to achieve his potential.

But Glass's words were still in his mind ...

62

'Don? You OK?'

He kept advancing towards her. Marina felt her heart quicken. This wasn't the Don she knew.

'Don . . .'

He reached her. 'What are you doing in here, Marina?'

'Looking for you.' Her voice a lot more level and calm than she felt.

He looked behind her at the door. She caught the look, knew immediately what he was thinking. A self-locking handle. She hadn't locked it. She made swift mental calculations, adding up whether she could turn, beat him to it.

Get out into the corridor. Run.

Then another voice entered her head. Muddied her thinking. *But this is Don we're talking about . . .*

'Did they send you?' Don's voice low, hard.

'Did who send me, Don?'

'Them,' he said. 'Glass and . . . and that lot.'

'No. No one sent me. I just came looking for you. I wanted to talk to you.'

He stopped. Frowned. 'Why? What about?'

'Phil,' she said.

At the mention of his adoptive son, Don sighed. The tension leaving his body, his shoulders sagging, legs bending. No threat in him any more. More like the old man she knew, Marina thought.

'So you know, then.' His voice tired.

'Know what? Don, I wish I did.'

'What d'you mean?'

'I wish he'd tell me what's wrong. There's something going on with him. Something . . . not right,' said Marina. 'At first I thought it was us. Me. Me and him, I mean, our relationship. But it's not that. It's more than just that.'

He moved nearer to her. The overhead light flickering, glinting off his eyes.

Marina moved backwards. 'Were you going to hurt me when I came in here, Don?'

He looked surprised. 'Hurt you? Good God, no. Why would I want to hurt you, Marina?'

'I don't know. You tell me. It looked like I'd interrupted you in the middle of something that you didn't want me to know about. Looked like you were pretty angry about it.'

'Oh. That.' Don gave a shamefaced smile. 'Sorry.' He patted his side, beneath his jacket. 'Needed a bit of . . . extra reading. Not strictly speaking legal extra reading.'

Marina returned the smile. 'I see. Just don't do it again.'

'I'm sorry. I won't. But you have to be careful in here. Have to know who you can trust and who . . . who . . . you know.'

'And who *can* you trust, Don?'

'I'm sorry. Of course I can trust you. I'm sorry.'

They stood looking at each other, saying nothing. The only sound in the records room the fizzing and spitting of the overhead strips.

'You wanted to talk to me about Phil,' said Don eventually, his voice carrying the weight of the world within it.

'Yes, I do.'

He shook his head. 'Where to start?' He gave a quick look round as if fearful of being overheard, leaned in close to her. 'D'you know anywhere round here that does coffee? Good coffee, I mean. Not the failed biological warfare experiments they serve in the machines in here.'

'Yeah. I do. Want to go?'

'I think that's a good idea. And then I can tell you. About Phil . . . '

63

Donna screamed.

Felt her arm being wrenched from its socket, pushed hard up her back. Heard – and felt – the tearing sound through her body. She screamed again. The pain increased.

'Yeah,' said the copper's voice between gasps, 'that's it. On your knees now, bitch.'

And that did it. That one word.

Bitch.

Donna hated it. Refused to hear it. Certainly wouldn't let a punter get away with saying it, no matter how much he paid her. Well, maybe she had done in the past, when she'd been desperate, but she had insisted on extra. Up front. And hated herself for it afterwards. Told the john there were plenty of girls who made a living that way, but she wasn't one of them.

Bitch.

She hated it. Wouldn't take it. It was one of the two things she couldn't abide, the other being a slap in the face. Anyone did that to her, she would turn round, punch them out. Same as the word. Bitch.

It worked on her like spinach on Popeye. Gave her super strength. Made her super angry.

Super fucking angry.

She felt Rose Martin pushing her down, felt her knees start to buckle.

'That's it, you fucking bitch, go on—'

And the world turned scarlet, spun off its axis.

Donna didn't kneel, didn't go anywhere near the floor. She lifted her right foot, brought it down as hard as possible on Rose Martin's right instep.

The policewoman screamed.

Donna felt the grip loosening. She wouldn't get another chance. Leave it too long and it would just make her angry. She stamped down again, harder this time. Caught the copper's shin as she did it.

Another scream, another loosening of her grip.

Donna pushed down with her arm, as hard as she could. Got it loose, bent it back, shoved her elbow with all her strength into Rose Martin's ribs. Caught her right on the diaphragm. Felt the air huff out of her.

Donna turned quickly, saw Rose Martin preparing to come back at her. Without thinking too much about it, she reached over to the bedside table, picked up the lamp. It was small, light and cheap, but it would have to do. She swung it as hard as she could. It connected with Rose Martin's cheekbone. She followed through, put all her strength into the shot. Saw the copper's head snap back, her body spin round.

Rose Martin hit the side of the bed, fell to the floor.

Donna threw the lamp aside, brought her leg back, took aim, let loose a kick. Rose Martin screamed. Donna heard and felt ribs splinter and crack. She swung her foot back, ready to do it again. Feeling the adrenalin course through her, loving the sense of power it gave her. She smiled. Kicking a copper. Brilliant.

But her jubilation was cut short. Rose Martin grabbed her ankle, caught it in mid-swing, twisted.

Donna's turn to scream. She felt her knee twist, heard cartilage rip, felt her leg go in the wrong direction. She tried to move with the twist, minimise the injury. She spun, hitting the floor hard.

Saw Rose Martin claw herself up on to her knees, arm wrapped round her shattered ribs, moving towards her, intent on keeping going.

Donna looked round the room for weapons, couldn't see any.

She felt for the kitchen knife. Lying there, she fumbled the blade from her pocket, hoped she had it to hand before Rose Martin started on her again. She pulled it free. Rose Martin was on her. Donna drew the blade back, gripping the handle, ready to stab.

But didn't.

A scream rent the air. The two women paused, stared at the source.

Ben was standing in the doorway. His face white, a horror-film death mask, he stared at the two women.

Rose Martin pulled her blow. Put her arm down. Donna lowered the knife. Sat up on her elbows.

'Ben. Come here . . . '

Ben didn't move.

'It's all right,' said Rose Martin, looking straight at the boy but unable to hold his eyes. 'I'm a police officer.'

'Yeah,' said Donna, gasping for breath. 'Like that's gonna reassure him.'

Rose sighed, looked at her. Donna looked back. The fight gone from the pair of them. A numb kind of embarrassment replacing it.

Rose looked at the knife. 'I think you'd better give that to me.'

Donna glanced at it, then at Rose. Reluctantly handed it over. Rose pocketed it. Gripped the edge of the bed, tried to stand.

'Want a hand?'

Donna was trying to get up too.

'I'll manage.'

The two women got painfully to their feet. Stood looking at each other.

Donna's first thought was to run, but she tamped it down. Yes, she had been about to attack a police officer with a knife. Yes, she had shattered her ribs. But that police officer had broken into her house and seriously assaulted her. So she imagined she wasn't going down for this. And judging by the look on Rose Martin's face, she was thinking something similar.

Donna looked at Ben. 'Go an' put the kettle on. There's a love.'

The boy, still unblinking, disappeared from the bedroom.

The two women looked at each other.

'You set me up,' said Rose Martin.

'Sorry,' said Donna. 'I had to get away. As soon as I knew somethin' bad had happened to Faith, just like she said it would, I knew I had to run.'

Rose frowned. 'What d'you mean, just like she said it would?'

'She said that if something happened to her, if she died mysteriously, I was to take Ben and run. Because he'd be next. And then me.'

Rose looked like she wanted to believe her, but seemed to have some way to go first. 'So why are you back here?'

Donna shrugged, attempted nonchalance. Failed. 'Forgot somethin'.'

'What?'

She hesitated. And Rose was on her.

'I said what?'

Donna sighed. No point in lying now. 'Faith left a book. A diary. Tellin' everythin' about who was after her, what had happened. She said it would be worth somethin' to the right people.'

'So where is it?'

Donna shrugged again. 'Dunno.'

'You haven't found it?'

'Not yet.'

Rose Martin smiled. 'Then I think we'll look for it together, don't you?'

Donna knew she had no choice. She nodded.

The two women, their bodies aching, their anger spent on each other, began the search.

64

The Gardener was out again. And it felt good. No, better than that. It felt right.

He had waited until the policeman had gone, then made his appearance. Because he had work to do.

Oh yes.

And he was looking forward to it.

The sacrifice was being returned to him. All he had to do was go and pick it up.

He walked to the stretch of road, waited in the agreed place. Up the hill by the park. Under a tree. No one would speak to him, or even look at him. He was a non-person. Just like Paul was. But the Gardener didn't mind that. In fact, he liked it. Fed on the energy of it. People ignored him. But he was more powerful than any of them realised. He was only letting them live as they walked past because it was too much trouble to kill them. He had the power of life and death over all of them.

If only they knew it.

Today was going to be special. The sacrifice would be returned and the ceremony could begin. And the future of the Garden would be assured.

Then another thought came into his head. And when it did, his heart felt like a sinking stone inside his chest. He sighed, whatever happiness, energy he had been feeling draining out of him.

He had nowhere to perform the sacrifice.

The house was gone. All his tools, his ritual with it. The cage . . . the cage was gone . . .

But there was another. He smiled to himself. Felt the stone lift in his chest. An even more sacred space. He had never attempted to do a sacrifice there before. But it made sense. It was the perfect place.

Perfect.

He was still thinking, still planning when his lift arrived. The driver had a baseball cap on and his collar turned up, but the Gardener still recognised him. He got in beside him.

The Portreeve didn't look happy. He looked scared.

The Gardener said nothing to him. Just waited until he pulled away, then yanked his hood up.

Smelled the rich, loamy smell. Felt comforted by it. Charged.

Beside him, he felt the Portreeve's fear increase.

Good.

Good . . .

65

Phil pulled up at the hospital. Parked, went inside. Flashed his warrant card at reception, asked where the boy under police surveillance was. Ignored the double-take the receptionist gave to his clothing.

He thanked her, went on his way.

He walked down corridors, mentally following the instructions he'd been given. As he rounded the final corner, he was expecting to find Anni, but was greeted instead by DCI Glass.

Phil stopped walking. His heart sank. 'Afternoon, sir,' he said, as neutrally as he could.

Glass turned, about to say something in return, stopped. 'What . . . what's that?'

Phil kept a smile off his face. 'What's what, sir?'

Glass pointed at him. 'That . . . that . . . What are you wearing?'

'I think you can see what it is, sir.' Phil again kept his voice neutral.

'A . . . a bow tie. An officer of mine is wearing a bow tie.' Glass shook his head.

'You said I needed to smarten myself up, sir. I thought a tweed jacket and bow tie would do the trick. They're very fashionable at the moment, I believe, sir. Very on trend.'

Glass's lips became thin, bloodless. 'Are you taking the piss?'

'Not at all, sir. It's just the kind of thing that'll play well in media briefings. The cameras'll love it. Sir.'

Glass's face changed colour, deepened to an unattractive shade of heart-attack red. Well at least he's in the right place, thought Phil. Glass moved in closer. No smile now, not even the pretence of one.

'The cameras'll love it, will they? The cameras'll love it. No they won't, Detective Inspector. No they won't.' His voice dropped to a dangerous whisper. 'Because you are going nowhere near a camera. You are going nowhere near a case in my department ever again. You are suspended from duty. Forthwith.'

Phil felt anger rise within him. He knew the best thing to do would be to keep it contained, but he also knew that wasn't an option. Not after what Glass had just said. 'On what grounds?'

A nasty smile smeared itself over Glass's features. 'I think that speaks for itself. Insubordination. Incompetence. Negligence. Not following correct procedures. How does that sound so far?'

Phil stepped in close to Glass. The DCI flinched. 'Bullshit and you know it. All I have to do is phone the Super at Chelmsford. He knows me. He'll back me up.'

'He'll also want to preserve the chain of command. He'll want to be seen to be following grievance procedure. He's open to scrutiny as well. He has his own job to think about before yours.'

'So that's it, is it? I'm out.'

'You most certainly are.'

A smile flitted across Phil's features. 'Then since I'm no longer a police officer, you won't mind if I do this.' He pulled his arm back, ready to punch the DCI.

Glass stood his ground, stared straight into Phil's eyes. 'I'd think twice before you do that, if I were you.'

'Why? You're no longer my superior officer, and I'm no longer on the case.'

'I'm thinking of your safety, Detective Inspector.'

'My safety?'

'Yes. You hit me and I'll fucking kill you.'

His stare level, icy. Phil didn't doubt the sincerity behind his words.

'I've read your file, Brennan. I know you've got previous where this is concerned. I know you've struck your superiors before and got away with it. Well not this one. Hit me and it'll be the last thing you ever do.'

Phil stared at him.

Glass smiled. 'That's better. Now run along home. The proper police have got work to do.'

Phil felt suddenly ridiculous standing there in a bow tie, even more so with the rage he was feeling inside him. He wanted so much to punch Glass. So, so much.

Glass laughed. 'Don't. Hit me, you go down. And you don't get back up again.'

Anni came round the corner, stopped dead when she saw the two men before her.

'Boss? What ... what's happening?'

Phil turned. Tried to speak. No words came out.

'I've just relieved DI Brennan of his position,' said Glass. 'From now on, you answer directly to me, Detective Constable Hepburn. Clear?'

Anni turned to Phil. 'What the hell's happened? Has he gone mental?'

'Keep talking like that, DC Hepburn,' said Glass, 'and you'll be next.'

Anni stared at the DCI, then shook her head, restraining herself.

Glass caught the look. 'Just get him out of here,' he said, turning and walking away, shoulders and back bunched with tension.

Anni looked back at Phil. 'And what are you wearing?'

'A bow tie,' he said, then sighed. 'It seemed like a good idea at the time.' Another sigh. He looked directly at Anni, turning his back on Glass, his voice a whisper. 'I don't know what's wrong with me ... '

Any kind of answer was cut short by a sound from the boy's room. Phil knew immediately what it was. Not a car backfiring, he thought; that's just a cliché. It was followed by a scream.

He and Anni looked at each other.

'Was that ...?'

'This way,' said Anni. 'Come on.'

She ran round the corner, Phil following. The door to the boy's room was open. Darkness inside.

'I was only away for a couple of minutes,' Anni said. 'I left Jenny Swan, the psychologist, in there with him. He should be ... '

She stopped talking as they entered the room. Jenny Swan was lying on the floor, unmoving. Blood pooling underneath her head. On the bed, the boy was backed up to the headboard, as far as he could go without burrowing into the wall behind him. Screaming. Screaming for his life.

Before him, standing at the side of the bed, was a man Phil hadn't seen before.

The man realised he wasn't alone, turned.

'Stay where you are,' he shouted. 'Don't come any closer. I mean it . . .'

And that was when Phil saw the gun.

66

Mickey leaned back, fingers interlaced behind his head, stretched his body. Felt the pull of the muscles down his arms, his sides. He flexed, stretched again. Took a deep breath, let it go. Relaxed again.

He hated paperwork. Loathed it. Despised it. Some people, Milhouse for one, were natural-born desk jockeys. They loved nothing better than sitting in front of a computer screen, trawling through virtual facts and figures in an unreal world, emerging with something real and concrete at the end. Mickey couldn't do that. He was built for action. He hated to admit it, knew the admission made him sound like some muscle-bound thug, the kind that volunteered for riot-squad work, but it was the truth. Not the riot-squad stuff; he couldn't stand the kind of officers that arm of the job attracted. Just the action element. Thief-taking. Catching criminals. That kind of thing. Proper police work. Not sitting here in front of a screen, getting eye strain.

But he had found out some interesting things. He had to admit that. The time hadn't been wasted.

So that was something.

And the office felt better when Glass wasn't there. Mickey had had reservations about him before the chat outside. An instinctive distrust of the man. Or a dislike. For Mickey, the two things were often the same.

But Glass's words kept running around his mind. Was the DCI right? Had he allied himself too closely with Phil? Would it impact on his career? He shook his head. Now wasn't the time to be thinking about things like that.

He rubbed his eyes, looked again at the screen. Richard Shaw. Tricky Dicky. Hadn't been so clever about hiding his paper trail as he thought he had. Certainly not if Mickey could find it.

He rubbed his eyes again. Couldn't stand another second looking at this screen. He needed to get out.

Mickey smiled to himself, took his phone out. Perfect, he thought. Just the excuse.

'I want to meet,' he said by way of greeting. 'Now.'

Fifteen minutes later, he was on the footbridge overlooking Balkerne Hill. On one side was the old Roman wall bordering the town centre. The Hole in the Wall pub built into the corner. On the opposite side, the upmarket suburb of St Mary's. Beneath him, traffic roared down the dual carriageways in and out of the town.

'Hello, Stuart,' he said.

Stuart was already there, staring down at the road. He looked up as Mickey approached.

'You know I don't like meeting in broad daylight,' he said, eyes darting round, checking for spies. 'Especially not somewhere like this.'

Mickey smiled. 'Perfect place, Stuart. Beats hanging round in some back alley or the corner of a dodgy boozer. Up here . . . no one's looking. You're ignored. You're safe.'

Stuart, Mickey could tell, didn't look convinced.

'So what did you want to see me about?' he said, a sigh of resignation in his voice.

Mickey looked at him. Stuart had been an informant longer than Mickey had been in Colchester. He had provided information for the previous DS in MIS and had seemed perfectly happy to let the arrangement continue with his successor. Today he looked rough. But then, Mickey thought, he always looked rough.

Stuart was tall and thin, and his black Cuban-heeled suede boots had seen much better days. Probably when John Lennon was divorcing Cynthia. His jeans were also black, drainpipe-cut, barely clinging to his drainpipe legs. A once-black T-shirt now gone grey, proclaiming the name of some band Stuart was keeping the faith for. One that had split up, re-formed, split up again and had three of its founder members die through various forms of self abuse. A black waistcoat and the same black leather jacket he always wore, so old it had come back into fashion at least three times without him noticing it. And his hair was a filthy nest of artificially blackened spikes. He looked old enough to have been a mod, but dressed as if the last tribe he had followed had been punk, and seemed to have lost the energy to reinvent himself since.

He claimed to be a poet. Although Mickey had never heard of him having anything published. He claimed he used to be a rock star. Although no one could ever remember him doing any gigs or releasing any records. He had always endorsed the sex, drugs and rock 'n' roll lifestyle. Well, the drugs at any rate, thought Mickey. Still, he seemed to know everyone in the area, some good, most bad, and had a knack of finding things out from circles Mickey could never get into.

'Tricky Dicky Shaw,' said Mickey.

Stuart frowned. 'Tricky Dicky Shaw ... there's a blast from the past ...'

'His son's been in town,' said Mickey. 'Calling himself Adam Weaver. Just been killed at the Halstead Manor Hotel.'

'Heard about that,' said Stuart. 'Any idea who did it?'

'I was going to ask you that.'

'Oh. Right.' He nodded. 'Tricky Dicky Shaw ... well I never ...'

'D'you think you could have a bit of a nose-around? Find something out for me?'

Stuart shrugged. 'Sure. See what I can do.' He screwed up his face again. Concentrating. 'Adam Weaver ... that name rings a bell.'

'Good. Give you something to go on.'

'When d'you want to hear something?'

'When you've got something to tell me. Sooner rather than later would be good, though.'

'Right you are, Mr Philips.'

'OK. Call me when you've got something.' Mickey turned to walk away. Stuart stopped him. Mickey turned.

'Couldn't give me a bit in advance, could you? On account?'

Mickey sighed. He had been expecting this and come prepared, but it was a ritual he had to go through. He dug into his pocket, pulled out a tenner. 'Here you go.'

'Much appreciated, Mr Philips. Hey, have I ever told you you've got the same name as the guy who discovered Elvis and Johnny Cash?'

'Only every time we meet, Stuart,' said Mickey with a weary smile. 'And it's only the surname, as you know. Ring me when you've got something.'

'Right you are.'

Mickey walked off. It wasn't a car chase, he reasoned, but it beat doing paperwork.

67

The Minories café was tucked away at the back of the art gallery of the same name at the top of East Hill, opposite the castle, in a sprawling Georgian building. With its stripped wooden floors and mismatched furniture, not to mention the huge cakes and quiches, it was a favourite lunch haunt of Marina's. Now she was there with Don, because it was the place where they were least likely to come across police officers.

They had taken a seat at one of the outdoor tables, the weather being just warm enough to allow it. They had sat as far away as possible from anyone else, mindful that they didn't want anyone overhearing their conversation.

Marina stared at her empty coffee mug, the dregs drying round the rim like geological strata, dating the time they had sat there. She blinked as if coming out of a trance, leaned back, looked round.

The garden, with its odd assortment of architectural features, its archways and vaults dotted about seemingly at random, always reminded her of a mini Portmeirion. But she wasn't noticing that now. She was taking in what Don had said, letting the words settle.

'Oh my God . . . '

What he had told her had made the day fall away. It had been like hearing the most unreal and unfamiliar things in the most real and familiar of settings. That had just heightened the effect of what he had said.

'Oh my God . . . ' she said again. There were no other words to express what she had just heard.

'I'm sorry you had to hear it like this,' Don said, eyes on his own coffee mug. Not empty like Marina's, since he had been doing most of the talking, but cold. Unwanted. 'I'm sorry you had to hear it at all, really.'

'No, no, it's . . . ' She shook her head. 'Poor Phil . . . '

'I always knew I'd have to tell him one day. Well, I thought I would. But I hoped it would never come to it.' He leaned forward, placed his hand on hers. She left it there. 'I certainly never imagined it would all come out this way. Never in a million years.'

'I'll bet.'

'I thought all that was over. In the past.' He sighed. 'I wished it was.' Shook his head. 'I really . . . ' Sighed again.

Marina wanted a cigarette. She hadn't smoked for years, not since she was a student trying to impress other students. But whenever she got stressed, she could feel the burning smoke being pulled down her throat, entering her lungs. Soothing her, comforting her. She knew the effect was imaginary, illusory, and had resisted it. But it was calling her now. More strongly than she had felt for years.

Don sat back. Removed his hand from hers. 'So anyway. Now you know.'

'Yes,' she replied blankly, not fully engaging with the words, 'now I know. And it explains a lot.'

'How so?'

'Phil's behaviour. He thinks he's cracking up. Seeing things

291

that aren't there, being . . . I don't know, haunted by ghosts he doesn't understand. By ghosts he thinks don't exist.'

'Oh they exist all right,' said Don. 'They're all too real.'

'Poor Phil . . .' Marina shook her head.

'The question I suppose I should ask,' said Don, 'is now that you know, what are you going to do about it?'

'That's one question,' said Marina, 'yes. Probably the most important question. But there's another.'

Don waited.

'What does it mean for this case?'

Another sigh from Don. 'Well,' he said. 'That's where this comes in . . .'

He took the stolen report from inside his jacket, laid it on the table before them. They both looked at it, Marina frowning.

'I think we'd better get more coffee,' said Don. 'This might take some time.'

68

Mickey was back in the office, printing out copies of his findings on Richard Shaw, looking at his watch, thinking it would be time to go home after he had done that, when his phone rang.

He checked the display. A number without a name attached. He answered.

'Detective Sergeant Philips.'

'Oh,' said a voice on the other end. 'Oh. Very formal.'

Female and familiar, Mickey thought. And in those few words, holding a lot of promise.

'Who is this?'

'Oh, sorry. I should have said. I just automatically assumed you would know. Sorry. It's Lynn. Lynn Windsor.'

As soon as she said her name, Mickey received a mental image of the solicitor. It was an image he was happy to look at.

'How can I help you, Lynn?'

'Well I don't know, exactly ... ' Her voice dropped, as if she wanted to say something private but was afraid of being overheard.

'Take your time,' he said. Then realised he was smiling. Very unprofessional, he thought, but he made no effort to stop.

'I've ...' Her voice trailed off. 'I don't know ...'

'It's all right,' he said, sensing that she needed encouragement. 'Take your time.'

She sighed. 'I've ...' Her voice dropped even further. 'I've discovered something. Something ...' Another sigh. 'Look, it's probably nothing. Nothing important. But I just thought, you know, what with everything that's been going on in the last couple of days ...'

'You've found something you think is important and you want me to take a look at it.'

The relief in her voice was palpable. 'Exactly. Look, I'm sorry, it's probably nothing, like I said, but I just ... Can I see you? Tonight?'

If the smile Mickey had experienced on hearing her voice hadn't been professional, the erection he felt stirring certainly wasn't. 'Yeah, sure ... when and where?'

I think it would be better if you came round to my flat,' she said, voice low and breathless. 'Will that be OK?'

'Sure ...'

'I'll give you directions.'

She did so.

'See you soon,' she said. 'Oh, one thing, Mickey ...'

'I'm still here.'

Her voice took on a breathy aspect. 'Don't tell anyone. Please.'

His own voice had dropped to a whisper. 'Well it's not correct procedure, strictly speaking ...'

'Please, Mickey. Please. I'm taking a ... a big risk coming to you about this. If anyone finds out about it ...' Another sigh.

'Well . . . '

'Please, Mickey, I'm begging you.' And she was. Her voice was doing exactly that. 'Keep this to yourself. If anyone else found out about this . . . please . . . '

He sighed. 'OK.'

'Promise?'

'I promise.'

'Good. You won't regret it.' And she rang off.

Mickey pocketed his phone. Sat staring at the screen.

Wondering whether he had just done the right thing.

Wondering if he was about to make things worse.

69

'Found it.'

Donna stopped what she was doing, looked up. She had been sitting on the bedroom floor, pulling out drawer after drawer, rifling through the life she had spent with Faith. She hadn't been enjoying it. It was like a betrayal of trust, no matter that Faith was dead. She felt like a horrible, venal relative, tearing up the family home looking for a will, seeing what she could get out of it for herself.

Which in a way was exactly what she was doing.

Except, she kept telling herself, it was the only way she could keep both herself and Ben alive. And if she made a little money from it too, so much the better. She was sure that was what Faith would have wanted. It was what she had been doing herself. When she died.

Donna had been getting sidetracked, seeing clothes Faith would never wear again, remembering times when she had worn them. Places they had gone together. Fun they had had. If she had kept on like that, she would have found herself tearing up. So when Rose shouted, she was glad of the distraction.

She looked up, felt the pain in her knee, tried to ignore it.

Rose was in Ben's room. The boy had been exiled to the living room, stuck in front of a DVD. Donna had thought that was for the best. She didn't want him to see the two of them tear the house apart.

Rose entered the bedroom holding aloft a blue exercise book. Donna looked at it. She could remember Faith buying it, coming home from Wilkinson's with it. *I'm writin' my life story*, she had said, and they had both laughed. And that had been the last Donna had thought of it.

Until now.

Rose sat on the edge of the bed, one arm wrapped protectively round her damaged ribs. 'Have a look at this,' she said. 'See if it means anything to you.'

Donna pulled herself off the floor, sat next to the police officer.

Rose opened the book. The two women started to read.

They didn't move.

'Oh my God . . . ' Rose was stunned.

Donna said nothing. There was nothing more to say.

They read on.

70

'Just put the gun down,' said Phil. 'Don't do anything stupid.' He looked down at the prone figure of the psychologist, wanted to amend his words: *don't do anything even more stupid*. But didn't think it would help.

'Too late for that,' said the gunman. 'Much too late.'

Phil realised just how terrified the gunman was. And a man carrying a gun with that level of fear was a perfect recipe for disaster.

'Come on,' he said, edging forward incrementally, his voice low and reasonable. 'Just put it down. Let's talk.'

Phil became conscious of Anni at his side. The one team member trained in hostage negotiation. He stepped back, allowing her to move forward. Looked at her, gave an imperceptible nod. She returned it, acknowledged it with her eyes.

'What's your name?' she said, edging nearer to the gunman.

The man looked confused, head turning from one of them to the other, then back to the child, screaming in the bed.

'I'm Anni,' she said. 'Tell me your name and we can talk.'

The man opened his mouth as if to speak, jaws working, lips moving, but no sound emerged.

Phil watched as a rivulet of sweat formed on the man's forehead and ran over his eyebrow, down the side of his face. He shook his head, clearly irritated by it, waving his gun as he did so. Phil's fingers curled to a fist, opened once more. His body tensed, ready to grab the man.

And then his phone rang.

The man swung the gun on him. Phil stared down the barrel as it shook.

'I'm turning it off,' he said, taking the phone from his pocket, making a clear show of pressing the button. 'See,' he said, dropping it back into his pocket. 'It's off.'

Anni stared at him. He moved back.

'Come on,' said Anni, eyes never leaving the man, voice never wavering. 'Just tell me your name, then we can get all this sorted out.'

His mouth moved again. Phil was reminded of a cow chewing the cud.

'S-s-s ... Samuel ... '

Anni summoned up a smile. 'OK, Samuel.' She slowly took the lapels of her jacket between finger and thumb, opened it slowly. 'I'm unarmed, Samuel, look. No gun.' She let the jacket drop back into place. 'And my colleague' – she nodded towards Phil – 'he's not armed either. Just his phone. So you put your gun down, OK? Then we can talk.'

All the time edging closer, closer ...

'I'm ... I'm finished,' said Samuel, more sweat springing from his features. 'Whatever happens, I'm finished ... '

'It's not that bad,' said Anni. 'Not yet. We can still salvage the situation.' Edging closer, closer ... 'Come on, Samuel ... '

'No,' he said. 'You don't understand ... I have to do this. If I ... if I don't do this, I've lost everything. I'm finished. Either way, I'm finished ... '

'Why, Samuel? Why are you finished? You don't need to do this.'

'I do!' Shouted. 'I've got to . . . got to . . . ' Tears sprang from his eyes, mingled on his cheeks with the sweat.

Phil risked a look at the boy on the bed. He had stopped screaming, was staring, wide-eyed, between the adults in the room. Phil kept focused, kept his attention on the gunman.

'Who says you have to do this, Samuel?' Anni was asking. 'Who? Taking the boy isn't your idea, I can see that. So whose is it? Who's told you to take him?'

'The . . . the Elders . . . '

'The Elders?' said Anni. 'Why do they want the boy?'

'They . . . they need him for the . . . the . . . sacrifice . . . Oh God . . . ' Fresh tears came, along with sobs.

His gun arm wavered. Phil edged ever closer.

Suddenly the gunman looked round, saw what Phil was doing. Swung his gun wildly in his direction. 'Get back! Get back! Don't make me shoot you too . . . please . . . '

'Just keep calm, Samuel,' said Anni, trying not to let the tension show in her voice. 'Keep calm. Everything will be fine if you keep calm . . . '

He swung back towards her. 'No it won't, no it won't . . . it'll never be fine again. Nothing will ever be fine again, don't you see? Nothing . . . '

Anni was still moving forward. 'Come on, Samuel, give it up now and we can get some damage limitation in place. Come on . . . ' She edged closer, closer . . .

There was a commotion at the door behind them. Glass came running in, saw what was happening. Phil turned to him, mouth open, ready to shout at him to stay back, but the DCI ran forward.

'What the fuck are you doing here?' he shouted at Phil,

grabbing him by the lapels, trying to wrestle him out of the room. 'I thought I told you to leave ...'

Phil, stunned by his superior officer's reaction, couldn't immediately fight back. He allowed his legs to be taken away, fell sideways to the floor, Glass still hanging on to him.

Anni, trying not to be distracted by what was happening, kept her attention on the gunman and the child. Samuel, staring wildly at what was going on before him, didn't know what to do. He raised his hand, pointed the gun at Anni.

Phil looked up, over Glass's shoulder, saw what was going to happen. Tried to call out.

Too late. The gun went off.

Anni spun round, a bright crimson flower bursting from her upper chest.

'No!' screamed Phil, trying to throw Glass off him. The DCI wouldn't move.

'Oh my God ...' Samuel stared at the gun in his hand, at Anni lying on the floor pumping blood, at the boy in the bed. 'What have I done? No ...' More tears began to well. A look of resignation came into his eyes. He turned to the boy, grabbed him from the bed. 'Come on, you're coming with me ...' Pulled him along with him, tubes and needles snapping off as he did so, the boy screaming.

Samuel made it out of the door and away down the corridor.

Phil managed to throw off Glass, stood up. He looked down at Anni, who was still breathing, looked to the empty bed. A hand grabbed his ankle.

'No you don't ...'

Phil turned round, aimed a kick at Glass's head.

'Fuck off,' he shouted.

Glass fell backwards, hand to the side of his head. Phil looked again at Anni. She had her right hand over the wound, was squeezing hard to staunch the blood. Phil knelt down beside her.

'Go . . . ' she managed to say. 'Go and get the boy . . . '

Phil nodded, stood up.

On the floor behind him, Glass's phone began to ring. Phil ignored it.

He ran out of the room and down the corridor.

71

Rose closed the blue exercise book. Sat back. Said nothing. Next to her on the edge of the bed, Donna did likewise. The sound of children's TV crept up the stairs, inconsequential and incongruous after what they had just read.

'My God ...' Donna's voice was small, cracked. 'She never ... she never said ... I had no idea ...'

'Why would you?' said Rose. Earlier, there would have been anger behind the words, sneering, snarling. Contempt. But now there was nothing of the sort. Just genuine enquiry, genuine concern. The words in the book had knocked all that out of her. 'If this is true ...'

Donna looked at her. 'You doubt it? Of course it's true. Faith wouldn't have lied. Not about that. Someone knew, didn't they? Someone else believed it, tried to stop her. And now she's ... she's ...'

Donna had felt numb while reading the book. Too emotionally stunned to feel anything. Faith's words had shocked her into immobility. But now, the book finished, the words permeating her brain, she felt the tears well up behind her eyes.

She didn't try to stop them. Fight them back. They weren't a sign of weakness. Not this time. They were a sign of solidarity. Faith deserved her tears. Especially after what she had endured.

She felt an arm round her shoulders. Rose. She should have been surprised at the other woman's touch, especially given what she knew about her, but she wasn't. No one could have read that account and not been touched.

They sat like that for what seemed an eternity. Charlie and Lola on the TV downstairs were having the kind of happy, perky life that no child in this house had ever had.

Eventually Donna leaned forward. Took a tissue from her pocket, blew her nose, rubbed her eyes. She looked at Rose.

'What . . . what should we do?'

Rose stared straight ahead. Eyes on the window, the street; beyond the window, the street. Donna was aware of a kind of steel entering her gaze. A calculating anger. The light glinted off the knife she had taken from Donna, nestling in her inside pocket.

'Make a couple of calls,' she said, 'then we call him.'

Donna frowned. 'D'you think that's a good idea? What . . . what if it was him who . . . '

'One of those calls is insurance. Then we call him. If it was him . . . '

Rose took the knife out of her jacket pocket. Played the light off it. Watched it glinting and sparkling. She looked at Donna.

'Let's just call him. See what he has to say.'

Donna nodded.

Stared ahead at what Rose had been looking at. Thought she could see it.

Or something like it.

72

Mickey pressed the buzzer. Waited.

The flat was a new-build, one of many that had sprung up in the town centre in recent years. He lived in one like it. But not too like it. This one was much more upmarket than his. Next to the River Colne, down by Hythe Quay. Mickey remembered the place well. He had encountered a very nasty murderer on the other side of the river less than a year ago.

A voice came over the intercom. 'Hello?'

Mickey paused. Who was he? Mickey Philips, was that too informal? DS Philips, was that too formal? What?

'DS Philips . . . Mickey Philips.'

Compromise. Both.

'Oh, hi, Mickey.' Lynn Windsor's voice, full of light and warmth. 'Buzzing you in. Come on up. Third floor.'

Mickey walked up the stairs. This place was definitely more upmarket than his own flat. Carpeted, the fixtures and fittings all top quality. It hadn't just been built; the block had been designed.

And it was a world away from the dead bodies he associated with the area.

Or at least he hoped so.

He reached Lynn Windsor's flat. Held his knuckle up, ready to knock on the door. Hesitated. Was this right? He wasn't following procedure. If anything went wrong, he would be in trouble. But what could go wrong? He was here to talk, that was all. Just talk. She had some information for him. That was it. Just talk.

He repeated the phrase to himself while he stood there. Saying it over and over in his head. Hoping to convince himself that it was true.

The door was opened from the inside. He put his hand down, feeling stupid.

'Hi,' said Lynn Windsor. 'I thought I heard you there. Come in.'

She opened the door wide. Mickey stepped inside and she closed it behind him.

He looked down the corridor towards the living room. The lights were down low. There was music playing. He didn't recognise it. Something slow, languorous. But with a beat behind it, a rhythm. Sexy, he thought. Seductive.

'Go on in,' she said from behind him.

He was aware of her perfume, her breath on his neck. He walked down the hallway. Entered the living room. It looked like something out of *House Beautiful* magazine. The corner unit, the lighting. The TV and music system were state-of-the-art. The pictures on the wall. Even the books on the bookshelf looked perfect.

'Nice ... er, nice place you've got here.'

'Thank you. I can't take much credit for it, I'm afraid. This is how it was when I moved in.' She laughed. 'I feel like I'm just squatting. Drink?'

'Erm ...'

'I've got some beer in the fridge.'

'Yeah. Yeah. Beer's fine.'

She walked off into the kitchen, called back to him. 'Make yourself comfortable.'

He tried to. Perched himself on the edge of the sofa.

Lynn re-entered holding a bottle of beer. 'Bottle OK, or would you prefer a glass?'

He told her the bottle was just fine.

She sat down near him on the sofa. He looked at her properly for the first time that evening. Her hair was up and she was wearing a long silk robe, as if she had just come out of the shower. He guessed by the structure of her body beneath the silk that she was wearing something fitting under it. She gathered her legs up beneath her, curled herself comfortable. Picked up her glass of clear fizzy liquid. Ice cubes chinking.

She reached across, met his bottle with her glass. 'Cheers.'

'Cheers.'

They drank.

Mickey put his bottle down on a glass-topped side table, conscious of the wet ring he would leave. 'So,' he said, 'you wanted to see me. You've got something to tell me?'

She looked down at her drink, smiled. 'I do.'

'What is it?'

She placed her drink on a similar side table. Turned to him. Eyes locked on his. He felt an erection beginning an involuntary stir.

'There's lots to tell you. But there's something I have to do first.' She edged nearer to him on the sofa.

'What?'

'This.'

She leaned across, took his face in her hands, kissed him full on the mouth.

He tried not to respond. Told himself afterwards that he'd

really tried. But he didn't. As soon as her mouth was on his, his tongue was in her mouth. Locked with hers, exploring.

He felt her body pressed against his, felt his erection spring right up.

She pulled back from him, smiling all the while.

'That's better,' she said.

She pulled at the silk tie of her robe. Slid it apart. He saw what she was wearing underneath. It took his breath away.

'I hope you don't think I was being presumptuous,' she said, working the robe slowly over her shoulders, letting it fall down her back. Knowing his eyes were devouring her black-underwear-clad body, her stockinged legs. 'But I think you feel the same way about me as I do about you, don't you?'

'But . . . don't you have . . . have something to tell me . . .?'

'Later,' she said. 'First, this. Is that OK with you?'

Mickey didn't answer. Just pulled the silk robe all the way off her.

Made no pretence at not responding any more.

Didn't think about anything but devouring Lynn Windsor's body.

73

Phil ran down the corridor, fast as he could. But Samuel was quicker. Whoever he was, thought Phil as he ran, the man certainly knew the layout of the building.

He had picked up the child. The boy was so small and thin, he had fitted under his arm. Allowed Samuel to move more quickly.

Phil reached the end of the corridor, found himself at a crossroads. He stopped, looked round, bent double, hands on knees, while he caught his breath. The corridors all looked alike to him. He hadn't been reading the ward signs as he ran, just following Samuel. He didn't know whether he had been down here before. He looked to his right, his left, straight ahead. Couldn't see any sign of the man or the boy. He listened. Hoping to hear screams, commotion. Follow the trail.

Nothing. Except his own ragged breathing.

Then: a scream. From the corridor on his left. He looked down there, could see nothing. The scream continued. Accompanied by the sound of running feet. Chest aching, Phil gave chase.

He ran, seeing the main entrance up ahead. People were

milling about, staff, patients and visitors alike. Screams and sobbing. Phil ran to the doors. He was grabbed by a security guard.

'Stay inside, please, sir, it's not safe.'

Phil tried to shrug him off. The security man tightened his grip.

'I said stay inside. The police have been called.'

Phil fumbled in his jacket pocket, flashed his warrant card.

'Sorry, sir . . . ' The guard let him go.

Phil ran through the double doors. Samuel was standing outside the building, the boy in front of him. Whenever someone made a move towards him, he brandished the gun.

'Get back,' he was shouting, 'get back, please . . . ' He sounded exhausted, tearful.

Phil stepped in front of him. Samuel immediately swung the gun towards him.

'Please, just . . . just leave me alone . . . '

'Let the boy go,' said Phil, moving towards him. 'Come on, Samuel, just let him go . . . '

The gun was still pointing at Phil. 'No . . . stay there . . . ' Pleading with him.

He's weakening, thought Phil. *I can take him.*

He walked towards the gunman.

'Get back!'

'It's over, Samuel. It ends now.'

'I'll . . . I'll shoot you . . . '

'No you won't.' Phil kept walking, across the car park.

'Yes, yes . . . I will . . . '

Phil stopped. A 4x4 was racing towards them, showing no signs of slowing down. He jumped back, out of the way. Samuel stayed where he was. The 4x4 screeched to a halt, the passenger-side door opening. Phil saw movement.

The boy had gone.

He ran forward. The driver's face was hidden. The passenger looked back at him.

Phil saw who it was. And felt like the life had been punched out of him. 'No, no . . . '

He fell to his knees, unmoving, as the 4x4 revved up, sped away.

Behind him, Glass ran out of the building, made straight for his own car. Drove away. Phil didn't even notice he had gone.

In front of him, Samuel raised the gun, placed it beneath his chin.

'I'm sorry, I'm sorry . . . '

Fired.

The car park came alive with screams.

But Phil didn't notice. All he could see was the face of the passenger. The rough sacking hood. The dark, bottomless eyes.

The man who had haunted his dreams.

He was real.

74

There was a knock at the door. Donna and Rose exchanged looks. They knew who it would be.

'I'll go,' said Donna.

She stood up from the sofa where the two women had been sitting, crossed to the front door. Opened it. DCI Brian Glass swept in.

'Where is she?' He ignored Donna, looked round the room.

'I'm here,' said Rose, standing up. Trying to ignore the pain. 'And I know what you've done.' Her voice hard, cold. Like Donna imagined an executioner's would sound. 'I know everything.'

Glass stayed where he was. Sighed. He looked at his watch. 'I don't have time for this.'

'Yes you do,' said Rose. 'Because it's all here.' She held up the notebook.

Glass said nothing. Just stared at her. Undisguised hatred in his eyes.

Feeding on his hatred, Rose smiled. 'Did you think I wouldn't work it out? Is that it? You didn't think I'd investigate?'

Glass said nothing. Stood there. Donna watched him. She had seen plenty of men like him before. Violence came off him in waves like aftershave.

Rose continued. 'Give the dead whore to the basket case, is that what you thought? The fuck-up. The mental patient. Give her a promotion too, but don't tell the rest of the station. Keep it between the two of us. That way you could always deny it later. Claim it was just ... just a sign, a sign of how fucking ... delusional I was ...'

Glass sighed. 'I don't have time for this.'

'Oh you do,' said Rose, and the knife was suddenly in her hand. 'You fucking do. You'll stand there and you'll listen. Because I've worked it all out. Who was Faith running from? Who was she meeting out in the woods at Wakes Colne? You. Now how do I know that? Checked the CCTV. No cameras on the street where you picked her up, but I gave them your registration number and they've got a perfect chain of you leaving the town centre and driving down Colchester Road out to the Wakes Colne woods. With a female passenger.' She smiled. 'Yeah. You're logged. You're in the system. You and Faith.'

Glass stared at her, his breathing low, shallow.

'She was trying to get money out of you, wasn't she? Taking the book to you before taking it somewhere else. And you didn't want that, did you?' Rose moved in closer to him, the blade dancing before him. 'Did you?'

Glass swallowed. 'No.'

'No. That's right. So you tried to kill her. What the hell, eh? Another dead whore, no one would lose sleep over her. Put much effort into looking for her killer. Just another punter that got a bit too handy, right?'

He said nothing.

'Except she ran, didn't she? Got away from you and ran.

313

And if those two cars hadn't been coming round the corner when they were, she would have got away, wouldn't she? Exposed you to the world.'

Glass's eyes didn't leave the blade. He licked his lips.

'How am I doing so far?'

A flicker of a smile. 'Pretty good. Not everything, but not bad.'

'Enough, though, eh?' She nodded. 'Enough to implicate you.' She laughed. It hurt her ribs, but she didn't notice. 'Give it to the headcase to investigate. Couple of days of getting nowhere, then it could be all dropped. And that would have been that.' She brought the blade up close to him. 'But it didn't work out like you planned, did it?'

'No,' he said, 'it didn't. But there's still time to remedy the situation.'

While she was still wondering what those words meant, Glass reached out, twisted her wrist with one hand, grabbed the knife with the other. Rose screamed, tried to get the knife back. Glass was too quick for her. And too strong. Before she could make a grab for him, he had pushed forward with the knife, stabbing her.

She looked up, surprised. He pulled the blade out, did it again. And again. And again. Face a mask of hatred.

Donna screamed.

On the stairs behind her, Ben screamed too.

Glass turned to the pair of them, the blade swinging before him.

Donna stood up, calculating the distance between herself and the front door. She knew she wouldn't get there in time. She still had her coffee mug in her hand. Not stopping to think, and trying to ignore the knife, she stepped up to Glass, swung the mug into the side of his head. Caught him behind the ear. He sighed, went down.

She turned to Ben.

'Come on, run . . .'

He raced down the stairs and the pair of them were straight out of the door.

Behind them, Rose had her arms stretched over her stomach.

'No . . . no . . . no . . .'

She watched, fascinated, as the blood pumped out of her. Cradled her own glistening innards.

She didn't have time to cry.

Didn't have time to feel anger or injustice at what was happening.

All she had time to do was die.

75

Grabbing Ben's wrist, Donna ran. She didn't know where; just as far away as possible from what was happening behind her.

She reached the end of the road. Two men stood blocking her way.

She stopped running. Recognised them.

'Oh no . . . no . . .'

The two men from the car. The ones she had injured.

'No . . .'

They were on her.

The one with the bandaged face smiled. Grabbed her tight.

'Now we've got you,' he said.

Donna wanted to scream, cry, fight.

But she didn't.

She just stood there.

No fight left in her.

76

The circus had arrived at the hospital.

Police cars, incident support units, the full works. The only things missing, for obvious reasons, were ambulances.

The car park had been taped off, the front of the building likewise. Samuel's body was still lying there waiting to be examined.

Don and Marina got out of their car, ran to the front doors. Phil was sitting on the steps. Marina sat down beside him.

'Phil?'

He just stared straight ahead. Didn't even acknowledge she was there.

'Phil, it's me. Marina . . . '

She held his hand, stroked it. Nothing. She glanced back at Don, a look of mutual concern flashing between them. She tried again.

'Phil . . . '

No good, she thought; he was catatonic with shock.

Don sat on the other side of him.

'Phil, it's me. Don. Phil, son, are you . . . are you there?'

Nothing.

Marina kept stroking his hand. She leaned into him.

'Marina . . . ' His voice small, as if coming from the far end of a long, dark tunnel.

Marina squeezed his hand harder. 'Yes, Phil, I'm here.'

He turned to her. And she saw something in his eyes she hoped she would never see again. Pain. Hurt. And a total lack of hope.

'He's real, Marina. The man from my dream. He's real. He was here . . . '

She held his hand even harder.

'Oh God . . . oh God . . . '

Not letting him go.

PART THREE

WINTER KILLS

77

It was the first time Brian Glass had ever killed anyone.

He had been responsible for deaths, but not directly. Not with his own hands. He sat on the sofa in Donna Warren's house, stared at the body on the floor. He had seen post-mortems before, watched while body parts were removed and weighed, cut and prodded, listened while decisions were made as to causes of death. But that was all afterwards. This was now.

Now he had the body of Rose Martin on the floor in front of him. He stared at it, transfixed. Her middle section was a confusion of red, lumpy gore. He couldn't identify organs or body parts; it was all just a mess. Her blood was all over the room. He knew that a blood-splatter expert could recreate what had happened from the various sprays and gushes, but right now he was content to just sit there and stare at it. Like an artist in his studio.

But it was the face that fascinated him the most. Minutes ago, it had been so full of animation. Eyes alight and burning with hatred, mouth spewing forth truths he hadn't wanted to hear. And now this. Nothing. Mouth slack, empty of words and sounds, eyes dull and staring, like a gutted fish on a marble slab.

He didn't feel bad about what he had done. On the contrary. He felt elated.

He just had to make sure he got away with it, that was all.

He rubbed his head. It was still sore from where Donna Warren had hit him. Tender to the touch. He had a bruise, a lump coming. At first he had been livid with rage that she – and the boy – had got away. He knew that following them wasn't an option. Causing a scene in public, brandishing a knife on a street – even in New Town – would attract attention. So he had had to let them go. But now, sitting here, he thought that was the best thing that could have happened. Because now he had a scapegoat. Now he had a murderer.

He knew what to do. Leave the body to be found. By him, later. And then shift all the blame on to Donna Warren. Make his later visit an explanation for how his DNA came to be in the house; let his verbal testimony be enough to catch and convict her. Take charge of the interviews. Make sure they went his way.

Oh yes. This would be easy.

And he had planned how to explain his sudden disappearance from the hospital too. He was giving chase to the person who had abducted the boy. And he had lost him. Simple. In fact, once he was certain the 4x4 was well away, he had put in a call asking for assistance in finding it. Covering himself. Muddying the waters further.

And Phil . . . He had looked in no fit state to say anything against him.

Glass nodded. Good. All good.

He stared at Rose Martin's body once again.

It was the first time he had killed someone.

But it wouldn't be the last.

78

The night was moving in. Bringing with it the chill of autumn, the threat of winter. But inside Phil and Marina's house in Wivenhoe, the windows were closed, the curtains and blinds drawn. The night was being kept at bay.

Or it should have been.

Because Phil could feel the night inside him. Deep within.

He sat in an armchair, staring straight ahead. Marina and Don stood in front of him, concern etched on their faces.

'Shall I give you a hand upstairs with him?' Don said. 'Get him into bed?'

Marina looked down at Phil. His eyes were open, but there was no movement. Whatever he was seeing wasn't in the room with them. It wasn't even in the present. Her heart broke to see him that way.

'No,' she said, 'leave him there.'

'But he needs rest, Marina. He needs—'

'Yes, Don,' she said, voice low, but calm and firm, 'he needs rest. But there's something he needs before that. Answers.'

She locked eyes with the older man. He couldn't hold her look, turned away.

'He needs to confront this, Don. It's gone on long enough. It's gone on his whole life.'

Don shook his head. When he spoke, his voice was barely above a whisper. 'I don't want . . . I don't want him hurt.'

Marina almost laughed. She gestured towards Phil. 'Look at him, Don. D'you think he could be hurt any more than he is already?'

Don sighed, eventually shook his head. 'No,' he said, 'I suppose not.' He sighed. 'Let's do it. Let's get him sorted out.' Each word was dragged out of him, like a chained concrete block being picked up and moved.

Marina took a deep breath, then another. She sat down opposite Phil, took his hand in her own. It felt cool, dry. 'Phil?'

His eyes flickered. Like a weak current of electricity had been passed between them.

'Phil. It's me. Marina. I want to talk to you. Can we do that? Can we talk?'

An imperceptible nod of the head.

'Good.' Still holding his hand. 'I just want to ask . . . who did you see, Phil? In the car, who was it?'

'The face . . . the face from my dream . . . ' His eyes closed, face contorted, as if seeing it all over again.

'OK. Good. The face from your dream. Good. What was he in the dream? What was he doing?'

'He was . . . I was in the cage, the cage of bones, in the cellar . . . and he was . . . ' He looked away, shook his head, as if trying to get the image out of his mind.

'You're doing fine, Phil. Just keep going.'

'I was in the cage and he was coming towards me, and . . . those eyes . . . in the hood, those eyes . . . '

'What about those eyes, Phil?'

'Dark . . . dark . . . like looking into something black and bottomless . . . '

324

'And he was hooded?'

Phil nodded. 'And then . . . and then he was there, outside the hospital . . . there . . . real . . . '

Marina looked at Don, who nodded too, grave-faced.

'Don's here, Phil. He's going to talk to you. He's got . . . things to talk to you about.'

She slid her hand from his, moved away. Don sat next to him. Leaned in to him.

'Phil? It's me. Don. I've got . . . I've got something to tell you. About the hooded figure. The man who kept you caged in your dreams. OK?'

Another imperceptible nod.

Don took a deep breath. Another. Ready as he would ever be. 'He's real, Phil. That's why he was at the hospital. He's real. And I know who he is.'

Phil opened his eyes, stared at Don. 'How . . .? How . . .?' His voice small, tiny, like a child's. A lost child's.

'Because I know him, Phil. I've come across him before. And I'm going to tell you all about it. This is about you and your life. Are you ready for this?'

'Will it . . . will it stop the nightmares?'

'Hopefully.'

Phil swallowed. Hard.

'Then I'm ready.'

79

The car drove through the night-time streets. Dwindling, emptying of people and traffic the further it moved away from the centre of town.

In the back, Donna tried to control her heartbeat. It was slamming against her chest, almost up into her throat. She hadn't felt like this since Bench gave her some of that nearly pure charlie that time at a party. But that was a pleasant experience. Well, at least until the nosebleeds started. This was anything but.

Beside her, Ben sat staring out of the window. Not wanting to look at her, too scared to look at the men in front.

Donna had tried talking to them. No response. They had just pulled them into the car, driven away.

'Wait,' Donna had said, 'there's someone in my house. A copper. She's been stabbed. You've ... you've got to go back ...'

One of the men had turned round, stared at her. Anger in his red, painful-looking eyes. She recognised him as the one she had pepper-sprayed in the face.

'Stabbed?' he said. 'Your speciality, is it?'

'What? No, I . . .'

He turned as far round in the passenger seat as he could go, looked her right in the face. Flecks of foam and spittle flew off his lips as he spoke. 'You know what you did? You put my partner in the hospital. He's fighting for his fucking life after what you did to him. D'you know that?'

A Scottish accent, she thought, her mind temporarily displaced by fear. She hadn't been expecting that. She said nothing.

'Bitch,' he said.

'Easy,' said the driver. His voice was more dispassionate. She responded immediately to that, wanted to cling on to it. Dispassionate meant he wasn't going to hurt her. Then her mind flicked over some of the punters she had had who had seemed dispassionate. At first. It wasn't a comforting thought.

Donna was breathing hard, terrified. She wanted to say something that would make this man calm down, that would take away the imminent threat from him.

'Please,' she said, 'I'm sorry.'

Her words just seemed to make him more angry. 'You're sorry? You're fucking sorry? You humiliated me, you nearly killed him . . .'

She sat back, eyes closed, preparing herself for a blow.

It didn't come. She opened her eyes.

He had turned back round, was staring out through the windscreen. The driver was silent, just kept driving.

Donna said nothing.

And that was how it had been all journey.

Ben startled her away from her thoughts, pulling at her hand. She looked down at him.

'I'm scared,' he whispered.

Me too, she wanted to reply. But stopped herself. That was what she wanted to say, but not what he needed to hear. He was just a kid; he needed her to be strong. To tell him lies that he hoped would come true. Like Father Christmas and life is fair, that kind of thing.

She summoned up a smile. 'It's going to be all right,' she whispered back. And squeezed his hand.

He looked up at her once more, his eyes meeting hers, trusting in her words.

And in that instant, her heart broke.

She looked up again, spoke to the men in front.

'Where are we going?'

'You'll find out soon enough,' said the one with sore eyes, not even bothering to glance round this time.

She looked down at Ben once more, then out of the window. She didn't know which was worse. This journey or the eventual destination.

She felt Ben's hand squeeze hers all the tighter.

Wished she could believe in lies too.

80

'There's no easy way to do this, no easy way to tell you . . . '

Don sighed. Felt Marina looking at him. Continued.

'Right. There was a commune. This was in the seventies, round about then. You know the type. Hippy dropout place. All kaftans and cheesecloth and children running about naked. That kind of thing. Beads and badly played guitars and free love.' His face darkened. 'Or at least it was, in the beginning.'

He took a sip of coffee, continued.

'The Garden. That was the name.'

Something flickered behind Phil's closed eyes. 'The Garden. But that's—'

'Don't interrupt, Phil.' Don's voice was not harsh, just firm. 'It's better that I tell you this without interruption. And you just listen.' He cleared his throat, continued. 'Like I said, the Garden started off with the best of intentions, the way these things always do.' He sighed. 'But along the way, like always happens, that initial vision, such as it was, got corrupted.'

Another mouthful of coffee. He wished it were something stronger.

'Brainwashing. That's how the allegations went. Not just a commune, but a cult. And abuse. All kinds of abuse. Sexual, psychological, physical. That was bad enough. But then other rumours started. Even nastier ones. That the communists, for want of a better word, were being hired out. Pimped out, sold, even.'

'In what way?' Phil couldn't help asking the question. He was too much of a detective.

Don didn't seem to mind this time. 'As sexual slaves,' he said. 'All ages. Rich perverts could get in touch, have a look at the menu, decide what they wanted. Sliding scale of payment depending on who they wanted and what they wanted them for.'

Another sigh. He shook his head.

'We heard that some rich sicko wanted a couple of adults to chase on his estate instead of foxes. They never came back. Torn apart by hounds, we reckoned. And women. Lots of women. Some of them came back. But not all. And I doubt the ones that did were ever the same.' His voice caught. 'And the kids . . . '

He took a moment, composed himself.

Silence thudded inside the house.

'Anyway,' Don said, clearing his throat, 'a couple of them escaped. Man and a woman, with a couple of kids. Boy and a girl. Just . . . just young. They came to us. Not immediately, of course. Took them a while to trust us. We were the enemy, after all.'

No bitterness in his voice, just a wistfulness.

'But they spoke to us. To me. I was a DI then. They wanted what was going on at the Garden stopped. Couldn't bear to see their dream go sour. Couldn't bear what was happening. It took a hell of a lot for them to get away. A hell of a lot. And they wouldn't talk unless we guaranteed protection. So I did.'

More silence.

'I arranged for the family to go into a safe house with twenty-four-hour protection. They were a really nice couple. A lovely family. I spent a lot of time with them. He had been a journalist before they joined the commune. She was gorgeous. And so were the kids.' He nodded. 'Yes. Especially considering what they'd been through. And when we got them there, they talked. Told us everything. Everything . . . '

His voice tailed away, his words getting lost in memories. Not pleasant ones. He brought himself back, continued.

'The Garden had started out OK. Guy in charge had genuinely believed he was doing some good. But then others got involved. Took over the running of it. They were . . . bad. Very bad. And that's when everything changed.'

Another sip of coffee. It had gone cold. Don didn't care.

'So we made plans to raid the commune. Gary and Laura, that was their names, gave us as much detail as they could. Layouts, who lived where, access in and out, as much as they knew. But we had to be careful. There'd been the Jonestown massacre in America a few years before, and we didn't want a repeat of that. We didn't think it was likely, not in Colchester, but we couldn't take any chances. They had them pretty brainwashed by now, half starved, ready to do anything they were told. So it took us a while to formulate a plan and get it implemented.'

He sighed again.

'And when we did finally move on the Garden . . . it was deserted. Empty. Like they had all been . . . I don't know. Beamed away to the mothership. Completely deserted. Like a landlocked *Mary Celeste*. We never found them. Not one of them. Ever.'

Don drained his coffee mug.

'Well, Gary and Laura got to hear about this in their safe

house. And they went ballistic. Were terrified. They said they had to be moved because they would be next. There was a penalty for giving up the Garden, and it was death. They were in fear of their lives.' He paused. 'And with good reason.'

'What happened?' asked Phil.

Don was reluctant to let the words leave his mouth. But he knew he had to. 'They were killed. Murdered. In the safe house. Along with the uniforms who were watching over them.'

The silence in the house was pounding, turned up to ear-bleed level.

'And the . . . ' Phil's voice was also unsteady, 'the children?'

'They were spared. Left there.'

'Why?'

Don shook his head, trying to dislodge the memories. 'I don't know. To suffer? Because it was more cruel? I don't know.'

'What happened to them?'

'They were put into care.' Another sigh. Don really wanted a drink now. 'But that wasn't much better than the Garden had been. And they didn't even have their parents with them.' Don's voice shook. He struggled to get it under control. 'The girl . . . the little girl died. She wasn't well. Wasn't strong. She . . . she couldn't last.'

Phil hesitated before speaking. Wanting to hear the answer, but dreading it also. 'And . . . and . . . the boy?'

Don's eyes locked with his.

'I'm looking at him,' he said.

81

Mickey Philips lay on his side, mouth open, gently snoring. Lynn Windsor propped herself up on one elbow, watched him sleep.

It had been a good night. She had to admit that. Her expectations hadn't been high before he had called, but Mickey had surprised her. He was strong, manly; yes, she had expected that given the way he was and the job he did. But what she hadn't expected was his tenderness. And his attentiveness towards her. His confidence as a lover. She had never come just by being touched, had always found it difficult. But the way Mickey touched her ... And as for his oral skills ... she had never felt anything like it. Probably the best orgasm she had ever experienced.

So she watched him sleep. Not with love or tenderness, but with regret. Because this was the first and last time she would have him here.

She moved the duvet back, slid slowly out of bed. Naked, she walked round to where Mickey had left his clothes, throwing them in a heap on the floor in a hurry to be with her. She worked her way through his pockets. Looking for something specific. Found it in his trousers.

His iPhone.

She had told him he had better switch it off; that they didn't want to be disturbed. There had been a slight conflict in his features, but she had done something with her hips and arranged her underwear in such a way as to win the argument hands down. He had done what she had asked, Lynn watching, memorising his numerical pass code as he did so. Now she turned it on. Keyed in the number when asked. Waited. The icons came up. She went straight into his missed messages, his voicemail. Checked it. Several calls asking him to come back to work. There was an emergency. Lynn had smiled. She knew just what that would be. She deleted them all. Then she found his texts, started scrolling through.

There were plenty. She deleted all the ones from work, requesting he come back. Then she checked the others. Most were mundane, arranging drinks in the pub, five-a-side, that kind of thing. But one stuck out. Exactly the kind of thing she had been looking for. She read it:

Adam Weaver. Got some info on him. Business stuff. Import-export business with that Lithuanian bloke Balchunas. Harwich. Shipment coming in tonight. CALL ME NOW. IMPORTANT. AND BRING YOUR WALLET. Stuart

Anger stabbed at her, mingling with panic. Her face contorted with anger, eyes fiery slits.

How did he know? How? And who was Stuart? She felt herself breathing heavily, her hands shaking as she held the phone. She looked over at Mickey lying asleep in her bed. It would be so easy, she thought. Just to walk over there, cut his throat while he slept. No more Stuart, no more information he wasn't supposed to have.

Mickey stirred in his sleep, turned over.

She looked again at the message, concentrated. Decided what she could do about it. Really do about it. Got it.

She worked quickly through his contacts. Stuart was listed as: Stuart CI. Confidential Informant. Not much of a code name. She deleted his number, put her own in, checking first that he didn't have it. Then she got her own phone out and wrote him a text:

Adam Weaver. Got some info on him. Seriously gangstered up in Lithuania. Lots of enemies. Word is he was killed by Lithuanian hitman. Back in Lithuania by now. No need to call. Stuart

Pressed send. Heard his phone ping.

At the sound of the text coming through, Mickey stirred. Looking around, Lynn quickly replaced his phone in his trousers, remembering to turn it off again first. He turned over, opened his eyes.

'What you doin'?' Voice full of sleep.

'Just going to the bathroom. Back in a mo.'

'Don't be too long.'

She quickly went into the bathroom, waited a while until she thought he would be asleep again. She still had to re-input his informant's number in his phone, take hers out. She couldn't do that if he was awake.

When she came back out into the bedroom, he was sitting up in bed, waiting for her.

'Missed you,' he said, pulling back the duvet.

She gave him a smile, slid in alongside him. Looked down at his erection. Summoned up a smile.

'Don't you ever stop?' She giggled as she said it.

'With you here? Nope.'

She felt his arms round her, his mouth on her body. He

would never check, she thought. His phone. Never connect it with her. Or at least she hoped not.

She lay back, felt him work his magic on her body once more.

Abandoned all earlier thoughts she had had about him. Compartmentalised her rage at him, let it go.

It'll be a shame to miss this, she thought. *A real shame.*

But some things are more important.

82

The boy was scared. Terrified. But back in the cage where
he belonged.

The Gardener stood at the other side of the bars, studied
him. Head to one side, beneath the hood he was smiling.

'Back where you belong ... Thought you'd got away, did
you? Eh? No ... you're too important. Yes ... Too important.
The future of the Garden depends on you ... Yes ...'

The boy pulled away, sat at the back, staring. Trying not to
cry, not even to whimper.

The Gardener turned, surveyed the space. This was good.
This was *right*. He didn't know why he hadn't thought of it
before.

It had been a struggle, getting everything in, especially
since he couldn't go the other way, his usual way. The police
still had that blocked off. But he already had enough of the
things he needed to hand. Another tool set. Another workbench. Already there. And the walls had the symbols on them.
Of course they did. That had been one of the first things he
had done when he moved in.

The symbols. The cycle of life. The seasons of life. Birth to death to rebirth. And on. And on. Paul had taught him well. Made him understand.

Paul. He could hear him now, from where he was. Crying softly, pleading. He ignored him. Looked at the symbols.

Everything had its season, everything had its time. Everything in the garden lived, everything died. Paul's words. And the Gardener had taken them to heart. Because the Gardener wanted the Garden to continue. And it had done. But not without sacrifices.

Every season. Every solstice. Every equinox. A child had to be sacrificed in order for the Garden to continue to flourish, to thrive. He had made the rest of the Elders understand that. If they wanted to do what they did with the Garden, he had to be responsible for making it grow, keeping it alive.

And he had done. For years. So many, he had lost count. Select an offspring, prepare it, sacrifice it. And keep the Garden alive.

The offering was never wasted. Blood and bone and flesh were reused, put back to work. It helped feed the Garden. It helped it grow. Made it strong. And it needed it now. More than ever. That was why this boy – this sacrifice – was so important. Because he had been there. Had seen for himself what was happening. The Garden was dying.

The rest of the Elders could talk, about new blood, about revitalisation, about all those things. But if he didn't keep the sacrifices going, if he didn't appease the earth the Garden grew in, it would never flourish again. And it had to.

It had to.

There was another reason for the sacrifices.

He enjoyed them.

Fed on the screams, the cries. Luxuriated in the blood. The power.

All seasons under his control. Birth, death and rebirth. All down to him.

At his behest.

He turned back to the boy, who cowered away from him. Chain rattling and clanking as he did so.

'You should be honoured,' he said. 'You have been chosen. Soon. Soon . . . '

He turned away once more.

Ignored the boy's cries.

Ignored Paul's.

Went to pick some flowers.

83

Phil felt numb. Like his body had become disconnected from his brain, the nerve endings deadened, unresponsive. The room seemed to tunnel away from him. He was viewing his partner and the man he had regarded as his father from the wrong end of a telescope.

The feeling didn't last. The raging conflicting emotions that Don's announcement had triggered in him had built up and were now unleashed, adrenalin crashing into his system, like the kind of rush he would get from a car crash.

He didn't know who to look at, to speak to first. His eyes swivelled, settled on Marina.

'You knew?' he said, the adrenalin becoming knife-like, stabbing him, bleeding internal betrayal, 'You knew?'

'Just before you did,' she said, eyes imploring him to believe her, not wanting to hurt him even more. 'Don and I talked, just before we came to the hospital. I said you should be told.'

There was nothing more he could say to her. He turned to Don. He knew there were more subtle, complex emotions that his body and mind were struggling to get him to feel, but he couldn't process them at the moment. For now he wanted to feel something direct, something visceral. He felt the anger rise within him once more.

'You knew,' he said, his voice dangerously low, 'you knew all this time. All those years. All my life ... ' His hands twisted and twined. 'And you never said anything ... '

Don sighed, shook his head. Looked at the floor, then back to Phil before continuing. 'We thought it best ... you didn't know.' His voice weary, tired.

Phil nodded, lips pulled tightly across his mouth. 'Right. So ... ' Hands still twisting. 'Every time ... every time I asked about my parents, my real parents, you told me you didn't know.'

Don said nothing, found the floor between his feet fascinating.

Phil kept going. 'Every time ... you talked me out of going. Out of going to look for them. Every time. When I was younger. Every time ... '

Don looked up. Pain in his eyes. He seemed to be hurting as much as Phil was himself. His face appeared frozen in pain, unable to release the words he wanted to say.

'You always said I'd never find them,' Phil continued. 'That you'd tried and they didn't want to be found. That they were nowhere in the system. Every time ... You lied to me, Don ... Lied to me ... And a sister ... a sister ... '

'It was better you didn't know ... ' Tears had sprung into Don's eyes as he found his voice.

'Better?' Phil gave a harsh, bitter laugh. 'Better? Shouldn't that have been my decision?'

Don said nothing, mouth contorting once more.

Phil's voice was getting louder. 'Shouldn't it?'

'No.' Don's voice as loud as Phil's. 'Perhaps if it had been an ordinary adoption, yes. If there is such a thing. But not in this case. No.'

'Why not?' Shouting now.

'Because you weren't there ... You didn't see what I saw ...' Don's voice ragged, breaking. His hand went to his face, rubbing his eyes, tears streaming round the edges of his fists.

Silence fell once more, hitting the room with the force of a bomb. The three of them sat, barely moving. Questions rising like fearful bubbles in Phil's mind, letting them pop, dissolve away, unanswered.

But not all of them.

He turned to Marina. 'The nightmares,' he said. 'The designs on the wall. The cage. The guy in the mask.' Hands twisting, locking and unlocking once more. 'Why? Why all of that?'

'Because they were real,' she said, voice calm and low. Soothing him. 'They were all part of your life. Aspects of your life.'

'But I ... I didn't know. I couldn't remember any of it ...'

'No,' she said, 'you wouldn't. You were very young at the time. Your mind was still forming. And if you'd been lucky, it might not have left any impression. But because the memories were so horrific, so traumatic, your brain just ... shut them off. Buried them. Repressed them deep inside you.'

Phil nodded.

'So why now ...'

'Like I said, it was too horrific. Your mind buried the past, but you still experienced it. It couldn't get rid of it completely. It can't. Because it still happened to you. So the memories lay dormant somewhere within your mind. Buried at the back. Just waiting for some trigger, some event to spark them off again. And this was it.'

'Right ...' Phil's mind was buzzing. Like a nest of wasps in his head. Marina spoke, cutting through the noise.

'Can you remember your parents at all?'

Phil closed his eyes. All he could hear was the humming. 'No . . .'

'Probably just as well,' she said. 'If you were there when they were killed . . . that won't be a memory you'll be in a hurry to access.'

The wave of anger was receding within Phil. But questions were still buzzing and fizzing, his head aching from everything he had to process. He didn't know what to think, what to say. What question to ask first. Don and Marina said nothing. Waited.

'The panic attacks,' he said eventually. 'Are they connected? Do they have anything to do with . . . all this?'

'I would imagine so,' said Marina. 'Displacement. Because your childhood trauma was repressed, you've never dealt with it, never been able to confront it head on. It's always been there; it's just attacked you in different ways.'

'And the job doesn't help,' said Don.

Phil nodded. His body seemed to be relaxing more now, the adrenalin leaching out of his system. He was starting to feel weary. Another question occurred to him.

'The hotel. Why did I think I'd been there before?'

'Because you had,' said Don. 'You used to live there. That hotel was where the Garden used to be.'

Phil sighed. Rubbed his forehead with the back of his hand. Silence fell once more.

Eventually Don spoke.

'I'm . . . sorry, son. I didn't . . . didn't know what to do for the best. Me or your mother.' He corrected himself. 'Eileen.'

Phil was now beyond tiredness. He managed a weary smile. 'It's OK,' he said. 'I can still call her mother.'

Don nodded. Gave a small smile. Looked at Marina, who warily returned it.

'It's going to take me an awfully long time to come to terms with this,' Phil said. 'A hell of a long time. But I'll try my best.' He dredged up another smile. 'Something Marina always says. Family is more than biology.' He sighed. 'Yeah . . .'

He felt Marina's hand on his. 'I think it's time for bed,' she said.

Phil, almost asleep by now, just nodded.

84

Mickey keyed himself in, opened the office door, entered. He had left Lynn's early, stopped off at his flat to change clothes and grab a quick shower. She had said he could have one at her flat, even offered to share it with him. He had been tempted. Very tempted. But had refused in the end. Night-time lust was one thing. But the morning mindset was something else. He even thought he sensed relief from Lynn that he had declined. Obviously she took her work seriously too. Something else they had in common.

As he had driven away, he had felt guilty for some reason. Not because of anything he had done, or that Lynn had done – he had thoroughly enjoyed himself. They both had. He kept re-enacting scenes over and over in his head, replaying the best bits – and there were many – on the drive to work. And in the shower before that. But something was niggling at him. Something still felt wrong.

He knew what it was, but he didn't want to admit it to himself. He had slept with someone who was involved – even tangentially – in the investigation he was working on. And he could have compromised that investigation by doing so.

Pulling through the gates of the station and parking up, he tried to banish those thoughts from his head. Concentrate on the good bits instead. They should see him through the day. Or at least until he could see Lynn again. Not that they had made arrangements, but he was sure it was only a matter of time. It had to be.

Entering the office with takeaway coffee, he was immediately hit by the activity. The noise, the bustle. It hadn't been like this the day before. What had happened? Had the investigation made a breakthrough in some way? And if it had, why hadn't someone let him know about it? He looked round, hoping someone could tell him, bring him up to speed. Wondering what it was he should know.

He didn't have to wait long. Glass had seen him enter, was striding towards him. Face like a lightning-struck tree.

'Where the bloody hell have you been?' Said loud enough to make others stop what they were doing, stare at Mickey.

Mickey frowned. 'Sorry?'

Glass crossed the office, reached him. 'I said where the hell have you been? Don't you answer your phone?'

'Yeah, course. It never rang. It's been on all night.' His eyes darted away from Glass's face, not wanting to be caught out in a lie. He knew he had turned it off the night before, at Lynn's insistence. Something else to feel guilty about, if he allowed it. But he had turned it back on before leaving her flat this morning. And there'd been nothing showing. No missed calls, no voicemail, no messages. Except one from Stuart that he hadn't had time to check. He took the phone out of his pocket, held it up for Glass to see. 'No new messages, no missed calls, no voicemails. See? Nothing.'

Glass seemed to be temporarily lost for words. He stared at Mickey, narrowing his eyes. 'You'd better not be lying to me, DS Philips.'

'Why would I lie? What do I have to gain from that? I showed you the phone; nobody called me. Or if they did, they didn't have the right number.'

Glass stared once more, unblinking, as if that was all the answer Mickey was going to get.

Mickey had to ask. 'So what's happened? What have I missed?'

Glass gave a snort masquerading as a laugh. 'What haven't you missed, you mean. Briefing room. Five minutes.'

He made to walk away. Mickey stopped him. 'Where's Phil?'

A smile twitched at the corners of Glass's mouth. 'Suspended, DS Philips. If you'd left your phone on, you would know.' He walked off.

Mickey stared after him, mouth open, wondering whether he had just heard him right.

Phil? Suspended?

Shaking his head, he made his way to his desk. Sat down, still trying to get his head round the news.

He took a sip of his coffee.

Was struck by another thought. If they'd been calling him all night, even though his phone had been switched off, where had all the calls gone?

He shook his head, tried to get his mind in gear, prepare for the morning briefing.

85

Marina watched Mickey enter the briefing room. He looked over at her, frowning, quizzical. Questions in his face.

He knows about Phil, she thought. Knows he's been suspended and wants to know why. But he doesn't know everything. He doesn't know the night I've just had . . .

Mickey sat down, still watching her. She returned his look, not able to say anything, not even sure what she was supposed to be conveying. She didn't smile.

Glass entered. Brisk, businesslike. Placed a folder on the desk, stood before it, eyes sweeping the room. Marina detected a twitch of a smile at the corners of his mouth. It just made her despise the man even more. Especially in light of what Don had told her about him yesterday.

'Right,' said Glass, 'let's get started. Run through what's been happening.' His eyes locked on to Mickey's. 'Especially for those of you who don't know.'

Marina saw Mickey's face redden, his eyes harden. How to alienate your staff in one go, she thought. Very impressive people-management skills.

'Finn, the boy who was found in the cellar on East Hill, was forcibly taken from the General Hospital yesterday evening. The person who abducted him ...' he looked down at his notes, 'Samuel Lister, was an executive at the hospital. No prior convictions, no previous arrests, nothing. Clean as. As you're all probably aware, he handed the child over to person or persons unknown and killed himself in the car park.'

Marina watched Mickey's response. He looked round the room, an undercurrent of desperation to his actions. 'Where's Anni?'

Glass stared at him.

'Detective Constable Anni Hepburn. Where is she?'

Glass sighed as if Mickey was no more than an irritant. 'Detective Constable Hepburn is undergoing treatment in the General for a gunshot wound received during the abduction of the boy.'

'Is she OK?'

'She's well. The wound wasn't serious, as far as we can gather.'

Relief flooded through Mickey's body. He slumped back into his seat. Glass looked down at his notes once more, continued. 'Jenny Swan, the child psychologist working with the boy, hasn't been so lucky. She's in intensive care. It's touch-and-go. Right. Updates.'

'What about the person who drove the boy away?' said Jane Gosling. 'Any news?'

'Just getting to that.' Glass looked towards Adrian Wren. 'Adrian?'

Adrian Wren stood up. 'Nothing much on CCTV,' he said. He took out photos from a file on the desk before him, handed them round. 'This is the image from the hospital's cameras of the vehicle driving away. As you can see, it's a green four-by-four, a Range Rover. Old, well-used. I've tried to get close-ups of the driver and any passengers there might be.' He handed out another photo. Marina looked at it. The driver's face was obscured. And where the passenger's head should have been was just a shapeless, faceless mass of darkness.

The hood, she thought. He was wearing the hood.

'It looks like he's wearing something over his face,' said Adrian. 'Making sure we can't see him.'

'A hood,' said Marina. All eyes turned to her. 'It was a hood. I saw it first hand at the hospital. Looked like it was made out of sacking, hessian, something like that.'

'That rules out a joke-shop mask, then,' said Mickey.

'We only had a partial on the number plate. We've put it through the computer but can't get a match. We reckon the plates were stolen, if not the vehicle itself.'

'What about CCTV from the town?'

'We've looked. Nothing. Either they took a route out of town that avoided the cameras, or they've gone to ground somewhere. DCI Glass gave chase but lost them. He's given a description of the car to all uniforms. We've had the helicopter out looking for it. Nothing. But we're still looking.'

He sat down again.

'Thank you, Adrian,' said Glass. He turned to Mickey. 'DS Philips. Your turn.'

Mickey stood up. Marina could tell he wasn't happy. She wondered whether he would use this opportunity to say something, or whether he would just make his report.

He opened his mouth to speak.

She would soon find out.

86

Phil opened his eyes.

And in those first few, blissful seconds he was nothing. Could have been anyone, anywhere. His identity as yet unwritten, his mind still clinging to sleep, not yet caught up to his waking body. It didn't stay that way for long. Within seconds he knew where he was, what had happened.

And who he was.

He groaned, turned over. Closed his eyes again.

He replayed the events of the previous night once more, stopping to examine them in close-up detail. Again and again, over and over. Trying to work out what he thought, what he felt. Whether everything being out in the open now was a relief to him, had put his mind at rest over his parentage, or whether it had just brought along another layer of problems, of uncertainties.

Eventually he sighed, opened his eyes. Can't lie here all day, he thought, sitting upright. Then remembered he was suspended.

With another sigh, he flopped back down on the pillow. Found another level of unhappiness just for that. He checked the time. Realised Marina must have left him to sleep. He listened. No Josephina. He remembered. She had stayed at Don and Eileen's last night.

Not wanting to spend the day lying in bed, he threw the duvet off, got up. His problems wouldn't be solved by staying there all day. But he still needed somewhere to go, something to do.

He went into the bathroom, turned on the shower.

Smiled.

He knew where he could go first.

87

Mickey stood up. Looked round the briefing room. Too many empty chairs, he thought. Too many missing faces. Then looked at Glass. Too many faces here I'd rather not see.

He glanced down at his notes, back to the room.

'Any news on the murder of Adam Weaver?' Glass looked at him, waiting for an answer.

Mickey paused. Remembered the text message from Stuart. It didn't seem right, he thought. He didn't know whether that was because it wasn't what he had expected to hear or because it wasn't what he had wanted to hear. Perhaps both. It didn't feel right. But it was what he had heard, so he had to share it with the team.

'I've been asking around,' he said to the room. 'Put a few feelers out. And I've had something back from an informant.'

Glass leaned forward, interested.

'Nothing much, just saying that he hasn't heard anything locally about it. Reckons the word going round is that it was a hit. A professional hit.'

'From here?' asked Glass.

'From Lithuania,' said Mickey, trying to mask the disbelief in his voice. 'That's all he's heard.'

Glass nodded. 'That runs current with my thinking, too,' he said. 'If that's the case – and it's looking increasingly like it is – then I think we can safely say the killer is back in Lithuania by now.'

'Yeah,' said Mickey by way of agreement, 'but it still doesn't add up. The way he was killed, the murder weapon, none of it points to a professional hit.'

'Why not?' said Glass.

'Because it was a knife, for a start,' Mickey said. 'You'd have to get close up to do that. And if you want to get close up, the other word that goes along with that is personal. A hitman would have used a bullet, done it from a distance. Quick and clean. Then gone.'

'Maybe they do things differently in the east,' said Glass, hint of a smile.

'And there's also the amount of blows. Nick Lines still hasn't come up with a definite number. At last count it was about twenty. All this screams out that Weaver knew his killer. That it was personal.'

'Yet all you've heard points to the contrary,' said Glass. He seemed to be thinking, deeply. Came to a decision. 'Right, DS Philips. If you've got intuition on something, I always think it's best to let it play out. So keep looking into it.'

'Thank you, sir.'

'But don't expect too much. And don't stop looking into the other angles too.'

'Right, sir.'

'Thank you, DS Philips.'

Mickey, clearly unhappy, sat down. Jane Gosling leaned across to him. 'Looks like someone's going to get a free holiday in Vilnius,' she said. 'Toss you for it.'

Mickey smiled, sat back.

Glass was looking round once more. 'Marina?'

Marina checked her notes, stood up. Mickey looked at her. She was well-dressed as usual, made-up. But she looked drawn, haggard. Like she had been up all night. Mickey remembered how she and Phil had looked when they came into work the previous day. Together, but apart. He didn't like to speculate on what was going on between the two of them. But he didn't think it was anything good.

'OK,' she said, 'I've now made a full analysis of the markings on both the cellar wall and the house opposite. I've cross-referenced them with every existing bit of data I could get my hands on and I think I can state, quite confidently, that they are calendars.'

She handed out photos of the wall markings.

'At first I thought they might be influenced by the zodiac, but that's not the case. They're seasonal.' She held the photo up, pointed to the relevant section. 'See here? This is the summer solstice. And here? The autumnal equinox. And so on. The way it's been positioned on the wall has the equinox at the top. If you look closely, you'll see that it's been painted over. Made to rotate. Whichever event is happening is always the uppermost one.'

'When's the autumnal equinox, then?' asked Mickey.

'Good question,' said Marina. 'Now. Today's the last day of it. And based on what we've discovered so far about the boy and what he's told us about his life – which isn't much, to be honest – I think it's safe to say that we've got a serial killer operating here.'

88

Glass looked sceptical. 'Without wanting to bring any of your calculations and conclusions into doubt, Ms Esposito, because I'm sure they're all perfectly valid, I have to ask, are you sure about this?'

'Yes. I am. I wouldn't make a statement such as that lightly.'

'I'm sure you wouldn't, but a serial killer . . . '

'I've dealt with them before . . . '

Mickey saw her hesitate. He could tell why. She didn't want to use Glass's first name, too familiar. Nor did she want to use his rank. Too formal. She settled for not saying his name at all.

'So I do believe I know what I'm talking about.'

'What's the evidence?'

'Well, circumstantial, I'll admit. But we found that child in a cage on the equinox. The cellar was prepared and dressed for the enactment of a ritual.'

'We've had preliminary DNA back,' said Adrian. 'That was definitely blood on the workbench and the tools.'

'Thank you,' said Marina. 'It was set for a ritual murder. And based on calculations made using the calendar on the wall, whoever does this does it at regular intervals. Four times a year. Multiply that by however many years he's been doing it . . . ' She shrugged. 'Serial killer.'

'And why would he do it?' asked Glass. 'What would he get out of it?'

'I don't know,' said Marina. 'This one seems a little hazy. Obviously the main reason is because he enjoys it. Whatever self-justification they use, however they dress it up, the bottom line is because it gives them a sexual thrill. But there's something more to this one than that. The calendar, the tools . . . I think he believes he's doing this for a reason. An important reason. Find that out and we're well on the way to finding him.'

Glass nodded. 'Good. Thank you.'

'There's something else,' Marina said. 'The window of opportunity. As I said, today is the last day of the autumn equinox. Finn, the boy, was abducted from the hospital last night. The killer wants this ritual to go ahead. We have to find where he is by midnight tonight to have any hope of seeing that boy alive again.'

Silence round the room.

'He'll have somewhere else,' she continued. 'Not the East Hill place, but somewhere like it. Find that and you find him. And hopefully the boy.'

'Do we know where?' asked Glass.

'No,' said Marina. 'But I'm setting up a geographical profile. See what I can get from that.'

'If he's been killing all this time,' asked Jane, 'where are the bodies?'

'Good question,' said Marina.

'We've had the radar out in the wasteland between the two houses,' said Adrian. 'Nothing yet, but they're still trying. The bodies have to be somewhere.'

'Thank you,' said Glass.

Marina sat down. Mickey watched her. There was something she was holding back, he thought. Something she had kept to herself. He didn't judge her for it, just wondered why. After all, he was doing the same thing himself.

'Well, there we have it,' said Glass. 'That's where we are at the moment. I want the boy to be our number-one priority. Find the car. Find him. Stop whoever this is from doing whatever it is he wants to do.'

Well put, thought Mickey, leaning back, arms folded.

'I've put in a request for extra staff,' Glass continued. 'Hopefully they should be with us later today.' He swept the room with his eyes once more, making sure he had made contact with everyone. 'As most of you are probably aware, Detective Inspector Brennan is suspended from duty and will take no further part in this investigation. I realise that will come as something of a shock to you. But please believe me when I tell you I had no choice. He was insubordinate and his judgement just plain wrong. He could have put this investigation into severe jeopardy, and even worse, put your lives in danger. I'm afraid he left me with no choice.'

Glass sighed as he spoke, like he had just made the most difficult decision of his life. Mickey didn't believe a word of it.

'In the meantime, Detective Sergeant Philips will be running both investigations – and MIS – and reporting directly to me.'

Mickey looked up, unable to hide the surprise on his face.

'Any questions?'

There weren't.

'Good.' Glass stood up. 'Everyone has a job to do. Let's do it. And see if we can save that little boy's life.'

The team stood up, started filing out. Glass stayed where he was.

'Marina? Could I have a word, please?'

Marina nodded, turned to follow Glass.

Mickey didn't know what that was about. But he doubted it was anything good.

89

'H^{ey.}'

Anni slowly opened her eyes, looked up. It took a long time for them to focus, but when they did, she managed a small smile.

Hi,' she said, her eyes closing again.

Phil sat down on a bedside chair. Anni was in a private room in the General. Three quarters of one wall was given over to windows. It was tranquil, restful. Bright and airy. The opposite of Finn's darkened room.

Phil had had trouble dressing to come out. His working clothes were far more casual than most people's, so he could just have put them on. But if he did that, he would feel like a fraud for not going to work. So he had compromised. Jeans, Converses, jacket and T-shirt instead of collar and tie.

'How are you feeling?' he asked, his voice low, so as not to disturb her.

She opened her eyes once more. 'Like I've been shot,' she said, smiling again.

Phil returned the smile. 'Does it hurt?'

'Not much.' Her speech was slurred. 'Would be a lot worse

if they hadn't pumped me so full of morphine. Mmm ...'
Another dreamy smile, eyes closing once more.

Phil had spoken to the nurse on his way in. Anni had been
rushed straight into surgery and operated on. The bullet
had gone through her body, leaving a nearly clean trail. It had
slightly nicked her shoulder blade. The bone fragments
had been found, the wound patched up.

'They say the bullet didn't hit anything too important,' she
said, her voice dreamy. 'But it's going to hurt like hell once the
drugs wear off.'

'You'd better stay on them, then.'

'Is that any kind of advice for my boss to be giving me?' She
managed a small laugh. 'Should be ... ashamed of yourself ...'

Talking seemed to become an effort. Phil sat silently beside
her, waiting until she drew strength, felt like speaking once
more.

Anni's eyes opened again. Not without effort; a frown
creased her forehead. 'Where's Mickey? Why hasn't he come
to see me?'

Phil found her concern touching. Knew that neither of
them would ever admit how they felt about the other, no
matter how obvious it was to everyone else on the team.
'Don't know,' he said. 'I haven't heard from him. Maybe he
doesn't know yet.'

Another frown. 'You haven't heard from him? Why?'

'I've been suspended, Anni, remember? I'm no longer in
charge of the investigation. Or MIS.'

Her eyes closed once more. 'Oh. Right.'

'That's it? Oh right? I thought you'd be a bit more concerned than that.'

'I am,' she said. 'Very. And I'm sure I'd show it if I wasn't
so heavily medicated.'

They both smiled.

'Glass. Never liked that man.'

'Have to agree with you.'

Another frown creased her forehead. 'Jenny Swan ... she was in the room too. He got her first. How is she?'

Phil rubbed his chin. 'Not good. I spoke to the nurse. It's still touch-and-go. Lister might have been a bad shot with you, but he was closer to Jenny Swan. She wasn't so lucky.'

Anni managed a small nod. Said nothing.

They sat in silence for a while. Eventually Anni broke it.

'She was reaching him. Finn. I'm sure she was.'

'How?'

'She'd managed to communicate with him, got him talking. Got him opening up.'

Phil said nothing. Waited. Anni marshalled her strength, kept talking.

'Apparently he lived in the Garden ... ' she said.

'Right,' said Phil, a shiver running through him at her words. 'But the Garden was a commune. It ... it vanished years ago.'

'Don't know about that,' she said. 'He said that's where he lived. The Garden.'

Phil tried to keep the eagerness, the desperation from his voice. 'Did he say where it was? What it was like?'

'Said it was ... metal. All metal.'

'Metal? What, you mean indoors?'

'Always inside, he said. Never out. That's one of the reasons he was so freaked out by coming here. Said he'd never seen outdoors before. I mean he didn't say it like that, but that's what he meant.'

'My God ... '

'Yeah. Said the light told them when to get up and when to go to bed.'

'The light?'

'Artificial light, we reckoned.'

'Was he . . . I don't know, underground? Did he give any clues as to where this place was?'

Anni shook her head. Her face creased. The movement had hurt her. 'No. Just . . . said . . . there was a lot of coughing. People always coughing. Lot of . . . It sounded like they didn't live that long.'

Phil sat back, trying to process what she had said, the words spinning round his mind.

He looked down at her once more. The effort of talking had severely weakened her. She was almost asleep. He didn't want to stay any longer, hamper her recovery.

'I'd better go,' he said.

She gave a dreamy nod.

'I'll come back and see you, though.'

Another slow nod. 'Bring Mickey . . . '

'I will.'

He stood up. Not knowing whether to give her hand a squeeze or even kiss her on the forehead. Just something, some human interaction to show that he cared. He squeezed her hand. She smiled. And slipped away into sleep.

He left her.

Walking back to his car, he realised he hadn't checked his voicemail for a whole day. He took his phone out, called. Listened.

His eyes widened, face changed expression.

Then he ran to his car as fast as he could.

90

'You wanted to see me.'

Marina had followed Glass into his office. Stood before the desk. He had sat down, looked at his computer screen, checked a file lying open in front of him. Trying to make her feel like a subordinate, she thought. Make himself feel superior. She didn't have time for his games.

No reply.

She checked her watch, turned for the door. 'You're obviously busy,' she said. 'I'll come back later.'

Glass looked up quickly. 'No, no. We'll do this now.'

She turned. Waited. His choice of words didn't fill her with confidence.

'Take a seat.'

'I'd rather stand. I'm in the middle of something and have to get back to it.'

Glass had to concede defeat. But it was clear he didn't like it. 'As you wish. Now I'm a big admirer of your work, Marina. Excellent. Out there, in the briefing, the conclusions you reached, the empirical evidence you based them on, great. I know a lot of officers in the force can't see the need for a psychologist, especially a full-time one, on the payroll, but I'm not one of them. It's the way forward, definitely.'

He sat back. Marina, taking that as her cue to speak, did so. 'Thank you.'

There's a 'but' coming, she thought. He's just preparing me for it.

'However,' he said.

A 'however' not a 'but'. She raised her eyebrow. Glass didn't notice.

'I'm afraid I can't have you on the team at the moment.'

Anger buzzed inside her at his words. She pushed it down, controlled it. Directed it.

'Why not?'

He opened his hands as if that explained everything. 'Because of who your partner is,' he said. 'You're compromised.'

She tried to keep the anger down. Failed. 'I'm sorry? Because of who my partner is? Would you say that to a male member of staff?'

Glass looked genuinely puzzled. 'What does that have to do with anything?'

She moved towards the desk, towering over him. 'You wouldn't say that to a male member of staff about his partner, because you'd assume he could manage to make decisions and reach independent conclusions without asking the little woman. But obviously you don't think I can do the same.'

'I never said—'

'Doesn't that sound like sexism to you? It does to me. And I'm sure my union rep would think so.'

Glass looked flustered. Clearly this wasn't the way he had intended the meeting to go. Marina had the advantage. She pressed it.

'Is my professionalism being called into question? Am I not doing my job at the level expected of me?'

'Well, yes . . .'

'Yes. I would think so. Especially as you've just sat there and said as much before taking me off the investigation. If you think I'm not capable of doing my job, then fair enough, but—'

The door opened. Mickey entered. He looked between the two of them, sensed the atmosphere.

'Sorry, sir,' he said to Glass. 'I'll come back later.'

'You may as well stay, Mickey,' Marina said, turning to him. 'Our leader here is just suspending me.'

'What?'

'Apparently I'm compromised. Not because of my work, you understand, but because of who I live with. That renders me incapable of working efficiently.'

Glass stood up. Clearly angry now. 'I only said—'

Mickey cut him off. 'No. I'm sorry, sir, but you're wrong.'

Glass looked like he couldn't believe what he was hearing. 'What? What did you say to me?'

'Marina is a very valuable member of the team, sir. Highly rated, with a proven track record.'

'We can get another psychologist in, if that's what you—'

'We've done that before, sir. It didn't end well. There's no other psychologist I'd rather have working alongside me.'

'Are you questioning my decision, DS Philips?'

'I suppose I must be, sir.'

'As your superior officer—'

'With all due respect, sir, I'm in charge of this team. You put me in charge yourself. And as the leader of this investigation, I want Marina to stay. She's too valuable to lose.'

Glass stared at the pair of them. Marina saw the anger in his eyes turn to hatred. His hands started twitching. She could well imagine what he wanted to do with those hands.

He couldn't speak. Too angry. Instead he walked round the desk, pushed his way past and out the door. They watched him stride across the main office and through the double doors. He tried to slam them but they wouldn't allow it.

Neither of them spoke for a few seconds. Then Marina turned to Mickey.

'Thank you.'

He smiled, sighing with relief. 'No problem. I'm not having him get rid of another one.'

'Good.'

'But,' said Mickey with a smile, 'it's time to get back to work.'

Marina gave a mock salute. 'Yes, sir.'

She walked out of the office, back to her own desk.

91

'Here,' said Phil. 'This is the one.'

Phil stood on the pavement outside Donna Warren's house. Don beside him. They both stopped, stared at it.

'Looks empty,' said Don.

'Yeah.' Phil walked up the front path. 'I'll knock anyway.'

He had phoned Don as soon as he had listened to his voicemail. He couldn't believe who it was from.

'Hi,' she had started, clearly uneasy. 'It's . . . Rose Martin. Detective Sergeant Rose Martin, in case you've forgotten, which I doubt you have. Or I should say, Detective Inspector.' Then a sigh. 'If that's actually real. Anyway. I'm . . . I need to talk to you. About Glass. Brian Glass. He's your DCI now.' Another pause while she tried to find the correct words. 'Don't trust him. Really. Seriously, don't trust him. He's dirty. Bent. And I've got evidence. There's a book. It's here. In my hand. It's . . . you wouldn't believe it. The stuff in it. You just . . . ' Another sigh. Then a laugh. 'I can't believe I'm calling you. You, of all people.' Another laugh. 'Considering how much I fucking hate you. And you know that. That's not news.' Another sigh. 'But you're honest. And I can trust you.

And I need someone I can trust.' She paused again. When she spoke, it sounded like the words were reluctant to come. Her voice small and hesitant. Stumbling. 'And you did save my life. And I never really thanked you for that. Not with everything ... ' She cleared her throat. 'Anyway. I'm rambling.' Then her voice stronger, back to business. 'Listen. This is important. If you don't hear from me again, come to this address.' She gave out the address of the house they were now standing outside. 'Meet Donna. Donna Warren. Talk to her. She'll tell you everything. And she'll have the book. It's a cheap blue exercise book. You must get it. Read it.' Another pause. 'I'm going to call him now. Glass. Give him a chance to explain himself. To turn himself in. It not ... ' A longer pause. So long that Phil thought she must have hung up. When she spoke again, her voice was uneven. 'Nice knowing you. Well it wasn't, but you know what I mean.' Then the sound of the line going dead. Quickly.

Phil had checked the time of the call, tried to remember where he'd been, what he'd been doing. He'd been at the hospital, talking to Samuel. He remembered that Glass's phone had rung at the same time. He knew who that would have been. Glass had disappeared straight afterwards.

He had phoned Don.

'Not gone in to work?' he had asked him.

'Reckon they can do without me for one day,' Don had replied. 'Reckon you might need me more.'

Phil hadn't answered.

He had met Don on Barrack Street. Played him the voicemail.

'What d'you think?' he had asked him.

'Sounds legit,' the ex-copper had said. 'On the level. She wouldn't have gone to all that trouble of calling you, you especially, if it wasn't important.'

Phil agreed.

'And Glass . . . ' said Don. 'I reckon she's right about him.'

'How d'you mean?'

'I've got my doubts about him too. Had them for years.'

Phil had stared at him.

'I was going to share them with you.'

'When?' said Phil, bitterness in his voice. 'When I was older?'

'Sorry.' Don sighed. 'Look, how are you? Bearing up, I mean.'

'I'm fine,' said Phil, clearly lying. 'Jim Dandy.'

'Maybe we should—'

'We'll talk later. Let's deal with this first.'

He knocked on the door. They waited for a reply. There wasn't one.

He tried again, harder this time. He received nothing but sore knuckles.

'Not in,' said Don.

Phil stepped away from the door, cupped his hands round his face, peered in through the filthy front window.

He straightened up, looked at Don.

'We'd better break in,' he said.

92

Mickey was back at his desk. Doing what he hated most. Paperwork. Or rather electronic work, as most of the things he was following up were all online.

He had kept his head down after Glass had stormed out, and in the absence of anything else happening, or any other leads to follow up, kept trying to track down the Shaw connection. Find out where it all intersected.

And then his phone rang.

At first he thought it must be Lynn. She probably wanted to tell him what a great night she had had, wondering when they might do it again. He was smiling as he went to answer it.

He took it out of his pocket, checked the screen. Number Unknown. His heart sank slightly, his hopes dashed, his fantasy put on hold. Probably a sales call, he thought, and made to answer it, ready to tell whoever it was that he wasn't interested and to never call him again.

'Detective Sergeant Philips.'

That should spook them, he thought. Make them hang up, even.

But it wasn't a sales call.

'What's the matter with you, then?'

Mickey was taken aback. The voice was indignant, angry. But familiar.

'Sorry?' he said.

'Sorry? Yeah, you fuckin' should be.'

He placed who it was. Stuart. His informant. 'What should I be sorry for, Stuart?'

'For all the bloody effort I've put in for you, that's what.'

Mickey was on the back foot, really confused now. Let him talk, he thought, fill him in. 'Effort?'

'Yeah, effort. It wasn't easy finding out all that stuff, you know. Risked life and limb, I did.'

'What stuff?'

'What you asked me. You havin' a thick day or somethin'?'

Mickey smiled. 'You risked life and limb? To tell me Weaver was probably killed by some Lithuanian hitman?'

There was a pause.

'What? What the fuck you talkin' about? Hitman? I didn't leave no message about no hitman.'

Mickey was interested now. He leaned forward, covering the mouthpiece so the rest of the office couldn't hear what he was saying.

'What message *did* you leave, Stuart?'

An angry sigh. 'I left . . . You know what I left. You must have got it. What's the matter? Can't you work your phone now?'

Mickey took the phone away from his ear, checked the display. Number Unknown. He replaced it.

'I think we'd better talk, Stuart.'

'Damn right we should talk. That's what I've been telling you, haven't I?'

'When?'

'Soon as. Red hot, this is. As you should know.'

Mickey was standing up. 'Usual place. Ten minutes.'

'Gotcha. And bring your foldin'. You're gonna need it.'

'One other thing,' said Mickey. 'You calling me on a new phone?'

'Yeah,' said Stuart. 'That's right. Made of money, me. No, same old phone. You should know, you've got my number. Or you're supposed to have.'

He hung up. Mickey broke the connection, looked down at his phone.

He knew something hadn't been right with Stuart's message. It wasn't just his copper's intuition; it was something definite.

He sat down again, checked his phone once more, writing down the number that Stuart had just called him on, checking it against the one in his phone's memory.

They didn't match.

Mickey sat back, rubbed his chin. Tried to think it through. He checked through all his other numbers, trying to find a match. Nothing. There had to be something. Maybe he'd entered Stuart's number wrongly. No. Completely different number. And he'd called him on it yesterday. He hadn't received any calls from Glass, either. All night. Admittedly, he hadn't had his phone on, but they should have been there when he turned it on in the morning.

No. Couldn't be.

Not wanting to believe what his intuition was telling him, he took out the business card Lynn Windsor had given him. Checked the mobile number on it against the one Stuart was supposed to have texted him on.

Direct match.

He sat back again.

No. Couldn't be.

373

It felt like his whole world had undergone a seismic shift. This finding had taken him – and the investigation – into completely new territory. He had to do something about this, formulate some plan.

But first he had to go and meet Stuart.

Standing up, taking his phone with him, he left the office.

93

Phil looked at the lock on Donna Warren's front door, tried to find a way to open it.

'Think we'll have to break it down,' he said.

'What, and alert the whole street?' said Don. 'Give it here.'

Phil stepped out of the way and allowed Don to move in front of the door. He fished inside his jacket pocket, brought out a small silver object.

'What's that?' said Phil.

'Lock pick,' Don replied calmly. 'We all used to carry them. Back in the day, as you youngsters are so fond of saying.' He shook his head. 'Call yourself a copper. You lot, I tell you. Don't know you're born.'

It didn't take him long. Phil stood all the while looking up and down the street, checking for twitching curtains, interfering or challenging neighbours, someone calling the police.

Ultimately he decided they were safe. It wasn't, he concluded, that kind of neighbourhood.

'And,' said Don, 'we're back in the room.'

The door opened. The two men entered, closing it quietly behind them.

'Don't touch anything,' said Phil. 'Don't move.'

'And don't teach your grandmother to suck eggs,' said Don.

They stayed where they were, just inside the doorway. Phil saw close-up what he had glimpsed through the window. Rose Martin's lifeless body sprawled on the floor.

'Oh God . . .'

'She didn't die easily,' said Don.

'They never do,' said Phil, and sighed. 'We're too late. Too bloody late.'

He looked down again. The body had been there a while. It was starting to lose its resemblance to the person it had once been, her spirit having long since departed, turning into something else, just another collection of matter, another organic component of the planet.

'That phone message,' said Don. 'She must have gone to meet him straight afterwards.'

Phil nodded, not taking his eyes off the body. 'He ran out of the hospital when you turned up. When Lister killed himself.'

'D'you reckon he did this?'

Phil sighed. 'I wouldn't like to think that another officer could be responsible. But . . .' He shrugged. 'It looks that way. Circumstantially, anyway.'

He kept staring at the body.

'Poor Rose . . .'

'Thought you didn't like her.'

'I didn't. But that doesn't mean . . .' Another sigh. 'I saved her life once.'

'She said.'

'Why couldn't I have done it again?'

Don turned to him. 'Now don't start all that.'

'What d'you mean?'

'All that blaming yourself. That leads to a very dark place, believe me. And you don't want to go there.'

You mean again, Phil said to himself. 'No. Suppose not.'

'There was nothing you could have done. She knew that what she was doing was risky. She shouldn't have done it.'

'No.' Still staring. 'But ... why?' Another sigh. 'I don't know. Maybe she couldn't believe one of her work colleagues was a murderer either.'

'Maybe. We'll never know.'

Phil looked up. 'What about the other woman? Donna Warren, was that her name?'

From where he stood, Don looked through into the kitchen. 'Don't think she's here.' He turned to Phil. 'You don't suppose she did this, do you?'

'Do you?'

Don didn't answer.

'We both know who we've got in mind for this.' Phil scoped the room once more, trying not to dwell on Rose's body. 'Can't see this book anywhere.'

'How did she describe it?' said Don.

'A cheap blue exercise book. Let's look upstairs.'

They went slowly up the stairs. Careful not to touch the handrails or walls. Don following Phil's indentations on the stair carpet. They went into the main bedroom.

'Looks like there's been a fight in here.'

Don scanned the room. 'But no book.'

Phil turned to him. 'You know what I think? We're not going to find it. It's not here.'

'I agree. We'd better go.'

They turned round, made their way downstairs without touching anything once more. At the bottom, Don turned to Phil.

'I think you-know-who must have it.'

Phil gave a grim smile. 'You-know-who? Have we jumped into Harry Potter land now?'

Don frowned. 'What?'

'Never mind. You're right. Glass'll have it by now. We'd better—'

'Is this what you're looking for, gentlemen?'

They both turned, startled by the voice. Two men, suited and tied, were standing in the kitchen doorway. One was holding up a cheap blue exercise book in a plastic evidence bag. The other was holding a gun.

The one holding the gun spoke. 'I think we'd better go somewhere a bit more private, don't you?'

Phil shrugged. 'Whatever you say.'

'Move.'

They moved.

94

Mickey walked back on to the footbridge overlooking Balkerne Hill. It felt like more than a day since he had last been here. The air felt colder. The sky heavier, darker. The cars beneath seemed to be moving faster, louder. Everything seemed heightened to Mickey.

Once again, Stuart was waiting for him. His leather jacket pulled tight around his skinny frame, cigarette clamped in the corner of his mouth, sucking down smoke seemingly to keep himself warm.

He turned as soon as Mickey approached. Looked anxious. Scared.

'So tell me what's happened,' said Mickey, coming to stand alongside him.

'It was there in the text I sent you,' said Stuart, sucking the final dregs of life out of his roll-up, flicking the butt over the railing.

'Pretend I never got it,' said Mickey.

Stuart frowned. 'Did you or didn't you?'

'Just pretend.'

Stuart nodded, pointed to Mickey as if about to impart

wisdom. 'Ah, now, y'see, that's why I never commit anything to paper. I mean, that's bad enough, but electronics is worse, innit? I mean, you never know who's listenin' in. Someone could be listenin' in to us now, couldn't they?'

Mickey frowned, lost. 'What? Who?'

Stuart pointed up to the clouds. 'Up there. Satellites. They can beam right in from space with pinpoint accuracy, listen in to what we're sayin'. Take photos an' all. They can.'

'Right. So what did this text say?'

Stuart sighed, shook his head. A teacher exasperated that his thick pupil had failed to grasp the lesson. 'That I'd found out somethin' about this Weaver guy. Like you asked me to.'

'What did you find out?'

'He runs this import-export company with this Lithuanian guy. An' we all know what import-export means, don't we?'

'Covers a multitude,' said Mickey.

'Yeah. An' none of it legal.'

'What Lithuanian guy?'

Stuart screwed up his eyes, tried to think. 'Bul . . . Bol . . . '

'Balchunas?' said Mickey. 'Is that the name?'

Stuart clicked his fingers. 'Yeah, that's him. Balchunas. Yeah. That's the fella.'

'And that's it? That's the big news?'

'Course it's not. Don't be stupid. I heard they got a big shipment comin' in tonight.'

'Of what? Drugs?'

Stuart shrugged. 'Dunno. Prob'ly. He's into all sorts of iffy stuff, what I heard. But just a big shipment. That's all I . . . my sources could tell me.'

'And it was definitely tonight?'

'Yeah.' He rubbed his stubbly chin. 'Worth a lot of money, I reckon.'

'Thought you didn't know what was in it?'

Stuart looked confused. 'What? The shipment? No, I meant me. My information, what I've just told you. That's what's worth a lot of money.' He shook his head as if he was dealing with an idiot.

'So where's this shipment coming in to? Did you hear that?'

'Harwich. Well, the ship's comin' in there. Then they're takin' it to their lock-up. Well, I say lock-up. It's this place they got outside of Harwich, along the coast. Huge, it is. Where their base of operations is.'

Mickey took out his notepad, started writing this down.

'Can't miss it,' said Stuart. 'Full of those metal containers, the ones that come off the ships and get put on to lorries, know what I mean? Piled up high, they are. Huge. Like a big tin city.'

'And that's definitely tonight.' A statement requiring clarification, not a question.

'Definitely. Stake my life on it.' He reconsidered. 'Well, sure as I can be. From what I heard. You know what these things are like, don't you? You know what I mean.'

'What about time? Did you hear anything about that?'

Stuart raised his hands as if in surrender. He made an incredulous face. 'Come on, Mr Philips, do I look like I carry the shipping timetable on me?'

'Take an educated guess.'

Stuart sighed. 'When it's dark. Best I can do.'

Stuart stopped talking. Mickey looked at him. Knew that was as much as he was going to get from him.

'Thanks, Stuart.' He took out some money, peeled off a couple of notes, handed them over.

Stuart took them, looked at them. 'That it? I risked life and limb to get this for you, Mr Philips.'

'Really? When it's dark. Hardly the most accurate thing you've ever given me.'

Stuart sighed. Waited.

Mickey peeled off another note. Handed it over. Stuart took it, made it disappear inside his jacket like the others. Mickey had budgeted for the third note. It was a ritual they had got into. The way they transacted business.

'Be a bit more specific next time,' Mickey said, turning to go.

Stuart stopped him, hand on his arm. 'Mr Philips.'

Mickey turned.

'You want to watch yourself. They're bad people, this lot. Very bad people.'

'So why haven't I heard of them before this, then?'

'Because they've got some very heavy protection, I've heard. That's what makes them so bad.'

'I'll be careful,' Mickey said, and walked off the bridge.

Stuart stayed where he was. Lit another roll-up.

Stared down at the speeding traffic once again.

95

The place was at the bottom of North Station Road. It had been an old warehouse, converted to a hotel and Indian restaurant. But to Phil it still looked like an old warehouse. Stuck on a corner in between a car exhaust centre and another business in terminal decline, and opposite a row of greasy-looking fast-food outlets, it appeared that the minimum of renovation had been done.

The restaurant at the front was in darkness, the double doors locked. It looked to have been a long time since anyone had entered through them. Phil and Don, with the two suited men behind them, were marched down the side of the building and through a door marked 'Welcome' that clearly didn't mean it. It was the hotel entrance.

'Move.'

They moved.

The men hadn't spoken all during the journey. Phil had resisted showing them his warrant card at the house. Depending on who they were – or who had sent them – that might not be the best thing to do.

He had tried to engage them in conversation in the car, get

them to open up, find out where they were going. Nothing. No response. Instead he had sized them up. One more laid-back, treating it all as a job. The other one, with sore-looking red eyes, seemed more angry. Regarding the whole thing personally. He would be the one to look out for.

'I know this place,' said Phil, going through the double doors. 'Been raided loads of times by Immigration. Well, not just Immigration. Plenty of agencies.'

'Shut up and get inside.' The red-eyed one becoming exasperated. Irritated.

Phil and Don entered. There was no one about. A dimly lit hallway and an empty reception desk. Red Eye indicated upstairs. Phil and Don shared a look. Knowing they had no choice, they climbed the stairs.

A vacuum cleaner had been left on the landing along with a pile of bedding and towels for laundry, very dirty, very worn.

'Nice,' said Phil. 'Very ambient.'

Red Eye grabbed hold of him, turned him round. 'That's enough of your lip. Now get in there.'

He gestured towards a cheap, plain wooden door. Number six. Phil opened it, entered.

It was an unimpressive hotel room. Cheaply furnished, badly maintained. Worn carpet, dirty bedcover, threadbare net curtains. In one corner, made from plastic sheeting, was an ill-conceived en suite shower room, mildewed at the joints. On the bed was a woman, mixed race, light-skinned, cheaply dressed, with a small child clinging to her.

Red Eye closed the door behind them. He turned to the woman on the bed.

'Recognise these two?'

The woman looked very scared as she answered. Scared but defiant. 'Should I?'

'You tell me. We found them breaking into your house.'

The woman's eyes jumped wide in shock. Then she recovered, examined Phil. He knew she had identified him as police.

'No,' she said. 'I don't.'

'Good.'

Red Eye put his gun away, motioned Phil and Don to sit on the bed. They did so.

'Right,' said Red Eye, 'you're no friend of hers.' It was clear from his tone what he thought of the woman. 'That might be a good or a bad thing, depending. So who are you, then?'

'I'm going to put my hand inside my jacket,' said Phil, 'and bring it out very slowly.'

The two men shared a look. It was clear they realised from his words what, if not who, he was.

He produced his warrant card. Showed it to them. 'Detective Inspector Phil Brennan. This is Don Brennan, my . . . ' He hesitated. Looked at the old man. Then back to the other two men. 'Father. And an ex-detective. Brought in to advise on a current case. And you are?'

The two men looked at each other, then back at Phil and Don. They too reached into their jackets, produced warrant cards.

'Detective Inspector Al Fennell,' Red Eye's partner said.

Detective Sergeant Barry Clemens,' said Red Eye. 'SOCA. Serious Organised Crime Agency.'

They put their warrant cards away.

Phil nodded. He had been expecting something like that, his suspicions having been raised on the journey. He hadn't got a gangster vibe from them, or even a common criminal one. He'd wondered if they were from some special security outfit. He wasn't far wrong.

'Do you often kidnap fellow police officers at gunpoint?' he said, feeling anger rise at his treatment. 'Is that your standard operating procedure?'

'You'd broken into a house we had under surveillance,' said Fennell, his voice dispassionate, eminently reasonable. 'We had no idea who you were. We brought you back here for questioning.'

'SOCA?' said Don. He turned to Phil. 'Aren't they supposed to tell you if they're in the area?'

'Yes,' said Phil. 'They are.' He looked at the two men, clearly not happy. 'So? I'm a DI in MIS. If anyone should have been informed about your presence it would have been me.'

'Ordinarily, yes,' said Fennell.

'And if it had been any other kind of operation, you would have been,' said Clemens.

'But?' said Phil.

'This one's different. More delicate.' Fennell.

'Especially,' said Clemens, 'given who you are and where you work.'

'Not to mention who you work for.'

Phil frowned. They were confusing him. 'Are you two a double act?' he said. 'The way you finish each other's—'

'Sandwiches,' said Don.

The woman on the bed laughed. Phil smiled. Fennell and Clemens just looked irritated.

'All right,' said Phil. 'Why should who I work for make a difference?'

'Do you know Detective Chief Inspector Brian Glass?' asked Fennell.

It wasn't the question Phil had been expecting them to start with, but somehow it seemed like the right one. 'Yes,' he said, guardedly. 'I do.'

Don wasn't so guarded. 'And he's a bastard.'

Clemens smiled. It made his eyes water.

'Then I think we're all going to get along,' he said.

96

'The first thing we have to do,' said the Portreeve, 'is to welcome our new member.' He pointed to the left. 'The Missionary.'

The new Missionary smiled. 'Is good to be here. Thank you.'

'Unfortunately we don't have time for any further pleasantries. Down to business. Thank you for coming to such a hastily convened meeting. I'm sure you think we could have done all this by phone, but with things getting to a critical point, it may be too risky.'

They were back in their usual meeting room, round the table. There was no water this time.

The Portreeve looked along the table. 'Teacher?'

The Missionary laughed. The Lawmaker stared at him. He didn't laugh any more.

'Perfect from my point of view. Couldn't have been better. In every respect. Mission accomplished. He took the bait and the information was successfully planted. And I quite enjoyed planting it too.'

The Portreeve shifted uncomfortably in his seat.

'Sorry.' The Teacher hesitated, then continued. 'But everything went to plan.'

The Lawmaker leaned forward. Had picked up something in the Teacher's hesitation. 'You sure about that?'

'Absolutely. Wouldn't mind doing it again.'

The Lawmaker sat back. 'That won't happen.'

The Portreeve turned to the Lawmaker. 'And you? How's things at your end?'

The Lawmaker waited until he was sure he had their full attention, then began. 'Fine, generally. The boy has been successfully returned. Our tracks have been well covered there. There's no way Lister can be traced back to us.'

'Shame to lose him,' said the Teacher. 'He was a good client.'

'There'll be others,' said the Lawmaker. 'The investigation is stalling. Into both Weaver's death and the boy's abduction. And it doesn't look like the escapee, Faith Luscombe, is going to trouble us either.'

'Care to elaborate?' said the Portreeve.

The Lawmaker shrugged. Clearly not happy to elaborate but going along with the request. 'One detective has been removed. There was a chance he could have been getting too close.'

'Removed?' The Portreeve.

'Suspended. And another has been removed also.'

'Suspended again?'

'No,' said the Lawmaker. 'This was in a more permanent capacity.'

There was silence round the table. Just the hum of the air-conditioning.

'Dead?' The Portreeve spat the word out like it would contaminate his mouth.

'Let's just say permanently removed,' said the Lawmaker, as nonchalantly as possible. 'We don't know who might be listening. She'd worked things out. Got too close. She had to go. Faith Luscombe's partner has been blamed and framed. So . . . ' The Lawmaker shrugged. 'Every cloud . . . '

The Portreeve leaned forward. 'You're sure about this? This isn't going to—'

'Come back and bite us on the arse?' said the Lawmaker. 'No. I'm sure of it.'

The Portreeve sat back, looking at the Lawmaker. Uneasy about the change that had come over him. He seemed calmer. Darker. As if during the events of the last few days he had really started to find himself. Discover his true personality. The Portreeve wasn't sure he liked it.

Wasn't sure he wouldn't be next.

'And the boy is back with the Gardener?' he asked.

'Yeah,' said the Lawmaker, folding his arms. 'I've been thinking about that.'

The others waited.

'We discussed this earlier. I think it's actually time to implement it.' He gestured to the Missionary. 'We have our new friend here. We have our new source of income just about to go online. We have no need of the, shall we say, old ways.'

Silence.

'Go on,' said the Teacher.

'Let's offer him up to the police. Let them have the collar. They catch a deranged serial killer, we have a diversion away from our shipment arriving.'

'That sounds like a plan,' said the Teacher. 'But what if he talks when he's been arrested?'

The Lawmaker shook his head. 'Credit me with some intelligence, please. He won't be arrested. There'll be a team of armed officers ready to take him down. And they will do.'

'Sounds . . . excellent,' said the Portreeve, unconvincingly. 'You sure you can make this work?'

'I'm sure.'

'D'you know where he'll be?'

The Lawmaker nodded. 'The back-up location. The one Faith Luscombe was taken to.'

'The one she escaped from,' said the Teacher.

Anger flared in the Lawmaker's eyes, just for a few seconds. But long enough to unnerve everyone else around the table.

'It'll be fine,' the Lawmaker said.

'So if the Gardener's going,' said the Teacher, 'what about the Garden? Will that go too?'

The Lawmaker smiled. 'I don't think so. I think it's about to be repopulated.'

'Good,' said the Portreeve, looking at his watch. 'Then I'll see you all later.' He looked round the table, ensuring eye contact with everyone there. 'And we mustn't lose our nerve. We're so close, and there's so much at stake. We can all look forward to a prosperous tomorrow.'

The Lawmaker leaned towards him. Smiled. It sent a shiver down the Portreeve's spine.

'My nerve's fine,' he said. 'How's yours?'

The meeting was over.

97

Marina was standing at her desk in the main MIS office, bent over, the space before her spread with charts and maps. Mickey approached, hovered by her side, moving slowly from foot to foot. Said nothing. Eventually she looked up.

'You all right there, Mickey?'

'How's it going?'

Marina sighed, straightened up. Pushed a hank of stray hair behind her ear. 'Slowly. I'm seeing if I can create a geographical profile of our would-be killer based on the calendar and where we know he's been.' She looked down again. 'Seeing if certain areas are more suited to different times of the year, that kind of thing.'

'Any luck?'

She looked up at him. 'Not yet. It takes a while to do this kind of profiling properly, and you need more information for effective triangulation. I was seeing if I could use the calendar as a short cut.' Her hair fell down, and once more she pushed it back. 'What can I do for you?'

Mickey looked round, as if nervous. Or fearful of eavesdroppers. 'Can I have a word?'

'Sure.'

'Not here.' Still looking round.

Marina did likewise. 'Where, then?'

'How about your office?'

'Come on.'

She picked up her bag, walked out of the office, Mickey following her. Down the corridor, up the stairs.

'How's Phil?' asked Mickey.

'He's . . . as well as can be expected,' said Marina, not turning to him, her face in profile.

'What a bastard.'

'The situation? Or Glass?'

'Both.'

'Couldn't agree more.' Said quietly, more for herself, he thought, than him.

They reached her office. She unlocked it.

'Take a seat.'

Mickey sat down in one of the two armchairs in the centre of the room. Marina took the other one. Crossed her legs, sat upright. Waiting. Then, realising that looked too formal, uncrossed them, leaned forward. Mickey could see she was trying not to make this chat into a therapy session. He hoped he could do the same.

'How can I help?'

Mickey's hands fidgeted. He tried to find the words. Marina waited.

'I've been . . . compromised.'

'In what way?'

Mickey heaved out a deep sigh. Started. 'With . . . someone connected to the investigation.'

'A suspect?'

'No,' he said, but sounded unsure. 'A . . . I don't even think she's a witness. But she's involved in some way.'

'Who?'

Mickey told her. All about meeting Lynn Windsor. Her phone call. Asking him to go round. Telling him she had something important for him to see. Asking him not to tell anyone else about their meeting.

'And did she? Have something for you to see?'

Mickey almost smiled. 'Oh yeah, but it wasn't anything to do with the investigation.'

Marina gave a small smile, nodded. Mickey continued.

'I spent the night,' he said. 'I know I shouldn't have done, shouldn't even have gone there. At least not without telling someone else first. And I shouldn't have been . . . '

'Thinking with your dick?'

Mickey reddened, studied the carpet. 'Yeah.'

'Don't worry,' Marina said. 'You're not the first and you won't be the last.' She smiled. 'How d'you think Phil and I got together?'

'I know,' he said, nodding, 'but it's not just that. There's something else.'

Marina waited while Mickey found the correct words, got himself in the right state to voice them.

'I think . . . I've been played.'

Marina frowned. 'In what way?'

'Just . . . something that happened earlier today. This morning. I turned my phone off. Last night. When I was with Lynn. When I turned it on this morning, there were no missed calls from Glass.'

'Should there have been?'

'Yeah. He'd been calling me all yesterday evening. Trying to get me back to work after what happened at the hospital. Loads of calls, apparently. I didn't get any of them.'

'Curious.'

'And that's not all. I had a few texts. One was from an

informant telling me, well, what I said in the briefing this morning. About Weaver being killed by a Lithuanian hitman.'

Marina nodded. 'And?'

I've just been to meet with my informant. He never said that at all. Said there was some shipment coming in tonight and we needed to be on it.'

Marina sat back. 'But how did—'

'That's not all,' said Mickey. 'When I checked again, I found that the number the text had come from, although it had my informer's name next to it, was Lynn Windsor's.'

'Get her in then. Get her questioned.'

'But what about . . . '

'I don't see that there's a problem. Not in this instance. This wouldn't have come to light if you hadn't slept with her. She must have done all this while you were sleeping.'

'She was walking around at one point . . . '

'Then bring her in.'

'Can't see Glass going for it, somehow.'

'You're running the investigation now, remember?'

Mickey smiled, nodded. 'True. If I bring her in for questioning, will you help?'

Marina smiled. 'It'll be a pleasure.'

Mickey stood up. 'Then I'll go and get her. Thanks for the chat.'

'Any time,' said Marina, watching Mickey leave the room.

She stood up too. Took out her phone, thought about calling Phil. Replaced it. Best let him have a little space to himself. *He'll call me when he needs me*, she thought.

She went back to work.

98

'So have SOCA had their budget cut, then?'

Phil was walking round the hotel room, picking things up, replacing them, grimacing with disgust at the dirt and mess in the place.

'No one would look for us in a place like this,' said Fennell.

'Not unless they were mental,' said Don.

Phil laughed. 'So why here?'

Clemens shrugged. 'We got a good deal.'

Phil smiled. 'Oh, I get it. That last Immigration raid. Were you lot behind it?'

The two men said nothing.

'Raid the place, close it down and just happen to get slipped a set of keys. Your own little base for your adventures. Very clever.'

'Look,' said Clemens, 'can we get down to business?'

'What, no cuppa?' Phil examined the tea-making accoutrements. Grimaced once more. 'Perhaps not.' He sat in a chair by the window. Hoped it would hold his weight.

'Tell me about DCI Glass,' he said.

Fennell obliged. 'We've had Glass under observation for some time.'

'He came to our attention a while ago. Picked him up on the radar because of his criminal activities.'

'Such as?' asked Don.

'Drugs,' said Fennell.

'People-trafficking. Sexual slavery,' said Clemens.

'Helping Eastern European criminal gangs get a foothold over here.'

'Why d'you think he wanted the job here?' said Clemens. 'Colchester's just next to Harwich. A nice little supply chain coming in from Europe.'

'Forgive me if this is an obvious question,' said Phil. 'But if you've got all this on him, why haven't you arrested him?'

'Because these things take time,' said Fennell.

'Getting a case together, doing it surreptitiously so he doesn't get wind of it, reeling in his known associates,' said Clemens.

'Making sure it's watertight . . . All takes time.'

'Plus,' said Clemens, 'we want him caught in the act.'

'Preferably with his associates,' said Fennell.

'So when's that going to happen?' asked Donna. Phil could see she was determined not to be ignored, sidelined. He admired that spirit in her. 'Today, tomorrow, when? You're just going to let him go till then?'

'Tonight,' said Fennell.

'There's a new shipment coming in through Harwich,' said Clemens. 'We're going to catch him there.'

'Shipment?' said Don. 'Of what?'

'People,' said Fennell.

'Girls,' said Clemens. 'Children. All from Eastern Europe.'

Phil saw Donna's head drop. Caught the look of despair in her eyes. She instinctively glanced towards the little boy. He looked exhausted. He had curled up on the side of the bed, was nodding off to sleep.

Donna looked up again. Phil could see the anger in her eyes. 'So that's it, is it? You're going to catch him at Harwich. What about what happened in my house? He murdered Rose Martin. He would've killed me an' Ben as well. Why didn't you get him then?'

'We're sorry about Rose Martin,' said Fennell.

'Sorry? Sorry? Sorry doesn't cut it, mate. You just going to leave her there?'

'Look,' said Clemens, his own anger rising, 'what happened to her was unfortunate. But we have to look at the bigger picture. You should too.'

'You bastard, you . . . ' Donna was off the bed and making her way across the room to Clemens. Fennell grabbed hold of her, restrained her.

'Donna,' he said, his voice low and reasonable, 'calm down.'

On the bed, Ben began to stir. He opened his eyes, saw what was happening, cowered back into the pillows.

'You're scaring the boy,' said Phil, standing up. 'Let her go.'

Fennell looked round, saw Ben. Let Donna go. She returned to the bed, sat next to the boy, an arm round him. Fennell kept talking.

'We did argue about what we should do with Rose Martin. We knew there would be enough of Glass's DNA in the house to implicate him, no matter how he tried to clean up.'

'And we also had a first-hand witness testimony,' said Clemens. 'Assuming you'd do it. So we weren't too bothered about that. We thought it might pay off to keep watching the house. See who else turned up.'

'And look who did,' said Don.

'But don't worry,' said Fennell, addressing Donna directly. 'A forensic team will be in there very shortly.'

'Our forensic team,' said Clemens. 'Not local. Wouldn't want the possibility of accidental contamination, would we?'

Phil stared at the man. He could understand why Donna would want to hit him.

Silence fell while everyone regathered. Eventually Don spoke.

'Glass,' he said, nodding to himself. 'Yeah. Always had him pegged as a bad 'un. Well, always suspected it, anyway.'

'You knew him, then?' said Fennell.

'Back in his uniform days,' said Don, 'when I was a DI in CID. A thug. He was always a thug. But a clever one. An ambitious one.'

'He still is,' said Clemens.

Don frowned. 'But something happened to him after the Garden case. He wasn't the same. He wasn't better, far from it. He was worse. Even cockier. Even more happy to throw his weight around. Like he had protection. Couldn't be touched.'

'And then what?' said Fennell.

'That's when his career took off,' said Don. 'And I hardly ever saw him again. We stopped moving in the same circles.'

'This Garden case,' said Clemens to Don. 'Tell us about it.'

99

'Paul Clunn,' said Don. That was his name. He founded the Garden.'

Phil listened once more. Tried not to think of the previous night.

'A city worker who had either a vision or a nervous break-down, depending how you look at it. Bought a country house and filled it with similarly afflicted souls.'

'Was Glass one of them?' said Clemens.

'No,' said Don. 'I'll get to him in a minute. Be patient.'

'When was this?' asked Fennell.

'Late sixties, early seventies,' said Don. 'Places like that were popular for a time. This one followed the usual pattern. Surround some vaguely charismatic leader with a load of fol-lowers desperate to hear what they think is the truth.'

'Strange name,' said Phil. 'Not the most charismatic.'

'I'm sure he overcompensated,' said Don. 'Anyway, it was ensured that the followers renounced all their worldly goods on the way in. Apparently that led them to find enlighten-ment.'

'And did it?' asked Clemens.

Don shrugged. 'As much as they could, I suppose. For a while, at any rate. The Garden certainly did. It became very wealthy.'

'Not surprised,' said Fennell.

'We looked into their finances,' said Don. 'They invested the money in property mainly.'

'Like the house at the bottom of East Hill,' said Phil.

'At one time,' said Don. 'Probably hidden by a paper trail now. But uncover that, and I'll bet you'll find it still leads back to the Elders.'

'The Elders?' said Phil.

'Clunn didn't do all this on his own,' said Don. 'He had helpers. Followers who shared his vision.'

'Or breakdown,' said Phil.

'Right. But these were more than followers. They became the Elders. They all had titles. Clunn was the Seer. The visionary. There was the Portreeve. He was in charge, ran things on a day-to-day basis. Guy who did that was called Robert Fenton.'

'Fenton?' said Phil. 'That name rings a bell . . . '

'He seemed all right,' said Don. 'Straight. Sharing in Clunn's vision. And June Boxtree. She was the Lawmaker. Same for her. There was another one. The Missionary. Responsible for recruitment. Used to take the good-looking young ones out on a weekend, stand them on street corners rattling a tin, engaging passers-by in conversation. Getting them to come to meetings. He scarpered when the place was raided.' Don smiled. It soon faded. 'But the other two . . . ' He shook his head. 'Bad. Very bad.'

'You remember all this well,' said Clemens.

'Like it was yesterday,' said Don. 'Every copper has his case, doesn't he? The one that haunts him. The one that still has him waking up in the middle of the night. Well this was mine. I remember it all right. Every single detail.'

'The other two?' prompted Fennell.

'Yes, the other two. One was called the Teacher. Gail Banks. A very nasty piece of work. A hard, cold woman. She hid her cruelty behind the Garden's peace and love. If she'd been born earlier and Irish, she'd have run the Magdalene laundries. And she'd have loved it. As it was, her heyday was the late sixties. So she became the most militant of feminists.'

'Accent on the militant,' said Fennell.

'Yes.' Don nodded. 'In the same way Hitler was militant. She was cut-price Germaine Greer. Having joyless sex with anyone just to prove a point. Or score one. Punishing the communists when they'd been bad. Especially the children. Especially the girls. But even her monstrousness wasn't as bad as the other player.'

'Who?' said Fennell.

'Richard Shaw.'

Phil couldn't believe what he was hearing. 'Not Tricky Dicky Shaw? The gangster?'

'The very same. Apparently when he came to the Garden he was genuine about it. Looking to change his life. Start over. That's what he said, anyway. And he was believed, welcomed in. Gave another name, of course.'

'Not Robin Banks, by any chance?' asked Phil.

Donna, arm curled round the sleeping Ben, laughed.

'No. George Weaver.'

Phil nodded. 'Of course. Makes sense.'

'We still don't know if he was just hiding out, lying low. Or whether he was genuine. Doesn't matter now. He told them he was an artist. Began to paint. And began to take an interest in horticulture. So he became one of the Elders too. Called himself the Gardener.'

'This Garden place,' said Donna, her voice quiet so as not

to wake Ben. 'Is it the same one as Faith talked about in her book?'

Don looked towards Fennell and Clemens.

'We'll come to that,' said Clemens. He looked at Don. 'Keep going.'

'Well the next thing that happened was that Banks and Shaw took over the running of the place. Sidelined the rest of the Elders, kept the Missionary on the streets the whole time.'

'And Clunn?'

'Made sure he was always doped up, out of his head. Permanently. There were rumours of ill-health, but nobody believed them. That was just a smokescreen so they could take over. Do what they wanted. And they did. Then it turned bad. Really bad.'

'How bad?' asked Donna. Fearful, like she wasn't sure she wanted to hear the answer.

'The communists were starved, driven half mad. They were pimped out to whoever wanted them, to do whatever they wanted with them. Some of them never made it back. Some of them wished they hadn't.'

'I've heard all this,' said Phil.

'Sorry,' said Don. 'That's when we raided the place.'

'And they were all gone,' said Phil, finishing for him.

Don nodded. 'They were gone. And that was the end of the Garden.'

Silence. Fennell and Clemens exchanged glances. Fennell nodded.

'No it wasn't,' said Clemens.

100

'The Garden didn't die,' said Fennell. 'It continued.'

'No it didn't,' said Don. 'We searched for it everywhere. We hunted down the properties owned by the Garden, looked there. Checked them all out. We couldn't find it anywhere. They sold the house, made it into a hotel.'

'It kept going,' said Fennell, brooking no argument. 'And it's still going now.'

'Yeah,' said Donna, 'it is. Faith escaped from it. She wrote about it. That's what's in the book. She got away from them. Someone she'd been hired out to bought her off them. And Ben.' Donna shuddered. 'An' he was just as bad. So she took Ben and ran. That's how she ended up with me. Well, eventually.'

'And she was trying to make a bit of money by selling the book to Glass,' said Clemens. 'The stupidest thing she could have done.'

Donna said nothing. Just glared at him.

'So where is it, if it's still going now?' asked Phil.

'We're not exactly sure,' said Fennell.

'But it does still exist,' said Clemens. 'And in a lot of

respects, it's the same as it used to be. They still pimp out the communists.'

'Except they're not really communists any more,' said Fennell. 'More like prisoners.'

'But they're still sold and hired.'

'You don't know where from, though?' said Phil.

Clemens shook his head. 'We know it's somewhere in the area. But we don't know any more than that.'

'And,' said Fennell, 'it's still run by the Elders.'

'What,' said Don, 'the same ones?'

'No,' said Fennell. 'Not exactly. Tricky Dicky Shaw disappeared after the raid. June Boxtree was never heard of again. The first Missionary never went back. We don't know what happened to him.'

'What about the others? Robert Fenton?' asked Phil.

'Resurfaced eventually,' said Clemens. 'Retrained as a solicitor. Opened a practice in Colchester.'

'I didn't know that,' said Don. 'Wasn't he arrested or anything?'

Fennell shook his head. 'Some kind of deal was struck. You know the kind of thing.'

Phil looked at Don. He could tell his father wasn't happy about that.

'And the rest of them?' said Don, bitterness showing in his voice.

'Like I said, Tricky Dicky was never found. Paul Clunn disappeared too.'

'Mind you,' said Clemens, 'he was so addled and mindfucked by that time that he could have wandered off a cliff and not noticed. Probably thought he could fly.'

'They didn't replace Clunn when he went. Didn't need to.'

Phil was thinking. The tramp. Paul? Hadn't that been his name? 'I think I've met him,' he said. He told them of his encounters with the tramp. Most of them. Not what he had discussed with him.

'I let him go,' he said eventually. 'Didn't think he could have done it. Like you said, brain completely addled. But he did have moments of lucidity. Few and far between.'

'What about Gail Banks?'

Phil could tell Don wasn't taking the news well. He didn't blame him. Something that had obsessed him all his working life – and beyond – reduced to these prosaic terms. He hoped that kind of thing wouldn't happen to him. But knew it probably would. It happened to every decent copper.

'Gail Banks?' said Clemens. 'Died of an Aids-related illness back in the nineties.'

'So who are the Elders now, if the original ones are all dead or retired?'

'Their titles are more code names now, really,' said Fennell.

'Something they use in case we're listening in.'

'And were you?' asked Don.

'When we could,' said Clemens.

'But that's inadmissible in court.'

'Which is why we want to catch Glass in the act,' said Fennell.

'Besides,' said Clemens, 'the names were something they could use in court anyway. Claim they weren't really pimping and selling people to rich perverts, just playing at secret societies. Pathetic.'

Phil thought for a moment. 'So how did you find out about all this? You were watching Glass.'

Fennell and Clemens both looked at him.

'Oh,' said Phil.

'Exactly,' said Clemens.

'He's one of them,' said Don, the fact piling bitterness upon bitterness for him.

'He's their new Lawmaker,' said Fennell. 'That's how we found out about them. Robert Fenton's son, Michael Fenton . . .'

'Of Fenton Associates,' said Phil.

'The very same,' said Clemens.

'. . . is the new Portreeve,' finished Fennell.

Don shook his head. He looked like he was broken, thought Phil. Like he had been betrayed by his memories.

'What about the rest of them?' said Phil. 'The Missionary? All those.'

'The Missionary, we think, was Adam Weaver,' said Fennell.

'Going out into the world, bringing back rich people. Or in his case, investors,' said Clemens.

'Until recently, obviously,' said Fennell.

'The Gardener,' said Phil. 'He's still out there. Still going.'

'We don't know anything about him. Apart from his old name. And that won't help us now.'

'True,' agreed Fennell. 'Doesn't matter, though. He's not central to this investigation.'

'But he's still torturing and killing children,' said Phil. 'Doesn't that count for anything?'

'Yes, it does,' said Fennell. 'But not as part of this investigation. We're after bringing down Glass and his people-trafficking scheme. That's the main objective.'

'Anything else,' said Clemens, 'is secondary.'

Phil said nothing. But he knew he had to do something.

'What about the Teacher?' said Don. 'Used to be Gail Banks. Who is it now?'

'Well,' said Fennell, 'Gail Banks had a daughter . . .'

101

Lynn Windsor didn't look happy to be there. In fact she looked furious.

Mickey watched her from behind the two-way glass of the observation room. Marina stood next to him.

'I can see what you saw in her,' she said.

'Saw being the operative word. I think our relationship's dead in the water.'

They both studied her once more. She was sitting behind the desk in the interview room, hands clasped before her on the table, back rigid. Anger and indignation keeping her upright.

Mickey had gone down to the offices of Fenton Associates, phoned her first, asked to meet her outside. He was hoping she would think it was something to do with the previous night, something he didn't want her work colleagues to hear. She did. Came to the front of the building.

'Hi,' she had said, eyes as bright as her smile.

He imagined her preparing that smile while she walked down, checking in the mirrors to see that it had the correct wattage.

He had brought her straight down. 'I need you to come down to the station.'

The smile had wavered. 'Why, what's wrong?'

'Can't say. I just need you to come with me straight away.' He had pointed to his car.

The smile disappeared completely. He watched her face closely, saw calculation. Knew what would come next.

'I think there's a mistake,' she said.

'No mistake, I'm afraid. We need to talk to you at the station. Straight away.'

He wouldn't let her go back inside the building, wouldn't let her get her jacket, bag or phone. 'Someone'll call work, tell them where you are.'

The drive to Southway had been silent. He hadn't even looked at her. Couldn't bear to. He knew she would be hating him. He could tell by the way her chest rose and fell in his peripheral vision.

He had put the radio on to fill the silence. Radio One.

'Love a bit of Lady Gaga,' he had said, after attempting to sing along. 'But I still don't know what she really looks like. You see her with that many disguises on, when you actually see what she looks like, you just can't recognise her, can you?'

Lynn hadn't answered.

And now he was observing her. Beneath the anger he sensed fear. She looked isolated, cut off. Good. That was how he wanted her. Suffering. And it had nothing to do with the way she had played him the previous night, he told himself. Oh no. Purely professional.

'Marina,' said Mickey.

She waited.

'Don't tell Anni about this.' He kept his eyes on the glass. 'About you and Lynn Windsor?'

Mickey nodded. 'Yeah. I don't want her to . . . think less of me. She's a good friend.'

'Right. I won't.'

'Thanks.' He sighed. 'I phoned the hospital. She's doing OK. Sleeping. I'll try to get to see her later.'

'She'd like that.'

'So would I.'

They stared at Lynn Windsor some more.

'Right,' Mickey said, 'how are we going to play this?'

'Same as usual. I'll be in here watching her. You get the questions going. I'll chip in as and when.'

Mickey nodded. Placed his earpiece in. 'Wish Phil was here. He's better at this than me.'

Marina gave a smile. Mickey sensed a sad, faraway quality to it. 'You'll be fine. You always are.'

He nodded. 'Right. In I go.'

He left the observation room. The door closed silently behind him.

Marina watched through the glass. Checked her mic. Everything was fine. She took a seat at the desk. As she did so, her phone rang.

She looked down at her bag, mentally chastising herself. She'd thought she had turned it off. Sighing, she picked it up, ready to kill it. Saw the readout. Phil. She looked at the window, saw Mickey enter the room. Looked at the phone.

Answered it.

'It's me,' said Phil.

'Hi,' said Marina, distracted by watching Mickey sit down. Lynn Windsor stare at him with undisguised hatred. 'How are you?'

'I'm fine. Listen, I've got some things to tell you.'

Marina felt torn once more. She wanted to talk to him –

needed to – but he had picked a terrible time. She had to tell him that. He would understand. He was a professional.

'Can we do this later? I'm sorry, but Mickey's just got someone in the interview room and I'm working the obs.'

'Who?' Phil said. 'Who's he got?'

'Lynn Windsor. The solicitor.'

She heard him cover the mouthpiece, say something she couldn't catch. There was someone else in the room with him. He came back to her. 'That's good. Keep her there. I've got some stuff to tell you. And I've got to tell you now.'

'Does it have to be now?'

'Yes. It concerns Lynn Windsor. And Brian Glass. How they're connected, and how dirty he is.'

'Stay on the line,' she said, heart suddenly racing. 'I may need you.'

'Pleasure to be back in business,' he said.

102

M ickey sat down opposite Lynn.

'Well,' he said, 'this is nice.'

'Is this how you repay all the women you've slept with?' said Lynn, with barely suppressed anger. 'Haul them in for questioning?'

'Not all of them. Only the special ones.'

'What d'you want to know? Who else I've slept with? Did I use protection? Have I had a check-up recently? Bit late for all that now.'

'Yeah,' he said, 'too late.'

She looked at the machine next to her. 'You going to record this? Because the first thing I'm going to say is that you slept with me. That anything I say consequently will be considered tainted testimony. That nothing will stand up in court.'

She sat back, pleased with herself.

Mickey smiled. 'Absolutely. I wasn't going to do this interview under caution, but if you'd prefer it that way, then fair enough.'

'I would.'

Mickey readied the recorder.

'You're doing great, Mickey,' said Marina in his ear. 'Keep her like that. Keep her angry. She thinks she's superior to you. Cleverer than you. She thinks she's going to beat this. She's so arrogant she hasn't asked for a solicitor. Thinks because she is one she knows it all. Even criminal law. Keep her that way.'

Mickey gave a small nod, hoped Marina caught it.

'Interview commencing at . . . ' He started talking for the benefit of the recorder. He gave his name, Lynn Windsor's name, cautioned her, stated the time. Got her to say she had turned down the offer of a solicitor. Then he was ready to start.

Her lips were curled at the edges. Ready for battle, thought Mickey. Ready to defeat him. He swallowed. Hoped that wouldn't be the case.

'Lynn, I—'

'Can I just stop you there, Detective Sergeant,' she said. She smiled. 'I realise I'm under caution and this is a formal interview. I should also like to state, for the recording, that last night you came round to my flat and had sex with me.'

She sat back, knowing what the repercussions of her statement would be, waiting for his response. She smiled. Mickey took his time.

'Yes I did,' he said eventually. 'I should say it was at your invitation. And that the sex was entirely consensual. And, I should add, highly enjoyable.'

She sat forward. That wasn't what she had expected him to say. Her eyes darted around the room.

'In fact,' continued Mickey, 'it was last night I wanted to talk to you about. You see, when I accepted your invitation to come over, I didn't consider you to be involved in the investigation I'm currently working on. However, as a result of spending the night with you, I'm not convinced of that at all.'

He reached into his pocket, brought out her business card. He had put it in a plastic bag. Thought it looked more official that way. He placed it on the table between them.

'Do you recognise this?'

She looked at it, looked back at him.

'Do you?'

She nodded.

'Can you speak up, please? For the benefit of the recording.'

'Yes,' she said croakily, her mouth suddenly dry.

'And what is it?'

She cleared her throat. 'My business card.'

'Right. Your business card. And could you look at that card for me, please?'

She bent over, looked at it.

'Could you confirm that's your mobile number on it?'

'Yes.' Fear began to dance in her eyes. *He knows*, her expression said.

Mickey suppressed a smile, fed off it, became more confident. He was circling, closing in on her. But he didn't want to get cocky, didn't want to lose the interview and her too. So he kept it controlled.

'Now, this is my mobile phone.' He took his phone out, placed it on the table. 'Could you tell me why your number appears in the address book?'

She shrugged. 'You must have put it there. Intending to see me again. It's not going to happen now.'

'All right, I'll rephrase the question. Can you tell me why your number is in my phone next to the name of one of my informants? And why the text message he sent me yesterday never got through? And why I received a different one instead with entirely different information in it? Can you explain any of that?'

Lynn Windsor said nothing. Just stared at him. Hatred burning in her eyes.

His mind flashed back to the way she had been the night before. It was hard to believe it was the same woman. He put the image out of his mind, concentrated.

'So you don't know how my informant's text was intercepted and changed.'

'No.'

'And your number substituted for his.'

'No.'

'Sure?'

She sighed. Aiming for irritated, unable to suppress the fear beneath it. 'This is ridiculous.' She was trying to inject strength into her voice, but it was too shaky. 'This is pathological. You're just ... just ... taking out your own guilt for sleeping with me on ... on ... like this.'

Mickey gave a pantomime frown. 'I don't feel guilty about what we did. Do you?'

Her eyes darted about the room once more, like sparrows trapped in a barn.

'If you're ... if you're quite finished, I'll ... I'll go ...'

Her hands on the table, trying to stand. Wanting to walk out. Wanting it all to end.

'Sit down, please, Lynn.' Mickey's voice strong, authoritative.

She sat down.

He heard Marina's voice in his ear.

'Right, Mickey, you've got her. Now. Trust me on this. Ask her about the Gardener.'

Mickey frowned.

'The Gardener. Just ask her where the Gardener is. And how you can find him. Trust me. Do it.'

Mickey leaned forward across the table. Hands together,

voice low, as if in conspiracy. *Us against the world*, his body language said. *You're in trouble but I'm the one who can get you out of it.*

'Lynn . . . '

She looked up at him. Up close, he saw the depth of fear in her eyes. He was glad he wasn't scared of whatever it was that was scaring her.

Or whoever.

'Lynn . . . where can I find the Gardener?'

And the fear he had just seen in her eyes was nothing compared to the fear that was there now.

103

The Gardener straightened up. Looked round. Smiled.

The sacrifice chamber had been filled with flowers. Bunches had been made up, colours and scents carefully combined, positioned at the correct stations round the room. The rest had been strewn over the floor. The smell was becoming overpowering in the confined space. Decay had already started.

Good. That was just how the Gardener wanted it. Needed it.

For the sacrifice.

The candles were in place too. But he had resisted the temptation to start burning them early. The room was cold and dark. He had put on another layer. Navigated by torch-light.

He looked over to the cage. The boy was silent. Curled up in a corner, still wearing the thin back-tied gown from the hospital. Bruises on his hands and arms where needles had been yanked out. Head tucked in. Shivering.

It didn't matter. Soon he would be beyond cold and beyond heat.

Soon he would be nothing more than the spark that kept the flame of the Garden alight. Keeping it alive.

Until the next sacrifice.

And the next.

He crossed to the workbench. Put the torch down. Picked up his first tool. A sickle. He didn't need to touch it. He could see how sharp it was just by looking. By the way it caught the torchlight, sent it bouncing round the walls. He replaced it. Picked up the torch again.

Turned and left the chamber.

There was nothing to do now except wait.

For the right time.

Wait.

And savour.

104

'The Gardener,' said Mickey once more, 'how can we find him?'

Lynn Windsor looked close to breaking down. She was shaking. Mickey had never seen anyone literally shake with fear.

'I ... I ...'

He pressed on. 'Just tell me, Lynn. It'll be so much easier for you if you do. Tell me. Where's the Gardener?'

'I ... I ... don't know ...'

He sighed. 'I think you can do better than that. You're so unhappy, so scared. Just tell me and it'll all feel much better. Come on.'

Heads nearly touching, hands nearly together, he was close to cracking her. He could feel it. One last try. A gentle push to take her over the edge.

'Come on, Lynn ...'

Then he heard Marina's voice once more. 'Good, Mickey. Here's something else. If that doesn't work, ask her about the Elders.'

Mickey gave a puzzled frown to the window. Small, so only Marina could catch it.

'Please. Trust me. Ask her about the Elders. Ask her where they are. She's the Teacher. Tell her you know that.'

Marina's voice disappeared. Mickey was left alone with Lynn Windsor. He didn't understand what Marina had said. But what she had fed him seemed to be having the right effect. So he would continue, pretend he felt more confident than he did. Use the words. See what they did.

'Lynn . . . what about the Elders? What would they say?'

Her head jerked up in shock. Her eyes, tearful, rimmed red and black from crying and make-up, locked on to his. Stared at him. Her hand reached out for his. Grasped it and clung on, like he was the last life raft on the *Titanic*.

'The Elders, Lynn. Would they be happy to see you here like this?'

She was shaking now, like she was about to fall apart. Both psychologically and physically, thought Mickey.

'That's right about the Elders, isn't it? You are the Teacher, after all.'

Mickey had no idea what he was saying, but he couldn't believe the effect the words were having on her.

'Come on. Just tell me . . .'

She looked up once more, imploring him, her mouth moving but no sound emerging.

'Come on, Lynn . . .' Mickey's voice barely above a whisper. The intimacy between them even deeper than that they had shared the previous night. 'Tell me. And it'll be all over . . .'

She reached forward for him, hands clinging desperately to him, working her way up his arms. Grabbing him, holding him, just about crawling over the table to be near him.

'Please . . .' Her voice was broken, almost shattered in pieces. A vocal manifestation of her mental state. 'Please, help me . . . help me . . .'

419

'I will,' said Mickey, whispering once more, not wanting to break the moment. 'I will. Tell me where the Gardener is and I'll help you. I promise.'

She put her head on his arms, sobbing.

'Tell me. Please.'

She looked up, mind made up, mouth open, ready to speak.

And then the door burst open.

'What the fuck's going on here?'

Mickey turned. DCI Glass was standing behind him.

And he didn't look happy.

105

'What the hell were you thinking of?'

Glass was in the observation room with Mickey and Marina. The room was so small, it was crowded with just one person in it. But three, standing there amidst all the old filing cabinets and broken office furniture, made it look massively overcrowded. It also made Glass seem even angrier. Mickey could almost feel the heat from the DCI's words as they left his mouth.

Behind them, Lynn Windsor sat at the table. Sobbing, wiping her eyes with a tissue. Next to her, a consoling arm around her shoulder, was her boss, Michael Fenton. His head close to hers, whispering. The sound was switched off. They couldn't hear what he was saying.

Mickey turned to Glass, realising that the question wasn't rhetorical and he was expecting an answer.

Marina got there first. 'In the absence of anyone else in the office, Mickey came to me,' she said. 'He had strong suspicions about Lynn Windsor. She'd been questioned already but he thought she would benefit from a more formal interview.'

Mickey studied Marina as she spoke. She was watching

Glass's responses, wary. As if she was measuring her words, careful of what she said to him. Mickey had found himself doing that with Glass because he didn't trust him, but Marina's actions confirmed that he was doing the right thing.

'And what made you think that?'

Again, Marina spoke before Mickey could. 'We received information that she was in some way connected with the abductor and would-be murderer of the boy taken from the hospital.'

'What kind of information?'

'Something to do with the Gardener?' Marina kept her face as blank as possible while she spoke.

The effect on Glass was immediate. It was clear he knew what she was talking about. It was equally clear that he was trying to pretend he didn't. He waited a few seconds, absorbing the information, letting his features settle down, preparing his response.

'What . . . what d'you mean? Who's the Gardener?'

'He's the person we believe is responsible for the boy's abduction,' said Mickey.

Glass turned to him. Face like stone, eyes like granite. 'And what would make you believe that?'

'Information received from an informant,' said Mickey. 'A confidential informant. It . . . involved Lynn Windsor. So I made the decision to bring her in for questioning.'

'But how could she . . . how could she know anything? She's a solicitor, for God's sake.'

'Yes,' said Marina, 'and solicitors never know anything, do they?'

'But she's not a criminal lawyer,' Glass explained, as if they were two retarded children. 'She's one of the most well-respected solicitors in the area.'

'And she may know something about the imminent murder

of a child,' said Mickey. 'If we had got her to talk, we could have saved that boy's life.'

'She can't know anything,' Glass said.

'And you're sure of that, are you?' said Marina.

Glass didn't reply. Just glared at her.

'You wouldn't want to stand in the way of a murder investigation, would you?' said Mickey.

Glass turned his stare on him.

'Sir,' Mickey added.

It seemed to Mickey that Glass was making a pretence of thinking. He came to a conclusion. 'You're right,' he said. 'We can't take the chance, can we?'

'Good,' said Mickey. He turned for the door. 'I'll just—'

'No,' said Glass, putting a restraining hand on his arm. 'I'll handle the interview. And it'll be done properly this time.'

'It was done properly last time,' said Mickey. 'Check the recording.'

Glass seemed to hesitate, stuck for what to do. He quickly made up his mind. 'I'll still handle the interview. But her solicitor will be present.' He looked round the observation room. 'And I'll do it in private.'

'Why?' said Mickey.

'In case she has anything of a . . . sensitive nature to reveal.' He turned to go, turned back again. 'Good, er, good work, DS Philips.'

He left the room.

Mickey turned to Marina, about to speak. She put her finger to her lips, looked at the door. They waited until Glass had entered the interview room and, along with Michael Fenton, escorted Lynn Windsor from the room.

Only then did Mickey speak.

'What was all that about?' he said. 'And where did you get all that stuff from?'

'I'll tell you later. Somewhere more private,' she said. 'All I can tell you at the moment, the most important thing at this time, is that Glass is dirty. He's as bent as they come.'

Mickey gave a small laugh. 'I think I'd guessed that.'

'And he's in this all the way.' Marina looked at her watch. 'Coffee time. Come on. I'm buying.'

They both left the room.

106

Phil's phone rang.

He thought it must be Marina calling him back, telling him what had happened in Mickey's interview with Lynn Windsor. But it wasn't. It was pathologist Nick Lines calling.

'I've got to take this,' Phil said to the others in the hotel room.

'Phil, it's Nick. How are you?'

'Suspended, believe it or not. How are you?'

There was a pause while Nick took in what Phil had just said. 'Sorry?'

'Suspended. DCI Glass has suspended me.'

'Why?'

'God knows. You'd better ask him.'

'I'm sorry to hear that.'

'It's OK,' said Phil. 'It's only temporary.' *I hope*, he added mentally. 'What can I do for you?'

'Well I've been trying to reach Rose Martin and can't get hold of her.'

'No,' said Phil, 'you won't. Can I help?'

'If you know where she is.'

Phil gave some thought to his answer. 'I don't think she's going to be around for a while.'

'Ah.'

'Yeah.' Let Nick think she was off the force again. Phil wouldn't contradict him.

'So can I help?'

'It was just something she was looking into. She found a brand on the foot of a dead girl. She asked if I could find a match anywhere for it.'

Phil stole a glance at Donna, back to the phone. 'And have you?'

'Not on a dead person, no. But that case you were working on, that boy from the cage, the one in the hospital. I spoke to a friend at the General. Apparently he's got one. I haven't seen the photos, but you've probably got access to them.' Then he realised what he had said. 'Sorry.'

'No problem. I'll pass the message across.'

'This suspension,' said Nick. 'You're going to fight it, I take it?'

'All the way.'

'With all you've got going on at the moment, you'd think Glass would need all the help he can get. He's making a big mistake.'

'Well obviously I agree with you. But don't worry.' Phil looked across at Fennell and Clemens. They were sitting on the bed, making plans for the raid later that night. 'I have a feeling our esteemed DCI won't be around much longer ...'

107

Glass sat down at the table in the interview room. A different interview room. One with no cameras or voice relay. A totally private room. For an impromptu Elders meeting.

Opposite him were Lynn Windsor and Michael Fenton. Lynn looked shattered, like she was barely there. Fenton's brow was furrowed. He had called Glass after Lynn had gone downstairs to meet someone and never come back. Mickey Philips had been identified, as had his car pulling away. The two Elders had arrived at the police station just in time.

Glass sensed that the others were on the verge of panic. He had to take control of the situation and do it quickly.

'We need a story,' he said. 'And fast. Concentrate. Think.'

Lynn Windsor started to speak. 'Look, Lawmaker—'

Glass cut her off. 'There's no need for that here. We're perfectly safe. No one's going to overhear us in this room. Talk freely. We need damage limitation. What have we got?'

Lynn tried to speak again. The words wouldn't come. Clearly she couldn't focus her mind. Her eyes dropped to the table, the floor. *Yeah*, thought Glass, *be ashamed*. He shook his head, turned away from her. *Useless*, he thought. *She almost gave us up. And I had such high hopes for her. Not any more.*

'You mentioned giving up the Gardener,' said Fenton. 'You said if we gave him up it would deflect attention from the shipment coming in tonight. Can you still do that? How has this changed things?'

Glass turned back to Lynn. 'What did he say to you?'

A weary, defeated sigh. 'I've told you . . . '

'Tell me again.'

'He said, tell me where the Gardener is. He said . . . ' Another sigh. It was such hard work. 'He said . . . that. Just that. Tell me where the Gardener is. Tell me where he is so we can stop him.'

'And that's it? Nothing else?'

She was about to speak, but stopped herself. She shook her head. 'No.' Her voice tiny, curled in on itself.

Glass studied her. 'You're lying. Tell me.'

Fenton leaned across the table. 'Don't talk to her like that . . . '

Glass looked up quickly, his eyes flashing at Fenton. 'Be quiet.'

Fenton caught the look. Was silenced.

'What else did he say?'

Another sigh that carried the weight of the world. 'He . . . he . . . called me . . . Teacher . . . '

The other two sat back.

'Oh my God . . . ' Fenton's hand went to his mouth.

'Said . . . said . . . he knew about the Elders . . . '

Glass felt the room zoom in and out of focus, like he was at both ends of a telescope simultaneously. He tried to blink everything else away. Concentrate. Focus.

'That's it,' Fenton was saying. 'It's all over. Might as well make a run for it now.' He made to stand up.

'No.' Glass leaned across the table, grabbed his wrist. Pulled him down again. 'We stick together. We work this out.'

'But they're on to us . . .'

'No they're not.' Glass shook his head. 'No they're not. They can't be. I'd have heard something. I'd know. And I've heard nothing.'

'But he knew . . .'

'Yes, he knew,' said Glass. 'But that doesn't mean he knows everything.' He looked back at Lynn. Lifted her head up by the chin, made eye contact. 'Did he mention the shipment? Tonight? Did he say anything about that?'

It took her a few seconds to focus. She shook her head. 'No . . .'

'You sure?' Searching her face for lies.

She shook her head once more. 'No . . . he didn't say . . .'

'Good.' Glass let her head go. It flopped back down. 'Good.' He sat back, thinking. Then leaned forward. 'Here's what we do. We stick to the plan.'

'But . . .'

'Listen. We stick to the plan. All of it. Where's the Gardener? At the farmhouse?'

'Probably,' said Fenton. 'That's his other place.'

'So he'll be doing the sacrifice there. Good. Right.' He slowly nodded his head. 'This is what'll happen. I'll announce to the squad that I've received some information. That the Gardener is at the farmhouse. I'll arrange for an armed response unit to accompany me. We'll break into the place, stop him.'

'But . . . isn't that dangerous?'

Glass gave a grim smile. 'For him, maybe. I'll be armed too. I'll make sure he doesn't get out alive. We rescue the boy, come back to town, everybody's happy. In the meantime, the shipment comes in at Harwich and everybody's happy there, too. Perfect diversionary tactic. And an impressive collar for Essex Police too. Perfect.'

Fenton rubbed his chin. 'It's risky. The farmhouse is where clients pick up and drop off. What if they see the place on the news? What if they come forward?'

Glass laughed. 'Come forward? After what they've done? I doubt it.'

'Is there anything there that links the place to us?'

Glass thought. 'It's where I took Faith Luscombe. Intending to move her back to the Garden. So I may have left some DNA traces there, but only small ones. And this way is better. I'll have a legitimate reason for being there. And I'll be in charge of the investigation. I'll be controlling everything. Don't worry. Just keep calm, play your part and everything will be fine.'

Lynn's head came up slowly. 'This information . . .'

Glass frowned. 'What information?'

'This information . . . about the Gardener . . . where did you get it from?'

'Nowhere. There is no information.'

'Did you . . . get it from me?'

He saw what she meant. Was she guilty, had she told them anything? What were the repercussions going to be for her? He thought. Came to a decision. Smiled at her.

'It'll be fine,' he said. 'You've got your solicitor with you, you'll be free to leave here on your own recognisance. You'll not be charged with anything. I'll just say the information came from . . . an informant. Don't worry. You won't be implicated.'

She nodded her head, grateful to hear what she wanted to hear. She wasn't aware of the silent exchange that passed between Fenton and Glass. Fenton's look said that he understood perfectly what Glass was doing. Glass's look asked whether Fenton wanted to challenge it. The way Fenton broke eye contact and looked away told him the answer was no.

Glass sat back. Looked at the other two. 'So that's it. Everything will go ahead as planned. Leave the Gardener to me. And hold your nerve. Everything will be fine if we all hold our nerve. Right?'

Fenton nodded.

Glass stood up, opened the door for them to leave. Fenton helped Lynn to her feet. As they passed the DCI on their way out, Glass whispered to Fenton, 'Look after her. She's very fragile. She may not last the night.'

Fenton, knowing exactly what he meant and wanting no part of it, hurried Lynn away down the corridor. Glass watched them go.

Smiling.

108

'Can I have your attention, please.'

Glass stood before the team, knocking on the window of the office behind him to get everyone listening. Mickey and Marina were at the back of the room, having received a text while they were out of the building having coffee. Marina had filled him in on Phil's phone call. Mickey had sat there. Jaw dropping further with each statement she made. He was so angry, felt so used and betrayed, that he hadn't wanted to return to the station. Marina had insisted.

'Let's see what he has to say,' she had said. 'So we know what he's doing and what we're dealing with.' Knowing she was right, Mickey had reluctantly agreed.

Now they stood there while Glass spoke. There was a gleam of triumphalism in his eyes.

'I've received new information,' he announced to the room, 'about the abductor of the boy Finn from the hospital. I know where he's taken him. If we're in time, we can stop him.'

Marina and Mickey exchanged looks. This wasn't what they had expected to hear.

'He's taken the boy to an abandoned farmhouse out near

Wakes Colne on the way to Halstead. He intends to kill him. We have to make sure he doesn't.

'An armed response unit have been contacted and are on their way. I will personally be taking charge of this. I will lead the unit. This man is armed and dangerous. We're taking no chances. Any questions?'

Mickey put his hand up. 'Where did this information come from?' Then adding, 'Sir.'

Glass looked irritated by the question. 'A confidential informant, DS Philips. I'm not at liberty to disclose that information.'

But Mickey kept going. 'Was it the one I've just had in the interview room?'

'Steady,' Marina whispered to him.

Glass was clearly annoyed now but couldn't show it with the whole room watching him. 'As I said, DS Philips, I'm not at liberty to say.'

'Will there be anybody from here on this team with you?' Mickey asked. 'We are MIS after all.'

'No,' said Glass. 'I'm the only one here who is firearm-trained. I'm the logical choice. I also don't want to give out a location for this farmhouse at the present time, as that information might leak and the abductor could run. And we wouldn't want that.' He looked quickly round the room, ready to stifle any more dissent. 'If there are no further questions, I must prepare. This is going to reflect well on the whole department. A huge morale boost, a great collar. Thank you.'

He walked out from behind the desk, through the room, past Marina and Mickey and swept out of the office. Silence followed his departure.

Marina turned to Mickey. 'Was that a "once more unto the breach" moment?'

People around her laughed. Mickey didn't.

'What was all that about?' he said to her. 'Where did he get that information from? Lynn Windsor?'

'I don't think it matters,' said Marina. 'He's playing a different game.' She thought for a moment. 'I've got to make a phone call.'

'Who to?'

'To your boss. Your proper boss. I think the team need a real briefing. Come on. We can't stay here.'

She turned and left. Mickey, confused but excited, followed.

109

The Hole in the Wall pub wasn't one of Mickey's favourite places to go in Colchester. In fact, it was one of his least favourite.

He associated it with the remnants of the town's counter-culture: indie kids, real-ale drinkers and students. Arty types, attracted by the theatre across the road. All mismatched wooden furniture and vintage leather sofas that you could sink into. That was the trouble. Once you were sunk in there, that was the day gone. And before you knew it, your life. Sitting there with your mates, drinking, arguing about something you'd read in the *Guardian*, dissecting the latest book or film or album, sorting the world out before it was your round. Even as a student he hadn't enjoyed places like this. They had made him feel uncomfortable. It was the waste. Talking when you could be doing something. But that, he thought, tipping his head back and putting the lager bottle to his lips, was just him.

Despite the alcohol, it wasn't a social gathering. They had needed somewhere to meet, not too far from the station, just far enough to not be discovered. And the pub was perfect.

The last place a clandestine police briefing would be expected to take place in.

Mickey looked round the table. Marina was sitting next to Phil, the pair of them looking a lot friendlier and more content than they had been recently. On the other side of Phil was Don Brennan. The older man looked thrilled to be back in the fray again. Rejuvenated. And enjoying the pint of dark beer that was in front of him. Across the table were two SOCA officers, Fennell and Clemens. Clemens seemed angry, itching to go. Fennell more measured. He, thought Mickey, would be the more approachable of the two. Although the way they sat, backs straight, wearing near-identical suits and ties, they could have been Mormons or Jehovah's Witnesses.

It was late afternoon. The pub was in its post-lunchtime lull, before the evening busy spell. Darkness was creeping in through the windows. They had managed to secure the largest table, furthest away from the bar. They went overlooked and unheard. But they kept their voices down just in case.

Phil made introductions, looked round the table. 'You'll be wondering why I've gathered you all here,' he said, smiling grimly. The smile dropped. 'Everyone's been brought up to speed. Everyone knows what's happening. It looks like this is the MIS team, not what's going on over in Southway.'

No one argued.

'Now we know the shipment's coming in tonight. But there's been an added complication. Mickey?'

'Glass won't be there,' he said. 'He's just announced that he's found the whereabouts of the Gardener, and he's leading a firearms team against him.'

'And he has to do that tonight?' said Clemens.

'It's a smokescreen,' said Marina. 'Something to divert attention away from his shipment arriving at Harwich. He establishes an alibi for himself and makes a high-profile arrest at the same time.'

And we miss out on him,' said Fennell.

'Not necessarily,' said Phil. 'You've still got his DNA all over Donna Warren's house. As well as Donna's first-hand testimony. You can get him that way. Plus the other Elders might want to roll over on him for a bit of leniency.'

Clemens shrugged. 'Possible. But we would have preferred a clean arrest.'

'I'm sure,' said Phil. 'But it'll still stick this way. He won't be able to wriggle out.

'And speaking of the raid,' he added, looking at the two SOCA officers, 'I won't be able to take an active part in it due to my suspension, I'm afraid.'

'That's all right,' said Clemens. 'We didn't invite you.'

'He means,' said Fennell, sugaring Clemens' words, 'that we haven't made provision for you.'

'No,' said Phil, 'but I think it's time you got us locals involved, don't you?'

'What did you have in mind?' said Fennell.

Phil pointed to Mickey. 'The finest detective sergeant in the county. Mickey Philips. Take him with you.'

'Well,' said Clemens, 'we don't—'

'I insist,' said Phil.

The two SOCA men looked at him, then at each other.

'It's time to play nicely,' said Phil.

Fennell nodded. 'You're right.'

'Good,' said Phil. 'Give the Super a ring in Chelmsford, tell him what's happening. Don't worry. He won't tell Glass. Not if he wants his career to continue.'

'Right,' said Fennell. He turned to Mickey. 'We've got a firearms unit coming up from London. They're on the way now.'

'OK,' said Mickey. 'Let's go and join them.'

'Which is all fine,' said Marina, 'but it still doesn't tell us where Glass is going to be. Where the farmhouse is. Or the Gardener. We don't know any of that.'

Phil thought for a moment. 'No,' he said, 'but I think I know someone who could tell us.'

'Who?' said Clemens.

'Remember I told you about that tramp? Paul?'

'The one you thought might be Paul Clunn,' said Fennell.

'That's him. If anyone knows where the Gardener is, and the farmhouse, it'll be him. In his own addled way.'

'And you know where he is?' asked Marina.

'I do. Want to come along?'

She did.

Phil smiled. 'Better bring your boots.'

'What about me?' said Don.

Phil looked at him. Mickey was aware of something passing between them. He wasn't sure what, though: he got the impression it could have been a father-and-son moment, or the sense of a baton being passed.

'Could you look after Donna and the boy?' asked Phil.

Don nodded. 'I'll call Eileen. Tell her we've got more coming round for dinner.'

'Thanks, Don.'

Don nodded. Looked away.

And in that gesture, that sad, defeated, redundant gesture, Mickey saw his own future. He was sure that Phil saw his too.

'Right.' Fennell looked at his watch. 'We'd better get going.'

Phil looked at Marina. 'So had we. Good luck, everyone. We'll need it.'

110

L ynn Windsor took a sip from her glass, looked out over the balcony.

It was dark now. She could see the lights along the other side of the river, the stream of car headlights heading away from the town centre. Beyond that she could see up the hill to the town centre. It should have been a beautiful sight. After all, she had paid enough for it. But she couldn't enjoy it. Not tonight. She couldn't enjoy anything tonight.

Another sip from the glass, larger this time.

Michael Fenton had been strange with her when he had driven her home. Distracted. Distant. But with a sadness to the distance. On the few occasions he had looked at her, it was with downcast, almost tearful eyes. She hadn't been able to hold his gaze either. They both knew without saying it that what would happen next wasn't going to be good.

He had let her out, driven quickly away. Started to say something, then stopped himself.

So she had come inside. Got changed, had a shower. Ignored the white wine in the fridge, gone straight to whisky.

And now she stood in her towelling bathrobe, drinking,

watching. All those other people. In their cars, on the streets, the trains, in their own homes. All those ordinary lives. Those brief lives.

At one time she would have called them boring. Living life blindfolded, she would have said. Unable to experience everything, do everything. Limited, bound by convention. By fear. Lynn hadn't been like that. She had prided herself on not being like that. She had wanted to experience everything, push herself to the extreme. She wanted to control, dominate. She wanted power, too. Had been brought up that way. Not just to feel superior, but to *be* superior.

She was her mother's daughter in every respect.

And look where it had got her.

Her hand trembled as it held the glass. She took another sip. Made it a mouthful. Felt the liquid burn as it travelled down inside her.

It was no more than she deserved.

What she had done, the things she had been responsible for, the lives she had ruined, ended ... Not her personally. Never her personally. But she had been there, in the background, pulling the strings. Dominating. Powerful.

Tears sprang into her eyes then. She looked down once more at the town. Thought of all the lives she had controlled, had taken. They could have still been here. They could have been like the people down there. Living their small, unimaginative lives. Beautiful lives, the kind she would never live.

Lynn thought of Mickey Philips. Of last night. He had given her a glimpse of another life. A better life. Happier. There had been a connection there, a real connection. And she had let it go. She'd had to. He would never have understood. Then she thought of that afternoon in the interview room. And how he had nearly reached her. A little bit more time ... and that would have been that.

She might as well have done. Told him what he wanted. She knew what was going to happen now. Knew she couldn't go back. She was tainted. No use. Just had to accept it.

Another mouthful. Her glass was empty. She reached down, tipped more in from the bottle. Replaced it on the deck. Heard a noise from behind her. She didn't turn round.

'I let myself in,' a familiar voice said.

He joined her on the balcony. She turned. Saw Glass's features looking out over the town. Another mouthful. It burned.

Neither of them spoke. For her, it was the silence of resignation. For him, she knew it must be the silence of anticipation.

'I know what you're here to do,' she said, taking another mouthful, vision swimming from all the whisky.

He sighed. 'This could have ended so differently, you know.'

'I know.' Another mouthful. Bigger this time.

'I had high hopes for you. Such high hopes . . . ' He stroked her shoulder.

She had felt his touch so many times before. Never tired of it. Now, she just wanted to fall into his embrace, sleep it all away.

She took another mouthful. The glass was empty. She refilled it.

'Careful,' he said, 'you don't want to drink it all. Lucky I brought you another.'

He placed an identical bottle next to the first one. Same brand, same size. She noticed he was wearing latex gloves.

'And here,' he said, reaching into his jacket pocket. He took out a brown plastic bottle, rattled it. 'Something to help you sleep.'

She took the bottle from him. Nodded.

'I'll wait while you do it,' he said.

'I thought you might.' Her mouth was dry despite all the liquid she had been pouring down it. She twisted the top off the bottle, shook out a few pills. Took them one at a time, swallowing them down with a mouthful of whisky.

He watched her all the while.

The pills went down easily. So easily.

'And another handful,' he said.

She did as she was told. The amount of whisky getting larger with each pill.

Her tears were falling freely now. She could hardly see the town, between the blur of salt water in her eyes and the alcohol affecting her vision. And now the pills. Could hardly see anything at all.

Her sobs became vocal. He shushed her. Not unkindly; tenderly. Like a lover would. She tried to be as quiet as she could.

Soon the pill bottle was empty. She let it drop on the deck.

'Good girl,' he said. 'Won't be long now.'

'Will you . . . will you wait with me . . . '

He looked at his watch. Back to her. She thought she saw a flash of irritation in his eyes. Blinked. It was gone.

'Yes,' he said. 'I'll wait.'

He stood next to her, watching.

She began to feel tired. Her head spinning. She closed her eyes.

'Take another drink,' his voice said.

She did so.

'Good girl.'

She closed her eyes once more. The town was slipping away. The balcony. The flat. Him. It was suddenly an effort to stand up. So she sat down. She heard glass breaking. Didn't have the energy to find out what it was, where it was. She just wanted to rest.

Then it was too hard to sit. She needed to lie down. She did so. Heard his voice.

'I'll see myself out.'

From the other end of a long, dark tunnel. Didn't have the strength, the words to answer him with. Let him go.

Tired. So tired. Sleep. She wanted sleep. It would be so peaceful.

So . . .

Lynn Windsor fell asleep.

111

'You ready, then?'

Marina nodded and got in the car. They set off for Halstead.

Neither spoke. *Johnny Cash: Unchained* provided the soundtrack.

'You OK?' Marina asked eventually, her voice low.

Johnny Cash was singing about how everything was done with a Southern accent where he came from. Some beautiful guitar work accompanying him.

Phil nodded as he drove. 'Working through it. You know.' He turned to her. Smiled. 'We'll get there.'

She placed her hand on his thigh. He kept it there.

The drive out to Halstead was busier than they had expected, catching the tail end of the evening rush-hour traffic. With the darkness had come rain, blowing across the road in front of them, hitting the windscreen like sheets of diamond-hard static. Cars were moving slowly on the twisting country roads, taking time on the hills, avoiding skids and spills.

They followed the villages along the River Colne, eventually arriving in Halstead.

Phil came to the crossroads in the town centre, went right. As he did so, he looked down the hill leading to the old mill at the bottom that represented the town centre. It was an old market town, the original architecture maintained, a place of decent restaurants, bars and pubs, upmarket independent furnishing stores. He and Marina had driven out for Sunday lunch a few times, bought a couple of little things for their new house. The shops were still hanging on. A few more empty ones than previously, a few more charity shops sprung up. He saw Marina looking.

'We'll have to come back here one Sunday,' he said.

She nodded. 'When this is over.'

'Yeah. When this is over.'

He drove out of the centre, down the hill towards the Halstead Manor Hotel. Pulled up in the gravel driveway. Johnny Cash was singing that it was so hard to see the rainbow through glasses as dark as his. Phil turned the music off. They looked at each other.

'Ready?' said Phil.

'You sure this is going to work?' said Marina. 'Asking a mad tramp what's going on?'

'Let's hope so,' he said.

'You sure he's not the murderer?'

'Wouldn't I have brought him in if he was?'

Marina shrugged. 'I don't know. You haven't been thinking straight these last few days.'

Phil sighed. 'I know. But I looked at him, looked in his eyes. It's not him, Marina. He's damaged, yes, troubled. But not a killer. He wanted the Garden to be a place of healing. Retreat.'

'And look what happened to that.'

'Let's go.'

They got out of the car. Seeing the rain start, they had both dressed practically. Jeans and boots. Waterproof jackets. Phil took a torch out of the boot of the car. 'This way.'

They walked off behind the back of the hotel, started down the bank towards the river. Phil swung the torch around. Picked up marks on the ground.

'Someone's been here,' he said.

'There was a murder here,' said Marina. 'I should think there have been a lot of people tramping around.'

'No,' said Phil, pointing to the path they were following. 'Look. There are fresh footprints. Fresh tracks. Someone's been down here recently.'

'Is that good?' asked Marina.

'If it's Paul,' said Phil, 'yes.'

'And if not?'

'Let's hope it's Paul,' he said.

They walked along the route as Phil remembered it. It was harder going in the dark, harder still in the rain. Secure footholds crumbled away to muddy nothing. Branches and trees used night as camouflage to entrap them. The two of them had to hold on to each other, help each other down and along.

'Here it is,' said Phil at last as they reached the river's edge. 'At least I think so.'

He swung the torch round. Listened. There was no sound except the rain hitting the water, the leaves. Like hot, sizzling fat or incessant machine-gun fire.

Along the muddy bank the torch picked out a larger area of darkness.

'There.'

They began to walk towards the cave mouth.

'This is it?' said Marina, stopping in front of it. 'The man who started the Garden. This is where he lives?'

'Yep. When he's not in one of his other properties dotted around town. All connected to the Garden, all derelict.'

She nodded. 'I could get a PhD out of him alone.' She peered into the cave mouth. 'Well, that looks inviting. What do we do, call to him? Leave food outside?'

'Or whisky,' said Phil. He swung the torch into the cave, stepped inside.

'Careful.'

'I am.' He walked on. 'I think someone's been here,' he called back.

Marina heard his voice echoing round the stone mouth.

'I think—'

Phil screamed. There was a clattering, smashing sound. Silence.

'Phil? Phil?' Marina ran into the cave mouth, still shouting. Panic rising inside her. 'Phil . . . Phil . . . '

'It's . . . all right . . . ' His voice, distant, distorted. Echoing.

'Where are you? Phil?'

'I'm . . . Don't come any closer. You'll do the same.'

'What?'

'There's a . . . an entranceway here. A slope. I didn't see it and I've just slid down it.'

She saw the faint glow of torchlight against the darkness, went towards it. She reached the lip of the shaft Phil had fallen down. Knelt before it. It was just big enough for one person to go down, as long as they weren't too wide. She could see him at the bottom, looking up. The sides, where the torchlight hit them, looked smooth. Too smooth to climb up again.

'How are you going to get out?'

'I don't know,' he said. 'Maybe Paul's down here. I'll ask him.'

'And maybe he isn't.' She sighed. 'Have you still got that tow rope in the boot?'

'Yeah, I think so.'

'I'll go and get it. Don't wander off.'

'Yeah, thanks. I'll bear that in mind.'

Marina stood up, made her way back out of the cave. She looked around, tried to get her bearings. The woods seemed scarier without Phil. Bigger, wilder. Things unseen lurking behind trees.

Trying to swallow down the panic that was threatening to rise within her, and telling herself there was nothing to be scared of, she set off in what she hoped was the direction they had come from. Back to the hotel, back to the car.

As quickly as she could.

112

The circus was on the move. Under cover of darkness and with the Super's reluctant, angry blessing. Mickey sat in the first van of the convoy, up front with Fennell and Clemens. Body armour on over his day clothes, the two SOCA officers doing the same.

The Super hadn't been happy when Fennell had called him. Engaging in a clandestine operation on his turf without his consent was exactly the kind of thing to make him angry. But Fennell, displaying great political skill, had won him round. Reminded him what a feather in his cap it would be for a people-trafficking operation to be halted on his manor. That the covert joint operation (he had stressed the word *joint*) would result in the rooting out and successful capture of a corrupt police officer. How such a superintendent would be looked on by the Home Office in the next round of budget cuts. When all this was pointed out, whatever misgivings the Super had were kept to himself.

Fennell had hung up, clearly happy with himself.

Yeah, thought Mickey, now we just have to carry all of that out. Because if we don't, it won't be the SOCA glory boys who'll take the blame. Not once they've involved the locals.

The convoy drove along the A120 towards Harwich. There were two ports on the mouth of the River Stour. Felixstowe and Harwich. Most of the heavy cargo, Fennell had informed them all at the briefing, came through Felixstowe. And as a result it was the more carefully guarded of the two. Weaver and Balchunas' cargo was coming in the Harwich side, where it would be less likely to be stopped and searched.

They would get in place for the shipment, identify it, follow it to the lock-up.

And then take them down.

The firearms unit was in the van behind. Mickey felt uncomfortable with them around. The cowboy outfit, Phil always called them. The shoot-first-fill-in-compliance-forms-later brigade. He must have caught Phil's allergy to them, Mickey thought, smiling to himself.

They were approaching Harwich, going round the roundabouts, heading down to the port itself.

Mickey always found Harwich a strange place. Away from the front, there were rabbit-warren streets of old Georgian houses, interesting local pubs and even a converted lighthouse. But the front, and the port, was different.

They drove along the front and round to the side, the convoy coming to a halt in a car park by the edge of the water.

Mickey got out, walked down to the sea.

It was raining fully now, and dark. The only sound was the tide lapping against the shore, rough waves crashing in, fizzing out as they withdrew. Mickey pulled his coat around him. He could feel the cold, the damp penetrate.

Felixstowe on the opposite side was lit up against the night. Etched against the darkness, it was all looming boxlike cranes and blinking lights. It looked sinister, alien. The port itself resembled a grounded alien spacecraft, no longer needing to cloak itself, wounded but still dangerous. The cranes along the shoreline, dark and top-heavy on foursquare legs, looked like the walkers from the old Star Wars films. Like they were the advance guard from the ship, about to come stomping across the estuary, all blackened and rusting, guns blazing.

Mickey shivered. Hoped it was just the cold.

Clemens got out of the van, came and stood beside him. He shook out a cigarette, lit up. Offered the pack to Mickey as an afterthought. Mickey refused.

Clemens had been silent on the journey. Mickey didn't know the man well enough to ask why.

'Just heard,' said Clemens, blowing smoke towards the other side of the estuary. 'My partner. Slipped into a coma.'

'I'm sorry,' said Mickey. Then thought. 'But isn't Fennell your partner?'

'Just drafted in. We know each other, have worked together before. But my other partner was sliced up a couple of days ago. He's been fighting for his life since then.'

Mickey didn't know what to say. Thought he wasn't expected to say anything, just listen.

'And you know who did it?'

'Who?'

'That slag back at the hotel. Her.'

Mickey said nothing. He could guess where this was going.

'And she's going to get away with it. Claim self-defence.'

'Was it?' asked Mickey. 'Self-defence?'

Clemens sighed. Shook his head. Blew more smoke. 'Didn't expect you to understand. Met your boss. See where you get it from now. Be trying to turn you into a *Guardian* reader too.'

Mickey hadn't taken to Clemens. Too quick to anger, too fast with his tongue. Looking for a fight. Not good traits to

451

have in someone who was supposed to be watching your back. He would have to be aware of that.

He didn't reply. Didn't rise to it.

The two men kept looking across the water, not speaking, each in their own world.

Others came out of the van to join them.

Then Fennell arrived, putting his phone away.

'Your boss said you were looking forward to doing some proper police work again,' he said to Mickey. 'Bit of thief-taking.'

Mickey gave a grim smile. 'Beats paperwork, I suppose.'

'Certainly does.' Fennell looked at his watch. 'Time to get organised.'

113

Phil tried to stand. Slowly, unsure of how much space there was between his body and the ceiling of the cave. Not much. Not enough for him to stand fully upright.

He checked himself out. No severe pains anywhere, nothing that indicated twisted ankles or broken bones. Just soreness resulting from the speed of the descent and the abruptness of the landing. He would hurt tomorrow.

If he could get out again.

He swung the torch around. The chamber he was in seemed to be a naturally occurring space that had been hollowed out further. Some of the rock looked smooth, age-worn; some looked hacked at, hewn.

He turned round slowly. Played the torch in front of him. Someone lived down here.

A bed frame of twisted, heavy branches held a mattress made from hessian sacking, straw and leaves spilling from loose seams. Some old blankets, holed and mildewed, had been thrown on to it. The whole thing stank.

He looked more closely at the bed, trained his torch on it. There was what looked like another bed next to it, in the shadows. At the foot of it a small broken table. Probably liberated from the hotel's bins, thought Phil. He shone the torch beam on the other bed. And recoiled as if he had been hit.

Laid out there were the remains of a mummified corpse. Clothing rotted away, skin like dusty old leather. Bones sticking through. But preserved, reverentially. Either side of it were candles.

Pulling his eyes away from the bed, he studied the small table. It had been painted with the same symbols as on the walls of the cellar at East Hill. The calendar. On it were several items, like the contents of someone's pockets but decades old, laid out as if they were offerings on an altar. Phil moved in closer to look. A cigarette lighter. Some beads. A watch, the leather strap all eaten away. A wallet.

He reached forward and, fearful that it might crumble to dust in his hands, slowly opened the wallet.

There was still money in there. Single pound notes. Ten-pound notes. Fives. All decades old. A library card, long out of date. He screwed up his eyes, tried to make out the name. Did so.

Paul Clunn.

'Oh my God . . .'

Then: a noise. Echoing.

Phil turned, swinging the torch, catching his head on the low ceiling. He rubbed at it. Kept looking round. Listening. All he could hear was the blood rushing in his ears.

He tried to blink the pain away, listen.

Nothing. No more sound. He shone the torch on the walls once more, this time noticing that the same design had been painted there. Old, the paint fading away to darkness.

It wasn't Paul who lived down here. Phil was sure of that. Whoever it was, it wasn't Paul.

The Gardener? Was it him?

He checked the entranceway he had come down. Looked for footholds. The rock was smooth, worn. The space just big enough for his body to pass through. He tried to climb up it. Couldn't get a grip. Slid back down again.

He looked round once more. Panic was beginning to set in. Phil hated confined spaces. Had always suffered from claustrophobia. Being underground just made it worse.

He tried once more to pull himself up the shaft. Thrust his elbows out, forced his body to move behind him. The space wasn't wide enough. He tried again.

And his elbows jammed against the sides. He couldn't move.

His breathing increased. He felt himself start to panic. He didn't want to stay here, stuck. He didn't know how long it would take Marina to return with the rope. There was only one thing for him to do.

He relaxed his arms. Felt able to move once more. Wriggled his body down the tunnel until he collapsed on to the floor, back in the same place he had started from.

He stood up as far as he could go. Looked around again. Whoever lived down here must have another way out, he reasoned. The entrance was only one way. He knelt down on the floor, played the beam of the torch round the base of the walls. Looking for cracks, other tunnels, anything.

There were a few. Most of them just looked like fissures, cracks in the rock. Not big enough to climb inside, just tapering away to nothing. But there was one that seemed to widen out into a tunnel. It was small, cramped. But big enough to get inside, pull himself along with his elbows. And push himself backwards if he had to.

Probably.

He heard the noise again. Echoing round the rock. It sounded like a cry.

Of pain. Of fear.

Was it an animal? Or a human? And more importantly, was it coming from the tunnel he was preparing to go down?

He had to find out.

He knelt down, stuck the torch between his teeth and, flattening down on to his stomach, pushed himself into the small space.

He remembered a similar situation a couple of years ago. He remembered what was waiting for him at the end of that tunnel. Felt his breathing increase at the memory, tried to control it. Save his energy for movement.

Then, not knowing whether he was going towards the sound or away from it, whether what was up ahead was worse than what he was leaving, he began to edge his way along.

114

The child was still shivering. Good. The Gardener liked that.

No he didn't. He loved that.

Made him even more excited. Made the anticipation all the sweeter.

The child gripped the bars of the cage. Pulling on them, rattling them, trying to escape. No good. Too well made.

He laughed at the boy. It ended up as a cough.

Deep, racking, bent double while the painful, angry barks came from his body, gasping for breath as his lungs, his chest burned.

Eventually the coughing fit subsided. He had something in his mouth. Lifting the hood up, he spat on the ground. Looked at it. Black-dark and glistening.

Blood.

The cough had weakened him. It was getting worse. Taking more out of him. Putting his body through more pain. Each spasm taking longer to recover from.

He pulled the hood back in place, looked down at the altar. His tools were laid out in their usual precise manner. Candles lit now on either side. He drew strength just from seeing them. Stood up straight. Looked at the boy.

Smiled. No laughing this time.

'Soon ... soon ...' He picked up the sharpened trowel. Played the candlelight off its gleaming blade. Sent mirror flashes of light on to the boy, who flinched each time the light caught him. That gave him an idea.

The Gardener smiled again. This was a good game. He angled the blade, caught the light, flashed it at the boy, who recoiled every time, moved away to a different spot in the cage. The Gardener giggled, changed the position of the blade, tried to catch the boy again. The boy whimpered, moved once more.

The Gardener loved this, could have played it for hours.

But he didn't have hours. He looked at the chart. It had to be done soon. It had to be done now.

He advanced on the cage.

Ready for the boy now.

Ready for the sacrifice.

So the Garden could live again.

115

'Wait for my signal. Have you got that? No one does anything until they get my signal. Understood?'

It was understood.

Glass had never felt so alive. He had forgotten just how good it felt to take down a villain. To feel the adrenalin and testosterone surge through his system, build up inside him like it was living lightning, ready to pulse from his fingertips, take out anyone who tried to stop him.

It wasn't living lightning. But the semi-automatic in his hands was the next best thing.

The firearms unit was in front of him. They were standing in the overgrown back yard of the farmhouse. The night was sin-black, hiding them from any eyes that might be watching. The farmhouse was boarded up. No lights showing. It seemed uninhabited. But it wasn't empty. Glass knew that. For a fact.

'Right,' he said to the unit. 'The target is in that building. My information tells me he'll be in the cellar. What plans we have indicate that that's in the front of the house, with a door going down to it from the kitchen, which is in the middle. That's where we're headed.'

He turned to the firearms unit's senior officer, Joe Wade. 'Now, Sergeant Wade has briefed you all. You know where you've got to be. I'll be going in through the front here with the A Team. Remember. This man is highly dangerous. Shoot to kill. And get that boy out alive.' One more look at the men. They stood there, all in body armour, guns held before them, looking like shock troops sent from the future. Glass's adrenalin and testosterone surged even more.

One more look at Sergeant Wade.

'On your signal, Sergeant.'

Wade gave the order. The unit moved in, surrounded the farmhouse.

On Wade's signal, the front and back doors were simultaneously battered down, the officers streaming in towards the middle of the house.

The only illumination inside came from the lights of the officers. Checking every corner of every room, securing each one before moving through the old house. It smelled of damp, abandon. The air stale, old. Dust rose as the officers tramped through.

Glass was loving it. What he was born for. A leader of men, gun in hand, ready for a righteous kill. As soon as he had picked up the gun, he had felt his finger begin to twitch. He had thought that itchy trigger fingers were an old cliché, but to his surprise he had found it to be actually true. And now, running through the farmhouse with the rest of the men, he wondered just how easy it would be to accidentally squeeze that trigger, take out one of the CO19 boys just for the hell of it.

He mentally slapped himself out of it. These were his own people. He had a job to do.

They reached the cellar door. Sergeant Wade looked to Glass, waiting for him to give the nod. Glass took a deep breath. Another. Nodded.

The door was battered to splinters. The unit rushed down the cellar steps. Glass followed. Finger wrapped round the trigger guard, hand ready to take off the safety, let it go.

But he didn't.

He stopped, stood still. They all did.

The cellar was empty.

Glass shone his torch round. Nothing. Clean.

He walked over to one corner, scrutinised it with his torch. A small pile of bones was stacked neatly against the bricks. He examined the wall. There had been a cage here. He knew that, had seen it himself. A smaller one than East Hill, an abandoned one, kept in reserve. It had been removed.

His head moved frantically from side to side. He swung the torch wildly, checking if he was hiding somewhere, ready to spring out at them. Nothing.

Glass sighed. Looked at Wade. The unit were pumped up, minds engaged for action. They looked disappointed, angry. Like volcanoes denied the chance to erupt. Violent lovers spurned a climax.

Glass rubbed his face with the back of his hand. Felt anger well up inside him. He wanted to strike out, hit something. Or someone.

'He's not here ... not here ...'

Wade looked around, checking for himself. He looked at Glass.

'He's not here, Sergeant ...'

'I can see that, sir.' Wade crossed to Glass. 'I think you'd better have a word with your informant, sir,' he said.

'Yes,' said Glass. 'I'd better.'

'Come on then, let's go,' said Wade.

The unit went back up the stairs, not wanting to believe they'd been denied action, swinging their guns around, checking just in case the target was waiting elsewhere in the house to surprise them.

They regrouped outside. Wade looked towards Glass.

'What do we do now, sir?'

Glass thought. There had to be somewhere else, had to be ... Think ...

'I ... I don't know, Sergeant ...'

Think ... He had dismantled the cage ... he would have put it somewhere else ... Think ...

Yes. He had it. He knew where it would be.

He turned to Wade. 'I'm sorry, Sergeant. You can stand your men down now. Thank you.'

Glass turned, began to walk away.

'Where are you going?' Wade called after him.

'To talk to my informant,' said Glass, without turning round. 'See what he's got to say for himself.'

He could still do it. Still make the kill, find the child.

Salvage something.

There was still time.

Glass hurried to his car, drove away as fast as he could.

116

'They've loaded up.' Fennell, his finger pressed to his ear-piece, turned to the rest of the group. 'The trucks have just left the port. They'll be on their way past here soon.'

The convoy had split up, and they were now parked in a superstore car park on the outskirts of Harwich. The store was closed, the car park – and the roads around it – deserted. Rain was still falling, the lights in the car park throwing out sporadic pools, no match for it and the darkness. The van was in the shadows of the main building. They couldn't be seen from the main road, but they had a clear view of the road coming up from the port.

Another van in the convoy had driven to the entrance of the import-export lock-up and was in place, waiting. Their target was a set of warehouses off a gated trading estate down past the oil refinery. They didn't want to move too quickly, give themselves away.

The third van was in place outside the port itself. Sitting next to the high metal railings with a clear view across the half-empty truck park to the offloading ramps. It was one of them who had called.

As soon as Fennell spoke, the mood in the van changed. There had been forced humour, tension building inane, unfunny things to hilarious levels, making the most unamusing utterances amusing. But his words changed all that. Now they were focused, ready. No more laughing. No more speaking. A team with a job to do.

Mickey looked across at Clemens. At first glance he seemed as concentrated as the rest of them. Eyes – and mind – narrowed down to the task before them. But Mickey studied him further. He was lost somewhere, out on his own. Lips curled, a slight smile of anticipation on them.

Mickey looked at Fennell. The other man was talking into his mic once more. Mickey felt he should have a quiet word, warn him that perhaps Clemens' head wasn't in the right place for this. That he could become a liability. But there was no way he would get a chance now. He just hoped someone else would pick him up on it.

And in the meantime, he would just have to watch him.

Fennell turned to them all once more. 'Any questions?'

'Yeah,' said Mickey. 'Do we know who's there? Balchunas? Anyone else?'

'We don't,' said Fennell. 'But we can expect him. And maybe Fenton, I don't know. Anything else?'

Mickey again. 'What the trucks are actually going to do once they're inside the gates, do we know that?'

Clemens turned to him. Sneered.

Mickey ignored him.

'Good question,' said Fennell. 'No, we don't. If things go according to plan, we step in, catch them in the act. Simple.'

'And if they don't?' someone else said.

'We improvise,' said Clemens. 'We do whatever we have to do to get them.'

'Right,' said Mickey.

Fennell turned back, in conversation once more. Mickey looked at Clemens again. His finger was never far from his trigger.

Fennell closed off his earpiece, turned to the rest of them. 'The trucks will be passing us at any moment.'

They watched. Several seconds later – although it felt like minutes – two trucks carrying metal containers passed them.

'There we go,' said Fennell.

They let a certain amount of counted time pass, then followed at a distance.

117

Donna walked to the window, pulled back the curtain, looked into the street. Satisfied there was no one watching her or the house, she let the curtain drop, returned to her seat.

'It's all right,' said Don, 'you're safe here.'

She nodded. Wanting to believe him. Knowing it was going to take more than words to make her feel that. Especially after what she had been through these past few days.

They had eaten, Eileen making a huge bowl of pasta carbonara. Both Donna and Ben had had thirds. She thought Ben would have just kept going if it hadn't run out. And it was good, too. Proper food, she thought. The kind she only ever saw on TV, or other people eating in a restaurant.

And wine with it. Not the cheap stuff from Ranjit's on the corner that she glugged by the bottleful and that left her burning inside for days afterwards, but proper stuff. Good stuff.

She had wanted to drink all of that, too. But had stopped herself. Made do with just one and a half glasses. Didn't want her hosts staring at her.

Don's wife had been very kind to her. She didn't seem to

mind the fact that Don had invited her and Ben along both for dinner and to sleep the night.

'It's no trouble,' she had said. 'We're always looking after Phil's daughter. And we used to do this a lot. Take in children, especially. When we were fostering.'

Donna had nodded. 'Right.'

She could remember what foster homes were like. Or the ones she had been in when her mother couldn't cope. Nothing like this one.

She had given a small smile. 'Don and Donna,' she'd said. 'I could be your daughter.' Her voice had trailed away.

Eileen had made a fuss of Ben. Got him something to drink, asked him if he wanted a bath, what his favourite TV show was, all of that. He was wary at first, not wanting to answer in case it was a trick. But Eileen had spoken to him clearly and honestly, and he had responded. He was now curled up in a bed upstairs, fast asleep.

And now she was sitting with Don and Eileen, in their living room, sipping from another bottle of wine. The room felt lovely. Warm. Safe. The armchair nearly big enough to sleep in. Donna could have done.

She could get used to this, she thought. Just stay here. Always.

She felt herself tearing up. Didn't want to cry. Struggled to hold it in.

She looked across at Don. He seemed friendly too. He had the feel of an ex-copper about him, but he didn't shove it in your face the way some of them did. Like some of her clients did, even. But now he seemed on edge, distracted.

'You heard from Phil?' Donna asked.

Don looked up, startled, as if she had woken him from a dream. 'No. No. I don't ... don't expect to. Not tonight.' He slumped back into his own thoughts.

Eileen leaned forward. 'So, Donna ... what about you? What are you going to do next?'

Donna had thought about that. She had followed Ben upstairs, had a bath after him. Lay there thinking. She couldn't go back to the way things had been. Not any more. Not after what she had just been through. She didn't want to go home, either. Not after everything that had happened there.

Maybe it was time to get herself sorted, she had thought. Get her head, her body straightened out. Maybe.

'I don't know, Eileen,' she said. 'I can't ... I don't want to go home. Not after ... you know.'

Eileen nodded.

'And there's Ben ... ' She sighed. 'I suppose he's ... ' She trailed off.

'You're all he's got,' said Eileen.

She was right. He was Donna's now. Whether she liked it or not. Her responsibility. And she had to act responsible.

Donna smiled. 'Maybe I'll write about what's happened,' she said. 'Get it turned into a film.'

Eileen smiled along with her. 'That would be fun.'

'Yeah,' said Donna, nodding, 'maybe I'll do that.'

Don stood up, went to the kitchen. She heard the fridge door open and close. Heard him rummaging around in a drawer for a bottle opener. The glug of beer into a glass. He returned with a pint, took a large mouthful, set it on the table beside him.

'Don't get drunk,' said Eileen.

'I'm not going to get drunk,' said Don, a trace of irritability in his words.

Eileen turned to Donna. Dropped her voice. 'Don's never left the police force. Not in his heart. It's difficult when he knows there's something big going on. Still wants to be there. In on the action.'

'I can hear you, you know.'

Eileen turned to him. Smiled. 'I know you can.'

Donna saw love in that smile. Silence fell.

'Well I don't know about you,' she said, 'but I'm glad I'm not there. Too much excitement. And not the right kind, you know what I mean?'

'I quite agree,' said Eileen.

Don sighed.

'Let's see what's on the telly,' said Eileen, searching for the remote.

They heard a cry from upstairs. Donna stood up, ready to run.

'It's all right,' said Eileen. 'It sounds like Josephina turning over in her sleep. Nothing to worry about.'

Donna sat down once more. Eileen was still looking for the remote. She found it, but before switching on the TV, she turned to Donna. 'You responded like a mother,' she said.

Donna stared at her. 'What? What you on about?' But she knew. She could feel her face reddening at the words.

Eileen smiled once more. 'That's what a mother would do. Her first thought. Protect her child, whatever.'

Donna took a mouthful of wine. Another. Until she had drained the glass.

She thought about Eileen's words. Her own actions.

'Yeah,' she said, heart full of love, full of fear. 'Maybe I've . . . maybe I've gained a son.'

She stopped speaking. Felt herself tearing up once more. Wouldn't allow it to happen. Forced herself under control.

Eileen looked away. Fumbled with the remote, turned the TV on. *Spooks*. Impossibly beautiful spies saving the world in implausibly ridiculous ways.

'Oh,' she said, more to fill the silence than anything else, 'I like this. Although I thought it was better when that handsome one was in it.'

'Yeah,' said Don, bitterness curling the edges of his words, 'let's watch someone else save the world, shall we?'

The three of them fell into silence once more.

Eileen looked over at Don. She felt for him. Donna could see why. It couldn't be easy to feel redundant. Especially when he'd been in the bar with the rest of them earlier on. Especially when it was all he wanted to do.

'So you've gained a son?' said Don, quietly, apology in his eyes as he looked at Donna.

She nodded.

'That's good,' he said. 'Very good. You look after him, mind.'

'I will.' And she knew, as she said the words, that she would.

Don sighed. 'I just hope I've still got one . . .'

The three of them fell back into silence and watched while the impossibly beautiful people saved the world.

118

Phil clawed his way down the tunnel. Slowly, elbows tucked underneath his body, arms and shoulders scraping the sides as he pulled himself along, his body being dragged over the uneven, jagged rocks. The ceiling was low. He could barely bring his head up to look forward.

Someone had been along this tunnel before him. That didn't make it any easier, though. The rocks were centuries old, not about to be smoothed down any time soon.

The tunnel twisted, turned. Phil, torch clamped between his teeth, had no option but to follow it. He noticed other fissures in the walls as he went, the beam of light swinging from side to side as he turned his head in the cramped space. Some were larger than others; a couple looked big enough to get his body into. He wondered whether he ought to try one of them.

Then he stopped. The tunnel forked before him. Two rocky pools of darkness ahead, leading off in different directions. He tried to look behind him. Couldn't. Wondered if he could crawl backwards, shuffle back the way he had come. Marina might be there by now, Calling down to him, throwing a rope for him to climb up.

He tried. Elbows moving in reverse, pushing his body back-wards over the rough rock, away from the light in front of him, back into the darkness. His shoulders hitting the low ceiling as he went, scraping pain down his back, gasping, crying out.

He stopped, unable to move any further. Flattened his body out, dropped. Sighed. Dust flew up in front of him.

He tried not to panic. No good; he could feel it bubbling up inside him. He hated confined spaces, felt claustrophobic even in a lift. Why had he done this? Why had he subjected himself to it?

Because he'd heard a cry, the rational side of his brain told him. He'd heard something that sounded like a person in pain. Or an animal.

Or a child.

And finding the skeleton back there had given him no choice.

He sighed once more, craned his head upwards as far as he could, looked in front of him.

The torch fell from his mouth, slick with saliva. He groped round for it in the semi-darkness, his hand still tucked under his body, unable to move too much. Found it. Tried to wipe away the grit and dust the handle was now coated with, replace it in his mouth.

He looked ahead once more. The fork in the tunnel. Which way to go.

He closed his eyes, listened. Any sound, any cry . . .

Kept listening.

Heard nothing.

Panic attacked him once more, clawing at him, making his body want to get up, jump around, stretch. Kick out at being enclosed. Scream.

He bit down on the torch handle to stop himself from

doing that. Let out a strangled cry instead, forced his body to remain still. Not to kick. He wouldn't just injure himself; he could bring the whole cave roof down on his head.

The wave of panic subsided. He lay still, breathing deeply, not caring about the grit, the dust he was inhaling. He moved forward towards the fork, still listening.

Nothing.

He tried something else. Taking the torch from his mouth, he turned it off. Lay there in absolute silence, pitch blackness.

Maybe this is what it's like to be dead, he thought. Lying all alone, still, cold, in the darkness. In nothingness.

No. That wasn't death, he thought. That was just self-pity. He wasn't dead yet. He had a job to do. He listened once more. Waited while his eyes focused on the darkness, studied the two tunnels ahead of him. There was a faint, flickering light coming from the one on the left. That was the one to aim for.

Turning the torch on once more, he crawled towards it with renewed vigour.

It was even narrower than the previous tunnel. Lower. Phil struggled to pull himself along. Started to worry whether it was going to get narrower still, whether he would just end up wedged inside it. Whether that was the sound he had heard: a child or an animal that had gone exploring and become trapped down here, stuck immovably in the rock. Wondered whether that would be his fate.

Tried to shake those thoughts from his head, keep going.

He felt air on his face. A small breeze, blowing towards him. It didn't last long. There was something at the end of the tunnel. Adrenalised by this, he tried to ignore the pain of the rock as it gripped him harder, squeezed him tighter, and began to move faster towards the air, the flickering light.

He rounded another corner. And saw the exit ahead of him.

Smaller than the entrance, but he could still get through it, if he pushed himself. He had to. He reached it. Pulled himself through. Ignored the pain screaming from his shoulders, his ribs, the jagged rocks as they cut into him through his clothes; just kept going. He managed to pull his legs out. And he was free.

He lay on the stone floor, gasping for air, willing his injured body to mend.

Eventually he opened his eyes. Looked round.

And felt his body shiver.

It looked like a chamber dug beneath a graveyard. Skulls and bones lined the walls. He wasn't sure if they had been piled there or if they were actually the walls themselves. There were a lot of them. The floor he was lying on was flagged, old. He recognised it, but couldn't place it. It was strewn with flowers.

He pulled his body into a sitting position, ignoring the pain as he did so. He knew what he would see next. Wasn't disappointed. An altar. And beyond it, a cage of bones.

And in the cage was Finn. Cowering, terrified.

Phil tried to pull himself to his feet, cross the floor to help the boy. He stood up, head throbbing, spinning. Heard a noise behind him.

He turned.

And there was the figure from his dream.

A hood of sacking and a stained leather apron. In his hand, something sharp and gleaming.

Moving quickly towards him.

Phil raised his hands, tried to stop him, tried to cry out. But his body wouldn't move, his mouth wouldn't work. He wanted to fight him off, call for help.

Nothing.

The figure was in front of him now. Eyes like darkness. Eyes like death.

He raised his hand.

And Phil was back in blackness again.

119

'Here it comes . . . '

Fennell's voice once more.

The van had followed the two trucks as they made their way to the lock-up. Not wanting to raise suspicion, they had driven past as the trucks turned in, went through the gates.

Now they were parked up down the road, waiting for the other van to arrive.

The road was deserted. Nothing out but the rain and them.

The two other vans arrived. Clemens caressed the trigger of his gun. Mickey tried not to look at him.

Instead he looked at Fennell. 'What's the signal?'

'Wait for it,' Fennell said. 'We're just checking everyone's in position . . . '

Mickey said nothing. Around him he was aware of the rest of the team, all pumped up and ready to go. Guns ready. Heads focused.

He tried to look out through the windscreen, see what was going on beyond the gates. All he could see was a high metal fence topped with razor wire, arc lights aiming inside the compound. There was a large warehouse in the centre, where the two trucks had gone. The rest of the space was taken up with metal containers. Hundreds of them, piled tall and wide, like a modernist architect's dream city. Multicoloured high-rises.

The door of the warehouse was still open.

'Not yet . . . ' said Fennell. 'Wait . . . '

Mickey kept watching. A green 4x4 drove up from behind a stack of containers. He frowned. A green 4x4 . . . Why was that . . .

He knew. Finn, the boy, had been abducted from the hospital in a green 4x4. He would bet anything that this was the same one. He told Fennell.

'Good,' Fennell said. 'A bit more evidence.'

Still no one spoke. Everyone watched.

Waiting for the signal.

120

'Phil? Phil . . .'

Marina stood at the mouth of the cave, called inside.

It had taken her longer than she realised to reach the car and get the rope. The forest had been treacherous, the rain making it much harder. She had slipped down bank sides, been hit and scratched by branches and walked round in circles twice. But she had made it back to the hotel and the car eventually and had returned with the rope.

And now there was no reply.

'Phil . . .'

Nothing.

'Stop messing about. Come on, Phil.'

Still no reply.

Marina was getting worried now. Maybe something had happened to him down there. Maybe he had hurt himself.

Maybe he had been attacked.

Wrapping the rope over one shoulder, she knelt by the opening, peered down. She had expected to see Phil's torch down there, but there was nothing. She couldn't see a thing. She was about to straighten up, take out her phone and try to call him, when she felt something being pressed into the back of her neck.

Something hard and metallic.

She knew a gun when she felt one.

She also knew the voice that went with it.

'Well, well, well,' it said. 'Fancy meeting you here . . .'

121

Phil opened his eyes. And felt panic begin to overwhelm him. He was in the cage.

His nightmare had come true.

He looked round. Next to him, Finn was curled as far into the corner as he could go. The boy's eyes were staring, vacant. Shock, thought Phil. He didn't blame him.

Phil's head was spinning from where the Gardener had hit him. He felt dizzy, nauseous. His body was tired and sore from the crawl through the tunnel. And the panic was still rising within him. Knowing it wouldn't be of any help to give in to it, he tried to tamp it down, control it. Do something constructive instead.

He looked through the bars of the cage. The Gardener was at the altar. Head down, waving his hand over twin candles at either side, reciting some kind of invocation. He hadn't noticed that Phil was awake. Good.

Finn managed to focus, stared at Phil. Moved further away from him.

'It's OK,' whispered Phil, 'I'm a friend. I'm here to help you. Get you out.'

He saw the boy mouth the word 'friend'. Hoped he could live up to the description.

Phil grabbed hold of the bars of the cage. Twisted.

Nothing.

He kept going, twisting, pulling as hard as he could.

Nothing. The bone wouldn't give.

Again. Harder this time, forcing it.

And there it was. A crack. The smallest of splinterings in the bone. But something to work on. He kept twisting.

The Gardener looked up. Saw what he was doing. Picked up one of the blades from the table, came towards him. Phil took his hands off the bars, stayed where he was.

Up close, the Gardener's mask looked terrifying. It was the absence of humanity, of features to talk to. Like a horror-film scarecrow come to life. Probably why he had done it in the first place, thought Phil.

Phil was determined not to be scared, intimidated by the figure before him. After all, he had seen him without his mask, talked to him, even.

If his guess was right.

'I assume,' he said, his voice louder and more confident than he felt, 'that the mummy on the bed back there is Paul Clunn?'

The Gardener stopped moving. Put his head on one side, listening. Phil kept talking.

'His body. I found it back there. Was he your first? Is that when you decided you liked it?'

The Gardener remained still, said nothing.

'What's the matter?' said Phil, voice still loud. 'Lost for words? Not like you.'

'You don't know me ...' The voice coming from underneath the hood was low, growling. Like he was perpetually trying to clear his throat and failing.

481

'Oh yes I do,' said Phil. 'I do.'

'Who . . . I'm . . . '

'The Gardener, yeah, I know that. But that's just the hood, isn't it? That's just your mask. You put that on and you're him. Take it off, and you're—'

The Gardener stepped forward, raised his hand. The blade clutched in his fist gleamed.

Phil jumped back. His heart was racing, pounding in his chest. He had been close to death before, but this was different. This was a death he had dreamed about. A death foretold. This was something he had to stop. No matter how terrified he was.

And he was very scared indeed.

Not just because of the maniac holding the knife. But because of what he represented. He was a nightmare. He had power over Phil.

And Phil had to stop that.

'You going to cut me now, is that it?' he said, hoping his voice didn't display the shake in his body. 'That the way you deal with everything?'

The Gardener grunted, slashed the air in front of the cage. On the floor beside him, Phil heard Finn flinch, whimper.

'Very good,' said Phil, mock-applauding. 'Very good. That all you can do?'

The Gardener stepped right up to the bars. 'I can kill you . . . '

'Yeah,' said Phil, aiming for nonchalance, hoping his voice could carry it off, 'but where's the fun in that? Tell you what, let's have a little chat first. Yeah?'

And before the Gardener could reply, he reached his hand through the bars and pulled the hood off his head.

The Gardener drew back, shocked. And Phil stared at him.

Paul. The tramp.

But younger-looking. Mad, wild eyes.

And angry.

With a scream, he flung himself at the bars, blade out-stretched.

122

The warehouse doors clanked into life, began rolling down.

'Wait for it . . . ' Fennell was staring at them.

Along with everyone else.

'Right,' he said into his mic, 'into positions, first wave. Disable CCTV.'

As Mickey watched from the van, two armed officers moved to either side of the main gates, reached up, cut the wires on the CCTV cameras.

'Good.'

The warehouse doors kept closing.

Mickey looked over at Clemens. He was staring at the warehouse but seeing past it.

The warehouse doors closed. Fennell turned to the team.

'Ready? Go, go, go . . . '

Adrenalin pumping, the driver switched on the motor, turned the engine over. Full beams. The other vans did likewise. Turned towards the gates.

Aimed straight for them.

123

'Just stand up,' said Glass. 'Slowly.'

Marina, her back to him still, started to straighten up.

'Well,' he said, 'I didn't think I'd find you here, Dr Esposito. The last person, in fact. Where's your boyfriend?'

Marina nodded towards the mouth of the cave. 'Down there.'

Glass laughed. 'Really?'

'Yes,' said Marina. 'Really.'

'Well I don't reckon much for his chances, then.' Glass laughed. Stopped suddenly. 'No,' he said, more to himself than her, 'he might get the collar. No, I can't let . . .'

Marina straightened up fully. Turned. Glass hadn't noticed the handful of dirt, gravel and stones she had picked up. But he did when she flung it in his eyes.

He screamed, hands going to his face.

'Bitch!'

With his eyes closed and still holding the gun, he tried to find her.

'Come here . . .'

Marina looked round quickly, assessing her options. If she

ran, he would find her. No matter how much she had slowed him down, he would catch her. She wasn't good in the woods, in the rain, in the dark.

That left only one option.

She looked straight ahead and, not giving herself enough time to think, jumped straight down the opening into the cave.

124

The Gardener lunged for Phil, blade out.

Phil knew he had to do something, tried a gamble. He stepped back. Held up the hood. 'Careful. You don't want this damaged, do you?'

The Gardener stopped. Stared at him. Eyes glowing with a deep, dark hatred. 'Give me that.'

'What, this?' Phil had thought the hood would be important to him. He held it higher up and further back. 'You want this?'

'Give it to me!' The Gardener screaming, madness and rage in his voice. 'Give it to me . . . ' He broke down into a coughing fit.

Phil watched him. He didn't look well. It seemed like it was only madness and hatred that was keeping him going.

'Let me out of here,' said Phil, his voice as calm and reasonable as he could make it, 'and we'll talk.'

Coughing was his only answer. The Gardener bent double, back heaving.

Eventually he straightened up. There was blood round his mouth. He ignored it, simply wiping it away on his sleeve. Stared at Phil.

'Stay there,' he said. 'Give me my face back . . .'

'No,' said Phil. 'Talk first. Mask later.'

The Gardener continued to stare, mouth open, breathing heavily, wheezing like a Tardis. Bloodied strings of saliva crisscrossed his lips, oscillated with each breath.

'I know who you are,' said Phil.

The Gardener said nothing.

'Richard Shaw, right? Tricky Dicky Shaw. Psychotic ex-gangster.'

The Gardener cocked his head on one side, frowned, as if remembering a song he hadn't heard in years.

'Well you might not be a gangster, but you're still psychotic. What happened?'

'Richard Shaw . . . is dead . . .'

'No,' said Phil. 'Paul Clunn is dead.'

'No . . .' The Gardener shook his head. 'Richard Shaw . . . no longer exists.'

'Neither does Paul Clunn. I've seen the body.'

'Paul was the best man I ever met. He . . . he saved my life . . .'

'And that's how you repaid him.'

'No . . .' His head shaking more violently now. 'No . . . When Richard Shaw came here, came to the Garden, he was . . . destroyed. He needed help. Rebuilding. He was seeking the truth. And he found it. Paul showed him.'

'And you killed him.'

Another shake of the head. 'No. No. No. Wrong. All wrong.'

'What happened, then?'

'Took his soul. He lives.' He hit his chest. Winced in pain, coughed. 'In here. Keep him in the cave. In here.'

'Of course. The cave. It's inside you.'

'He saved my life. Was a . . . a visionary. Made me an artist.

488

And he was . . . he was . . . dying. Cancer. We tried to save him. Gave him drugs, chanted . . . But no. Nothing. That was why he did the Garden. He knew. Knew he was dying. Wanted to . . . to . . . make a difference . . .'

The Gardener's eyes were shining. Lost to the present. Phil waited, knew there would be more.

'He spoke to me alone. Asked me to . . . to . . . to kill him. To pass him over, he said. Be one with the earth. The Garden was in good hands, he said. The Elders . . . So I did. I made sure he didn't suffer. Did what he wanted. And I cried. Killing him. And then . . .' He turned his head upwards. Phil saw tears in his eyes. 'Then here he was . . . in me . . .'

Phil had no idea whether what the Gardener was telling him was true. He didn't care. He just wanted to get out of there and take Finn with him.

'Paul . . . was the greatest man who ever lived. He showed Richard Shaw what he could become. Opened the light that shone inside him. Turned him into . . . me. The Gardener.'

'How?'

'Told me I had to look out for the Garden. Tend it. Whatever happened, I had to tend the Garden.'

'And this is your idea of tending the Garden. Killing the people in it.'

Another shake of the head, but more to himself this time. Like he was explaining it to himself. 'No . . . no . . . you don't understand. I had to. Sacrifice. There had to be . . . sacrifice. To the earth. The seasons. For the Garden to grow.'

'So you sacrificed children all this time. You killed children.' Phil couldn't keep the anger and disgust from his voice. He looked down at Finn, saw the boy huddled shivering in the corner. Eyes wide, staring. Face wet from crying.

'No,' said the Gardener, 'they're passing over. Not killed. Just passing over.'

'Where?'

'The earth. Part of life itself. The glorious cycle. Paul went first. He knew. Made it right for the rest to follow ...'

Phil couldn't believe what he was hearing. 'And that's how you justify it, is it? How many have you killed, Dicky?'

'Don't call me that!'

'How many? You've been doing this for years, haven't you?'

'Needed to. To keep the Garden flourishing ...'

'For years. And you've never been stopped, never been caught.'

'No.' The Gardener shook his head. A smile played on his lips. 'I grew my own.'

Anger rose within Phil. 'For sacrifice? You had children bred to kill?'

'The Garden has to survive. You don't understand ...'

'Oh I understand that bit. I understand why you think you were doing it. But it wasn't just that, was it?' Phil grabbed the bars of the cage. Knuckles white. 'You do it because you enjoy it.'

Another smile from the Gardener. Eyes wet and glittering and insane. 'You've got to enjoy your work ...'

His words hit Phil almost physically. Like he had been punched in the stomach, the head. He thought of the calendar, the solstices and equinoxes marked. A sacrifice for each one. Four a year. And all those years ...

He couldn't come up with a number. Didn't want to come up with a number.

All those bodies, those unmarked children's graves ...

While he was distracted, the Gardener made a grab for the hood. Phil noticed what he was doing in time, jumped back.

'Stay where you are,' he said. 'Get back.'

'Make me ...' The blade shining in the light.

Phil picked up the hood, held it above his head. Began to pull it down. The Gardener saw what he was doing.

'No ... no ... you can't ... can't wear it ... only ... only me ...'

'You killed your own son,' said Phil, the hood on top of his head. 'Adam Weaver. So don't give me that bullshit about the Garden. You killed your own son.'

'No! He was Richard Shaw's son. Long ago. But not any more. He wanted the Garden ended. They told me. He had to be stopped. No son.'

'So you killed him.' Phil pulled the hood down further.

'No!'

The Gardener jumped forward again. Phil wasn't so fast this time. The Gardener made a grab for the hood, slashing through the bars with his blade. He caught Phil on the back of the hand. Phil let go of the hood. The Gardener grabbed it before it could fall to the floor. Scuttled away from the cage. Pulled it over his head once more.

Phil looked down at his hand. Blood was pouring out. He had to do something. Quickly.

'The boy,' said the Gardener, pointing his blade at Finn. 'Now. It's time.' He swung the blade at Phil. 'You, afterwards.'

Phil thought desperately. He located the spot in the bars that he had cracked with his twisting. Grabbed hold of it again. Tried to ignore the pain in his hand, his body. Twisted. Kept twisting.

It cracked once more. Louder this time.

'No ...'

The Gardener turned, moved towards him.

Phil stared at him, watching him advancing. Saw his nightmare made real. Saw his past, his haunted childhood before him. Looked down at Finn. Knew that it could have been him there. If Don and Eileen hadn't saved him. He could have been one of the dead children. Unknown in life, lying in an unmarked grave.

He thought of his own daughter. Of Josephina.

He looked at Finn once more. He had to do something.

For the boy.

For himself.

For the past and the future.

He lifted his leg, aimed a kick at the weakened bar. It cracked. Again. It cracked further. Again. The whole thing was splintering now.

The Gardener tried to push himself against the bars, stick his blade into the space Phil had created. Phil grabbed his wrist, twisted. The Gardener screamed, held on to the blade. Another twist. The blade dropped.

With his other hand, Phil punched the Gardener. The air knocked out of him, the man staggered back. Phil picked up the blade, forced himself through the gap he had made.

The Gardener had recovered, stood before him by the altar.

'You're going to die,' he shouted from beneath the hood.

Phil saw the curved, razor-sharp shape of a sickle in his hand.

The Gardener ran towards him, arm raised, screaming.

125

The van sped towards the gates. The driver changed up, increased speed.

Mickey, along with the rest of the team, braced himself for impact.

Bull bars connected with metal. The van bumped from the impact. The driver put his foot down, kept going. The gates gave. The team cheered, Mickey included.

They were in.

The other two vans followed.

The first van came to a halt before the warehouse's closed doors. The second one drove round the back; the third stayed just inside the gates, blocking any exit.

The men piled out. Ran towards the warehouse. Dim light came from the windows at the front and sides, seeping round the blinds. There was a normal-sized door by the side of the main entrance. The enforcer was brought out of the van; a heavily gloved officer took up position. Brought it back. Forward. Again. Again.

The lock broke, the frame splintered.

They were in.

Mickey ran in with them. Inside was a wide strip-lit area. On either side were rows and rows of shelves rising high to the ceiling, going back deep into shadow. Filled with all manner of appliances, consumer electricals, household items, sports equipment. All compartmentalised and catalogued. It screamed 'legit'. Perfect cover.

The two trucks sat in the main area. In front of them was the green 4x4. A couple of leather-jacketed, mulleted, heavy-set men were opening the doors on the back of the containers. Out stepped young women, some no more than children, blinking and squinting into the artificial light. Dressed in filthy clothes, some in rags. All thin, pale.

Mickey paused, stared.

The girls screamed when they saw the police, ran back inside.

The two men had pulled out their weapons, but they soon realised they were outnumbered. They slowly put their hands in the air.

Clemens stepped forward. Grabbed the nearest heavy, smashed the butt of his gun into his face. The man grunted, staggered back, hands to his face, blood fountaining from where his nose had suddenly split. Clemens followed him, did it again. The man went down, whimpering.

Clemens turned to the other man, who held his hands out before him, backed away.

'Stop it . . . ' Fennell was staring at Clemens. He backed off, panting for breath, chewing his lip, smiling.

Mickey looked round. Couldn't see Balchunas or Fenton.

Fennell was shouting orders.

'Fan out, find the ringleaders. Don't let them get away.'

The team did so. Officers running down the aisles, all round the shelves.

Mickey joined them. He glimpsed a shadow flitting from one side of a row to the other, at the far end of the warehouse.

494

Ran down after it. Reached the end of the row. Looked round the corner.

Nothing.

Checked along to his left, his right. His left once more.

Saw the shadow again.

Ran towards it.

As he approached the end of the next row, squinting against the gloom, he didn't see the cricket bat being swung towards him until it was almost too late.

He managed to twist his body out of the way of the shot, letting it connect with his shoulder rather than his head, the intended target. He let out a gasp of pain, grabbed where he had been injured. Dropped his gun.

The bat came at him again.

He opened his eyes just in time to see it coming, managed to scramble out of the way. Then turned to see who his attacker was.

Balchunas. Eyes wide with fear and desperation. Panic and anger. Not good combinations.

'Get back . . . let me . . . let me go . . . bastard . . . you bastard . . .'

He swung again.

This time Mickey was ready for him. He waited until the bat had been swung and was out of the way. Then grabbed Balchunas' arm, pulled it backwards. Balchunas screamed. Mickey kept pulling. Balchunas dropped the bat; Mickey forced his arm behind his back.

As he did so, he felt the Lithuanian being pulled away from him.

'I've got him.'

Mickey turned. Clemens was standing next to him, twisting Balchunas' other arm. The Lithuanian tried to drop to his knees, whimpered.

'Please, no . . . no. . . stop . . . please . . .'

Mickey let go. Stepped back. Was about to argue when movement caught his eye. A back door was opened and closed again quickly. He saw in silhouette who had gone through. Fenton. He looked at Clemens.

'Look after him. If you injure him, I'll have you.'

Before Clemens could answer, Mickey was off.

Out of the warehouse, into the night.

After Fenton.

126

The sickle came down towards Phil's face.

He jumped backwards, got out of its path. The Gardener was breathing heavily from the exertion.

Phil dodged round him, ran to the altar. Picked up another blade, turned. Just as the sickle came towards him once more. It caught his arm, cutting through his jacket. He felt a slash of pain as it sliced into his flesh. Blood started to seep through the edges of the tear.

The Gardener advanced. His madness gave him strength, negated the age difference. Phil moved behind the altar, picked up a candle, threw it at the Gardener's face. It hit the hood, fell to the floor. Sputtered, went out.

Loss of blood was starting to make Phil light-headed. He had to focus, concentrate. Just to stay alive.

The Gardener swung, missed.

Phil used that to his advantage, went on the offensive. Swung his own blade. Connected with the Gardener's chest. The Gardener screamed, clutched himself where blood started to seep through. He screamed in rage, came at Phil again.

Phil upended the altar, threw it into his path. The Gardener stopped.

In the cage, Finn began to scream. The Gardener turned. 'Shut up . . . shut up . . . '

Phil was weakening. Stars dancing before his eyes. He couldn't see straight. He needed to rest.

The Gardener was weakening too. Phil could see it. But he wouldn't stop. He came at Phil again.

Phil tried to move out of the way, but was too tired.

The blade came towards him.

Phil couldn't move.

127

'Phil?'

Marina looked round the chamber. Took her iPhone from her pocket, turned on the flashlight.

'Phil?'

There was no sign of him. She shone the torch round, listened. Looked behind her. Glass hadn't followed. That was something. But that didn't mean he wouldn't. She had to do something. Make a decision. Another look round.

'Phil?' Louder this time.

Nothing. She shone the torch once more, found the bed. Crossed to it. Made the same discovery Phil had made.

'Oh my God . . . oh my God . . . '

She looked round once more, frantically this time. She knew, rationally, that the skeleton couldn't hurt her, wouldn't rise up and chase her, but that didn't mean she wasn't scared by it.

Or by the person who had done that.

She tried to find another entrance or exit to the chamber. Felt all along the walls, the floor. Found a tunnel. She knelt down, listened.

Heard voices. Screaming, shouting.

'Phil . . .'

Giving a quick glance behind her to make sure Glass wasn't following her, and wanting to get out of the chamber as quickly as possible, she crawled inside.

128

Mickey ran. Through puddles and potholes. The rain was still lashing, the lighting in this part of the yard pooled and sporadic. He viewed the night like a static-filled TV screen.

He ran away from the warehouse, down an alleyway between the stacked containers. Fenton still ahead of him. The night, the rain, covering him. Fenton ducked round a corner. Mickey increased his speed.

He ran round the corner. Stopped.

No sign of Fenton.

Mickey slowed, stopped running. Looked round.

The area had opened out, enough space for a truck or two to get between the stacked containers. Open ground. Nowhere he could hide.

But he had gone. Disappeared.

Mickey looked up, thinking he might have climbed above him, tried to escape that way. Squinting against the rain, hand shielding his eyes from the lights. Couldn't make out anything. No figure was there.

He looked round again. There was nowhere Fenton could have gone. Nowhere.

Mickey sighed. Shook his head.

Impossible.

He looked again. Walked down the side of the containers. On his left-hand side, at the base of the biggest stack, there was a shadow that didn't seem to belong. Mickey moved closer. Stopped beside it.

It was a slight shadow, and if he hadn't been looking, he would have missed it. He moved nearer, examined it. A doorway had been cut into the metal side of one of the containers. Secured with two bolts. Padlocked. The bolts were undone, the padlock open. The door hung slightly ajar, casting the shadow.

This was where Fenton had gone. He had tried to close the door behind him but couldn't bolt it.

Mickey opened the door, stepped inside. Gun drawn. Ready.

He was completely unprepared for the sight that greeted him.

129

Phil froze as the blade came towards him.

Finn screamed. 'No . . . no . . . he'll kill you . . . no . . . '

The boy's voice undid the spell. Phil jumped, moving quickly out of the way as the sickle cleaved the air he had just occupied.

His head spun. His arm was beginning to feel numb.

The Gardener came again.

Phil pivoted once more, moved just in time.

He couldn't keep this up. He was weakening, blood loss making him faint. Adrenalin was pumping hard round his system but that just speeded up the rate at which he was losing blood.

He stumbled, almost fell. Couldn't. Wouldn't allow himself to. Willed himself to keep upright.

The Gardener was coming again. Nearly as bloodied as Phil was, but still going. Phil knew that this time would be it. Either he would go, or the Gardener would.

He tried to stall him.

'Take your hood off . . . '

The Gardener ignored him.

'Take it off. I want to see your face . . .'

The Gardener made a sound that could have been laughter or could have been him clearing his throat. Still holding the sickle with one hand, he reached up, tugged the hood from his head.

'That's better. I can see you now.'

The Gardener threw the hood to the floor. Smiled. 'I'll get you this time.'

'You'll have to,' said Phil, hoping he could remain upright long enough to finish this. 'It's getting late. The equinox is nearly over. You're going to miss it . . .'

Enraged, the Gardener moved swiftly forward.

'Phil . . . look out . . .'

A voice. Behind them. Phil recognised it straight away.

The Gardener turned, surprise etched on his features.

Phil didn't stop to think. He was on him straight away. He sliced the blade across the Gardener's throat. Jumped quickly back as the blood arced out of his neck, spraying him.

The Gardener dropped the sickle, put his hands to his throat. Gurgling sounds coming from his mouth. He tried to stop the flow of blood by pushing his fingers into the wound. Pushing and pushing. More gurgling. The blood spurted faster. Harder.

Phil watched him. No emotion in his face.

The Gardener sank to his knees, hitting the flagged floor with a thud. He looked up at Phil, eyes asking for an explanation.

Phil had none to give. Just stared at him.

The Gardener pitched forward. Head hitting the stone with a thud. He lay there, eyes wide, staring, as the blood slowed to a trickle, stopped altogether.

Phil sighed. Felt his legs give way.

Marina ran to his side. 'I've got you,' she said. 'I've got you.'

He put his arm around her, let her take his weight. He looked at the cage, at the boy inside it. 'You ... you saved my ... my ... life ...' Phil smiled.

Marina walked him across to Finn.

'Let's get you out of here ...'

Finn had stopped crying, stopped screaming. There was disbelief in his eyes.

He wouldn't – couldn't – believe it was all over.

It wasn't.

130

Mickey stopped dead. Stared.

The breath knocked from his body.

Inside the container was like a shanty town. Old mattresses were spread over the rusted wet metal floor. Stained, disgusting and damp, they had old blankets on them, people lying there.

And what people. Filthy. Emaciated. Barefoot. Wearing clothes that were little more than rags. Strings of low-wattage bulbs hung from the ceiling, some blown, casting pale, depressing pools, a shadowed glow.

Mickey walked further into the container. The few people there stared at him, pulled away from him. No one spoke. He stepped into the centre. Peered ahead. It wasn't just one container. He could see where the back wall had been cut from the first container, the jagged, rusted edges welded to the next one along. Light bulbs were strung through there too. More mattresses, more walking-dead people.

He felt like one of the Allied soldiers at the end of the Second World War, walking into Belsen.

He realised, horrified, where he was.

In the Garden.

He walked slowly ahead, looking around all the time. Looking for Fenton, eyes, senses taken by what was before him.

The smell was appalling. Human decay, human waste. The noise, a low moaning, keening. The terminally unwell, too tired to cry out. Adults shielded children as he passed. He communicated terror by his presence. Another smell in the background: food. A rotting vegetable soup smell. Like reheated three-day-old kitchen waste.

He moved forward, eyes becoming accustomed to the gloom. He knew there would be no point asking if Fenton had come in here. He didn't even know if they could speak English.

Finn came from here. Poor kid, thought Mickey. Poor, poor kid.

He stepped through into the next container. This one had a square hole cut into the ceiling. A metal ladder had been placed there. Mickey, looking around and not seeing Fenton, climbed upwards.

He came out on another level, much the same as the ground floor, though this one was slightly better. Washing was strung out – old, worn, but with a semblance of being clean – and the mattresses weren't quite so stained as the ones down below. But then these ones didn't have pooling rainwater soaking through them. Water ran down the walls, though. Mickey felt the damp in his chest immediately.

He looked round. The same layout as downstairs, but still no Fenton. He was about to begin walking round that floor when he felt a tugging on his leg.

He froze, stared down. A woman, huddled and scared, was looking up at him. Flinching away, too frightened to make direct eye contact. His first response had been to pull away.

But he fought it. Stayed where he was. The woman didn't want to hurt him. She was telling him something.

She pointed to a ladder in the next container along. With her fingers mimed travelling upwards. Mickey did the same. She nodded.

He knew where Fenton had gone.

He forced a smile, nodded. Mouthed a thank-you to her.

She just cast her head down as if expecting a blow from him.

Mickey moved quickly to the bottom of the next ladder. Started to climb.

Ready for Fenton.

He reached the top floor. There were no lights here, so he had to wait a few seconds, allow his eyes to get accustomed to the gloom. He focused. It was deserted, no people up here. As if it took too much effort for them to get this far. He saw that the bulbs stretched out as on the other floors, but a constant stream of water had rendered them useless. But possibly live, so he kept away from them.

The rain was battering the metal ceiling. If I had to live here, thought Mickey, it would drive me mad. He thought of the inhabitants downstairs. It explained a lot.

He took his torch out, swung it round, checking out the layout. He caught water coming in, so hard and persistent it seemed like it was raining inside.

And then, several containers along, water shining and splashing all around, he saw a shadow move.

Fenton.

Mickey quickly made his way through the cut-out walls, splashing in rusty brown puddles, careful not to touch the electric wires hanging from overhead.

He saw the shadow flit around another corner. Shone his torch at it.

Dead end.

He had him.

'Fenton ...' Mickey's voice echoed off the metal walls. 'Give yourself up. I'm armed and you're surrounded. You won't get out of here.'

Nothing. The rain the only response.

Mickey lowered his voice, tried a calmer approach. 'Come on, Michael. It's over. Let's talk, hey?'

He heard a scream.

The shadow had detached itself from the back wall and was coming straight towards him. Mickey didn't have time to react before Fenton was on him, punching and clawing at his face and head, screaming all the while.

He closed his eyes as Fenton's fingers tried to push inside his eye sockets, gouge out his eyeballs. His turn to scream.

He wrapped his hands round Fenton's wrists, tried to prise his hands away. He couldn't. He worked his way along, grabbed hold of Fenton's fingers, tried to pull them out. They wouldn't budge.

He felt Fenton's thumb sink into his left eye socket. The pain was becoming intense. He needed to do something drastic. Taking Fenton's index finger with both hands, he pushed it back as far as it would go, heard the snap.

Fenton let out an animal howl. Mickey felt the pain in his eyes stop. He grabbed Fenton's neck with his left hand, punched his face as hard as he could with his right.

Fenton fell backwards.

Mickey scrambled to his feet, eyes still stinging. Fenton was backing away from him.

'Get off me! Get away from me!'

'Come on, Michael, let's go ... ' Mickey, walking towards him.

Fenton turned, got to his feet. Made a break back the way

he had come. Mickey reached out for him, but he was beyond his reach.

Fenton turned to see if Mickey was behind him, turned back again. And tripped over the welded metal ridge between the containers.

Mickey reached out for him, but Fenton fell backwards, away from him.

'No,' called Mickey, 'don't—'

As Fenton fell, he reached up for something to steady himself. Found the soaking wet electrical cable running along the ceiling. He pulled, it detached itself and he slipped back, taking it with him as he went.

'No . . .'

Mickey stepped back. Well away from Fenton now.

The cable, worn and uninsulated, hit the pools of water in the container. Fenton, holding on to it, screamed.

Mickey couldn't watch.

He turned away, the stench of burning flesh and singeing hair in his nostrils. Heard the wire sparking and humming.

He ran for the stairs.

Wanting to put as much distance between himself and Fenton – and the Garden – as possible.

131

'Come on,' said Phil, 'let's . . . let's get you out of here . . . '
With Marina supporting him, he crossed to the cage.
He was still carrying the blade he had used on the Gardener.
Now he dropped it, began untying the binding, opening the
door. Finn just stared at him, eyes wide. Phil smiled. It was an
effort.

'Told you I was a friend,' he said. 'Told you I would get you
out.'

For the first time, there was the ghost of a smile on the
boy's face. Terrified to believe the words, desperately hoping
they were true.

Phil fumbled with the bindings, had to stop.

'I'm sorry, I . . . '

'You've lost a lot of blood, Phil,' said Marina. 'You're going
to pass out. Here. Let me.'

She moved in front of him, took over the untying. Phil
held on to the bars to steady himself. Tried hard to keep his
eyes open. He felt like he wanted to sleep. His body telling
him to just let go, drift away. He moved about, blinked,
fought it.

Caught a glimpse of movement at the far end of the chamber. Blinked again. Saw what it was.

Glass. Standing there holding a gun.

He blinked again. Hallucinating, he thought.

'Stand away from the cage,' Glass said.

Marina turned also. Stopped what she was doing.

'How did you get in here?' she said.

'Through the door,' said Glass, as if explaining a simple fact to a dull child. 'This chamber is directly beneath the chapel in the hotel. It was used for ... oh, I don't know. Hiding Cavaliers from Roundheads. Something like that.'

'And the Gardener was here all the time,' said Marina.

'Ever since the Garden was forcibly evicted,' said Glass. 'And all down to me, too. If it hadn't been for me, they wouldn't have had anywhere to go.'

'You arranged for their disappearance.' Marina staring at him.

He gave a small, bobbing smile. 'I did. Went to them, told them what was going to happen. Offered them an escape route. And gave them my terms and conditions.'

'Which were?'

'I wanted to be one of them. An Elder. Because I could see the potential even then. They soon came round to my way of thinking.'

'And that's it, is it?' said Marina. 'All this? Just for money?'

Glass shrugged. 'And power. And influence. The usual stuff.'

'You sold out your job. Yourself. Just for that.'

'Oh, please. What would I have become if I hadn't done that? Don Brennan? Old and redundant. Nothing. Him?' He gestured to Phil. 'No. The Elders allowed me to become the person I always knew I could be. Always should have been. They made me. They created me. But I don't expect you to

512

understand. Your mind's too small. Boring. That's what you psychologists do. Make the spectacular mundane.'

She was about to answer, but he cut her off.

'I'm not here to talk about the past. I'm all about the future. Mine in particular.'

'Not . . . mine?' said Phil with an effort.

'You don't have one,' said Glass. He looked round. Saw the Gardener lying on the floor, blood pooled round his body. 'You got rid of him. Good. Saved me the trouble. Of course, I can't let you leave here. Not alive.'

Phil tried to come up with an answer, couldn't get his mind to work fast enough. Marina spoke once more.

'Let it go, Brian,' she said. 'It's over. Finished. You're finished.'

'Shut up,' he said. 'Move away from the cage. Or I'll shoot you.'

'Why? You're going to do that anyway. It's over, Brian. There's a team of SOCA officers at the warehouse now, intercepting your incoming shipment. Mickey's with them too.' Marina looked at her watch. 'Should be all wrapped up about now.'

Glass looked like he was about to explode. 'You're lying . . . '

'Yeah, that's right, Brian. I'm lying. I'm making all of that up. I've plucked that information from thin air and flung it at you just to get a response. That's what we psychologists do.'

Glass started to breathe heavily. He looked around as if trapped. 'But I can still . . . still take the . . . the credit for this . . . I can . . . '

He pointed the gun at the Gardener, then at Marina and Phil. His earlier composure had slipped away following Marina's words.

'Bastards, you bastards . . . '

Hand shaking.

'You've . . . you've ruined everything . . . '

He moved closer to them. Stepped across the body of the Gardener, round the upended altar, right in front of them.

Phil was aware of some movement behind him. He couldn't focus strongly enough to make out what it was.

'Put the . . . put the gun down, Glass . . . ' he said.

'Shut up.' Moving nearer.

'Why not just run?' said Marina. 'Start now. We won't try to stop you.'

'Oh you won't, will you? Well that's good of you.'

Marina tried to move away from the cage, take Phil with her.

'Stay where you are.' The gun trained on her, finger tightening on the trigger.

'Make your mind up,' said Marina. 'Move away from the cage, stay where you are . . . Honestly, Brian, what d'you mean? Which one is it?'

He didn't answer.

'Come on, Brian, be consistent. Man of action like you. Natural-born leader. Should be able to speak your mind and get people to do it.'

She moved once more. Nearer to him.

'Is this right?' she said. 'Or should I move back again?' She took a pace backwards. 'You tell me, Brian, which is it?'

Phil watched her, puzzled. She seemed to be deliberately trying to provoke Glass. He didn't know why. She couldn't get the gun off him; she wasn't physically strong enough to overpower him. And Phil couldn't do anything. She was going to get herself killed.

He opened his mouth to say something, didn't get the chance.

Glass was staring at Marina, trying to think what to do, angry at her interruptions. He didn't see Finn creeping up behind him.

The boy had slipped out of the cage. That had been what Phil had heard behind him. Marina had seen Finn, known what he was doing. Let him.

Finn had picked up the blade Phil had dropped, crept round behind Glass. While the DCI was looking between the pair of them, while Marina's words had been throwing him off balance, the boy had moved.

'So what's it to be, Brian? Come on, make a decision. Haven't got all night.'

'Shut up . . . shut up . . .'

Finn slipped his arm round Glass's body. Pushed the razor-sharp blade between his ribs, as far as it would go. Hard.

Glass's eyes widened. Two white-rimmed bullseyes. He dropped his gun. Finn pulled the blade out, did it again. Glass jumped. And again.

And now Glass screamed as he realised what had happened to him. Screamed and kept screaming.

Marina looked at Finn. He had the blade raised once more, ready to stab him.

'No more, Finn,' she said, her voice calm, reasonable.

'Him,' whispered Finn, 'him . . . he kept us in the Garden . . . he hurt Mother . . . he hurt me . . .'

'And he can't hurt you any more. No more. Put the knife down, Finn.'

Finn did as he was told, let the blade drop at his feet.

'Good. Come here.'

The boy went to her. She put her arm round him.

Glass fell to the floor.

Phil looked between them. Glass. The Gardener. Marina and the boy. He must have frowned.

'It's what mothers do,' Marina said, 'for their families to survive.'

Then Phil's world went black.

515

PART FOUR

SPRING AWAKENING

132

'And about time. What time d'you call this?'

Mickey smiled. 'Well you're feeling better.'

Anni Hepburn was sitting up in the hospital bed, back propped on pillows, arm and shoulder supported and bandaged. She was smiling and, apart from the occasional wince and grimace, looking relaxed. Mickey sat down on the chair beside her.

Anni put down the book she had been reading. David Nicholls. *One Day*.

It was almost a week since that night at Harwich. Since Mickey had confronted the extreme horror of what humans could do to other humans in the name of exploitation. He had seen some bad things before. Almost on a daily basis in his job. But that ...

That night he hadn't been able to sleep. Not without self-medicating himself into oblivion with a bottle of whisky. He had woken up with a raging hangover and the realisation that what he had witnessed had actually happened.

But he had resolved to change things.

'I've been busy,' he said.

'I'll bet. And here's me stuck in this bed. Missing all the fun.'

Mickey opened his mouth to reply, came out with a different response. 'There'll be plenty left for you to do when you get up. Don't worry about that.'

And there would be. With the deaths of the other Elders, Balchunas had been left to carry the blame. He had immediately started bargaining, but soon discovered he had very little to bargain with. He had been caught in his own warehouse with two containers of illegally trafficked young women. Also on the site was a prison made out of containers.

'Ongoing inquiries?' said Anni.

Mickey nodded. 'The Elders, as they called themselves, left very detailed notes. Who their clients were, what kind of things they enjoyed, how much they paid, where and when . . . all of that. And their customers weren't short of a bob or two, either.'

'Which means they'll be fighting all the way.'

'Absolutely. We crack one of the biggest cases in ages, lawyers have a field day. Going to tie the courts up for years. And then there's the Gardener. Whole country's being torn apart looking for the remains of his victims. He's going to be bigger than the Wests, Shipman, all of them put together.' He looked at her. 'So yeah, plenty of work for you to do. Hurry back.'

'Yeah, great.' Anni's smile dropped. 'Look, I . . . heard about your girlfriend. I'm sorry.'

'She wasn't my girlfriend.' Said very quickly.

'Right.'

'She wasn't. She was . . . she used me for information. I was in the way and I . . . ' He shrugged. Couldn't look at her. 'That was it, really.'

'She killed herself when she couldn't take it any more.'

Anni's voice quiet, light. Not wanting to disturb the surface tension of the room.

'Seems that way.' He sighed. 'Maybe it was my fault. Maybe I rode her too hard in the interview room, made her face up to what she'd done. Maybe I could have . . . ' He sighed again. 'I don't know.'

'You couldn't have done any more, Mickey,' said Anni. 'Like you said, she faced up to what she'd done. What she'd been a part of. And couldn't live with herself. It wasn't your fault. So don't blame yourself.'

He nodded, tried to appear convinced by her words.

They lapsed into silence.

'Jenny Swan didn't make it,' said Anni. 'She tried, she was a fighter, but . . . '

'I heard,' said Mickey. 'Clemens, one of the SOCA guys, nearly lost his partner. But he's pulled through.'

'Well that's something.'

'They were all right, those two. In the end. Recommended Phil and me for promotion.'

Anni tried to sit up, fired by his words. 'Really?'

'Yeah. Phil to DCI, me to DI.'

'Wow.'

'But Phil doesn't want it. So that means . . . '

'You'll be staying where you are.'

He looked right at her. Eye to eye. 'I'm staying where I am.'

Silence once more.

The wind blew dead leaves against the window. They could feel a faint draught coming through, the world outside penetrating the room inside.

'I've been thinking,' said Mickey, after deliberation.

'Me too,' said Anni. 'Haven't been able to do much else in here.' She pointed to the TV. 'Except watch *Clash of the Titans* on pay-per-view. Again.'

'When you're up and about, d'you want to ...' He felt himself reddening. 'D'you fancy going out one night?' He suddenly found the window beside her hugely interesting.

Anni smiled. To herself. 'You asking me out on a date?'

Mickey didn't trust himself to answer immediately. He feared his tongue would trip his words.

'Yeah,' he said eventually. 'Yeah, a date.' He looked at her this time. Saw her smile. For him.

'Yeah,' she said, 'I'd really like that. I'd love that.'

He tried to hold her hand, but it was strapped up. Settled for touching her arm.

'Ow.'

Sorry.'

They both laughed. Kept looking at each other.

Outside, it was a miserable day.

But inside, the room was warm.

133

Donna had never had a good time with religion. Standing outside the church of St James and St Paul on East Hill, she thought of turning, walking away. Not going in.

But she bit down on her fear. Pulled the last bit of life from her cigarette, crushed it under her boot. Went into the church.

Inside, it was as she had expected. Dark. Polished wood. Stone. Tall stained-glass windows, high carved ceiling. All of it dwarfing the people inside. Making small lives seem smaller.

Don and Eileen were sitting about halfway back. Her first impulse was to go to them, join them in their pew. But she resisted. They might not want her with them. Might not welcome her. So she sat near the back. Easier to escape when it was all over.

Donna hated funerals. She had been to Faith's just a couple of days before. It hadn't been anything like this. Much simpler. A nearby church, the crematorium, then drinks at the Shakespeare. She had sent Ben to school. He didn't need to be there, she had reasoned. His mother wouldn't be.

She had witnessed the vicar glance at his watch while he

talked about Faith, seen her cheap wooden coffin go through the curtains, then watched while people she barely knew used her death as an excuse to get hammered. Later she had picked Ben up from school, taken him out in town for a meal. Watching him eat, laugh and tell her about his day at school, she became determined to honour Faith's memory in a better way. And do something for herself – and Ben – while she was at it.

She looked round the church. A lot of coppers there. Some she recognised. Not always happily. Part of her wished she hadn't come. But part of her knew she had had no choice.

The service went on. Phil was asked to speak.

She had liked him. A decent copper, a decent man. All too rare. She watched as he stood at the lectern, fumbled to take his papers from his pocket since his arm was strapped up, looked round the church.

'Rose Martin,' he said, and glanced down at his notes, 'was one of my officers for a time. And in that time I came to know her well. She was ... ' He paused, glanced down at a very attractive dark-haired woman who had been sitting next to him. She nodded. He looked up, kept going. 'She was all the things a good police officer should have been. Conscientious. Hard-working. Loyal.' He swallowed hard. 'And that she should die in this way is ... particularly upsetting. Now, we didn't always see eye to eye, Rose and me. But we were on the same side. And she knew it. When she needed an ally, when she needed help, she came to me.' He sighed. 'And I wish I could have saved her. I wish ... ' He stopped talking, trailed off. Looked at the stained glass. 'I wish she was still here. I wish I wasn't standing here saying this. In the end, I was proud to know her.'

There was more, talking of Rose's achievements, her accomplishments. But Donna tuned out. That was just cop talk. Nothing to do with her. Nothing to do with the woman she had known briefly, who had died in her house.

Died in her house. A lot had changed in the few weeks since that had happened, thought Donna. A lot. She wanted to move on. Not sell her body any more, not take her anger out on the world. She had responsibilities now, she had Ben to look after. She had to look after herself, for his sake if nothing else. After what she had been through recently, she owed it to him. And Faith. And herself.

So she had gone to St Quinlan's Trust, asked for help, enrolled in some classes. And she had felt good about herself. The first positive thing she had done in ages. She had a long way to go, but she had made a start.

Someone else was up now, another copper, talking about Rose. Donna tuned out again. She had come, paid her respects, that was enough. She could just slip out the back door, no one would notice.

And that was when she noticed Don turning round, looking at her. He smiled. Caught, she smiled back.

Now she would have to stay.

So she listened, and she stood and sat when they asked her to. She sang a hymn, or at least mouthed the words. And as she sat there, something came over her. Grief. She hadn't mourned Faith's passing. Not really. She had wanted to remain strong for Ben. But now, thinking of Rose, she let it all come out. Rose, this woman she had hated, who had hated her. Rose, who she had developed respect for, knew it had been reciprocated. Rose, who had died in her house.

She began to cry. Torrents of tears, flooding from her body. An unstoppable flow. She didn't scream, didn't cry, just let them come. Sat there, on her own, hunched forward, crying. For Rose. For Faith. For Ben. For what she had done with her life.

And then it was time to leave. Donna stood with the rest of them, tried to duck out. But couldn't quite move. She took a deep breath. Another. And felt cleansed. Purging the grief from her system had made her feel clear-headed.

Don came alongside her. 'How are you bearing up?'

Donna tried to smile. 'OK,' she said, her voice small and wet.

Eileen passed her a tissue. 'Take it, I've got plenty.'

Donna thanked her, took it.

They walked out of the church together.

'We're ... we're going back home,' said Don. 'There's a proper reception for Rose. But we're not going.'

'No,' said Donna.

'Would you like to come with us?' asked Eileen. 'Have a bit of lunch?'

Donna thought of their house. How warm it was, how safe it felt. And she was tempted. Very tempted.

Don and Donna. I could be your daughter ...

She shook her head. 'Thanks. But no. I've got to ...' *I've got to make my own way. I've got to make my own safe house.* 'I've got to go.'

'OK,' said Don. 'But you're welcome any time. Any time at all. You've got our number, give us a ring. Let's get together.'

Donna nodded. 'Thank you.' Turned and walked away.

Out of the dark and into the daylight.

134

The table was laid, the chicken roasting in the oven, the wine bottles open. Don, beer in hand, took over the kitchen on a Sunday, wouldn't let anyone else in. Insisted on doing the whole thing himself. Phil and Marina, exiled to the living room with their glasses of wine, joined Eileen, who was playing with Josephina on her mat.

An almost stereotypically happy family Sunday scene.

But the picture was distorted. Disguising just how difficult the last few weeks had been.

For all of them.

When Phil had recovered consciousness and was lying in a hospital bed, he had opened his eyes to find Marina by his side.

'Hey,' he had managed.

'Hey yourself,' she had replied.

He had felt good seeing her there, like it had all been worthwhile. And then he had drifted off again.

A few days later, he was up and talking. Mickey had been to see him, filled him in on what had happened; Don and Eileen too. And Marina. Always Marina.

They had sent him home with his arm strapped up and instructions to take it easy. He couldn't do anything else. But although his body wasn't responding, his mind was. And there were things he needed to talk about.

'How's Finn?' he had asked Marina, the night after he had been discharged from hospital. Sitting in an armchair in the living room, the Decemberists playing, drinking wine. Trying to relax. Not doing a good job of it.

Marina had looked up from her book. 'He's fine,' she had said. 'He's been reunited with his mother. We've got him counselling. We're getting all of them counselling. They're going to need it.'

Phil took a mouthful of wine.

'D'you think you did the right thing?'

'What d'you mean?'

Phil could tell from the look on her face that she knew exactly what he meant. It was what he had wanted to talk to her about since he had come round in hospital. And she had been expecting it.

'Down in the chamber. You encouraged Finn to kill Glass.'

'He was going to do it anyway. Or try. What could I do?'

'He's a damaged boy, Marina. What you allowed him to do could make him even worse. Unreachable, even.'

'Things weren't that simple, Phil, and you know it. What was I supposed to do? Tell him that I knew what he was about to do but strongly advise him not to do it? And then let Glass kill all of us?'

'But . . .'

'No, Phil. No buts. He'd just watched you kill the Gardener. He did the same thing to Glass. It wasn't a situation where middle-class morality applied.'

Phil said nothing.

'Finn will recover,' Marina said, leaning towards him over

528

the arm of the sofa. 'We'll make sure he gets the best help he can. We'll allow him the time to get better. He's confronted the worst thing in his life and faced it down. Now, with help, he'll hopefully be able to go on and lead as normal a life as possible.'

'But what about what happened to him in that room? In the Garden?'

'Remembered as a bad dream. Hopefully. Like what happened to you.'

Phil took a sip of wine.

'Like what happened to me,' he said. Took another sip. 'Hopefully.'

'Dinner in about ten minutes,' said Don now, popping his head round the door.

They all acknowledged his words.

Marina looked across at Phil.

She was getting him back. She was sure of it. Slowly. But he was coming back to her.

It had been difficult. Of course it had. And although she could empathise with him, she couldn't imagine what he had gone through. But he was accepting things. Moving on. Getting his life back together.

And she was so glad she was still a part of it.

She looked down at Josephina playing with Eileen. The little girl laughed at something Eileen did, then looked at Phil to see his reaction. He laughed too. Marina saw tears in the corners of his eyes. Saw the smile linger on his lips, reluctant to go. Knew how much love that man had in his heart.

Yes.

His arm was healing. She was sure he was healing inside too.

She was getting him back.

★

They sat round the table, food laid out before them. All hungry, all ready to start.

'Before we dive in,' said Phil, 'I just want to say something.'

Silence fell. Don and Eileen risked a look between them.

'It's been a funny few weeks, hasn't it?' said Phil.

No one spoke.

'I just wanted to say ...' he looked at Don and Eileen, 'thank you. For everything.'

Don started to say something; Phil kept going, talked over the top of him.

'Sorry, Don, you'll get your turn in a moment. I've thought long and hard about this, and I want to say it while it's still fresh in my head. What you two did for me ...' he looked at them again, 'I can't thank you enough. I can never thank you enough. You gave me a home. You gave me a childhood. You gave me a future.'

His voice caught. He stopped. No one moved. No one spoke. They waited. Phil continued.

'You kept some things from me. And yes, I was angry about that. But I've been thinking. And ...' He sighed. Shrugged. 'What else could you have done? I'm sure I would have done the same if it had been me. And you did it for the best.'

He paused again.

'And because you did, I've got a family. Don, you've always said families are more than just biology. And you're right.' He looked round the table. 'I've got my family. Right here, Don.' He looked at him again. 'Dad.'

Don turned away, eyes wet.

Phil held his glass up.

'To family.'

They all joined in. Drank. Ate.
Together.
A happy family.
The tightrope holding.